PARACHUTES

PARACHUTES

KELLY YANG

Kᴛ KATHERINE TEGEN BOOKS
An Imprint of HarperCollins Publishers

Katherine Tegen Books is an imprint of HarperCollins Publishers.

Parachutes
www.epicreads.com

Library of Congress Control Number: 2019951312
ISBN 978-0-06-294108-4

Typography by Laura Mock
20 21 22 23 24   PC/LSCH   10 9 8 7 6 5 4 3 2 1

First Edition

To those who did not believe me,
you broke me with your decision.
And to those who stepped forward
and spoke your truth, despite the odds,
you put me back together again.

one

Claire

Shanghai, China

I lie in bed listening for the shuffle of my father's slippers. It's 7:30 a.m. My father, if he were home, would be in the kitchen, sitting down to his breakfast: three egg whites, scrambled, with oatmeal—doctor's orders—which he would remark to Tressy, our maid, were either overcooked or undercooked, just so he could get up and go rummaging around the kitchen for one of the taro buns he's not supposed to eat but that my mother secretly buys for him anyway. She buys them for him because she hopes the sweet gooey taro will somehow lure him away from his mistress, providing the kind of warmth and stickiness that will make him want to come home.

Except that his mistress also knows to buy him taro buns.

I've never met her, but the other week, she tried to add

me on WeChat. I stared at her picture for almost an hour, trying to decide if she was prettier than my mom. She looked about twenty-five—half my father's age—with long flowing hair, styled curly and tinted red at the tips. Her hand was running casually through her hair, pulling her shirt up just enough to reveal her milky-white skin. The whole thing looked so effortless and staged at the same time, the kind of shot I try and try to take but can never get right.

I deleted the friend request and didn't tell my mom about it, though maybe I should have. It was bold of her to reach out to me. There have been others, I'm sure. But none of them dared make contact.

I close my eyes, sinking back into my bed, trying not to think about what this means. Or where my dad is, for that matter.

The softness of my mother's hand on my cheek wakes me hours later. My mom's sitting on the bed, staring at me. Like a creep.

"Mom, ew, what are you doing?" I squirm away from the light pouring in from the window, burying my face in the sheets.

"It's nearly noon," she says in Mandarin. She's wearing big Chanel sunglasses.

"You okay?" I ask her, peering at her sunglasses.

She nods. "Oh, yeah, just allergies. Probably from the pollution," she lies.

I glance out the window. The Shanghai sky, normally

gross and gray, looks peacefully white today, like those might actually be clouds we're seeing.

Her shades slide down an inch, and when I turn to look at her, I catch a glimpse of her red, swollen eyes underneath.

"Is it Dad?" I ask gently.

She pushes her sunglasses up firmly, like a shield.

"No, of course not. He's just working," she says. I don't know who she's lying to—me or herself.

She reaches out a hand. "Hey, let's go out for dinner tonight!" she says, her face brightening.

I hesitate—I have *so* much homework—but her eyes say, *I need this.*

"Sure, Mom."

It takes me six hours to slog through the homework my teachers assigned me. I'm in eleventh grade at a local school in Shanghai, which means every day I'm a slave to my taskmaster. First math, then science, then English, and then Chinese, my weakest subject, despite the latest fancy tutor my mom got me. Her name is Ms. Chen, but I call her Sticky Fingers for the way she licks her fingers after polishing off the plate of fruit that Tressy brings us when I'm being tutored. When she's not busy eating fruit, she's barking at me what to write for my essay so I'll get a high mark, literally word for word, as though I'm not capable of producing my own thoughts. I always throw away the paper after she leaves.

My friends and I sometimes watch American movies about teenagers hatching plots and going to crazy places, and we're like, when do they have time to do this? In China, every second of my day is usually decided by someone else.

When the last of my assignments is finally done, I walk upstairs to my mom's room. I can hear Snowy's bell, our poodle. If Snowy's still in there, it means my mom's probably forgotten about dinner. She never lets Snowy in her room when she's getting dressed, for fear of Snowy chewing up her Louboutins. I'm about to turn when the door swings open. My mom's in her satin robe, her hair's up in a towel, and she's holding a glass of chilled rosé. Adele plays in the background.

"Go put on something nice," she tells me. "We're going to M."

M on the Bund is one of my mother's favorite restaurants, right on the water, a tourist attraction but in a good way. My mom used to take me there when I was little, usually after I'd just won a swim meet. Now she takes me only when she's all out of girlfriends. She usually goes out with Auntie Maggie and Auntie Pearl, women who share her love of complaining and laser skin treatments.

We sit at the corner table, overlooking the balcony. My mom's in a Costume National wool gray dress, chic but not loud, thank God, unlike some of her other clothes. I'm in black pants and a white shirt. Unlike my mom, who likes her clothes colorful and tight, I opt for understated and functional.

Mom sips champagne while making small talk with the waiter. She's a regular, and he kisses up to her so shamelessly I have to look away. She orders for us while I gaze out the window at the boats going up and down the Bund, tourists taking pictures, the Oriental Pearl Tower. There's a roller coaster inside. When I was little, I used to go on it with my dad. I smile at the memory.

The waiter finally leaves us alone.

"Did you know your father and I met here?" she asks. She points to the foyer, where the hostess, in pencil-thin stilettos, balances delicately behind the white marble table. "Right over there."

She's told me the story a thousand times. She was a college student at Fudan, working as a hostess that summer. He was an executive with a considerable expense account. It was love at first sight. And a trip to Cartier shortly after.

"I was just nineteen!" my mom reminds me. "Not much older than you. So young."

Her cheeks flush with nostalgia, and I settle in for a trip down memory lane. I try to take a sip of her champagne, but she moves the flute out of reach.

I protest, "Aw, c'mon."

"I was so beautiful then," she continues, ignoring me.

"You're still beautiful," I remind her. I can't tell you how many classmates—the guys especially—have commented on my mom's appearance.

"Your mom's gorgeous," they'd say, usually followed by "You sure she's your mom?" *Har har har.*

It used to bother me that she looked so much younger than all the other moms. I guess that's what happens when you get started at twenty. She used to joke that we were both still kids. She'd ask me, "What do you want to be when you grow up?" and I'd ask her back, "What do *you* want to be when *you* grow up?" And she'd laugh and laugh.

I don't know when she stopped laughing. She shakes her head at the champagne, pursing her lips.

"I'm getting old," she sighs. She grows quiet, eyes welling up. I hope that's not what she's blaming Dad's infidelity on.

My phone dings. It's a WeChat voice message from my boyfriend, Teddy. He's a year older and studying hard for his gaokao. The Chinese college entrance exams are so intense that girls take birth control pills to avoid getting their period during that week and construction work is halted, traffic diverted near the examination halls so as to not disturb the students. So far, though, he still has time to mess around. I try to tap out of the app, but my finger accidentally presses Play.

"Hey, babe, just thinking about the other day, in the back of the library. It was so—"

I shut off the message and, for the next two minutes, sit there with my face melting off my skull. My mom is silent.

She knows about me and Teddy, but she still thinks of high school dating as a "I'll walk you to class, you walk me to class" type of thing.

"Have you and Teddy . . ." She fumbles to get the words out.

"No!" I exclaim. "Of course not."

My mom's eyes scan me like a human lie detector. I remind myself I have nothing to hide. We haven't done anything more than make out. Though lately, he's been asking me for pics. He swears he won't show them to anyone else. I haven't indulged him, but I haven't flat out said no either.

"Promise me you'll save yourself for someone special," my mom says. "A Fortune 500 CEO perhaps. Or second-generation scion. Someone *better*."

Better than me or better than Teddy?

"Teddy's a nice guy," I say.

"A nice guy?" She laughs, waving her champagne flute in the air. "You think that's what's going to pay for all this? A nice guy?"

"No, *I'm* going to pay for all this," I snap. "I have a brain, remember."

She considers her words carefully. "So use it to get into a good school. Trust me, it'll be a lot harder to meet a good husband once you're out of school. I was lucky to have met your father when I did."

I raise my eyebrow at her.

"I'm just trying to watch out for you," she says, her voice

softening. She reaches out a hand, and my anger thaws.

I look over at my mom, sitting there, so lonely, sneaking glances at her phone, pretending to be smoothing out her napkin when we both know she's checking to see if he's called. He hasn't.

Gently, my mother lifts her champagne flute and sets it down in front of me, a peace offering. I take a sip.

The next day, my mother drags me to lunch at my nai nai's house. Nai Nai is my grandmother on my dad's side, a fierce widow with a head of white curls and a mouth that makes my mom want to crawl into a Qing vase before Nai Nai even opens it. I kiss Nai Nai on both cheeks as she sits at her throne in the dining room. She's holding court—my aunts, uncles, and cousins all gathered around her. They make no attempt to scoot over when my mom walks into the dining room, so she's forced to take the last remaining seat, at the end of the table. My father, if he were here, would sit at the head of the table and my mother next to him. But per usual, he's not here.

"Nai Nai," I greet her.

My grandmother's face blooms. "Claire." She smiles. However she feels about my mom, she dotes on me because I'm her eldest grandchild. Nai Nai waves to her maids to set a place for me next to her, and I look to my aunts and uncles, who reluctantly instruct my little cousins to scoot down.

"How are your studies, Claire?" my grandmother asks.

"Her studies are good," my mom answers for me from the other end. I can tell she takes the question as more a probe into her tiger-momming skills. "I've got her the best tutors in Shanghai!" my mother says.

But Nai Nai barely looks at her, keeping her eyes steady on me. My aunts and uncles jump in with various tutor recommendations.

"Did you hear about the white guy who's tutoring Chinese?" Aunt Linda asks.

Uncle Lu puts down his jade chopsticks. "Why is everyone in this country so obsessed with lao wai? Not *everything* done by a white person is better!"

"I hear he's pretty good, actually," one of my other aunts responds. She snatches up the last two remaining tiger prawns and puts them on the plate in front of her son, Jeremy. Jeremy keeps his eyes glued to his iPad, while one of my grandmother's maids feeds him.

My mom sighs loudly and tells my aunts and uncles my new Chinese tutor, the one who makes me copy down her words, costs two thousand renminbi an hour. The brag, masked as a complaint, shuts up my aunts momentarily.

"Anyone can just pay some money. That doesn't mean a thing," my grandmother remarks.

My mom's cheeks color. I'd almost feel sorry for her if I didn't dislike my Chinese tutor so much.

"Actually, the tutor is very important," my mom says.

"Claire's teacher at school even said. You don't know the local schools in Shanghai these days; you really need to get the right tutor or you don't stand a chance."

"I'll be fine," I say. Contrary to what my mother thinks, I like Chinese writing. I don't need to memorize someone else's words and cough them up on my exam. I can write my own, thank you.

My mom sighs. "You see what I have to deal with?" She looks to me and motions at me with her chopsticks. "You're doing what the tutor says. You're writing what she tells you to write on the exam!"

"Yes, Claire," my aunt Linda remarks. "Don't be stupid!"

"Can I have her number?" Aunt June asks, pulling out her phone.

"No! I'm not doing it," I say. I'm not copying. I don't care if it gets me a hundred, it's not *my* hundred. My mom shoots me a stern look. All my aunts and uncles jump in, yapping about my future, my grades, the gaokao.

Here we go again, life by committee. I roll my eyes. No wonder my dad never comes to these things. My grandmother puts up a hand to silence the chatter. She takes my hand in hers and peers into my eyes. I'm hopeful she'll take my side, but instead she says, "Your mother's right; you can't hit a stone with an egg."

I yank my hand away, flushing.

"She won't. James and I will make sure of it," my mom assures Nai Nai.

My grandmother turns to my mom. "And how is that husband of yours?"

I glance over at her. Mom's smile has vanished, and she's folding the napkin in her hands, trying to buy some time as she works out the best response.

Life by committee's a bitch.

two

Dani

East Covina, California

Do you ever get the feeling like everyone's looking at you but no one actually sees you? I mean, they see you—they see you standing on the stage, receiving your headmistress commendation; your frizzy hair; your ratty shoes; your mom in the back squirreling away stale cookies—that they see, but they don't see *you*.

"Dammit, Dani, how many times do I have to tell you?" my band teacher, Mr. Rufus, yells, "It's an F sharp, not an F! And please clean out your flute. That sound you're making—that noise—that's the sound of spit!"

My face turns red as I reach for my wipe. The entire band sits back and lets out an exaggerated sigh as they wait for me to finish.

"Ever heard of lessons?" Connor, who sits next to me,

mutters under his breath.

Connor O'Brien. I remind myself he wears tighty-whities stained yellow and keeps his mom's Crisco cooking oil under his bed to use as lube. I know because I clean his room every Tuesday after school when he's at lacrosse practice. I've probably cleaned the houses of about half the people in band, not that they would know. Everyone always books their maid for when they're out.

Yes, I've heard of lessons, I want to hiss back. You ever heard of pre-foreclosure? Splitting a $3.99 cheeseburger from Burger King for dinner while your mom fills up on free soda refills?

I glance over at Zach, my other neighbor. Zach's the captain of the American Prep swim team. He also happens to be last-chair clarinet and because I'm last-chair flute, we sit right next to each other. I'll admit that's one of the only reasons I like band. Unfortunately, we've never talked. And I've never cleaned his room. I'm not even sure where he lives. I think he might be a scholarship student too, like me and Ming.

Ming mouths to me *You ready?* from her seat as first-chair violin. I nod. She's from China and here on a music scholarship, and she's also my coworker, cleaning houses with me after school.

"All right, let's take it from the top," Mr. Rufus says, looking to Ming. The trumpets get their sheet music back out. The French horns put down their phones. As Ming lifts her violin, the entire string section takes their cue from her. I smile. It's nice to see her leading the other kids, even if we secretly scrub their toilets.

After practice, Ming catches up to me. She's carrying her black violin case, balancing it delicately on her slim shoulders. She hand-carried it from China, and even though the edges are frayed, she refuses to get a new one, kind of like me with my debate shoes. She told me once that when she was ten, she had a chance to be on *China's Got Talent* but her parents couldn't afford to fly her to Shanghai. So when Mrs. Mandalay, our headmistress, discovered her during one of her recruiting trips to China and offered her a full scholarship, Ming jumped at the chance to attend American Prep to pursue music.

"We walking over to Rosa's after school together?" she asks. Rosa's our boss at Budget Maids. I talked her into letting Ming work there, even though it's not exactly legal—Ming's on a student visa. But her scholarship covers only tuition and a tiny stipend for housing, so she needs the money.

"Can't. I have debate training today," I tell her. "I'll come after!"

Ming sticks out her lower lip. "When are they going to announce who they're sending to compete in the Snider Cup?" she asks.

At the mention of Snider, I suck in a breath. Mr. Connelly, my debate coach, has been training us for the tournament all year. My entire college admissions strategy next year is riding on Snider. All the top coaches are going to be there, including the coach of Yale, my dream school. Their team is undefeated this year.

"Soon, I think," I tell her.

"You'll definitely get picked," she assures me as she starts heading out. "Mr. Connelly loves you."

I smile, grateful for the words. My coach has been encouraging, though right now my most immediate problem is coming up with the money to pay for Snider. Flights and hotels aren't cheap, and my mom doesn't exactly have air miles like all the other kids' parents. She works for Budget Maids too, scrubbing toilets to try to put food on the table. That's what my grandmother did and her mother before her. I am going to be the first girl in my family to break the cycle. But first I gotta get into college.

I put my flute back in its case and wait around until all my classmates leave before returning the loaned flute back to its loaned-instruments cubby.

After school, I push open the door to debate training. As usual, Mr. Connelly greets me with a smile.

"Dani! How's my Thunder Girl?" he asks.

I roll my eyes at the term. Ever since one of the judges at a recent tournament called my speech "thundering," Mr. Connelly has been calling me that.

"You ready to go up against Heather today?"

"Yeah, Thunder Girl, you ready?" Heather jokes. I laugh and tell her I was born ready. My teammates, for the most part, are friendly. There's an unspoken understanding that my situation is different from theirs, and so sometimes they don't invite me to things, like if they're all going to an expensive restaurant after a tournament to celebrate.

As he divides us into teams, Mr. Connelly reminds us that he'll be looking closely at our performance in practice as well as in the next two tournaments to see who gets to go to Snider. As much as we've all been trying to avoid it, the simple math stares us in the face: there are ten of us, and only six get to go.

"So today when you debate, don't hold back!" Mr. Connelly urges. He tells us the motion—"This house would eliminate tracking in schools"—and asks me to begin the debate.

I get up and walk to the front of the room, while my teammates pull out pieces of paper to scribble down responses to my opening statement.

"Close your eyes and picture your ideal audience," Mr. Connelly says.

The ideal audience is a concept Mr. Connelly came up with. It basically means closing your eyes and picturing someone—could be a real person, could be fictional—who is patient, kind, thoughtful, smart, and who desperately wants to hear what you have to say. It's kind of embarrassing, but my ideal person *is* Mr. Connelly. He's been my ideal person ever since he pulled me aside freshman year and said to me, "You have a voice. Let me help you find it."

I think about that first year, how he spotted my mom $20 because she was so behind on bills she couldn't pay for a pair of Payless black pumps for me to wear to the tournament. And at the tournament, when he asked me why my parents didn't come and I told him I don't have a dad and my mom's busy cleaning houses, he gave me a hug and said, "Well, you have me." Yup, he's my ideal person. I don't even have to close my eyes.

I take a deep breath and smile at him.

"Ladies and gentlemen," I begin. "Tracking is a modern form of segregation. Kids are labeled from an early age based on how they do on a few tests and are then divided into separate tracks for the rest of their schooling. It's based on the erroneous belief that we as human beings don't change, that once ignorant, always ignorant. Once poor, always poor."

I set forth evidence and examples, talk about systemic bias and racial bias and how it oozes into our subconscious and convinces us that we're not good enough. I think about how people like my mom's boss, Rosa (though I don't say it), looks at my mom and says she shouldn't be sending a child to private school. *You are a maid. What are you doing sending a kid to private school?*

"And so, I ask you to look in your hearts and ask yourself,

17

what is the purpose of education? Is it to keep people in their place? Or is it to lift people up? I believe it's the latter and so should you."

"Bravo," Mr. Connelly says. He stands up and claps even though he's not supposed to. The debate's not over yet. He's supposed to wait. The fact is not lost on my teammates, and I catch a few eye rolls as I sit down.

Mr. Connelly leans over and whispers, "You're going to be amazing at Snider, Thunder Girl."

Later after practice, I'm putting books away at my locker, bending down to tie my shoes, when I overhear some of my debate teammates talking as they walk past.

"Did you hear him gush over how good her speech was?" Heather asks.

I freeze, hiding my face behind my locker. Are they talking about me?

"He's just going easy on her because she's a scholarship student," Josh says.

"It's so unfair. It's not like she paid to be here," Audrey adds. "We all have to pay for her."

Wow. And here I thought we were all equals.

I fume as I walk over to Rosa's after training. I can't believe what my teammates said; *I* thought we were a group of principled individuals. That's what I loved about debating: we may come from different worlds, but we believe in the same things—justice, ethics, equality. Evidently they're just a bunch of words to score points from judges. They don't really mean it.

The door to Budget Maids bangs against the wall as I push it open.

"Dani, where have you been? You're late!" Rosa scolds me as she snaps her fingers, *chop chop*. "Get your uniform on."

I glance at Ming, who already has hers on. Her cut-off denim shorts peek out from underneath it. Rosa makes us wear these ridiculous black-and-white maid uniforms that have *Budget Maid* on them, complete with hat and surgical mask, like some sort of half Pilgrim, half nurse. She says they make us look professional.

"I don't get it," I say, reaching for mine in my locker and putting it on. "Why does the client care what we wear as long as we get the job done?"

"How many times do I have to explain it to you?" Rosa asks, cutting the air with her hands. "It's not just about getting the job done. It's about brand building."

I roll my eyes. Rosa's been taking e-MBA classes. That's where she gets terms like that from, which she likes to throw around to remind us she's not just a boss, she's a CEO.

She hands me and Ming our next address, one I don't recognize. My mom and I have this rule—if it's a new address, I don't go. Someone else can go and clean it for the first time, just in case there's something dodgy with the client. But maybe it's okay. I glance over at my mom's sweater hanging by her locker. Ming will be there with me, and besides, I really need the money, especially if I'm going to Snider. Round-trip tickets to Boston cost $500, and that's just for the flight, that's not even including a hotel. Every dollar counts.

Ming stuffs the address in her pocket. Her parents aren't here to tell her where she can and cannot clean. I don't even think they know about her part-time maid job. She nods to Rosa and says, "Okay."

I help Ming with the cleaning supplies, and we head to the truck. Rosa's husband, Eduardo, drives us. As we shuttle over to the address in North Hills, where the houses are twice as expensive and the people twice as likely to accuse us of stealing, I fidget in my seat, looking over at Ming. I want to tell her what Heather and those jerks said at debate, but she has her eyes firmly glued to her window.

We arrive in North Hills and make our way up the winding driveway to the impressive Mediterranean mansion perched above. With its lush lawn and wraparound balcony overlooking sprawling views of Los Angeles, it's got to be worth at least two to three million dollars. Property prices have been going through the roof lately. Ming points to a jade statue of a dragon near the doorstep, muttering, "Crazy-rich Asians."

"Gotta love them!" Eduardo says, beaming. He and Rosa are big fans, both of the movie and of the people, who buy up houses in North Hills and hire Budget Maids to keep them clean. He teases Ming, "Those are your people!"

Ming shakes her head as she lugs the cleaning supplies out of the car. "Not my people. We crazy poor Asians," she says, pointing a thumb to her chest.

I get out of the car and smooth out my maid's outfit. Together we walk over to the house. Eduardo waits until we've found the key under the mat before backing out the car.

"Call me when you're nearly done," he hollers as we open the front door.

Once we're inside, Ming and I drop our cleaning supplies on the floor. I take off my surgical mask. We look up at the forty-foot ceilings in the living room.

"Holy shit, it's like a museum," I say.

A single crystal chandelier hangs from the center of the ceiling, made even more dramatic by the gigantic mirrors along the walls and the white marble floors.

"Or a concert hall," Ming adds.

She lifts her hands up and pretends to play the violin, humming the melody. I smile and go into the kitchen to get us some sodas. There are a couple of dirty dishes piled in a corner and some pizza boxes on the floor. That's it. This will be a cinch to clean.

Light floods in through the French doors. I stand for a while, taking a moment to look out at the pool as I sip my soda, trying to imagine what it would be like to live in a place like this.

Ming's testing the cleaning sprays against the mirrored coffee table when I get back to the living room. I notice she's wearing a new thin leather hair band. I wonder if she made it herself. It looks good on her. I hand her a soda and kneel down beside her. I'm about to tell her what happened at training when she turns and drops her own news.

"So yesterday my host dad was walking around the kitchen in his underwear, *again*. And he reaches in there and he readjusts." Ming puts down her soda and gets up and demonstrates, reaching for her crotch.

"Ew," I say.

"And then he takes the same hand and hands me my plate."

The look on Ming's face is so priceless, I start laughing, even though it's not funny. Ming's host dad is a middle-aged out-of-work truck driver named Kevin Malone who has a drinking problem, two little kids he can barely support, and no business watching over teenage girls. But he somehow discovered that hosting foreign students was an easy way to make money, and, as luck would have it, Ming got assigned to him, mostly because he was cheap. The school only gives her $600 a month for her housing stipend.

"Can you get another host family?" I ask her. "Or tell him to put some clothes on?"

She takes a sip of her soda and shakes her head. "The other host families, they're all too expensive," she says. She's afraid of upsetting the school if she asks for more money.

I can relate. I've thought many times of asking Mrs. Mandalay, our headmistress, if the school will cover my debate travel, but I've never been able to do it. Every time I've opened my mouth, I've promptly closed it and ran over to Rosa instead to ask for more addresses.

"It's not like my parents can help." Ming sighs. She doesn't talk much about her parents. I know they're not like the parents of the other Chinese kids at our school who drive around in Porsches and Teslas armed with their parents' American Express black cards.

"You want me to talk to your host dad?" I ask. I'd love to straighten him out!

But Ming shakes her head. "It's okay. It is his house, and I guess he has the right to wear—"

A noise from upstairs cuts her off. What the . . . ? Is someone home? Ming and I walk quickly up the marble staircase to the bedrooms. We follow the sound to the master, where we push open the door and walk in on two people having sex. The guy, not much older than us, peers at me and Ming as a topless girl sits on top of him. An amused look crosses his face as he looks at us.

"Wanna join in?" he asks.

three

Claire

My mother and I wait outside my Chinese teacher's office. The Shanghai traffic hums from the window. My mother shakes her head as she stares at my pitiful Chinese essay exam in her hand. I can feel her disappointment—her anxiety— with every labored breath she takes.

"I can't believe you did this," she says. She points to the big forty-two out of one hundred on the top of my paper. That's what I got for writing my own words instead of memorizing my tutor's. It probably didn't help that I wrote on the importance of incorporating student voices in school decision-making. I should have just picked a safer topic, like the dangers of internet addiction.

"You can't believe I tried to write my own paper?" I ask sarcastically.

"Don't get sassy with me. This isn't about you writing your own paper. This is about you never *listening*," she says.

"Always wanting to do things your way." The paper shakes as she scolds me. A few teachers walk by and give us dirty looks. My mom hushes but struggles to maintain her composure.

"This is China," she hisses. "You go to a local school. You told me yourself your Chinese teacher encouraged you guys to work with your tutors."

"So?"

"So why'd you think she said that?" my mom asks. "Why do you think she gave out the exam questions in advance?"

I look away. Yeah, well, that may be the game, but I don't like the rules. The door opens and my Chinese teacher, Zhou Lao Shi, walks out. She issues my mom a tight smile and gestures for us to come in.

"Mrs. Wang, Claire," Zhou Lao Shi says, running a hand through her thick streak of white roots, which run skunklike through her dyed-black hair.

My mom takes a seat and thanks her for seeing us. Gently she pulls out my exam. "I want to talk to you about Claire's grade."

I glance over at Zhou Lao Shi, but she sits there, expressionless, as she does throughout most of class.

"I know what she wrote wasn't perfect, but a forty-two?"

Zhou Lao Shi barely blinks. My mother's words have no effect. I nudge my mom with my elbow—*Maybe we should go.* This is a woman who's used to being bribed, questioned, tipped, and threatened by parents all day long. It's going to take at least five thousand renminbi just to get her to move an eyebrow.

"Claire received a forty-two out of one hundred. That is her grade," Zhou Lao Shi says.

My mom sets down her Birkin. She always dresses up when she comes to school; she says it's so the teacher treats us better. I think it's so she can impress the other moms. She crosses her wide-leg Balmain pants and tries again. "Perhaps because you're comparing it to the other students. But are you aware that some of the other kids plagiarized for this exam—"

"Mom!" I exclaim. *Has she lost her mind?* I get that she wants me to get a higher score, but to squeal on my class-mates for cheating?

"I'll have to investigate that," Zhou Lao Shi says tersely, and gets up. "I'm afraid our time is up."

We've offended her. My mother knows it too. She ditches her tough-lady approach and throws herself at my Chinese teacher's feet. "Please, it's my fault. I didn't get Claire the right tutor. Punish *me*, not her."

Her wet, desperate eyes look into Zhou Lao Shi's stern, ruthless ones.

"I'm sure there will be another opportunity coming up soon," Zhou Lao Shi says. "Hopefully, you will see to it next time that Claire's prepared."

In the car on the way home, my mom curses Zhou Lao Shi. "What kind of turtle-egg Chinese teacher is that? She didn't even care that her students are copying their tutors!"

Yeah, well, neither did my mom until twenty minutes ago. Still, I appreciate her standing up for me. I rest my head against the massaging neck pillows my mom got for our Audi as Patrick, our driver, glances in the rearview mirror.

"It's everywhere! At my son's school, a teacher got busted for selling seats in the front row of her classroom," Patrick chimes in.

"What if I went to international school?" I ask.

My mom tucks a lock of my hair behind my ears. "You know the rules. You don't have a foreign passport, honey," she says.

It's so unfair. While some of my friends' parents had the foresight to give birth to them in America, my parents were too busy scrambling to get their wedding photos taken before my mom started showing.

When we get back to our villa, my father is waiting for us in the living room.

"Dad!" I exclaim. What's he doing here in the middle of the day? My mom must have texted him *EMERGENCY*. I'm glad at least one good thing came out of my refusal to cheat.

"Hi, sunflower," he says, walking over and kissing the top of my head. The sound of my nickname on his lips makes me want to forget about the fact that I flunked Chinese, that I haven't seen him in weeks. "I heard about your teacher."

My mom kicks off her Manolos and plops down on the couch. "What a pompous ass," she says, calling to Tressy to get us some Pellegrino. "You can just tell she's one of those people who love wielding her power and just milking it, drop by drop. Is she like that in class?"

I sit down beside her while Tressy brings over three tall glasses of sparkling water and think about the question. I want to say, *Yeah, Zhou Lao Shi is arrogant*, but what I really want to know is *How do you do this? How do you just carry on and have a conversation with your spouse, whom you haven't seen in weeks and literally have no idea where he's been, like nothing happened?*

"You know, I've been thinking . . . ," my dad says, walking over and taking a seat next to us on the couch. "What about going to America for school?"

My mom puts her sparkling water down and sits up.

"There's a guy in my office. He was telling me about this school in California . . ."

"You mean for college, right?" I ask. I've been considering it myself, going to America or the UK for university.

"No, I mean now, right now. For the rest of your junior year and your senior year," my dad says excitedly.

He's kidding, right?

"What are you talking about?" my mom asks for the both of us.

Thank you.

"I'm talking about getting out of this broken system,"

28

my dad says. "You said it yourself, Claire's teacher is insane. And it's not going to be any better next year, what with the gaokao. And if you don't do well . . ."

"Ugh, I don't even want to think about that," my mom groans, closing her eyes and massaging them with her fingers. "Your mother's going to kill me."

I want to say to them I *won't* not do well! I swear I won't! But then again, I did just get a forty-two. My mom sits sullen on the couch, head buried in her hands, contemplating her future . . . because if you're a Chinese mom whose sole measure of success is how well your offspring does, when your offspring screws up, *you* screw up.

"If you go to America now, you won't need to do the gaokao," my dad says. He's offering us an out, and judging from the depressed look on my mom's face, I don't know who needs it more, me or her. "You can graduate and go to a college in the US. One of the UCs."

"You can't just get into one of the UCs," I say. He says it like they're M&M's.

"Yes, you can," he insists. "There are so many of them!" He takes out his hands and starts listing UCs. "And besides, even if you don't, at least you'll still be foreign-educated."

My mom mouths the words. The gears are turning in her head. *Foreign-educated. I can work with that.*

"I'm not going," I say to the two of them, nipping this crazy talk in the bud. I am not about to run off to another country just because I failed one exam. "Sorry. I refuse to go to boarding school."

"Who said anything about boarding school?" my dad asks. "Wash your own clothes? Eat cafeteria food? Live with roommates?" He shudders at the thought. "Besides, you don't have time to take the SSAT."

OMG, he's actually serious. I thought this was all angry talk, which is why I indulged him, but now, looking into his manic eyes, I wonder how long he's been thinking about this. Maybe I should have just memorized my tutor's stupid words.

My mom chews her fingernail. "It would make things a lot easier," she says. "And when you come back, think of how much you'll stand out."

"I don't want to stand out," I say.

"Well, you should!" she retorts. "There are 1.3 billion people here! Why do you think people are always shopping, trying to grab whatever label and slap it on their asses? To stand out!"

I roll my eyes. Please, with the shopping psychology.

"Your mother's right," my dad says. "We have to be smart. This is the right move for your future."

"And what about my friends? What about my boyfriend?" I ask. My eyes water under my contacts at the thought that I might not be able to see Teddy again, that we'll have to Skype . . .

"What boyfriend?" my dad asks. He turns to my mom. "You didn't tell me she had a boyfriend."

"He's not a boyfriend," my mom quickly denies, trying to calm him down. Her eyes urge me to go along. She always does this, whenever my dad gets mad at me, and I used to love that about her, but lately, it's made me wonder. Why do we always have to massage the truth for him?

"Yes, he is," I say. "Which you would know if you actually lived here."

"Claire!" my mom shouts.

My dad jumps up from the couch, his face red. But I don't let him off the hook.

"Where have you been?" I ask, following him to the kitchen.

"I've . . . I've been traveling," he mutters.

Ah yes, "traveling." The word my dad uses to avoid any and all responsibility. *Why didn't you come to my swim meet?* I would ask. *Oh, was that today? Sorry, I've been traveling so much, I can't remember*, he would say.

I cross my arms. My dad reaches into his pocket for his second favorite get-out-of-jail card—his phone.

"I have a deal blowing up," he says, fingers tapping his phone. "I have to go back to the office."

I look to my mom for help. Is he just going to walk away from this? Finally, we're talking about it, having the conversation we should have had many years ago, and he's just going to walk away? My mom's frown carries the same heavy weight of disappointment, but she says nothing.

"Did you know Mom cries herself to sleep at night?" I blurt out. I don't know what else to say to get his attention.

My mom jumps from the couch and walks over to us. "Stop it," she orders. She starts apologizing to my dad, saying I'm not myself, I'm too stressed out, too upset over my grade. Why does she always do this? Why is she so afraid of him?

A second passes. Then another. My dad takes his hand and slips it into my mom's, accepting her apology, and the two of them stand side by side in the kind of nauseating solidarity that makes me sad for womankind.

My dad looks to me and says, "It's true I've been working a lot of late nights at the office," by way of explanation.

"Yeah, right," I mutter.

My mom shoots me a look. *Watch it.*

"But I'm going to be home more often from now on," he promises. My mom looks like she doesn't know if she believes it, but she'll take it. "I'm going to be more involved, starting with your education. First thing next week, I'm going to take you to the agent who's going to help get you into the American high school."

I turn to my mom and plead with her. I promise her the moon and the stars—I'll write whatever the tutor wants me to write; I'll get better grades; I'll never talk back, ever. "Please, Mom, I don't want to go to America," I beg. "Where am I even going to live?"

"Oh, don't worry, the agent will take care of it," my dad says. "You're going to American Preparatory. It's in LA. And you're going to live with a wonderful host family."

My dad dishes out the death sentence like it's dessert.

four

Dani

I try to push the image of the guy having sex in the big Mediterranean house out of my head as I ride the bus home from the agency. We didn't have time to wait for Eduardo. Ming and I got out of there as fast as we could, Ming nearly tripping with her chunky boots on the dragon statue by the door. I've seen some weird stuff cleaning houses, but this is a first. And the way he said, *Wanna join in?* Like it was a video game. I hope when I finally have sex, it's with a guy who respects me.

"Mom?" I call as I walk inside my house. "I thought you were picking me up today from the agency?"

I waited for her for a half hour, trying her on her cell.

"Dani!" my mother answers from the spare bedroom. "Come in here and help me!"

I dump my backpack on the floor and walk over to see her kneeling, reaching under the bed. Three large trash bags sit next to her, and she's pulling out more junk from underneath the bed: newspapers, old Christmas ornaments, little bottles of shampoo she's been hoarding.

"What are you doing?" I ask.

"Clearing out this room," she says, sitting cross-legged on the floor in her whitish stretch pants. For all her separating other people's laundry all day long, my mom never bothers to separate her own whites. Says it wastes too much water. As a result, her whites are gray.

"Why?" I ask.

We never use the spare bedroom. Ever since my dad left, it's been just the two of us. My mom's relatives are all back in the Philippines. I've met my grandparents only once, as they're too old and weak to make the trip from Manila to the US. Still, my mom prides herself on the fact that we have a spare bedroom. "See? We're not strapped. We have extra," she'd say.

"I'm renting out the room!" she announces to me.

"What?" The news cramps my throat. "To who?" I ask.

"A nice girl from China, you'll like her," she says. "She's gonna go to your school. Her parents are paying us two thousand dollars a month just for her to live with us!"

I don't know what to say—$2,000 is a lot more than Ming pays Underwear Kevin. On the other hand, we'd be giving up so much more than a room.

My mom frowns. "Look, you know the property taxes are going up, the mortgage payments are killing us . . . ," she says. My eyes slide over to the stack of tax bills on top of the trash bag. She doesn't have to remind me. My dad may have left us this house, but he didn't own it. Not even close.

"What if we didn't send so much money back to the Philippines to Lola and Lolo . . . ," I suggest. Every month, my mom sends $500 back to my grandparents in the Philippines. That check's the first one in the mail before any of the other bills get paid.

"You know I have to send money home!" my mom protests. "We're Filipino; that's what we do—we take care of each other!"

So take care of us, I want to say.

"Let's not fight. It's going to be okay. We'll take her in, and we'll make her feel at home," my mom says. "I'll cook her Chinese food. Pick her up from school . . ."

Funny how my mom will remember to pick up this girl, a girl she's never met, but she doesn't remember to pick me up, her own daughter, from the agency. I cross my arms. "So you're basically just going to be her mom. You're renting yourself out."

I can hear Mr. Connelly's voice in my head shouting, "Whoa! Tone it down!"

My mom sticks her hands into her pockets. "What will you have me do?" she asks. "Beg Rosa for more money?"

I can hear Rosa's shrill laugh in my head, *Poverty's the result of laziness. A smart person grabs opportunity by the throat.* That's what she did when she stole my mom's idea. The two of them used to work for an old lady, cleaning her house together. One day, my mom got the idea that they go off on their own and start a house-cleaning business. There were more and more wealthy Chinese families moving in, buying up houses, and they needed people to help keep them clean. But before Mom could do it, Rosa went out and bought a van with her husband's money. Now there are ten vans and twenty-five of us cleaning for Rosa. Ideas are cheap, vans are expensive, according to Rosa.

My mom looks down at the mattress, her face tired.

"My coach is probably going to pick me for Snider," I tell her, hoping my good news will cheer her up. Ever since I can remember, I've been using my good news to try to fill the void my dad left.

Her face blooms. "That's great!" she gushes, pulling me into her arms.

I smile and breathe in her pride as she holds me. "But I need quiet, Mom," I tell her. "I can't have someone else living here, distracting me while I'm trying to train."

My mom swats at my concern. "She won't distract you. And besides, a little distraction could be good for you in case . . ."

I pull away. I know what's at the end of that sentence, and she's wrong. My mom thinks my debating is like a hot night in Vegas. Everything good comes to a disappointing end. But it won't. I'll show her. And when I win, our lives are going to change. I'm going to get into Yale, and we won't have to ever worry about not making another mortgage payment again.

I get to band early the next day to take my loaned flute out before anyone sees. Zach is also there. As I'm cleaning my flute, Zach blows too hard on his clarinet and makes an *eek* sound. He turns red and apologizes to me. And I think maybe today's the day when we'll finally talk, like in one of those romantic comedies where the dorky girl somehow ends up with the hot guy and it turns out she's not really so dorky, it was just the glasses.

But no. We don't talk. He just goes back to playing his sheet music, and I sit there, wishing I was his sheet music.

Ming walks over. "You ready for the fund-raiser tonight?"

Mrs. Mandalay requires us full-scholarship students to attend the American Prep cocktail fund-raisers she's always putting on to solicit donations for the school's already inflated endowment. It's an opportunity for new parents to ingratiate themselves with her, usually in the form of a five-figure or six-figure check. But at least there's good food. I usually have to make a speech, and Ming does a solo performance. All the new parents ooh and aah and it feels a bit like we're on display at a zoo. I remind myself it's a small price to pay. My old public school had more security checks than an airport.

"You guys going to that thing too?" Zach asks.

My head snaps. Did he just speak?

"Yeah, are you?" Ming asks. She smiles at me, raising her eyebrows suggestively. She knows *all about* my crush on Zach.

Zach nods and goes back to fiddling with his reed.

I can hardly sit still the rest of the day, thinking about the fact that Zach's going to be at the fund-raiser tonight. The sports-scholarship students don't usually have to come to these things. If he's going, he'll hear my speech. I walk through the halls, reciting it in my head. It's the same one I made the other day, about tracking in schools. And it has to be perfect. I'm so immersed in my speech that when Mr. Connelly calls my name in the hallway, it takes me a second to respond.

"Dani!" Mr. Connelly calls. I turn around. Jokingly, Mr. Connelly waves his hand up and down in front of my eyes. "Earth to Dani! What's up? You thinking about your boy-friend?" he teases.

I blush. "I don't have a boyfriend," I tell him.

"Really?" he asks. "Hey, I'm glad I bumped into you. I'm thinking about making you team captain for the next tournament. You think you can handle that?"

My eyes widen. That would be *amazing*. I've never been team captain before. It's usually Heather or Audrey. I nod enthusiastically.

"Good!" Mr. Connelly grins. "I'll see you at practice on Wednesday, Thunder Girl!"

o o o

I'm still smiling later that day when I walk into the annual-fund cocktail fund-raiser. I'm in my formal debate attire—black dress and pumps, the same ones I wear for debate. *And* just in case I get close to Zach, a spritz of the sample Lancôme perfume one of my mom's clients threw away and she fished out of the trash. The auditorium is lit up and packed with parents, mostly from China. Ming is in the corner tuning her violin. As the caterer offers me a glass of water, Mrs. Mandalay waves at me. Her wild red hair bounces above her shoulders as she strolls over to me in her power suit, looking every bit like the tough-as-nails headmistress who single-handedly quadrupled our school enrollment.

"There you are, Dani!" she says. "Are you ready?"

"Yes, ma'am," I say. I hold up my note cards. I look around for Zach but don't see him. Mr. Connelly is in the corner, talking to a parent. He waves, and when the parent turns around to get another glass of wine, pretends to shoot himself in the head.

I stifle a laugh.

Mrs. Mandalay walks up onto the stage and calls everyone's attention.

"Ladies and gentlemen," Mrs. Mandalay says, stepping up to the podium. "Welcome to the annual-fund cocktail fund-raiser. We thank you for spending the evening with us, and by spend I mean *spend*."

There's a wave of laughs. Mrs. Mandalay is the Olympic champion of fund-raising. She can squeeze a quarter out of a squirrel. She once got $200 out of my mom, a check that thankfully bounced the next day. Ever since then, I've told my mom to stay clear of these events.

I'm up first. Mrs. Mandalay introduces me to the podium.

As I take the stage, I look out at the room full of people. Eager prospective parents mixed with bored alumni roped in to attend through guilt. I smile at all of them. To me it's all the same. I welcome the chance to fire up any crowd.

Tonight is no exception. As I deliver my last line, the room bellows, "Bravo!" The alumni clap, while the parents' eyes go wide. I can tell what they're thinking—*Wow. I want my kid to speak like that girl. Maybe if they come to this school, they will.* One by one, they whip out their checkbooks.

"Danielle De La Cruz." Mrs. Mandalay beams. She looks at me and nods, pleased. "We're so proud to have students like Dani at our school, thanks to the generous donations to our annual fund!"

The crowd cheers. As Ming steps onto the stage with her violin and fills the room with the soothing sound of Brahms, the crowd takes out their phones and snaps pictures of the talented young violin prodigy.

When Ming finishes, the room erupts in thunderous applause. Ming bows and walks over to the mic with her violin. Slowly, she begins her speech, one that I've heard many times before, describing how she was a poor girl in a Chinese village with a love for violin, an instrument her parents neither understood nor knew how to support, when Mrs. Mandalay offered her the opportunity to come to America.

Ming looks to our headmistress. "Thank you, Mrs. Mandalay. You gave me the chance to be who I am," she says with a smile. She delivers the line with the perfect combination of emotion, and the crowd eats it up. Mrs. Mandalay puts a hand over her heart. I make a mental note to ask Ming later, does she really mean it? Or is it just part of the performance?

Afterward, Mrs. Mandalay moves on to the live auction, and Ming and I walk offstage as parents happily drunk bid on useless items like a personalized walking tour of the city led by a high school student. I fight the urge to slump down on one of the chairs and kick off my heels, but I know I can't. We all have our roles. Mine is to smile and say thank you.

Mr. Connelly walks over and gives me a hug. "You were great," he says to me. I introduce him to Ming, and he congratulates her as well, telling her how proud and honored the faculty is to have her at the school. Before he leaves, he leans in and whispers into my ear, "Get used to it. You're going to have to do a *lot* of these when you get into Yale."

I smile. I turn to Ming after he's gone and ask her if she's seen Zach. Ming rolls up the long sleeves of her formal velvet dress and shakes her head.

"Hey, did you mean what you said about Mrs. Mandalay changing your life?" I ask her.

She nods.

"Because your parents didn't understand why you play the violin?"

She shakes her head. She leans over, as if to tell me a secret, then hesitates. I furrow my eyebrows, *What is it?*

"No, because I'm gay," she finally says.

five

Claire

I glare at my Chinese teacher in class. Her lack of ethics has doomed me to a lifetime of American burgers.

At lunch, my friends crowd around me, analyzing the pros and cons of going, while I look over at Teddy. He's sitting at the senior table with his friends, but he's not talking to them. His rice sits untouched while he scrolls on his phone.

What are you thinking? I text.

He looks up at me but doesn't text back, instead he puts his phone away. He's mad. He hasn't said a word to me since I told him the news this morning.

I wait for him after school, and we walk the long way home, where the Old Northern Gate was. Shanghai used to have many gates. The gates separated the concessions in Old Shanghai. There's the former French concession, where the French dignitaries used to live. There's the British and

American enclaves, ceded as a result of the Opium War.

I think about that, about all the concessions I've made over the years, pieces of me carved out to please my parents. Maybe this is just another one. I'd like to think that, like Shanghai, eventually I'll get it all back.

I look over at Teddy. *Say something.* We cut through People's Park. He stares at the umbrellas on the ground, fingers squeezed into his pockets. It's a marriage market day. The sidewalks are lined with umbrellas. On each umbrella, there's a piece of paper taped to it advertising an unmarried girl. They call them "leftover women," meaning women over thirty who have not yet married, a fate considered worse than death. Desperate mothers crowd the parks trying to marry off their girls by umbrella—no doubt, my mother's worst nightmare.

"You're gonna go and fall in love with one of those big-nose Americans," Teddy finally says.

His voice is raw and vulnerable. I had no idea he was hurting this bad.

"I won't!" I promise.

"And it'll be so unfair because they won't even appreciate how pretty you are," he continues. "All Chinese girls look the same to them! They'd be just as happy with ugly Yan!"

Yan's a girl in our school who has tiny eyes and single eyelids. I have double eyelids and long lashes, the source of envy from my classmates. What my classmates don't know is I used to have single eyelids too, until my mother took me to Korea, at my grandmother's suggestion, to have my eyes done when I was ten. I bet Yan could look cute too if she went to Korea.

"Nothing's going to change," I assure him. "We'll Skype every day. Six a.m. California time, nine p.m. China time."

He shakes his head like he doesn't believe me. He parts his lips, and I think he's going to tell me to try harder to stand up to my parents, but instead he kisses me hard on the mouth. His lips are hungry, his hands traveling fast down my cheek to my neck.

"Whoa," I say, pushing away from him. I try to catch my breath. The umbrella mothers give Teddy a dirty look.

"C'mon, I want you to remember me," he says.

I shake my head at Teddy. "No," I say. Not like this. "And what do you mean *remember* you? I'm still going to be with you!"

"You say that, but you won't," he says. "You'll meet some other guy and you'll . . ."

I take a step toward him. Our hands touch.

"I won't," I say.

A man selling roses on a tricycle squeezes by us. Teddy looks down at the umbrellas and mutters, "Maybe we should just break up."

"What?"

"Well, you're going away and I've got the gaokao coming up," he says.

I can't believe it. And to use the gaokao of all things to break up with me.

"Fine. You want to break up? Let's break up." I let go of his hand and start running.

Teddy calls out for me. "Claire, wait—"

But it's too late. I race across the street and hail a taxi, the tears pooling in my eyes.

Two days later, there's a big black box waiting for me on the dining room table. I'm hoping it's from Teddy, apologizing. We haven't spoken since the day at the park, though I've spent hours glued to his WeChat, going through old pictures of us.

"It arrived this afternoon," Tressy says, setting down a plate of fried chicken.

I pop a piece of chicken in my mouth. "You preparing me for American food?" I ask. Tressy's been my nanny and our housekeeper since I was five. She's from the Philippines and is the only reason I speak good English.

The deliciousness of the chicken wing—golden, fried to perfection—catches me off guard. Another reason I can't go—Tressy's too good a cook.

"You can't tell my mom I ate this," I say to her. "Tell her I'm so upset I haven't eaten a thing."

Tressy promises she won't. She's good like that, always has been. Excitedly, she points to the box. "Are you going to open it?"

I wipe my fingers on a napkin and open the box. It's a baby-pink Prada bag inside. Calfskin leather. I stroke the soft pillowy leather, mind going to what outfits would go best with it, and close my eyes as I pick up the card. Please let it be from Teddy.

> *Dear Claire,*
> *Hope you like the bag. You can wear it in America!*
> *Love,*
> *Daddy*

I toss the card and the bag back in the box.

Tressy looks confused. "What's wrong?"

My mother walks in through the door as we're talking. "Oh, Claire, good, you're home. I just had lunch with your nai nai. She thinks you going to America is wonderful!" My mom points to the box. "Is that—?" she asks excitedly.

"I'm not keeping it," I say.

"What do you mean you're not keeping it?" She frowns. "Do you not like it?" She inspects the bag. "It is rather pink. You can always return it and get something else."

My mom is the queen of returning gifts and pocketing the money. This, in fact, is how she first started dating my dad. He'd buy her stuff, which she'd accept so she could return it and send the money back to her mother. Even now, she jokes about the hypothetical scenario in which if my dad ever leaves her, she'd sell all her Birkin bags, which can fetch anywhere from HKD$80,000 to $800,000 in Hong Kong, and invest the money in a nice apartment.

She walks over to me and puts her hands on my shoulders. "This is a good opportunity," she says. "Do you know, when I was your age, I would've died for the chance to go to America. . . ."

She glances out the window at the artificial lake in front of our house, and I catch her reflection in the window.

"Why didn't you?" I ask. Sure, returning gifts is a nice cushy gig, but why didn't she go for her own dreams?

"It would have been different if I had been a boy. . . ." She sighs. "Or if I had had one." She adds the last part so quietly that I almost don't hear it. But then I do, and it grinds into me.

"I can't help it if I'm all you guys got," I say.

According to Tressy, after my mom had me, she tried to get pregnant again, but each time it always ended in miscarriage. I was too little to understand, but I remember once hearing my grandmother talking about it, how it was such a pity my mom couldn't give my father a son. My mom dropped the teacup she was holding onto the ground. It was the only time I'd ever seen her publicly get mad at my grandmother.

Watching my mom grimace now, I know the pain has not entirely left.

"I'm sorry, Mom," I say. "I just . . . I don't want to go to America."

"I know," she says. "I don't want you to go either. You're all I have." She reaches and touches my cheek with her hand. When she speaks again, her voice is full of resolve. "Which is why you have to go."

I shake my head. "What if something goes wrong?" I ask.

She takes her iPhone out from her purse. "I'm one phone call away. If something goes wrong, I'll be right over," she promises.

I glance at her phone, trying not to think about the fact that half the time when I'm here and I call her, I can't find her because she's getting a massage.

"Who am I even going to be living with?" I ask.

My mother smiles. "The De La Cruzes," she says. "They have a daughter just your age. Her name is Dani."

six

Dani

At lunch the next day, I grab me and Ming some seats in the back. I can't believe she never told me she's gay. Does she have a girlfriend? Does anyone else know? But before I can ask her any of these questions, Zach walks over. It takes me a moment to process he's here, standing in front of me.

"Hey," he says, setting down his tray of food.

My mouth's full of sandwich, so I can't say hey back. I search the cafeteria for Ming and see her over by the sushi corner, pocketing soy sauce packets.

"You were great last night," he says.

My cheeks preheat like a Thanksgiving oven. So he *was* there!

"Did you mean all that stuff you said?" he asks.

"What?"

"About how it's wrong to track people. Just because someone's dumb at one point doesn't mean they're always dumb. Do you really believe that?" He peers at me with wide blue eyes.

"It's just not . . . like . . . ideal . . . is . . . I don't know," I say. Why is it that when I'm in front of a podium, I can come up with these eloquent lines and when I'm off the stage, I can't seem to find the words and end up sounding like a frog?

Zach pops a potato chip in his mouth.

"Me too," he says, nodding as he chews. "What you said."

I smile. Now we're two frogs.

"Hey, would you like to tutor me sometime?" he asks.

My face crumbles like my mom's puto seko that's been left out.

"It's just you're really smart. You're always reading when Mr. Rufus isn't looking," he says.

Victory! He's been watching me too in band!

"And I need to maintain a 3.0 for my sports scholarship."

"I'm on a scholarship too," I say.

"But you're like brilliant. And I'm . . ." He laughs nervously. "I guess you could say I'm not the sharpest knife in the drawer. I'm more like a spoon." He looks down at the plastic utensils on my tray. "I just thought because of what you said in your speech, maybe you'll want to help me . . . but if you don't want to . . . you know what, forget it!"

"No, no, no," I say. My fingers reach for his tray. *Stay.* "I'd love to help you."

"Really?" he asks.

"Yeah, of course." I ask him what subjects he needs help with as Ming starts walking over to us. She sees us talking, stops walking, and turns and goes back to the sushi corner.

"Everything," he confesses.

"That's fine," I tell him. I pull out my phone so we can exchange numbers. "We'll make a schedule."

"Thank you so much," he says. He flashes me his dimpled smile, and I feel my dopamine pathways flood. "I can't believe you're being so nice."

I want to tell him that's not it. *It's because I like you. That's why I look forward to band even though I hate band, just so I can sit next to you for forty-five minutes every other day. That I've been deliberately trying to get worse at flute just so I stay last chair and get to sit next to you.* But I don't tell him any of that today. Instead, I smile and say, "Of course."

Later that day, I'm kneeling in a house in North Hills, blotting up the spilled wine from a dinner party, when I look up and see Heather, my teammate from debate. She's standing in the living room, opening the door for an older guy. *Is this her house?* I pull up the surgical mask that Rosa makes me wear.

"Thanks so much for coming," she tells the guy, letting him in. "I just need you to draft my speech. We're debating on 'this house will tax inheritance at one hundred percent.'"

My jaw drops. Who is this guy? She wants him to *draft*

her speech? That's the motion we're debating on Wednesday.

"No problem," he says. "I just did that one with my team last week. We beat UCLA at El Camino."

"Well, try to tone it down, Coach Evans." She laughs as she guides him over to the couch and coffee table. "Remember, I'm only in high school."

Oh my God. Is Heather *buying* speeches from a college debate coach?

For the next half hour, I listen as Coach Evans feeds Heather line by line, exactly what she needs to say to win the debate. As they're wrapping up, Heather's mom walks down the stairs with her wallet. She pays him $500 cash.

"There's a bonus if she makes it to Snider," she says. "And of course the ten thousand dollars we talked about for the recommendation letter."

Coach Evans nods as he puts the money into the pocket of his faculty jacket. The whole time, I'm sitting eight feet away, completely invisible to them, scrubbing at their ivory wool carpet until my finger is rubbed raw and the burgundy stain seeps deep into my nails.

seven

Claire

In the weeks leading up to my departure date, my dad is home every night, my parents reunited by the happy news that I'm leaving for America. They take me to the agent, this guy who grins at me with yellow jigsaw teeth. He tells me everything's all set for my arrival, and my host family's so excited. My parents picked the De La Cruzes, figuring I'd be more comfortable living with a Filipino family, since Tressy has been taking care of me all my life. They take me to the consulate to get my visa. To the health insurance broker to get me international health insurance. My father gives me a platinum American Express credit card with an outrageously high limit and tells me to use it in emergencies. My mother tells me to use it whenever.

My grandmother throws me a goodbye party, which all my aunts and uncles come to. Nai Nai congratulates me on being the first of her grandkids to be educated abroad, while my parents stand by proudly and my cousins roll their eyes. I glance down at my phone. Teddy and I still haven't talked since the day at the park. I can't believe it's really over.

My girlfriends and I go to sing karaoke one last time while my mom runs around town doing last-minute shopping. She gets me a new backpack from MCM, makeup from Shu Uemura, beauty products from Dior, and a Moncler jacket, which I put back in the bag.

"Mom, I told you, it's always warm in LA," I say.

She takes the jacket, adds it to my mountain of clothes and says, "You never know." Then she dumps about a pound of pollution masks from Taobao on my bed.

I pick up one of the masks, confused.

"What are these for?" I ask. There are black and gray masks of varying thickness. I take the thickest one and put it on. It makes an *uuufff* sound when I breath in, like something out of *Star Wars*. "We don't even wear these here!"

My mom rolls her eyes. "That's because the pollution here covers up the UV. But in America, it's sunny all the time." She points a finger at me. "I won't have you coming back brown!"

I close my eyes, feeling the fury and frustration building inside. It brings me back to when I was twelve and my mom made me quit the swim team.

She had told me the coach said I didn't have what it takes. Swimming was my passion. I loved the way the water cocooned me from the outside world. It was the one activity that I did for *me*. Tearfully, I went to say goodbye to my coach and thanked him for all the years of training. I apologized for having wasted so much of his time. That's when I learned that he never said those words. My mother just didn't want me to keep swimming because she was concerned I was gaining too much muscle.

I blew up at her when I got home, and she'd blamed it on my grandmother. But I was mad at my mom. When you're always going along with a seventy-four-year-old madwoman, how are you any better than her?

I squeeze the pollution masks in my hand. Maybe it's not such a bad thing I'm leaving. I can finally take back control of my life.

On the car ride to the airport, I stare at my WeChat. Still no message from Teddy. He must know I'm leaving today. My friends made such a big deal about it at school yesterday, getting me flowers and balloons. I tap on his name to compose a message.

Hey. Just want to say bye. I'm leaving today . . .

I pause and delete it.

"The driver's picking you guys up at LAX," my dad says as we arrive at Pudong International Airport. "His name is Tong. We use him all the time."

My mom, who is going with me to LA, adds Tong's contact into her phone as Patrick, our driver, pulls up to the curb. We get out, and Patrick starts unloading all our suitcases—we have so many, thank God we're flying business. My dad jumps on a call.

When all the suitcases are loaded onto the cart, my dad gets off his call and we walk into the airport and check in. As the woman at the business-class counter hands us our boarding passes, I hear someone calling my name. I turn and see Teddy running toward us. He's carrying roses and a card.

"Claire!" he exclaims.

He throws his arms around me, a messy embrace of flowers and hair. I wait for him to catch his breath while my parents stare on.

"I'm sorry," he says. "I acted like an idiot."

They were the words I'd been waiting for, staring and willing them to appear on my phone. I smile at Teddy and kiss him, a long, wet kiss that makes my dad look away.

"It's okay," I say.

Teddy takes the flowers and presents them to me along with the card. I smile as I take a whiff.

"I'll be waiting on Skype every night," he says.

"Me too," I promise.

I stand on my tiptoes and hug him once more as he whispers, "I love you," in my ear. My dad walks over, gives Teddy an eyeful, and reminds me that it's time to go. Reluctantly, I let go of Teddy's hand. I give my dad a hug, eyes still glued to Teddy. My mom tugs me lightly, and I follow her, waving at Teddy and my dad as we walk through security.

When I look back, they are both gone.

On the plane, the tears come. My mom sits across the aisle and is too engrossed in a TV show to notice.

I make myself wait to open Teddy's card, slathering cucumber cooling gel on my eyelids to minimize the puffiness from my tears. I drink myself to oblivion, downing glass after glass of champagne. The flight attendant neither notices nor cares.

When I absolutely can't stand it any longer, I rip open the card. Teddy has written the words "DON'T FORGET ME" in all caps. Underneath, he has drawn three guys in color pencil. Two are American, one with blond hair and one with red hair. He made the American guys look ugly, with orange skin and pimples all over their face. As if that's not enough, they're both x-ed out. The third guy is circled. It's a self-portrait of Teddy, a smiling Chinese guy with the words "I'm belong to Claire" in English tattooed on his arm.

I laugh out loud at his grammatically incorrect tattoo and miss him so much I want to press the emergency exit lever and jump out. I start ugly crying all over again.

This time, my mom sits up. She unbuckles her seat belt, comes over, and puts her arm around my shoulders.

"It's okay." She shushes me.

"It's not okay!" I sob. "You're sending me to a foreign country to live with strangers!"

My mom digs through her Saint Laurent purse for tissues.

"You're making a scene," she says, ordering me to stop.

She hands me some tissues and tells me to wipe my face. But the tissue's too coarse and it only makes me cry more. My mom gives up and goes back to her seat. For the rest of the flight, she buries her face in a magazine and pretends she doesn't know me.

eight

Dani

My mother paces the house, nervously chewing on her fingernail as she dusts.

"Everything must be perfect," she says.

We're in the spare bedroom, trying to move the mattress into my mom's room. The smell of adobo wafts from the kitchen. We're switching mattresses so Claire, our guest, can have the good one. I try not to wrinkle my nose as I move the bed. We had found it lying on the side of the street. It was the perfect size and in good shape. But it had been sitting next to a trash dumpster for so long, even now, if you put your nose up to it, it still reeks of banana peels and sour wine.

The stench brings me to earlier today, cleaning the carpet in Heather's house. I can't believe she's buying her way to Snider. And the fact that a college debate coach would write her speeches for her, trading the most important thing a debater can have—his principles—for cash! It makes me sick, the privilege. If that's what my teammates are doing, do I even stand a chance?

"Dani!" my mom yells, jolting me from my thoughts. Her nails are digging into the mattress. "C'mon, put a little muscle into it!"

"Sorry," I say. I help her drag the mattress along the frayed brown carpet. "Are you sure about this?"

"Positive," she says, "She's our guest. She should get the nice bed."

I can't believe my mom's giving up her Tempur-Pedic memory-foam mattress. It's her most prized possession, the one decent thing my dad ever gave her before he left. They picked it out together. She told me the story a thousand times, how they both lay down on the bed, her with a swollen belly, him with his dirty shoes, which he took off before lying on the bed in the store. Less than a year later, when I was barely six months old, he split. But for that one moment, she said it was like lying on a cloud. And now she's giving her cloud to some girl she's never even met.

"I really think you're overdoing it," I say.

My mom stops moving the mattress for a second. "You've never been around rich people before," she says. A long time ago, my mom worked for a wealthy family in Hong Kong as a "helper." A helper is what the people in Hong Kong call a maid who lives with you.

I would have been humiliated if I'd ever been a helper, but my mom still talks about it with pride. How Madam was so important and Sir so successful. How they took her on trips and always stayed in the nicest hotels because "Madam never stayed anywhere less than five stars." How little John and Bennie, the two boys she watched, were so adorable. She talks about them as though they were her own kids.

Some days, I think she prefers her fake family to her real one. I think a part of her regrets ever leaving them, coming here and having me. On those days, I sit with my knees to my chest on the rancid mattress in the spare bedroom, thinking of how I'm gonna prove it to her. I'm gonna prove to her that I can do it. I'm gonna make it in this world, even if all those around me are cheating.

"All right, you guys ready? Heather, you're up first!" Mr. Connelly announces on Wednesday.

We're practicing in the auditorium, and Heather smiles as she gets up and goes to the podium. I squeeze my hands into balls, hoping she won't use the speech she bought off Coach Evans, that she'll somehow come to her senses, but she delivers line by line what he fed her. As she recites all the glorious reasons why we should tax inheritance at 100 percent, I almost want to laugh, because I'm pretty sure if we did tax inheritance at 100 percent, she wouldn't be able to afford the speech she's just given.

"Da-amn!" Mr. Connelly exclaims, slapping the seat in front of him and jumping up when she's done. "That was amazing, Heather!"

Heather beams.

I'm next. I wipe my sweaty palms on my jeans. I walk to the podium and try my best to debate the merits, even though it's extremely hard going up against a forty-year-old, two-time national-champion college debate coach masked as a teenager, which is effectively what Heather is.

"That was . . . good," Mr. Connelly says. I feel his letdown as I lean against the podium and squint into the light. "But with a little more feeling next time?"

I nod, shifting my weight as I take in Heather's delighted smile. When I get back to my seat, Mr. Connelly turns to me and asks, "Something wrong? You're usually so on fire."

Heather's totally cheating, I want to say.

Instead, I shake my head and vow to do better next time.

At the end of practice, Mr. Connelly tallies up our scores and announces who the team captain will be at our next tournament in Irvine. "Heather!" he says. He pulls me aside. "I'm sorry, Dani. I really wanted it to be you. But scores are scores. And Heather's are higher."

Heather walks over, chewing loudly on her gum as she puts a hand on my shoulder. "Oh well, there's always next time, Thunder Girl!"

Ming meets me after school. The two of us walk over to the agency together. I kick a rock as I tell her what happened with Heather.

"That's so messed up," she says. "And I thought America

64

was supposed to be different." Her shoulder droops, tired from carrying her violin case. I noticed she's stitched the words *Fearless Female* with string on her violin case. "Joanne's." She smiles, catching my gaze, referring to the fabric store one town over. She switches shoulders. "Anyway, you'll still beat her, trust me. Something at the tournament will trip her up. She can't memorize everything."

That's what I've been telling myself too. Still, the unfairness stings. Ming kicks a rock to me and tells me about her host dad. "Yesterday he offered me a beer. I told him I don't drink, and he got mad and said drinking's a part of American culture," she says.

"So what'd you do?" I ask.

"Well, he started screaming and yelling, and one of his kids started crying. So I took a sip."

Whoa. I stop walking. I know we'd been joking around a lot about Underwear Kevin, but this sounds serious. *Forcing a minor to drink?* I ask Ming if he's done it before.

Ming shakes her head. "No," she says. "And, really, I can handle it. Trust me, I've seen worse."

I don't know what that means. "Why don't you tell the school about it?" I ask. "They might be able to switch you to another host family."

"I don't want to make a big deal out of it. The school's been so kind and generous already," she says.

We walk along the quiet, residential streets. I look over at Ming. We still haven't had a chance to talk about what she told me. "So do your parents know . . . that you're gay?"

"No way," she says. "Hopefully they never will."

Ming kicks another rock, and I study her face.

"How about at school?" I ask.

"You're the first one."

Wow. I guard the honor with my heart.

"I'm so proud of you," I say.

Ming smiles as she lifts her hand to shield the sun out of her eyes. "Thanks," she says. "It feels pretty good."

"Are you going to start telling people?" I ask.

"Maybe." She shrugs. "But not back home." She lets out a long, labored sigh. "China's not like here. My family will never understand."

As she looks up at the palm trees and the vast blue sky, I think about how difficult things must have been for her back home to want to leave her family and come live with strangers in a foreign country.

nine

Claire

We arrive at LAX. The driver picks us up in a Mercedes SUV. I sit in the back, gazing out the window at the palm trees and the many people walking around in flip-flops.

"Why does everyone here look like they just woke up?" my mom asks, frowning at the pedestrians' sweatpants.

"Welcome to America! Where everyone walks around in gym clothes and nobody goes to the gym!" the driver says cheerfully.

My mom shakes her head at the people while I pull out my phone, tap on the Amazon app, and start shopping for flip-flops. When in Rome and all.

"Don't even think about it," my mom says, grabbing my phone. "I will not have my daughter dressed like a slob."

"Hey!" I protest, reaching out a hand for my phone.

She gives it back and turns to the driver. "What else is different?"

"Oh, a lot of things. You gotta be careful, especially at night. People have guns here," he says.

It takes us two and a half hours to get to East Covina, California, where my school and host family are. I thought the Shanghai traffic was bad, but it's nothing compared to Los Angeles traffic. By the time we arrive, it's already 6:00 p.m., too late to go to the school, so we head directly to the host family's house.

I notice there are many signs in Chinese in East Covina. Shops, restaurants, even banks have signs written in Chinese. If it weren't for the palm trees, I'd say we were still in Shanghai. Famished, I point to one of the restaurants, Sizzling Sichuan Garden, and ask if we could stop and eat there. My mom shakes her head.

"They're expecting us," she says. "I'm sure they'll have prepared dinner."

We arrive at the host family's house ten minutes later. It's much smaller than our villa in Shanghai. It barely has a yard and is sandwiched in between two much larger houses.

My mother turns to me and remarks, "Bad feng shui," as the screen door screeches open and a Filipina lady steps outside. She's petite and has a bubbly face, which reminds me of Tressy, and I instantly miss her.

"Are you the Wangs?" Mrs. De La Cruz asks. She beams and goes to shake the driver's hand. "You must be Mr. Wang."

"No, no, he's my driver," my mom cuts in, laughing

at the thought. My mother studied drama and English in university, so her oral English is actually decent. "I'm Mrs. Wang. This is Claire."

I smile politely.

"Claire, it's so good to meet you! I'm Maria De La Cruz," she says. "My daughter, Dani, is just your age."

I follow her gaze to the house and see a skinny girl with thick wavy hair and glasses, holding a book, standing behind the screen door. Mrs. De La Cruz, meanwhile, picks up one of our suitcases and starts moving it inside the house.

"C'mon, let me show you to your room," she says. "I have it all ready for you!"

We follow Mrs. De La Cruz inside. I mumble hi to the girl as we pass, and she mumbles hi back. Clearly she's as psyched about me being here as I am.

The living room is tiny and sparsely furnished. There's a gray couch, a coffee table, a cabinet with a cross hanging above it, and a TV. That's it. It's so bare, it reminds me of the inside of Tressy's room. I still remember the first time I stumbled inside. I was six. I remember looking around, at her small bed and wardrobe, and being confused. I asked her why she didn't sleep in one of the spare bedrooms upstairs, and she answered because she's not a member of the family.

"Of course you are," I had insisted. She spent more time taking care of me than my own mother did.

Tressy bent down and put her warm hands around my small cheeks. "Oh, sweet child," she said.

Later that night, I asked my mother if it would be all right if Tressy moved in to the room next to mine.

"No way! She's a maid. She needs to sleep in the maid's quarters," my mom said.

"But her room's so small," I said.

My mother crouched down in front of me and looked in my eyes. "It's small for us, but it's big for her."

The memory weighs in my mind as my mom stands in the De La Cruzes' living room.

"How long have you guys lived here?" she asks Mrs. De La Cruz. Dani sits down on the couch.

"Oh, a long time, madam. Since before Dani was born. It was her father's house," Mrs. De La Cruz explains.

My mom looks around the room. "And where is Mr. De La Cruz?" she asks.

Mrs. De La Cruz gazes down into her hands. "He left us, madam . . . a long time ago."

My mother stiffens. Mrs. De La Cruz has just uttered her literal worst nightmare. Now she really can't stop staring at her.

"So it'll just be us girls," Mrs. De La Cruz says brightly. "Would you like to see your room, Claire?"

I nod.

Dani gets up from the couch and leads me down the hallway. She asks me what grade I'm in, and I say eleventh. She's also a junior at American Prep.

"Oh, that's great," I say.

She compliments me on my English, and I shake my head shyly as she opens the door to my room.

My room, like the living room, is modest, with a queen bed, a small bureau for my clothes, and a desk. But at least it has a window, and as Dani reaches to open it, I instinctively reach for her to stop—*No, it's too polluted outside*—then remember we're not in Shanghai anymore.

"Sorry," I say.

Dani smiles. The first smile since we arrived. I sit down on the bed—sink down, rather, it's way softer than my bed in Shanghai—and Dani pulls up a chair. I ask her what the teachers at American Prep are like.

"Some of them are really good, like my debate coach," she says. "Others . . . could be better."

I inhale with jealousy at the word "coach." And then it dawns on me. My mother and grandmother aren't here breathing down my neck, telling me what to do. Maybe I can swim again.

"Are there a lot of Chinese kids?" I ask.

"*Oh yeah,*" Dani says.

Our mothers walk in. Mrs. De La Cruz sets my suitcases down, and my mother pushes down on my bed with her hand, feeling the firmness of the mattress.

"Everything looks good," she says to Mrs. De La Cruz, who seems genuinely happy to hear my mom say that. Then my mom turns to me and says in Chinese, "So Tong's going to take me to a hotel and—"

"Wait a minute, you're not staying here with me tonight?" I ask.

My mom looks at me. "There's only one bed!" she says.

"We can share," I fire back. Frantically, I get up from the bed. *Please don't leave me here with these strangers*, I plead with my eyes, at the same time readying myself for the all-too-possible scenario of her ditching me for the spa.

Mrs. De La Cruz jumps in. "You can have Dani's room, madam. Dani and I will share. You don't mind, do you, Dani?"

Dani scrunches her face. Oh, she minds.

"That won't be necessary," my mom says. "We'll be fine in Claire's room."

My mom kicks off her Marni sling-back pumps, and I'm almost tempted to grab them so she can't leave.

My mom and I sleep side by side. She tosses and turns, and despite what Mrs. De La Cruz says about how it's a Tempur-Pedic mattress, I can feel her shifting. With every move, the contents of my stomach jerk up and down like we're at sea. Mrs. De La Cruz made chicken afritada for dinner, a Filipino chicken stew, which, while delicious, was also heavier than I'm used to.

"Stop moving, Mom," I whisper. "You're making the whole bed shake."

"I can't help it," she hisses back. "This bed is too soft. How can anyone sleep on something so soft?"

She thrusts her body against the mattress, trying to find a comfortable spot. I feel the chicken ramming up against the back of my throat.

"Mom, I think I'm going to be—"

Before I can say the words, it happens. I don't have time to make it to the bathroom. I throw up, and it splatters on top of the blanket.

My mom jumps out of bed and screams.

"Tressy!" she yells, forgetting we're not in Shanghai.

I cover my mouth—there's more coming—and with my free hand, point to the trash can.

Instead of giving me the trash can, my mom starts waving her arms. "Don't! Stop it! Not here!"

I jump out of bed and run to the trash can, where I puke up the rest of the chicken.

When I look up, my mom's gone. She's not in the room.

Dani and Mrs. De La Cruz come running in. I cringe with embarrassment, wishing my mom hadn't woken them up, as I sit on the floor hugging the trash can.

"Don't worry! We'll help you!" Mrs. De La Cruz says. Dani quickly hands me a towel and leads me to the bathroom to wash up.

When I return, I see Mrs. De La Cruz bent over the floor, scrubbing up my mess while my mom pats awkwardly at the floor with flimsy squares of toilet paper, trying to help but making more of a mess. I can't remember the last time I've seen my mom clean. And it shows.

My mom's phone rings.

"It's your dad," she says. She looks to Mrs. De La Cruz. "Do you mind if I take this?"

"Go," Mrs. De La Cruz tells her. "We'll take care of this."

My mom puts an appreciative hand on Mrs. De La Cruz's back as she leaves. Dani takes her spot and scrubs next to her mom silently. In the silvery moonlight, I can see her frowning. I can't believe my mom would leave them to clean up my mess. Then again, of course she would. It's what she's been doing her whole life.

I bend down and join Dani and her mom. Mrs. De La Cruz squirts bleach on the floor, and the smell clogs my throat. Not at all how I imagined my first night in America.

ten

Dani

You should have seen my mom—"yes, madam," "no, madam." And the Wangs, the way they sat there at dinner like it was a restaurant. They didn't even offer to help clear the table or wash the dishes. And later, when Claire threw up, the way her mom just left us to clean up the mess, it docked on my forehead like raindrops how utterly spoiled they are.

Early the next morning, Claire's mom's driver takes us to school. Heads turn as Claire gets out of the car. She's in white frayed jeans and a blue silk tank top. Wisps of long jet-black hair fly in the wind as she throws her leather backpack over her shoulder. The boys stare at her—all legs and boobs and silky skin. Standing next to her, I feel myself disappearing into the background, like a pygmy seahorse.

Claire seems oblivious to all the eyeballs on her, or maybe she's just used to it. She moves her aviator glasses up to the top of her head as she follows her mom to the main office.

"I gotta go to class," I tell them. "Good luck today."

"Thanks. I'll see you later!" Claire says.

I open my mouth to say, "Maybe at lunch," then close it. I'm certain by lunchtime, she'll have firmly established herself at the top of the crazy-rich-Asian pecking order and she won't want to hang out with me and Ming.

Zach's at the library waiting for me after school when I arrive.

"You're here!" Zach says when I walk in. He looks and sounds so surprised.

"Of course I'm here," I say. I take a seat next to him.

"I was worried you weren't going to come," he says.

A few kids walk by. Zach opens his laptop and pulls up his English paper. Zach's not in the same English class as me. I take a look at what he's written, our fingers brushing as I pull the computer toward me. It's a narrative nonfiction piece about his mom. Zach wrote about the time his mom came home and she was really sick and he had to take care of her all by himself. As my eyes move across the page, I'm surprised by how honest it is. Yes, there are some grammatical mistakes. But there's also truth and pain to it.

"It's awful, right?" he asks. "Should I start over? Let's just start over."

I shake my head. "No, no," I tell him. "It's good. You just need to expand on it."

He looks relieved. I ask him questions to help him flesh out the details. How old was he when this happened? Seven. How'd he take care of her? He cleaned her up, put her to bed, and made her get up to drink water every couple of hours.

"What did she have, the flu?" I ask out of curiosity.

He looks down and shakes his head.

"No," he says quietly. "She was just drunk."

Oh. I follow his gaze to his hands. His fingernails are short, his knuckles calloused like mine. My mom says you can tell a lot about a person just by looking at their hands. I look at the worry in his eyes at what he's just revealed. It makes me want to tell him about all the times my mom's gone out looking for my dad in the wee hours of the morning.

But instead, I say, "That must have been really hard for you."

Zach shrugs. Doesn't elaborate. He rubs his nose and points to his essay. "So you think it can be fixed?" he asks.

"Oh yeah, totally," I say. I put my hands to the keyboard and start fixing his run-on sentences and his misplaced modifiers. I show him how to add some of the details in. Our arms touch as I type, and I keep mistyping, I'm so distracted. When he reads back the essay, a smile beams on his face.

"How'd you do that?" he asks.

"It's nothing," I say. "They're your details."

"But the way you put them together . . ." He marvels at

me like I'm a wizard. "It's better than anything I could have imagined."

I smile.

"Thanks for helping me . . . edit this? Cheat?" he jokes. "Seriously, I don't know what to call the magic you worked."

"Well, it's not cheating," I tell him, muttering under my breath. "What Heather does . . . that's cheating."

"Heather McLean?" he asks.

I bite my lip, not wanting to get into it, but Zach gazes at me with the same discerning eyes I'm used to sneaking glances at in band, and he gets it out of me.

"That's so messed up!" he exclaims. "You should call her out on it!"

I don't know about that.

"Once there was this guy who lied about being on the swim team for his college applications."

My eyes bulge.

"Oh yeah. Everyone knew," Zach says. "Even the coach, but he didn't want to say anything because the kid's parents were major donors."

"So what'd you do?" I ask Zach.

"I went up to him and told him if he didn't take it off, I'd tell the school," Zach says. I look up at him in awe.

Heather walks into the library as he's telling me this. Zach scoots closer to me, eyeing her as he leans over and says, "Seriously, you gotta say something. Don't let her get away with this shit."

○ ○ ○

"Heather!" I call out, running after her as she walks out of the library and down the hall. I can't believe I'm taking Zach's advice. "Your speech the other day, I was just wondering, what kind of research did you do?"

Heather flips her ash-brown hair to one side and texts on her phone. "Oh, you know, the usual," she says. She rattles off a list of periodicals: *The Economist*, *Foreign Policy*, and the *New York Times*. "Why?"

"It's just really similar to a speech I heard against UCLA at El Camino," I say. I'm completely making it up, I have no idea what they said at El Camino. But I remember Coach Evans mentioning this when he was over at her house.

Heather looks up from her phone, her cheeks crimson. "So?"

"So . . ." I take a deep breath, mustering up the strength. "Heather, we can't win at these tournaments if our speech is just copied from somewhere else. We have to come up with all original points."

She tosses her phone in her Kate Spade bag and crosses her arms at me. "*Every* argument is derivative," she informs me. "Every point is based on a previously established point. There are no original points!"

"Yeah, well, there's a difference between deriving and outright copying," I say.

This sets Heather off. "You're one to talk! You wouldn't be here if you didn't have extra help!"

My mouth dries, and I feel the expensive glass walls of our hallway closing in around me as Heather turns and walks away.

"Watch your back, Thunder Girl," she warns.

eleven

Claire

There are a *lot* of Chinese kids at American Prep. Mrs. Mandalay, the headmistress says they come from all over: Beijing, Chengdu, Shenzhen, etc. Many of them live with host families too, though some live alone, she says, as she leads us on a tour around the school.

"They love it here," Mrs. Mandalay says. "Some don't even want to leave for the holidays."

My mom pokes me. *Hear that?* I intend on catching the first flight back whenever there's so much as a long weekend.

"Do you guys have any . . ." My mom searches for the right word in English. She tells me in Mandarin.

"Discipline problems," I translate for her.

"Oh, no," Mrs. Mandalay is quick to say. "I assure you, all the kids here are very good."

My mom nods, satisfied, and turns her attention back to

her phone while I continue gazing at the Chinese kids. Many of them are carrying MCM backpacks. The girls wear shorts we would never get away with wearing in China. There's a couple in the corner making out. The boy has his hand inside the girl's shirt, and even when we walk past, they don't stop. I look over at my mom. She doesn't seem to notice.

The white students stare at me as I walk. They don't seem to be mixing with the Chinese kids. They keep to themselves. I can't tell if they are fascinated or disgusted by the arrival of yet another Asian person.

"How are the teachers?" I ask Mrs. Mandalay.

"We only recruit the finest!" Mrs. Mandalay declares. "And the ones who teach the international students are *especially* patient."

My eyebrows bunch together as I turn to her. "Wait a minute, we're not in the same classes as the American students?"

Mrs. Mandalay laughs. "Of course not, there are major language barriers, for one thing. And culturally, we just find it easier . . . for everyone."

I glance at my mom, but she's already moved on to other questions, specifically about dining. As she and Mrs. Mandalay talk, I fall quiet, thinking about what Mrs. Mandalay said. It's odd to move all the way over here to go to an American school and not take classes with American kids.

"Excuse me, Mrs. Mandalay, are you saying I'm not *allowed* to take classes with the local kids?" I interrupt.

The question catches Mrs. Mandalay by surprise, and she stops walking. She chews the inside of her cheek, glancing down at her watch. When she looks up, she's all smiles. "No, of course not! I'm not saying that at all! You just need to test into them, once you've proven you have a sufficient English proficiency."

Okay, that sounds better. Mrs. Mandalay jokes to my mom, "Your daughter's feisty—I like that! Are you sure she's not American?"

"Good God, I hope not!" my mom replies with a laugh. "We want an American education, not an American daughter."

After the tour, Mrs. Mandalay takes us to her office and gives me my schedule. I'm in English foundation, precalc, world history, biology, and psychology. She assigns me a student mentor, Jess Zhang, who comes over to the office looking like she's dressed for Milan Fashion Week. She's wearing the latest Fendi boots I'd had my eye on for weeks and greets my mom, "Ah yi hao."

My mom smiles. "So polite!" she remarks to me. My mom extends a warm hand and introduces us.

"Claire, you're from Shanghai?" Jess says in Mandarin, her eyes brightening. "I'm from Shanghai too! Well, originally, until we moved to Wuhan."

"Jess, do you mind taking Claire to class?" Mrs. Mandalay asks.

Jess nods at Mrs. Mandalay and says, "Follow me," in English. I note her English is nearly perfect, like mine. No accent. I wonder if she had a Filipina nanny too growing up, or did her mom just cram her full of tutors?

"C'mon, let's go, we're going to be late," Jess says.

I glance at my mom and muster a brave smile. This is it. This is what she wanted. For a second, she looks like she's having second thoughts. Regret washes over her face.

"She's going to do great here," Mrs. Mandalay assures her.

And the moment passes. My mom smiles at me and wishes me good luck.

"So you know any other parachutes here?" Jess asks as she walks.

"Parachute?" I ask.

"That's what they call us. Kids from China who come to the US on our own, without our parents. We parachute in . . . get it?" she tells me. Her silky hair flows over her white top. A few white boys holler at us as we walk.

"Hey, girl, you wanna meet at Panda Express this weekend?"

"Ignore them," Jess says, linking her arm with mine. She whispers in my ear, "American boys are all the same. They're all horny as hell and cheap as fuck. They never pay for dinner. What they lack in wallet size they make up in catcalls." She stops walking and smiles at me. "But they give the *best* shoulder rubs."

I laugh. Sounds like she has some experience.

"How long have you been here?" I ask.

She tells me she's been at the school for a little over two years. Like me, her parents were worried about the gaokao, so her mom made her come.

"I wouldn't talk to the bitch for months," she says. "But I'm glad I came. You should come out with us this weekend. We're going clubbing in San Gabriel Valley!"

I don't know. I'm not a big partier. Even in Shanghai, where people are a lot more relaxed about drinking, I wouldn't go crazy. I like to have a glass of Clicquot once in a while, sure. But you won't find me dancing on tables, downing Grey Goose and slurring my words. I'm confused though.

"Aren't we underage here?" I ask her.

She shrugs. "There are ways. . . . Don't worry about it."

When I don't say anything, Jess reaches out and touches my arm.

"Hey. We're all stuck in this together. We might as well have fun."

Jess pushes open the door to my English classroom, and the teacher, a white guy in his late forties in jeans and a wrinkled khaki shirt, turns to us.

"Welcome!" he says. "Or shall I say, huan ying." He turns to his class, full of Chinese kids, and asks, "Did I say that right?"

Some parachutes nod at his Chinese, others barely look up, as Jess goes to her seat. The kids around her are playing with their phones. The guys in the back are pounding so hard on the keyboards of their MacBooks, I wonder if they're gaming . . . in class?

"I'm Mr. Harvey," the teacher says to me.

"Claire," I say.

"Claire, that's a pretty name," he says. "Did you just make that up for yourself?"

My cheeks color. "No . . . I've had it since I was little," I tell him. Jess stifles a laugh from her seat at Mr. Harvey's reaction.

"Your English!" he exclaims. "Wow. It's amazing!"

Jess throws both palms over her cheeks at her desk in feigned surprise. That girl. She's too much. "Thanks, I speak it with our housekeeper at home . . . and my parents have taken me to San Francisco a few times."

"San Francisco, really?" Mr. Harvey asks. "Did you go to Angel Island? A lot of Chinese people came through Angel Island. Of course, now they fly through LAX." He laughs. He glances at the clock and tells me to go to my desk. "It's good to have you here, sweetheart."

Jess pats the empty seat next to hers and adds, "Yeah, sweetheart."

I slide into the desk next to Jess and get my computer out from my bag. I look around the room. I spot a couple of girls shopping online. My eyes stop at a Chinese boy sitting near the front. He has deep brown eyes and jet-black hair falling over perfectly chiseled cheekbones. A smile plays at his lips like he's enjoying his own private joke.

"Who's that?" I ask Jess.

Jess glances at the boy.

"Oh, dream on," she says. "That's Jay. His dad owns like half of Beijing."

Jay looks over at me, and I quickly shift my eyes.

"He's single too," Jess continues to dish. "I think. Can you imagine landing a guy like that? We've all been stalking him on WeChat for months."

My own WeChat dings. It's a text from Teddy.

Hey babe. How's your first day of school? I love you.

Mr. Harvey walks by and passes out the assignment for today. I quickly put my phone away and turn the piece of paper over.

Please write two paragraphs on your favorite American food and why.

NOTE: If you can't write the English, you may use Google Translate. 😊

I turn to Jess. He's kidding, right? *This* is the assignment?

She shrugs. "You can write whatever; they don't check. One time I literally wrote, 'This sucks balls.' And Mr. Harvey still wrote 'great job' at the top," Jess says.

The other kids in class have barely flipped their papers

over. That boy, Jay, is talking on his phone, while Mr. Harvey sits at his desk, with his feet up and his headphones on. His headphones! If this were in China, our teachers would be walking up and down the aisles, scrutinizing our every character stroke with their hawklike eyes.

Jess takes my paper and quickly scribbles, *I love hot dogs. They are my favorite American food because they are long. I love long foods.*

"Done!" she announces.

I look down in horror at what she wrote as she holds out her hand.

"Now give me your phone. Let's set up your Insta!" she squeals.

For the next half hour, Jess helps me set up my Insta in class while I erase what she wrote about hot dogs and try to write something meaningful. I end up going with minestrone soup and how I like it because it represents the melting pot of American society. When I'm done, Jess glances over at my essay and says, "Damn. Mr. Harvey might actually have to put on his reading glasses."

"How do we get out of here?" I ask her.

"What do you mean?" she says, handing me back my phone. She's made my Insta handle @ClairrreLA and posted a picture of her smiling and me writing my essay in the background with the caption "smartbitches."

I point at Mr. Harvey snoring at his desk. "He's *sleeping*!"

Jess glances at him and shrugs. "Whatever, could be worse," she says. "At least he's not straight-up racist. I heard the teachers in the normal stream, they write, 'Do not cheat' in Chinese and put it up in their classroom!"

I make a face. For real?

The bell rings, jolting Mr. Harvey awake. He scrambles to get out of his chair to collect the papers before his students leave. "Great class, guys! I can't wait to read these!" he exclaims.

Jess hands him our essays as we walk out. In the hallway, two Chinese girls run up to Jess. Their bracelets clink and clang as they run.

"Florence, Nancy, meet Claire," Jess says. "She's a new parachute."

They smile and compliment me on my backpack and my shoes. As we walk, they ask me about my host family.

"They're okay," I say. "It's this woman Maria De La Cruz and her daughter, Dani."

"You're so lucky you don't live with a guy," Jess says. She makes a face. "My host dad leaves the toilet seat up all the time. And, like, he always misses! There's pee everywhere!"

"My host," Nancy says of the ABC family she lives with, "she looks at me like I'm the shittiest thing to happen to Asian Americans since affirmative action."

"Wait, I thought *we're* Asian Americans now," I say.

"No, we weren't born here. That's why it's called ABC—American-born Chinese," Nancy explains. "God forbid we take up one of their precious few seats in uni. . . ."

"Or they're mistaken as one of us," Florence adds.

Wow. I had no idea. I turn to Florence and ask her who she lives with. She says she lives alone in an apartment.

"Florence's dad is a hedge fund mogul," Jess brags, rubbing her fingers together for money.

"Stop," Florence says, slightly embarrassed. "But, yeah, it's nice."

As we're walking, I notice all the parachutes are going one direction and the other kids a different one. It's the weirdest thing. An entire lane of black hair headed one way, and every other color of hair the other.

I point to the white kids as they walk past. "So they really don't take classes with us?" I ask.

"You sound *so* disappointed." Jess giggles. She flashes me a wicked smile. "Someone likes some milk with her tea!"

I blush hard. "No, no, no . . . that's not what I meant," I say. I try to explain I have a boyfriend. But no matter what I say, the girls won't stop teasing me. They make kissing lips at me and all the American boys stare as they walk by.

twelve

Dani

When I get to work later that afternoon, I find Ming sitting outside Budget Maids on the curb. She's in tears.

"He took away my violin," she says. "My host dad, he just grabbed it from me. I thought he was going to break it!"

I dig into my backpack for tissues and hand her a pack as I sit down next to her. She blows hard on her nose.

"I wasn't even practicing loud," she says. "I wasn't!"

I put my arm around her and try to calm her down. "I know," I say. Our heads touch. "You've got to get out of there. You can come and stay at my place for a while."

Ming twists away from me. "I just want my violin back," she says. "Please, Dani, help me get it back. It was a gift from my uncle!"

I pull out my phone and start scrolling through my contacts. I pause when I get to the headmistress's office, but Ming shakes her head.

I try to reason with her. What he did is not okay. He can't just take her violin, that's her personal property!

"There has to be another way," she says. "I don't want to go to the headmistress, okay?"

I rack my brain trying to think. "How about Mr. Rufus then? He can call your host dad and ask him to explain where your violin is." Having a school official call up Underwear Kevin might scare him, and Mr. Rufus will be extra motivated to help, since Ming's his star violinist.

Ming doesn't say anything.

"C'mon, we have to tell *someone*!" As I search up the direct number for Mr. Rufus, I tell her about the loaned-instruments program at school. It'll tide her over until she gets her violin back. Ming nods, rubbing her eyes and resting her head on my shoulder. She gazes out at the strip mall plaza, and I tell her about the confrontation I've just had with Heather.

"That's so mean," she says. "If it makes you feel any better, they call me foreign aid. And the parachutes—they call me an international mooch."

I put down my phone, so shocked to hear this. I thought all the parachutes would be so proud of her, I know I am!

"Well, not all of them," Ming sighs, tugging at the colorful braided bracelets on her wrists. "There is this one girl, Florence. She's pretty nice." Ming blushes. "And gorgeous," she adds. "She asked me to give her violin lessons sometime. . . ."

"Are you going to do it? Give her lessons?" I smile.

"I dunno . . . ," Ming says. "She's from a totally different world."

I understand Ming's hesitation. I tell Ming about having to clean up Claire's vomit last night.

Ming shakes her head. "That's why I don't want to ask her out . . . they're so spoiled."

But maybe Florence is different. I shouldn't let my experience with Claire color Ming's perception of her new crush.

"You should give her a chance," I encourage Ming.

"Maybe," Ming says. "First I have to get my violin back."

I text her Mr. Rufus's number as Rosa walks outside and shrieks at us to stop braiding our hair and get back to work.

thirteen

Claire

After school, my mom picks me up out front by the entrance. The driver gets out of the car and opens the door.

"So how was it?" my mom asks, taking off her sunglasses.

Different from my school in Shanghai, but interesting. I really liked my psychology class. In China, we don't get to take psychology until we're in college. The only class I didn't like was Mr. Harvey's. I don't care what Jess said, I'm totally testing out of his class.

"Did you make any friends?" my mom asks.

I tell her about Jess, Florence, and Nancy. It was clear by lunch from the way they carried themselves and the way the other parachutes looked at them that they were the queen bees. My mother smiles, proud that I've so quickly established myself with the crème de la crème of the parachutes hierarchy.

"And how about the guys?" she asks.

I shrug. I don't tell her about Jay. Knowing her, she'll probably start stalking him on WeChat. Besides, I have Teddy.

"They're okay," I say.

My mom tells the driver to take us to the mall. I furrow my eyebrows. *More* shopping?

"What?" My mother looks at me. "You don't think I'm going to let you keep sleeping on that god-awful mattress, do you?"

"It's fine. Plus they cleaned it."

My mom takes a deep breath. "Look, I know I'm not the most hands-on mom in the world . . ."

You think?

"But what I lack in . . . handiness, I make up in spending power," she says, patting her LV tote. She reaches for my school bag, peeling the heavy backpack off my shoulder, and I let her.

I nestle into the crook of her arm. As we drive over to the mall, my mom fiddles with her phone. I ask if she's texting Dad. My dad called to wish me luck this morning, but I was running late and couldn't talk.

"No, not with your dad." My mom sighs. The driver glances at us through the rearview mirror. "He's busy," she explains, more to him than to me. "It's not easy being the vice president of a big company. He's got so many projects going on."

I wish she'd stop making excuses for him. But maybe

it's a face thing. In China, everything is about saving face. Maybe she's just saying it to the driver, so he won't look down on her.

The car pulls into the mall parking lot, and my mom's face brightens the way it always does whenever she's within one hundred meters of a credit card machine. She reaches into her tote and pulls out a black pollution mask. As if that's not enough, she puts a huge Balenciaga visor over it. She steps out of the car looking like a well-heeled Darth Vader.

"Where's your mask?" my mom asks, pointing at my unprotected face.

Reluctantly, I fish mine out of my school bag. I haven't worn it all day.

"Mom, it looks silly here," I protest.

My mom gazes up at the blazing afternoon sun and barks from underneath the mask, "What's silly is you coming back to China looking like a pretzel. Now put it on!"

Teddy adjusts his laptop and stares into the screen as we Skype each other for the first time. The lighting is poor, and he moves the camera too close to his face, making his nose look like a garlic bulb.

"So tell me about the other Chinese kids," he says, yawning. It's midnight his time, 9:00 a.m. my time on Saturday.

"You're tired. . . . Let's do this another time," I say.

"No, no, no! I really want to know!" he insists. He opens

his eyes wide and rubs his face to try to wake up.

I start telling him about Jess and Florence when I hear Dani open her bedroom door. I get up and go out into the hallway. I have a question for her.

"Hey, what English class are you taking?" I ask her.

"AP English Literature," she says. "Why?"

I tell her I'm thinking of switching out of my class. I ask her who are the good English teachers.

She thinks for a second. "Mr. Connelly. He's my debate coach, but he also teaches English Two and English Three honors. But I think you might have to—"

"Test into them, I know," I say. I repeat the name a few times in my head *Connelly*, so I remember. "Are there any teachers I should avoid?" I ask.

Something catches Dani's eye. She peers into my room and points to my bed. "Is that a new bed?"

"Yeah." I smile. "Do you like it?"

She puts a hand over her stomach like she's having cramps. "What'd you do with the old bed?" she asks.

"We threw it away," I tell her. The delivery guys helped us chuck it. But now, judging by Dani's expression, maybe that was a mistake?

Dani calls out something to her mom in Tagalog, and Mrs. De La Cruz walks over. My mom follows her from the living room. I turn to my desk and see that Teddy has logged off.

"Why didn't you tell us you were going to throw away

the old bed?" Dani asks me and my mom.

My mom raises a sharp eyebrow at Dani's tone while Mrs. De La Cruz puts a hand on Dani's back, trying to calm her.

"Dani, it's okay!" she says.

"No, it's not okay, Mom!" Dani responds. "My dad got us that bed!"

There's a hitch in her voice as she says the words, and I suddenly realize how important it is to her. "Oh my God, I'm so sorry," I say. I run inside my room and grab my phone. "Maybe we can call them. Maybe they haven't thrown it out yet!"

As I google the number for Sealy, my mom reaches for her purse. She starts pulling out cash, and I'm so embarrassed, I pull her into my room and hiss, *"Put it away,"* in Mandarin. Can't she see? This is not something her money can solve. The mattress is *priceless*.

I dial the number for Sealy and explain the situation. We all crowd around my phone while the Sealy customer service rep puts me on hold. The whole time I'm saying, "I'm so sorry . . . I didn't know" to Dani, who doesn't say anything back, just stands there, trying to keep it together, staring at my new mattress like it doesn't belong there. Like I don't belong there.

Finally, the rep comes back on, only to say, unfortunately, the delivery guys have already discarded the mattress at the dump.

"Do you want me to go look for it?" I offer. "We can go

to the dump." I look over at my mom, who wrinkles her nose, a hard *no*.

Dani's mom says that won't be necessary, and my mom breathes out an audible sigh of relief.

"I will of course pay for the mattress," my mom says, getting her wallet out. "How's one thousand dollars?" She pulls out a thick wad of cash.

Mrs. De La Cruz and Dani are silent. I don't know if they're offended by my mom's offering or that she's offering too little. Awkwardly, my mom fumbles with her wallet and pulls out another stack of hundreds, increasing the amount to $2,000.

The cash lies cold on the table. "Now that that's settled," my mom says, turning to me, "I should be going back."

It takes me a minute to register. She's leaving. Like *leaving* leaving.

"But we just got here!" I say. It's only been two days.

"Yeah and now you're all settled in. Your classes are sorted. You've got a new bed. You have your Amex. And Dani and Maria here are going to take excellent care of you," she says, nodding at Dani and Mrs. De La Cruz standing next to her. I can't believe she's doing this right in front of them.

She holds out her arms for a hug. "I gotta go back. Your dad's in Shanghai all alone . . ." She doesn't have to say it. We both know what that means. "Don't make this harder than it has to be."

She looks at me with wet brown eyes. There are so many things I want to say to her. Like I need more than a bed. I need more than an Amex. But what's the use? I take a deep breath and walk into her open arms. My mom kisses my hair and says all the things: *Take good care of yourself. Don't eat too much fried American food. Take Uber, don't walk around by yourself.* And all I can do is nod.

Later that day, after my mom leaves for the airport, I call Jess. We go to the South Coast Plaza in Costa Mesa.

"I don't know why they're making you pay for their old bed. If it was so important to them, why'd they put it in *your* room?" Jess says, holding up an Alexander Wang lace camisole in front of a mirror.

"They didn't make us pay for it," I say. "We wanted to."

Jess puts the top back and gives me a look. "You know they're just taking advantage of you, right? I'll bet the mattress wasn't even special." She walks toward the shoes section. "So why'd your mom leave so soon?"

I groan, looking down at my phone to see if her flight's taken off. She's probably boarding. "To keep an eye on my dad," I mutter. I put a hand to my mouth. I can't believe I just said that to Jess. I barely know her.

"You know you can hire someone for that," Jess says, examining a pair of white crocodile-skin sandals.

I've never talked about it with anyone, not even to my best friends. I was always too embarrassed. Jess puts the shoes down and takes a seat next to me on the plush white chairs. In a low voice, she tells me her father too had wandering eyes for years, but her mom hired an agency and they took care of it.

"What do you mean 'took care of it'?" I ask.

"They brought in a mistress dispeller," she says, shrugging. "This young, hot guy to seduce my father's mistress away." She grins and taps my arm with her hand. "In China, there's always a private solution."

Wow. That sounds so wicked and brilliant at the same time. Also I can't believe her dad had a mistress too! I know it's common in China, but to hear someone else go through the same experience, it warms me in places I didn't even know were cold. I want to ask her what it was like for her and her mom, and now that her dad's back, are things okay? But Jess is more interested in unpacking her wallet than her feelings.

"C'mon, let's go to Gucci," she says, dumping all the stuff she's picked out on the sales counter and pulling out her Amex.

I can't believe she's buying so much. "Where do you even have space to put all that?" I ask. I can barely manage to squeeze all my clothes from China in my small closet. I'd taken a pic of the tiny closet and posted it this morning on my WeChat, to the horror of my girlfriends back home.

"My mom rented me two rooms. One for me and one for all my crap," she says.

I laugh. "What?" I ask.

"She can't put me here and not let me shop!" she cries. "I told the bitch, 'You want me gone? You better give me storage space.'"

I crack up so hard, the other shoppers look at me. I stroll over to the swimsuit section while she pays. I reach out with my finger and touch the stretch fabric.

"Hey, have you signed up for any extracurriculars?" I ask.

Jess shakes her head, making a face, like, *Ew, gross.* Then she spins around and flashes me a naughty smile. "But I am hooking up with my trainer. Does that count?"

fourteen
Dani

Claire's mom slid $6,000 cash in big bulging envelopes, three months' rent in advance, across the kitchen table before she left. Together with the $2,000 for the mattress, it's more cash than my mom and I have ever seen. Still, it does little to assuage the fact that they threw out my dad's mattress without even asking. And now it's gone.

The next morning, it's a Sunday and Claire sleeps in. Ming calls me at the crack of dawn to tell me it worked— Mr. Rufus scared the crap out of her host dad, and this morning he returned her violin to her.

"I'm glad he put the fear of God in him!" I giggle.

Ming laughs.

"Have you decided to call that girl Florence?" I ask.

"Not yet," Ming says. "But I added her on WhatsApp."

My mom calls my name, and I hang up with Ming to go help her make breakfast. She's making tocilog, a Filipino breakfast with fried egg and rice, and my stomach rumbles in hunger.

My mom works so hard during the week, cleaning an endless succession of houses and offices, that I hardly ever get to see her. But on Sunday mornings, we always make breakfast together.

"How are you doing in your classes?" she asks as she fries the eggs. "Your teachers happy with you? Remember, you need those recommendation letters."

I smile. My mom, though she's never gone to college, has been reading up on the admission process online at night. I hear her watching YouTube videos in her room.

"Don't worry, Mom," I assure her, setting the table. "I've got this."

We sit down to eat, and as usual, my mom takes one bite of her fried egg and insists she had a huge dinner. She sets the rest of her egg on my plate. She's always giving me her egg, ever since I can remember. And I'm always giving it right back to her, saying I had a big lunch at school. As I set the fried egg back on her plate, I ask her about the houses she's cleaned this week.

Rosa has her working the VIPs, houses up in the North Hills that are willing to pay extra for discretion and a maid willing to clean up the drugs and booze after a wild party. My mom shakes her head, telling me about her client who was passed out on the floor, just seventeen years old. I think about the couple having sex that I walked in on the other day. I'm tempted to tell her about it, but it'll only worry her. And she might make me stop cleaning, which will make it even harder for me to go to Snider.

Instead, I start doing the dishes. My mom kills herself cleaning everyone else's house, on her day off, she shouldn't have to clean.

At half past eleven, when my mom gets home from church, Claire saunters into the living room in her silk robe, yawning. She plops down on the couch and watches me as I cut up a lemon and run it down the garbage disposal in our sink.

"What are you doing that for?" she asks.

"To deodorize the garbage disposal," I mutter. *Duh.*

When I start the vacuum, Claire frowns. She covers her ears with her hands.

"Do you have to do that right now?" she says. "I just woke up."

Yes, I do. I have a tournament later. And what's with the attitude? You'd think she'd be more apologetic after chucking my dad's mattress. My mom walks over and switches off the vacuum.

"It's okay, honey," she tells me. "I'll finish the cleaning later."

No, it's *not* okay. It's her one day off. She should put up her feet! But my mom nods, urging me to let it go. I throw the cord in my hand down dramatically, glaring at Claire as I walk back to my room to get ready.

○ ○ ○

The tournament, in nearby Orange, is comprised of more beginner debaters from the local high schools. Still, Mr. Connelly reminds us to take it seriously, as it's all good practice for Snider. Just like at Snider, he'll be splitting us into groups of two today.

"Heather, looks like you're going to be paired up with . . . Dani!" he announces.

I groan under my breath. *Great.*

"Remember, just because you're on teams, I'm still going to be looking at your performance individually. So try to rake in best-speaker points!" He looks at me. "You hear me, Thunder Girl?"

Heather rolls her eyes as I nod. We scribble down our assigned motion—"This house would legalize prostitution"— and the organizer leads us to our assigned prep room. We have fifteen minutes to prepare.

"I'll be first speaker. What are our three points?" Heather says as soon as we walk into the room. I look at her puzzled—*Wait, you can't just call it.*

"We should flip a coin to see who gets to be first," I suggest.

Heather points to her Apple iWatch with her finger. "Hello! We only have fifteen minutes! You really want to fight about this for ten minutes? When we could be prepping? Ticktock!"

I hate that she's using our limited time against me. But

106

she does have a point. I slide into a chair. "Fine," I say.

We prep for the fifteen minutes. When the time's up, we have all three points mapped out. As first speaker, Heather is supposed to say the first two points, and I'm supposed the say the last point, which happens to be a highly sophisticated argument. I even came up with a model that proves why legalizing prostitution would have negative ramifications on society.

I walk back into the tournament room, pumped for my speech, when Heather walks up onstage, opens her mouth . . . and steals my point.

fifteen

Claire

My leg taps outside Mrs. Mandalay's office as I wait to talk to her about testing out of Mr. Harvey's class. Yesterday, we didn't do anything but play two truths and a lie in class, which was actually hilarious because that cute guy Jay said some really shocking things. His two truths and a lie were:

I once crashed a sports car that wasn't mine.
I can fly a helicopter.
I've never been naked in –10 degrees Celsius.

Guess which one his lie was. It doesn't involve transportation.

As soon as he said the word "naked," all the girls in the room blushed. Jess fanned herself, turning to me and mouthing, *"I'm dead."*

I giggled. I still can't believe she's messing around with

her personal trainer.

She told me they started a little over a month ago. It's purely physical. She would never "date" a white guy—her parents would kill her. And she swears it's going to end soon, he's going to UCSD in the fall.

"So he's older?" I asked her. "Are you being safe?"

"Of course I'm being safe!" she insisted. "I put, like, five condoms on him!"

I shake my head. That crazy girl.

I'd be okay with staying in the class with Jess if we had someone else as our teacher. Ms. Jones for instance, our substitute, is amazing. She's a warm and funny African American teacher with long braids, and she actually made us read. Unfortunately, she only taught us for one class. Mr. Harvey came back the next day, and it was back to playing categories.

Mrs. Mandalay's assistant nods at me and tells me to go in. I walk inside Mrs. Mandalay's office and take a seat.

"Claire, how are you adjusting?" Mrs. Mandalay asks, looking up from her laptop.

"Good," I say. "I was hoping to talk to you about my English class."

She puts down her black-rimmed reading glasses. "What about it?" she asks.

"I just . . . I've always enjoyed English, and I'd love to have a chance to take a class with"—I look down at my phone at the name of the teacher Dani had recommended—"Mr. Connelly."

Mrs. Mandalay shakes her head, lips puckering.

"That's not an option, I'm afraid. His classes are all full, and he only teaches honors," she replies quickly.

I wonder, How does she know I won't qualify for honors?

"Well, is there someone else who's teaching English Three?" I ask. "How about Ms. Jones?"

"Ms. Jones is just a substitute," she says. "And I have to warn you. English Three is tough. They're reading F. Scott Fitzgerald, *The Great Gatsby*."

"I love *The Great Gatsby*!" I tell her.

"The book? Not the movie with Leonardo DiCaprio," she clarifies. The condescension in her voice makes me look down.

She taps a few keys on her computer. "The only teacher who has a spot available in her English Three class is Mrs. Wallace," she tells me. "That is assuming you pass the test."

I walk out of Mrs. Mandalay's office with a date to take the English placement exam next Thursday at 9:00 a.m. As I head back to the cafeteria to tell Jess and the others, I pass by the auditorium and hear Dani's voice inside. I stop and peer through the door, listening to her for a few minutes.

Damn, she's good. I've heard her practicing in her room for the tournament this weekend. I was *in awe*. There are so many questions I want to ask her, like how did she learn to debate like that? How does she come up with such powerful lines, about individualism and diversity and justice? Does she really believe them?

I wish I had a chance to ask, but at dinner, Dani sits there and reads—*reads*—while I try to make conversation with her mom. I know she's still mad over the bed. Had I known it was going to cause this much of a problem, I would have never let my mom buy the stupid mattress.

Jess says Americans are like pendulums. You never know which way they'll swing. Dani's mom, though, is consistently nice. She's always complimenting me on my clothes and shoes. She's noticed that I don't really like to eat Filipino food, so she's been making more Chinese food. I feel fortunate, especially compared to Florence, who orders all her food from Uber Eats, and Jess, who says her host family just puts out bread and cheap bologna slices and tells her to make a sandwich.

I walk to the cafeteria and make my way to our table. Florence, Jess, and Nancy are picking at their lunches—the American cafeteria food is so calorie-rich compared to back home. I tell them about testing out of English, but they're too preoccupied staring at Jay, two tables down.

"I heard his family has a private plane," Nancy says.

No way. "If his family has a private plane, why would he come here?" I ask. Flashy clothes are one thing, but private planes are a whole other level of wealth, one that usually comes with bodyguards and a lot of supervision.

"Some of my dad's clients have private planes." Florence shrugs. "They're not that uncommon."

"Maybe his family doesn't like the prep schools," Nancy says. "All those rules . . ." She shudders. "Plus, it's so damn cold all the time in New England."

The girls sigh at Jay. "It should be illegal to be that rich and that hot."

"I bet he has a million girlfriends," Nancy says.

"I would *love* to be another one of them," Jess volunteers.

Florence rolls her eyes. "You guys, stop," she says. "He's just a guy." Before she could finish the rest of her sentence, there's an announcement on the school intercom.

"Attention, please. Will the student driving the gold Bentley please move your car out of the faculty parking space?" the loud voice boomed.

As we all look around the cafeteria, there's a wave of snickers from the Asian American table across from ours. "Move your car!" one of them, a girl, yells from the table. Florence whispers the name of the girl—Emma Lau— whose locker is next to Florence's.

Jess gets up, on behalf of the parachutes, and starts getting into it with Emma. "How do you know it's ours?" she asks.

"Uhhh . . . gold Bentley?" Emma responds. "Our parents would never buy us something so tacky."

Jess's face reddens even though it's not her car. "No, they're too busy clipping coupons for Walmart!" she yells.

The whole cafeteria erupts "OH!" as Nancy and I yank Jess down by her shirt and plead with her to let it go.

"It's not worth it," we urge in Mandarin.

"I need some water," Jess says, fuming.

I get Jess some water as Nancy and Florence try to calm her down. As I'm grabbing a couple of Smartwaters, I notice Jay standing in line. Casually, I get in line behind him and wait as he pays for his Coca-Cola, trying not to stare—he's even hotter up close.

My phone dings. It's a text from Teddy.

Hey babe. I had another dream about you and this time we were—

I click my phone shut before I can read the rest and stand there, face flushing. Lately, our Skype sessions have been getting a little . . . intense. It started accidentally, when Teddy sleepily described what he wanted to do to me if we were right next to each other. I think he was actually half asleep when he said it, but it was kind of hot. We've been Skyping ever since, sharing our fantasies. I tell myself it's not real. It's just on Skype. It's not like we're taking our clothes off or actually going to do any of the things we say we are when I get back to Shanghai. Still, my overactive imagination heats my skin.

When I look up, Jay's gone. I hand the cashier my waters and ten dollars. The cashier shakes her head at me.

"You're all good," she says.

"What do you mean?" I ask, confused.

She points her finger toward Jay. "He already paid for you."

sixteen

Dani

I can't believe Heather took my point in a public tournament. That's debate equivalent to sitting on my head and taking a shit. She grinned so hard when they announced she got thirty-seven more speaker points than me. In shock, I couldn't come up with a new point on the spot, and the judges marked me down big-time.

Afterward, Mr. Connelly pulls me aside. It takes every ounce of effort not to cry when he comforts me, "Hey, it's okay, we all have an off day sometimes."

I want to say to him, *No, I'm not having an off day! I'm having an on day, but she just took all my ons!*

"Get some rest," he says. "Let's talk tomorrow."

I nod, biting the inside of my cheek. I won't give Heather the satisfaction of seeing me cry.

"We'll go out for lunch," he says. He points a finger at

me. "I meant what I said to you when I first started training you. There's a champion in there, I know it."

I mope around the house the rest of Sunday. My mom's out getting groceries, so it's just me and Claire. Honestly, I wish she weren't there, and I know it's not her fault, but every time I look at her, she just reminds me of Heather. All that privilege, wealth, and entitlement, the fact that she can order anything—a car, a home, a mom.

I used to think debate was a way out from all that, but now I'm not so sure.

My Messenger dings.

Hey, you busy?

It's Zach.

No. Where are you? I text back.

I'm at the library.

I look around my room and grab my keys.

Be right there.

I grab a granola bar from my desk and head out. I stop for a second in front of Claire's room, debating whether to tell her I'm leaving. She's studying. I will say, that girl studies a lot. I head out without disturbing her.

Zach's sitting on the curb by the entrance of the library when I get there. His notes and papers from class are sprawled before him.

"I forgot the library closes early on Sundays," he says, frowning at his notes. "I'm in deep shit in bio, and we have a test."

I sit down next to him.

"What are you guys doing in bio?" I ask. I'm in AP, and he's in regular.

He tells me they're on cell cycles. Bio's probably my least favorite subject, but on a day like this, I welcome any and all distractions. I grab his notes and flip through them. He's gotten some of the terms mixed up, and I pull out a blank piece of paper from his notebook to draw out the difference between the interphase and the mitotic phase so he'll remember.

"And this"—I point to the line in the middle of an animal cell—"is how they split."

"And what's that line called?" Zach asks.

I tell him it's called the cleavage furrow. His left eyebrow tilts slightly as he looks at me.

"The *what* furrow?" he asks.

"The cleavage furrow," I say, blushing.

As I say this, his eyes wander down my neck. I tell myself it's nothing, just a biological reflex; boys are biologically incapable of talking about breasts or cleavage without checking it out. And, really, there's not that much to check out.

"Cleavage furrow, got it. Won't forget that," he says, blushing.

"Or Golgi vesicles," I add.

He smiles. He turns his head to one side. The rays of the sun hit his blond hair. "You're, like, the smartest girl I know," he says.

The comment comes out of nowhere and temporarily lifts me. Then the pride mixes with my disappointment of having just bombed at the tournament.

"What's wrong?" Zach asks.

I shake my head, not really wanting to say.

"What, you can tell me," he urges.

There's a gush of wind and some of his papers drift on the sidewalk, but Zach makes no attempt to get them.

I sigh and tell him what Heather pulled at the tournament. I don't know what it is with him, he has an uncanny ability to get things out of me. I'd like to blame it on his blue eyes, but I'm not even staring at them now. I'm looking down at my hands as they fiddle with the hole in my thrift-store cardigan.

"That's bullshit," Zach says. "I can't believe she did that."

It feels good to let it out, though my fists still tighten every time I think about Heather.

"Hey, next time you know what you do?" he asks, putting a casual hand on my arm. I glance down. It looks good there. "You feed her bad arguments."

I shake my head, reaching to help him gather up his loose papers off the ground. That's the thing. Heather was perfectly willing to let us lose as a team today, so long as she scored her individual speaker points, but I'm not. That's a line I'm not comfortable crossing.

Zach takes the loose papers and puts them in his backpack. We both get up. I smooth out my skirt as we head over to the bus station. He apologizes for not being able to give me a ride home, as his mom was using his car.

"No problem," I say.

I feel better. Zach thanks me for my help and hugs me goodbye before crossing the street to wait for his bus.

"Hey!" he calls out from the bus bench across the street. "You'll beat that speech-stealing, coach-bribing fraud! I know you will! She ain't got nothing on you!"

I grin at him, kicking my feet under the bench as I wait for the bus.

seventeen

Claire

Friday night, I'm Skyping with my mom. It's her Saturday morning. I've been in California a week. I miss the comforts of home, not having to make my own bed, not having to Uber everywhere. I miss Tressy. On the other hand, life by myself and not by committee is incredibly freeing. I can finally do whatever I want, and eat, say, drink whatever I want. There's no one here to stop me.

My mom's sipping tea and nibbling at a pineapple bun. She seems distracted when I tell her about my week. Judging by the silence in the house and the single plate setting, I'm guessing my dad did not come home again last night.

"You okay, Mom?" I ask. I think of what Jess said about the mistress-dispelling agencies. "You know . . . there are these places, these agencies we can go to."

I tell her about Jess's dad, thinking it might help, but it pisses her off. "You *talk* to your friends about this?" she asks.

Her anger catches me off guard. I feel the strings of guilt, curling around my neck, even as I remind myself I've done nothing wrong. I'm allowed to have friends. And I'm allowed to talk to my friends about things!

"We do not air our dirty laundry in public!" my mom commands. "You understand? And I'm certainly not going to go to some agency."

"Mom. It's more common than you think. Half the country—"

"I don't care about half the country. I care about this family. This is our own internal affair," she emphasizes, staring into the camera. Her voice is so loud on Skype, I have to lower the volume.

"I just . . ." I swallow. "I want you to know all the options."

My mom takes a long, sullen breath. Clearly, this conversation is not going the way either of us pictured.

I think about telling her about my English placement exam but decide against it. It's not a sure thing that I'll pass. Just like it's not a sure thing that that tycoon kid Jay paying for my waters meant anything.

"How's Nai Nai?" I ask instead.

My mom slumps back in her chair. "Good," she says. "She wants to know if you can buy her fish-oil capsules and mail them to her."

I'm confused. "Can't she buy them in China?" I ask. I'm pretty sure my grandmother's been eating fish-oil capsules every morning for years.

My mom rolls her eyes. "Of course she can. But she wants them from America."

"Why?" I ask.

My mom looks at me like, *Duh.* "Because everything's better from America!"

The girls come by later on Saturday night. Jess, Florence, and Nancy push open the door to my room. I look up from my SAT Verbal study guide. I don't know what to study for my English placement exam, so I've just been studying that. The girls are all dressed up. Jess crawls onto my bed, grabs the SAT book, and tosses it aside.

"Hey!" I protest. "I was studying that for my English placement exam!"

She ignores me and says, "We're going out." She says that a bouncer she knows texted her and he's gonna get us into a club. Florence and Nancy are already rummaging through my closet. Nancy holds up a silver-sequined plunge-neck Rachel Zoe dress from my closet.

"That's hot." Jess nods approvingly.

I shake my head. "It's not even mine," I tell her. It's one of my mom's dresses—Tressy must have gotten it mixed up when she was packing. "It's way too sexy!"

Jess whips out her phone. "Girl, you got a hundred and eighty followers," she says, swiping to my Instagram account.

"So?" I ask.

"So my dog has more followers than you," Jess says. She hands me the sequined dress and orders me to change. "C'mon. You gotta show a little honey if you wanna attract the bees."

I take the dress, wondering what kind of bees we are attracting here. Still, I climb out of my bed. I've been studying all weekend and could use a break. I bump into Dani on my way to the bathroom. She looks down at my dress, raises an eyebrow, but doesn't say anything. Her eyes glance over to my room, landing on my mountain of dirty laundry. She points to it. "When are you planning on doing that?" she asks.

I shrug. "Tomorrow?"

"You need to separate it into small batches or you'll break our machine," she says.

I roll my eyes and look over at my friends. *See what I mean?* This is literally all she ever says to me.

Jess crosses her arms at Dani and says, "If she breaks it, I'm sure you'll make her pay for it, like you did the mattress."

Dani's eyes widen in shock. She turns and stomps back to her room.

"Bitch," Jess says under her breath. I stand in the hallway, torn between calling after Dani and yelling at Jess. Why'd she have to say that?

Dani slams her door.

○ ○ ○

We snap selfies in the back of Jess's Porsche while she drives, the music blasting, the wind in our hair. Jess drives like a crazy person, swerving all over the place. It's terrifying—I have no idea where she got her license—and if I weren't so worried about my boobs falling out of my dress, I'd be clinging with both hands to my seat. I'm so Ubering back.

Guys honk at us, begging us to slow, asking us where we're going. The girls drink the attention up while I sit with one hand over my eyes, the other arm over my breasts.

We arrive in one piece, thank God, forty-five minutes later. Club Landmark in downtown Los Angeles is packed with people. There's a line to get in, which Jess skips. The bouncer, Steve, lets us in, doesn't ask for ID. Jess whispers in my ear as we walk inside, "He's cool. I've been here a thousand times." As we settle into a VIP booth in the back, Jess orders three bottles of Grey Goose.

Nancy and Florence snap pictures, flooding their social media with posts I hope our parents will never see. Thank God Insta's blocked in China. The music is so loud, I can feel my whole chest vibrating. The pic that Nancy and Florence just posted has Nancy sticking her butt way out and Florence looking like she's grinding into it. The caption reads, #girlsnightout.

"Claire! Come *on*, get into this pic!" they shout. I shake my head shyly, but Nancy and Florence pull on my arm and start snapping shots. They post and tag and heart and caption to the delight of their five thousand followers.

When I sit back down, three white guys walk over to our table.

"You girls look hot tonight," one of the guys says. "Where are you from?"

I open my mouth to say China, but Jess beats me to it.

"OC," she says.

The blond guy, who looks like a surfer dude, announces he's from the OC too. His friend laughs, unsatisfied with our answer, and asks again, "No, but where you *really* from?"

Jess looks confused. "My mother's uterus?" she tells them.

The guys say, "All right, all right," and chuckle. They ask if they can join us. Jess and Nancy quickly nod, eager to add some fresh arm candy to their Instas. Florence looks uneasy but scoots anyway to make room. I move down too, hands carefully holding my dress in place as I move. I regret not having gotten some double-sided tape. Jess pours me a vodka tonic while the blond surfer dude extends a hand.

"I'm Eric," he yells over the music.

"Claire," I say.

He compliments me on my dress, eyes lingering at my plunging neckline as he whispers, "You're just my type, Claire."

"What type is that?"

"Asian."

"That's not a type," I inform him.

"Sure it is," he says, smiling. He points to the dance floor. "You wanna dance?"

I shake my head. "No, I'm good."

The dance floor is so packed with sweaty bodies, it looks like the Shanghai subway during rush hour.

"C'mon, it'll be fun. You look like you could loosen up," he says, reaching for my hand and trying to pull me up.

What's *that* supposed to mean? "No," I tell him, looking over at the girls. Nancy is busy flirting with his friends, Florence has her eyes glued to her phone, and Jess is busy pouring drinks.

"It'll be *fun*," he insists, pulling on my arm.

"What's up?" Jess says, looking up at me from the drinks.

"I don't want to dance with this idiot," I say to her in Mandarin.

Eric releases my arm and whips out his phone. To my horror, he starts recording an Insta story. "Watch me persuade this Asian chick to dance," he says into the camera. Jess grabs the phone from him and deletes the story.

"She said she doesn't want to dance with you," she says. "Now fuck off."

Eric's eyes narrow in the blinking lights. He stands there a few seconds. Finally, he turns to his friends and says, "Let's go. These hoes ain't worth it."

Nancy and Florence flip them off and yell, "Keep walking!" as they slink away.

We get plastered, drinking vodka tonics while dancing.

When it comes time to settle the bill, the four of us can barely stand. The manager, an older Chinese business-woman in a blazer, comes over to our table. "How old are you girls?" she asks as she slides the bill across the table. "Your mama know you here?"

Jess laughs in her face. "My mama put me here," she says, slamming down her American Express card.

It's late when I get home. I stumble drunkenly into the house after my Uber drops me off. Once inside my room, I kick off my heels and take out my contacts. One of the heels accidentally lands against the wall and makes a *bang!* sound.

"SHUT UP!" I hear Dani shout.

"Sorry!" I apologize.

I undress in the moonlight of my room, my silver dress halfway down my naked body when I hear Skype on my computer ring. It's Teddy. I walk over, biting my lip as I smile and tap my finger lightly on the touchpad.

"Hey, I just wanted to say hi before I—" Teddy stops talking when he sees my half-naked body on the screen. The tiny silver sequins of my dress shine and blink. "Whoa."

Quickly he closes the door to his room.

"Heyyyy, sexy," I slur my words.

eighteen

Dani

Mr. Connelly insists on taking me to lunch off campus on Monday to cheer me up from my loss at the tournament in Orange. I tell him I have band at 2:00 p.m., but he says he'll write me a pass.

"It'll be fun!" Mr. Connelly says as he grabs his keys.

I follow him as we walk down the hall, feeling a bit nervous but mostly special. Isn't this what college kids do all the time? Go out to lunch with their professors? We pass Heather on the way out. She side-eyes me, shaking her head.

"Hey, Heather!" Mr. Connelly greets her. For a second, I'm petrified he's going to invite her to come along, but instead, he says, "Killer job this weekend. Keep it up!"

We get into Mr. Connelly's Volvo SUV, which I note has a car seat in the back. He never talks much about his personal life. I know he has two boys because sometimes they call him when we're training and I can overhear their voices, but he's not one of those teachers who constantly whips out their phones to show you their kids.

We drive over to Denny's. Mr. Connelly orders the all-day breakfast while I order a pastrami sandwich.

"Thanks for having lunch with me," he says, beaming. "I don't always get the company of such a beautiful, talented young woman."

I know he's just saying that to be nice, but I'm flattered. I smile.

"You still cleaning houses after school?" he asks.

I nod, looking down at the table. I reach for a sugar packet and fiddle with it. He's the only one at school who knows about my job, aside from Ming.

"I didn't mean to embarrass you," Mr. Connelly says. Gently, he reaches across the table and stills my sugar-packet-fiddling hands. He looks into my eyes. "You should be proud of what you do."

The waitress comes over with our food.

"I used to paint houses in college. Nothing wrong with that," he says, taking the pepper and putting it on his eggs and hash browns. "Be proud of where you come from, is all I'm saying." He chews his food, adding with a wink, "Especially when you're at Yale."

"I have to get in first."

"You will," he says. "I have confidence in you."

I smile and vault the words.

"I know the last few tournaments have been tough, and maybe it's my fault," he says. "Maybe I've been putting too much pressure on you."

I put down my sandwich. *That's not it.*

"It's just that I know you're capable," he says, loosening his pale blue tie. He waves his fork in the air as he ruminates. "You remind me of myself. I wasn't always the smartest student, or the fastest."

"Or the richest—" I add under my breath.

Mr. Connelly stops.

"I'm sorry," I quickly apologize. "I didn't mean—"

He holds up his hands, like, *No biggie.* "You're right. I wasn't the richest." He looks at me and ventures a guess. "Been comparing yourself to some of your teammates, I take it?" When I don't answer, he dabs his mouth with his napkin and nods.

He takes a long sip of his coffee. "So they're rich," he says. "Their parents drive around in fancy cars and have big houses, so what? Doesn't make them a better debater."

That's the thing! I lean across the table and tell him some of the other kids have private debate coaches. I don't say who, and I don't say what these coaches are doing for them. Still, it's enough to make his nostrils flare.

Mr. Connelly taps the rim of his coffee mug, absorbing the news.

"Well, you know, if you want, I could coach you," he says, looking up at me.

"You already coach me."

"No, I mean privately. For free of course," he offers.

My pupils flash with surprise.

"I'm serious," he says. "Dani, I believe in you. I'd be honored to."

I am speechless. And I am never without speech.

"Besides, the school needs you. They need you to win trophies so they can get the next group of full-paying kids in and get their parents to write big fat donations checks. That's how it works."

I laugh. "You make it sound like a scam," I say, munching on a fry.

"It is a scam!" he insists, grinning. His face grows more serious as he breaks off a piece of toast. "But Mrs. Mandalay, I have to hand it to her. Four years ago, the school was a dust bowl. It was smart, recruiting Chinese kids." He points at me with the toast. "So for purely selfish reasons I'd do it." He beams.

I smile at him.

On the drive back to school, I close my eyes and imagine, is this what having a father is like? If my dad hadn't left, are these the kind of soul-affirming conversations we'd have? I look over at Mr. Connelly, happily tapping on his steering wheel to the music. If I could choose, I'd want a dad just like him. It makes me want to write speeches all day long, just to try to live up to the version of me in his head.

nineteen

Claire

It feels so weird waking up, knowing what Teddy and I did last night. Was it the alcohol or all the nights of explicit sex talk on Skype culminating in us taking the next step? I always thought my first time undressing for a boy would be somewhere intimate, somewhere special, not sitting in a stranger's house, breasts illuminated by the neon green camera light of my MacBook Pro.

But he was so into it. Like *so* into it. He kept saying, "God, you're beautiful," his eyes like saucers, as he studied every freckle, shadow, and curve of my body, as if so he could re-create my breasts at any moment in his mind.

It's fascinating, to know that I have that kind of effect on a boy. My phone dings. It's a message from Teddy.

Are you ok? Last night was so special.

Aw. He's sweet.

Yes, I write back. Are you ok?

Never been better 😉, he replies.

I laugh.

I swipe over to Insta, where my eyes boggle at the number of followers I have. It says I now have 520 followers, thanks to last night and the tagged posts from Jess and the girls. I click on some of my new followers.

The profiles of strung-out-looking men and creepy randos stare back at me. A few of them slide into my DMs, and hesitantly, I tap to read their messages to me.

I want my yellow fever cured now, writes Bob, 38, a carpenter from North Carolina.

Me love you long time! writes Derek.

I can do things to your sexy Asian body that you didn't even know are possible 😉, writes another.

On and on they go, gross messages that make me want to wash my eyes out and never turn my phone back on. I immediately close Insta—I am tempted to delete it altogether—and call Jess.

"Wei?" she answers, sounding like she's half-asleep.

"Jess! I'm getting these sick disgusting DMs from rando creeps on my Insta!" I tell her.

Jess yawns. "Calm down," she says. "Show me the messages."

I tap back into Insta, screenshot the DMs, and send them to her. As I wait for her reply, I see that in the short span on our phone call, she's already posted three pics of her lying in bed, talking to me on the phone, in her silk slip, dreamily looking into the cam, hashtag #aboutlastnight.

"This isn't so bad. You should see the ones I get," she says.

"How do I get them to unfollow me?" I ask.

"You don't!" she snaps. "Look it's not *who* follows you. All people care about is the number!"

For some reason, when Jess says this, it makes me think of my mom, and I miss her. But even my mom would draw the line at using slutty pics to attract followers. I scroll down on the tagged pics of me from last night and my toes curl with regret.

"Jess, I need you to delete the pics of me right now," I say.

"No!" she exclaims. "I'm not doing that!"

My lungs fill with panic. "What do you mean you're not doing that?" I ask. "I look like a cheap whore!" What if my parents see this? What if colleges?

"You look amazing," Jess insists. "You *rocked* that dress."

The phone shakes in my hand. "Jess, you're not listening to me!" I all but scream. "I don't want it out there!"

There's a spell of silence, during which my stomach tightens into a knot as big as the mountain of dirty clothes sitting at my feet.

"Jess?" I ask.

I wait for her voice, and when it comes back on, it takes an entirely different tone.

"You know, you think you're so above it all. Too good

for English class, you gotta test out. Too precious for Instagram. Well, guess what? You're not that special," Jess yells. "I'll do whatever the hell I want with my Insta. It's *my* Insta."

And just like that, she hangs up on me. I sit in bed, wondering what just happened. I stare at my phone. What should I do? Should I call her back? I want to call Teddy, but he'd be so upset if he saw my pics and the DMs from the creepy guys. For the first time it hits me, how utterly alone I am in this big foreign country.

Five minutes later, Jess calls me back. I wipe my eyes as I try to pull myself together and take the call.

"Fine," Jess sighs. "I'll delete them. But you owe me."

I carry my pile of dirty clothes to the laundry room, dumping it onto the floor as I google "How to do laundry" on my phone. I snap a selfie of me sitting on the cold floor and post it on WeChat for my friends back home so they can see—this is my life now. I miss the simplicity of China, not having to deal with Instagram or followers (our WeChat accounts are not public). Thankfully, Jess took all the pics from last night off, but the stress and anxiety of this morning still lingers. What does she mean, I think I'm so "above it all"?

According to Google, the first step is to put your clothes in the machine. I dump my clothes into the washer in small batches, as Dani said, and put in the detergent. When I'm done, I stare at the control panel. Which button do I press?

Dani walks by as I'm trying to decide.

"Hey do you know which button I'm supposed to push?" I ask. She sighs at me, like, *OMG, really?* I ignore the judgment as she glances down at my clothes in the machine.

"You can't just wash reds with whites," she says. "You have to separate them. Haven't you ever done laundry before?"

"No, I have not," I inform her.

Dani mouths *Wow.* She starts pulling out my clothes and throwing them all on the floor.

"Hey!" I protest. "Those are expensive!"

"I don't care how expensive they are. You still need to separate them," she says. "Once it's all separated, call me."

I have no intention of calling her back. Instead, I sit down on the floor and YouTube "How to do laundry."

Twenty-five minutes later, I'm still in the laundry room, studying my SAT book, while I wait for the load to finish, when Dani walks by. She glances at my piles of clothes on the floor and the roaring laundry machine, which I've successfully loaded by myself. She inspects the setting on the machine—cold wash, cotton, medium batch.

"Good," she remarks.

As she's about to leave, I close my book and offer a truce of sorts. "Hey, sorry for my friends yesterday. They can be . . ." I try to find the right word. "A bit much."

Dani sits with the apology, then nods and points to my SAT book.

"You taking it soon?" she asks.

I tell her I'm studying for the placement exam to get out of my English class, but since I don't know exactly what to study, I'm just reviewing the SAT book.

"Who do you have again?" she asks.

"Mr. Harvey."

"Oh yeah, that guy's useless. You should definitely try to get out," she says. "But you shouldn't use SAT stuff to prep."

She goes to her room and comes back two minutes later with a syllabus from English III.

"How do you have this?" I ask. I thought she was in AP English.

"I . . . tutor a guy who's in it," she says. "They're probably going to test you on how to analyze literature, since that's what they're mostly learning in English Three. Poems, narrative nonfiction, that sort of stuff."

I take my phone out and snap a picture of the syllabus. "Thanks." I smile, handing it back to her. "If I have any questions, I'll come and ask you."

She takes her time responding. The two of us listen to the roar of the washing machine while I worry if I might have overstepped. But then she says, "Okay."

"Who do you tutor?" I ask.

She blushes. "Just some guy."

twenty

Dani

Ming laughs hysterically on the phone when I tell her Claire didn't know how to do the laundry.

"They live in such a different world, the fuerdai," she says, using a Chinese term to describe the rich second-generation kids of China. "In China, they would sometimes buy thirty tickets or rent out an entire movie theater just so they wouldn't have to sit next to the rest of us."

"Wow," I say, glancing at the wall Claire and I share. I wonder how Claire feels, not just having to sit next to me but to live with me.

"But not Florence though," Ming says. "We've been texting on WhatsApp. You know she lives in a house all by herself? Yesterday she invited me over there and she actually cooked dinner for us."

"Wow! So you asked her out?" I ask.

"She asked *me* out," Ming informs me. "Last week. I

wanted to tell you, but you were going through all that stuff with Heather."

I stare into the phone. "I'm here for you. You know that, right?" I ask. It's important to me that Ming understands no matter what kind of shit I'm going through, I always want to hear her happy news. "So? How was it?"

"It was great! She's different from the other parachutes."

I nod, thinking about the term. Lately, I've been thinking it doesn't apply just to foreign students. Heather and her friends are kind of parachutes too. They all have trust funds and safety nets protecting them if they fall. All I have is me. And if things don't work out for me, I'd free fall.

"By the way, today, when Kevin came into my room without knocking to give me a package from my parents, I asked him to please knock next time."

"Good for you!" I say to Ming. It's so great to hear she's standing up to Underwear Kevin. I ask her what was in the package, and she says just some Chinese medicine.

She asks me about debate. I tell her about Mr. Connelly's offer to coach me.

"That's *amazing*!"

"Yeah, but don't you think it's weird? Being coached on the side by my own coach?" I ask.

"Happens all the time in China," she assures me. "But never for free. That part is bizarre." We both think about that for a second.

"He must really believe in you," she concludes.

I get off the phone with Ming and go to the kitchen to return a glass when I step on something hard in the hallway. I hear a *crunch* under my feet. I lift my foot and see a hardened contact lens on the bottom of my feet.

Ugh!

Did Claire seriously take her contacts out and just flick them on the floor? I feel like banging on her door—what the hell! But then I think about my mom and how much the $2,000 a month means to her, and I swallow. I kneel to the ground, pick up the hardened contact off the floor, and put it in the trash.

The next day, after my morning-period classes, I duck out early to find Mr. Connelly in his classroom. I have a free period and thought this might be a good time to do our extra training.

"That is, if you're serious," I say to him.

"Of course I'm serious," he says with a smile. As luck would have it, he's also free until lunch.

The next hour flies by. We run motions, everything from banning junk food to the merits of investing in space travel. Because none of my teammates are around to rebut my statements, *he* personally debates against me. He throws me rebuttal after rebuttal, arguments so airtight, they leave me scrambling. The whole time, I'm sitting there thinking how incredibly lucky I am to be trained solo by one of the greatest debaters of our time, ranked thirteenth internationally when he was just nineteen. That's something not even Heather can brag about.

By the time we're done, it's a little after noon when we both collapse onto the chairs. Mr. Connelly tosses me a Gatorade.

"You want to grab a bite again?" he asks. "Off campus? C'mon, my treat."

I politely decline, shaking my head. It's already beyond generous that he's training me privately. Plus last time I was half an hour late for concert band and the entire orchestra had to stop when I came in. Mr. Rufus was pissed.

I tell Mr. Connelly I have to meet up with someone at lunch.

"A boy?" he teases me.

I blush. "Just someone I'm tutoring," I say.

"Well, I'm sure he's a very lucky guy," he says.

I get up from my seat. "Thank you again for the extra training."

"My pleasure," he says, reaching over and gripping my hand in his, a firm, unwavering hold that conveys the full extent of his confidence in me, and I'm both thrilled and enraptured. "Do you feel better now?"

I nod.

"Good," he says. "We'll show 'em at the next tournament. The other kids can get all the private coaches they want, but it won't make any difference. You wanna know why?" He leans in.

"Because you're better," he says with a wink.

Later that day, Zach and I sit in his old Honda Civic in the school parking lot. He's offered to give me a ride home. As I buckle up, I smile inside, thinking about Mr. Connelly's words. I can't believe I hit the coach jackpot.

Zach looks similarly stoked as he turns to me and tells me about his bio test, the one I helped him study for. "I can't believe Mr. Schwartz gave me an A!" he says, starting the car. "Even Mr. Schwartz couldn't believe it!"

I laugh, feet bumping up against a bag of repair tools.

"Sorry," he says. He scrunches up the bag of tools and tosses them in the back.

"Were you fixing the car?" I ask.

He looks at the tools and doesn't say anything for a long time, like he's trying to decide whether to tell me something. "I was fixing our trailer," he says finally. "My mom and I, we live over at Sun Grove Mobile Park."

"Oh." Surprise slips off my tongue. He catches it and looks away.

"We used to live in a house over by Ralphs," he explains. "But then the property prices started going up and the taxes . . ."

He doesn't have to explain to me about property taxes. "My mom and I recently started renting one of our rooms out," I tell him quietly. "We need the money. My dad left when I was a baby."

What happened? I just wanted to dip my toes in the water. I ended up fully submerged.

"So did my dad. I don't even think my mom knows who he is," he says. "She's not exactly a model mom."

"Mine either." I don't know why I say this. It's not a fair statement. My mom tries. She wasn't dealt the best card in life, but she tries.

He turns to me, amused.

"Really?" he asks as he turns on the radio. "Then how'd you end up so smart?"

I shake my head shyly, secretly thrilled.

"I'm just a normal girl," I say.

He laughs. The sound of his laughter is so addicting, and I try to memorize it. "You are most definitely *not* just a normal girl," he says.

Five minutes later, we arrive at my house.

"Do you want to come inside?" I ask him. It feels like we're on a date. Except it's four in the afternoon. And I'm hugging my textbooks like a life jacket.

"I gotta go home and help my mom," he declines. "But how about later this week? Are you free?"

I nod eagerly.

"Great, because I have an econ paper due," he says.

The anticipation—that he really wants to be with me—and the letdown, only because he needs my help with homework, are both so real.

Be cool, De La Cruz. Be cool. I remind myself I already have a kick-ass coach and a shot at Yale. Any more would be greedy.

"Sounds good," I say, smiling as I get out of the car.

Inside the house, I find my mom sitting on the couch. She's home early for a change!

"Look! Claire ordered us some flowers," she says, pointing to the bouquet of lilies on the coffee table.

I plop down on the couch.

Claire has discovered American online shopping. Every day a new box arrives. So far, she's ordered pants from Theory, T-shirts, bras, notebooks, makeup. Sometimes, she throws in a little something for my mom, which is nice, but it still doesn't make it okay for her to flick her contacts on the floor.

"Isn't that thoughtful of her?" my mom gushes. She leans over and smells the flowers, closing her eyes. "She's such a good girl, that Claire."

I roll my eyes. A good girl? *Please.* I heard her coming home at 3:00 a.m. from a hard night of partying.

"What's wrong?" my mom asks.

"Nothing," I say. "It's just that you're so into her." I didn't want to say it, but it's true, and it's a little disturbing.

My mom gets up to make some tea. "She's our client."

I snort at the word. Who does Mom think she is, Rosa?

As she puts on the water, my mom takes a breath,

collecting her thoughts. "Like it or not, I'm running a business. You're going to be out of here in a year and a half. And what am I going to do with the extra rooms?"

She could come with me—New Haven's not yet completely gentrified. I'm sure we can find a cheap two-bedroom apartment somewhere off campus. When I suggest this to my mom, she frowns.

"You don't know if you'll get in," she says. Which stings. A lot. "And I can't be by your side forever. You have to go out and live your own life, not worry about taking care of me."

"You take care of Lola and Lolo," I mutter.

My mom walks over and puts her tired, wrinkled hands on my shoulder. "I know, my anak," she sighs, calling me by the Tagalog word for "child." "But I don't want you to be burdened with the same."

I would never think of her as a burden. As she pours her tea, I curl up on the couch at the warm spot where the afternoon sun shines in, gazing at Claire's lilies.

twenty-one

Claire

The English test went better than I thought. As Dani predicted, it tested me mostly on literary and poetic devices. I won't get the results back for another week, but I'm feeling good. I even told my mom about it. I smile as I reread her response on WeChat.

Wow! That's great! I'm proud of you!

I put away my phone in Mr. Harvey's class and look over at Jay. Neither of us have said anything about the fact that he paid for my waters in the cafeteria. I was going to thank him, but then I waited too long, and now it'd be too awkward to bring it up.

In class Jay is quiet. I notice he sometimes smiles when he's texting on his phone, which makes me wonder if he's texting his girlfriend. Jess swears he's single, having done a huge amount of detective work on WeChat and Weibo.

She's mostly gotten over my asking her to take down the

pics, though she still brags that she increased my following by 430 percent in one night.

Every day I stare at my 520 followers. Maybe they'll move on. I haven't posted anything since. Or maybe they'll stay and I can reap the rewards of "having a following," which Jess says is just as important for one's future in the US as getting into better English classes.

I haven't told Teddy about any of the crazy Insta stuff. He wouldn't understand. He only uses WeChat and limits his posts to personal friends.

I tell the girls when we're out at dinner that Teddy and I started sexting.

"Claire!" Their eyebrows shoot up, impressed.

"Damn, girl," Jess says, cutting into her beef. "Didn't know you had it in you."

They ask me for details, and I tell them we've been doing it ever since the night at the club, 6:00 a.m. California time, 9:00 p.m. Shanghai time.

"I like the sweet texts I get from him afterward," I say. Sometimes Teddy sends me a bunch throughout his night, which make me feel less lonely throughout my day.

"They're so sweet afterward, aren't they?" Jess adds. She takes one last bite of her beef and puts her fork and knife down. She gestures to the waitress she's done.

"Oh, wait, don't throw that away." Florence points to the thick piece of beef still left on the plate. "We can wrap that up and give it to the homeless."

"You wanna feed Kobe beef to the homeless?" Jess starts cracking up, putting a hand on Florence's delicate shoulder. "Whoever ends up with this girl is one lucky guy."

Florence hands the waitress the plate to box up. "How do you know I haven't already found this person?"

We stare at her. "Is there something you're not telling us?"

Florence blushes and shakes her head. "No, I'm just kidding. I haven't."

The waitress returns with the doggy bag and the check. We all throw down credit cards, except Nancy, who digs inside her bag.

"Ugh, I forgot to move my credit cards from my other bag," she says.

"Don't worry, girl, I got you," Jess says, reaching for the check.

Later, as we're getting into our Ubers, I think about how nice it is that my new friends didn't judge me for the sexting. My girlfriends back home definitely would have judged.

Teddy's waiting for me later that night. We stay up late fooling around on Skype. The next morning, I come out of my room so flushed, I skip breakfast with Dani and her mom and instead grab a muffin at school.

The varsity swim team is in the cafeteria early in the morning, eating breakfast too. There are seven guys and three girls. I watch the way they eat, devouring their pancakes and eggs like there's no tomorrow. I miss that about swimming. I used to be able to eat like that.

Instead, I nibble on my tiny raspberry muffin all squished inside the plastic wrap. One of the swim guys walks over as I'm standing in front of the trash can, throwing the plastic wrap away. He accidentally bumps into me with his wet towel as he empties his tray.

"Sorry!" he apologizes. "Did I get you wet?"

I peer down at my shirt and wipe the spot the towel touched.

"It's okay," I say.

He moves his towel out of the way. "It's clean, I promise," he says. "Just has a little chlorine on it."

I breathe in deep, almost envious, remembering the days when I was bathed in the scent.

My phone dings. It's Teddy again.

Hey babe, yesterday was so hot. I'm still thinking about the way you looked when your fingers traveled down your stomach.

I blush hard and tap Close.

Two weeks go by, and there's still no word from Mrs. Mandalay about my test results. I'm getting worried.

"Why won't she just tell me?" I say to Jess on the phone. "Even if I bombed, just say it! Don't keep me waiting and waiting. I can handle it."

Jess mutters, "Be right back." I hear a guy in the background. There's music playing. Is she at the gym?

"Hey, Claire, I have to go," she says. "I'm at my trainer's."

"Oh . . . ," I say. It's funny how she never calls him her boyfriend. He's still just her trainer. "Okay, call me!" I linger for a second before adding, "Be safe."

I hang up the phone and glance at the time. It's 9:00 a.m. in China, too late to Skype Teddy. He's already in school. I think about texting my mom. Instead, I walk over to Dani's room, hesitating for a second at her door before knocking.

"Busy ako," she calls out to her mom in Tagalog.

"No . . . it's me," I say.

Dani opens the door. She takes off her headphones. I glance at her headphones, old worn-out Sonys, and wonder, Can she hear me and Teddy in the morning? Maybe I should buy her a better pair.

"What's up?" she asks, letting me into her room.

I lean against the wall and tell her about my English placement test.

"I don't know what to do," I tell her. "It's been two weeks!"

"You should definitely email Mrs. Mandalay. She probably just forgot. She's been so busy with fund-raisers lately," Dani tells me.

I cock my head. "Is that where you were going the other day?" I saw her walking out of the house in a sleek black dress. I was surprised. I didn't know she had such a nice body hiding underneath those sweats and hoodies.

Her body language says it's no big deal, but her face nods with pride.

"I had to go make a speech," Dani says.

I want to say, *Your speeches are amazing*, but I don't. She'd be too weirded out if she knew I listen to her from my room sometimes. As I would be too if she listened to me.

"So I should just email her?" I ask.

Dani nods.

I linger, hesitating. "But in China, if we nudge a teacher, let alone a headmistress, it's considered rude," I say.

"Well, here, nudging is considered adulting," she informs me. She pulls out her phone. "Speaking of which, my mom wants to know how to add your mom to WeChat."

"Sure, I can show you," I say, pulling out my phone. I use my own account handle on WeChat to add Dani to show her how to do it.

My phone dings as I'm adding Dani. This time it's a message from my dad.

What's this your mother tells me about an English placement test? Are you sure that's such a good idea? You've only just gotten there! You don't want to offend the school. CALL ME.

"Sorry, Dani. It's my dad," I say, excusing myself to go call him. I shake my head as I walk back to my room. It's amazing the double standard. My dad does whatever he wants, but when it comes to what *I* want to do, suddenly it's all about *Gee, how's this going to look?*

I'll tell him how it's going to look—like I'm taking charge of my life. And it's about time.

twenty-two

Dani

I browse around on WeChat, scrolling through Claire's wall or "Moments" as they're called on WeChat.

I stop on a pic of Claire sitting on the floor of our laundry room with a bunch of Chinese words written underneath. There's a translate option in WeChat, and I tap it, expecting the caption to read something like, *My first time doing laundry!* or *My roommate, Dani, helped me figure it out!*

Instead, the translation that stares back at me is: Slumming it in America. Can you guys believe this is my life now? 😔

The words hit me hard. I thought she was starting to like living with us. I thought that day when I helped her with her laundry, we actually kind of bonded.

I scroll through her other posts. I find two others of our house, besides the laundry room one, both equally whiny and snarky. There's one of her closet with the caption The depressing moment when you get up and realize this is your closet. 🫠 She also snapped a pic of our sink and wrote, Drinking water from the tap because that's what people do here. 😣

At dinner, I ignore Claire. We're having spaghetti, and as she hungrily digs into her food, I fight the urge to ask, *If you hate it here so much, why are you stuffing your face with my mom's meatballs?*

I take deep breaths in debate training the next day, trying to focus on the techniques Mr. Connelly went over with me in our private session. My voice builds and builds, in a palpable crescendo, as I deliver my speech in front of Heather and my other teammates.

"I believe in the power of one person to change the world, no matter who they are or where they come from. I believe in social justice, in education as a vehicle for social mobility. In standing up for the *truth*. Truth is what's going to prevail over money, over greed, over nepotism and legacy and cheating." I look to Heather as I say it. "Truth, ladies and gentleman, is ultimately how we're going to heal our society."

Mr. Connelly stands up and claps, not only him but all the custodian workers and technicians in the auditorium, *they're* standing and *they're* clapping. A smile stretches across my face, breathing it all in: the lights, the sounds, the adrenaline, the pride pulsating in my veins.

Heather McLean's face turns the same color as the

podium—a deep burnish brown with the threat of exploding lava underneath.

"That was incredible!" Mr. Connelly claps. He looks around at my teammates and asks, "Wasn't she incredible?"

A few mutter their assent. Most look at their feet. The doors in the back of the auditorium bang open, and Zach walks in. He must have heard the speech outside because he's clapping too. Mr. Connelly glances at Zach.

"Hey!" I say, walking offstage and over to him. "What are you doing here?"

"I came to watch you practice," Zach says, taking a seat. He looks to Mr. Connelly. "Is that okay?"

Mr. Connelly doesn't say anything but doesn't kick Zach out either. As Heather walks up to the podium, Zach nudges me with his elbow.

"Want me to boo her?" he whispers in my ear.

"No!" I whisper back. Mr. Connelly glances over at the two of us giggling.

"I'm booing her!" he insists.

He laughs and nudges me with his elbow as Heather clears her throat. No sooner does Heather start speaking then Mr. Connelly frowns at her to stop. "No, no, no. That was abysmal," he says. "It almost sounds like you're reading from the back of a cereal box."

Zach muffles a laugh.

"You have to put your feeling into it, like what Dani did," Mr. Connelly says, nodding at me.

Heather looks like she's about ready to strangle me as Mr. Connelly explains to her how to improve her delivery. Zach turns to me after training's over and gives me a high five.

"That was amazing!" he says.

I wait until all my teammates have left before answering, "Really?" I kind of wish Mr. Connelly hadn't gone on and on about me. "You didn't think it was too much?"

"The coach is giving you extra attention. That's a good thing!" Zach says.

He puts his arm around me and smiles and waves at Mr. Connelly as we walk out.

twenty-three

Claire

Teddy dings bright and early at 6:00 a.m. I groan into my sheets, still sleepy. I'm tempted for a second to ignore the call and sleep in. I was up late talking to my dad, which is sort of a mood killer. But then I think about Teddy waiting eagerly on the other end, and I reach for my phone. I tap Accept Voice Call instead of Video.

"Morning," I say to him.

"Hey!" he answers. "Can you see me? How come I can't see you? Switch over to video!"

I glance down at my phone. I know what he wants, but I just want to talk. I miss *talking* to him.

"I'm not really feeling all that hot," I say. "I'm kind of nervous about my English placement exam."

I was hoping he'd ask me about it and make me feel better, but he's more interested in something else.

"I'm sure you're still hot. C'mon, switch to video and take off your shirt."

I groan. "I gotta go. I have an early day at school," I say. After we hang up, I look around my room. My eyes land on the towel hanging on my chair. I think about the calm and clarity I used to get after a long swim, and I grab the towel and head out.

It's my first time at the school pool, and I find it behind the gym. Thankfully, it's always open so the swim team can train, even when school's not in session, and there's an extra lane open for non–swim team students. As I change in the locker room, I can hear the team practicing, the sound of the water sloshing as bodies thrust through it. My toes curl, itching for that warm-jelly feel of the water. It's been *so* long.

I plunge in, eyes wide open as the water grabs me and holds me. Like everything else in LA, the water is warm, much warmer than in Shanghai. I hold my breath, feeling the stillness in my lungs. I've always liked the first moment underwater. It reminds you that you still have control, even if it feels like your life is spinning out of control. All you have do is kick, and you'll be back on top.

I swim to the other side. Back and forth and back and forth, I do laps alongside the swim team, until my legs ache and my arms burn, and even then I don't stop. God, I've missed it. I swim for forty-five minutes straight with no breaks. By the time I'm done, the pool's mostly empty. The swim team has finished their practice. I hold on to the edge of the pool, trying to catch my breath.

The boy from the cafeteria the other day spots me and walks over to the edge of the pool. He has a blue swim cap on.

"Hey." He smiles. He puts a towel around his wet trunks and kneels down. Water pools around his feet. He has gentle blue eyes, the color of the water. And broad shoulders. Swimming shoulders. The kind of shoulders my mom and my grandma were so worried I'd have. They look good on him. "You've got great form."

"Thanks," I say.

I kick away from the edge and start swimming another lap. As I swim, I hear his voice calling out, "Don't hold your hand out for too long. Slice your hand into the water and go through the water. It's more efficient." I try it and get to the other side in less time. When I look back, he's gone.

By the time I'm done swimming, the other kids start arriving at school. I head to the parking lot, hoping to find Jess. Instead, I spy that girl Emma Lau, the one who gave Jess lip in the cafeteria.

Her mom calls to her in Mandarin as Emma gets out of the car, "Don't forget you have SAT tutoring after school!"

Emma turns and flips out at her mom. "I told you a million times, don't speak Chinese to me at school!" she yells.

I jerk back. *Whoa.*

"No pride," a voice says from behind me. I turn, and Jay

is standing next to me, watching Emma, shaking his head.

"Hey," I say to him in Chinese. "It's you."

He smiles. "It's you too," he answers. He locks his Lamborghini, parked in the first row and swings his backpack over his shoulder. The sun glistens in his eyes.

"Thanks for the waters," I say.

"What?" he asks, furrowing his eyebrows. He looks at me like he has no idea what I'm talking about, and I blush. I'm so embarrassed to have made a big deal out of it in my head when he doesn't even remember. He probably buys waters for every girl.

I shake my head. "Never mind," I say. A few parachutes walk by. The girls take in me and Jay. I wish Jess and the girls were here to see this, but they haven't arrived yet.

My phone rings. It's probably Teddy. I silence it with my finger.

One of Jay's friends calls out to him, and he turns to leave.

"See you around," he says to me.

I feel the slip of disappointment as Jay walks away, even as my vibrating phone reminds me I already have a boyfriend.

twenty-four

Dani

"Who was that in the back yesterday?" Mr. Connelly asks at our private coaching session the next day. He puts his feet up on his desk as I prepare the cue cards for my speech.

"That was just Zach," I tell him. I clear my voice to start making my speech, but Mr. Connelly isn't finished.

"Zach Cunningham?" Mr. Connelly asks. He seems amused by this as he shakes his head. "Didn't figure him to be your type."

I look down at the cue cards.

"He's kind of a lightweight, don't you think?"

I don't like where he's going with this, so I clear my voice and start my speech.

"Ladies and gentlemen . . . ," I begin.

Mr. Connelly cuts in again. "So how long have you guys been dating?" he asks.

I put down my cue cards. "We're not dating." Not yet anyway.

"C'mon, I saw his hand on your shoulder. That looked like dating," he says. Why's he so interested in this?

Mr. Connelly crosses his arms. "I just want to make sure your head's in the right place, that's all," he says. "That is, if you still care about going to Snider. . . ."

"Of course I care about Snider," I erupt. I steady my hands on the table.

"Then why are you wasting your time playing footsy with Junior?" he mutters under his breath.

I stare at him. I can't believe he just said that, almost like he's jealous. It's so patronizing. At the same time, all I can think about is the way he's looking at me, the sag of his shoulders as he shakes his head, like he'd picked the wrong racehorse. I pick up my backpack and slide out of my seat, the emotions unraveling inside me.

"I'm sorry, I have to go," I say.

I push open the classroom door and walk out into the hall. The chaos of seven hundred famished kids greets me, all headed to lunch. I scan the sea of heads, looking for Ming.

My phone dings in my bag.

I'm sorry, Mr. Connelly writes.

I don't respond.

Dani, are you there? I know you read that.

Dot dot dot.

I'm really sorry. I lost my mind back there, he writes. Will you forgive me?

I stare at the words.

Dani, please. Say something, he writes.

I feel a pang in my chest.

I just want to see you succeed. I care about you. I don't want you to throw your future away for some guy.

I swallow the knot in my throat as I text back, I'm not throwing my future away for any guy.

Three more dots.

Good, he writes.

twenty–five

Claire

I stare at Jay in English class, a smile playing at my lips. He sits three rows in front of me, slouching in his seat. Even the way he slouches is sexy. *Stop it.* I remind myself I'll be switching out of Mr. Harvey's class soon. Although maybe staying wouldn't be so terrible. *Stop.*

Ms. Jones, our substitute, is teaching us about "the hero's journey." It's this concept in creative writing, and I can't help but compare it to my own journey to America. How I rejected the call at first, but then I crossed over into the unfamiliar. And now I'm meeting people and going through all these little trials and tribulations before finally proving myself.

"And eventually, in the hero's journey, your protagonist will face the *ultimate* challenge, which will test what he or she is really made of," Ms. Jones explains, "in order to take back control of their life."

I repeat the line in my head and smile. I wish we could have Ms. Jones every day.

After class, I unlock my phone. There's an email from Mrs. Mandalay.

Dear Claire,

I'm pleased to report that your test results are sufficiently high to gain admission into English III. We are pleased to offer you a spot in Mrs. Wallace's class (period 3, room 412). You may start on Monday.

Stacey Webber

For and on behalf of

Headmistress Joanna Mandalay

I stare at the email, feeling a rush of pride. I show the email to Jess, who throws her arms around me.

"Congratulations!" Jess says. "We have to celebrate!"

Jay glances over at us. My phone dings again. I click on WeChat, hoping it's maybe my parents, but instead it's Teddy.

Babe, when are you coming online? I know you're in class but can't you sneak out for a bit? Teddy types. I'm getting huuuuuugely boooooorrrreeeedddd waiting for you. 😉

I blink at the words. They look so foreign in the middle of the day.

I just got my English results back. I passed! I text back.

He responds with a simple "yay." That's it.

163

○ ○ ○

I Skype Teddy later that night. There's a breeze coming in from the window, and I reach to close it.

"I think we should slow down," I tell him. "I just feel like all we do is physical stuff, and I want to talk to you about what's going on at school." I'm still so annoyed that all he wrote was "yay" earlier.

"What do you mean all we do is 'physical stuff'? We're not even physically together!" Teddy protests.

"You know what I mean . . ."

"So, what, you just want to go back to normal? And I'm supposed to forget all the things we did and said to each other online?"

I look down at my keyboard. I mean, he doesn't have to forget, I just don't want to continue. At least not right now.

Teddy shakes his head at me. "You know, if you had told me you were going to be breaking up with me, I wouldn't have wasted so much time with you. I could have been studying for gaokao!"

And there it is again. I reach to lower the volume of my laptop. "I'm not breaking up with you," I tell him.

"How's this different?" he challenges me.

Wow. And to think I actually thought he might enjoy slowing down and asking me about my day instead of just wanting me to take off my clothes.

I glare into the camera. "You're right, it's so over. I should have broken up with you the first time so you can study for your precious gaokao." I reach to click End Call, adding as I log off, "Which I hope you bomb!"

twenty-six

Dani

Maybe I'm making a bigger deal of the Mr. Connelly thing. Maybe he was just grilling me on my boyfriend in the fatherly kind of way. Aren't dads always being weird when it comes to whom their daughters date? Not that I would know. I text Ming when I get home.

Maybe it's like me with Underwear Kevin, Ming texts back. You just need to find a soft way of pushing back with Mr. Connelly.

I shake my head at the text. *No, it's not like you with Underwear Kevin!* I can't believe we're even talking about Mr. Connelly, my amazing, inspiring coach, in the same breath as him. I put away my phone as Claire walks into my room and announces she got into English III.

"That's great!" I offer. I'm happy for her, even though I'm still salty over her posts on WeChat. At least she hasn't posted more. I've been checking every night.

"Too bad I didn't get Mr. Connelly like you recom-mended," she says.

I purse my lips but don't say anything.

"Anyway, thanks again," she says. She reaches to give me a hug.

"No problem," I say, awkwardly hugging her back. I fight the urge to add, *It's the least I can do for you slumming it here with us.*

I tell Ming about it the next day as we're cleaning houses.

"She might have been just saying that though," Ming says, fluffing a pillow. "Haven't you ever done that? Say one thing to a group of people and a different thing to another?"

"No. I'm a debater. I have principles," I insist. Of course, even as I say this, I know it's not entirely true. I would never tell Heather and my other debate teammates that I clean houses after school.

"Well, I have," Ming says. She picks up another pillow. "All my friends in China think I'm dating a guy here. I even made up a fake WeChat account for him."

My eyebrows shoot up. "And what about your parents?" I ask. "You're just never going to tell them?"

"Nope," Ming says.

"And what if you meet the love of your life?"

Ming shrugs. "Florence hasn't told her parents either."

I turn off the vacuum.

"Whoa, did you just call Florence the love of your life?" I ask. I know they've been spending a lot of time together, but I didn't know it was serious.

"No, I don't know," Ming says, shaking her head. "You know what I mean."

I ask her how things are going between them.

"Great." Ming beams, tugging at the sheets. "Last night, I went over and we kissed for the first time."

I smile. "How was it?" I ask her.

"Incredible," Ming answers. She fluffs the pillow and hugs it to her chest, closing her eyes at the memory.

The look on her face makes me wonder when Zach and I will get there too. I can't wait.

Ming places the pillow back down on the bed. "Anyway, all I'm saying is maybe the posts you read, that's just China Claire . . ."

"Maybe . . . ," I say.

"Have you thought more about what you're going to do with Mr. Connelly?" Ming asks.

I shake my head. "Just gotta try to maneuver it, I guess. Not let him get any wrong ideas. . . ."

"That's the way to go," Ming says. Her eyes widen. "Speaking of awkward situations, you won't believe what I found out when I went to drop off my rent yesterday at the host agency. They're placing teenage Chinese girls in the homes of single men."

"What? I thought in order to be a host family, you had to be an actual family." I walk the vacuum across the room. I start tidying up the desk.

Ming shakes her head. "I overheard the sales team talking, and apparently, there are so many Chinese kids who need rooms, they're now just taking anyone," she says. "All you have to have is a spare bedroom. And go through a background check. That's it."

I shake my head as I straighten the desk, peeking at the papers lying on top. We're in the bedroom of Tiffany Davis, from geography class. And she's labeled all her Middle Eastern countries wrong.

"Can you imagine the stuff that goes *on*?" Ming asks, squirting the room with Febreze. "I'm thinking of working there on the weekends."

"At the host agency?" I ask.

She nods. "Who knows, maybe I can help them screen potential hosts," she says. "Make sure we don't get more Underwear Kevins in the system."

"Good for you," I say. I smile as we finish up the rest of the room, proud of her for using her experience to try to help other kids. "So when am I going to meet this Florence?"

"I'll introduce you when we're in school!"

twenty-seven

Claire

There are fifteen emails in my in-box from Teddy. They all
say more or less the same thing.

**Can we talk? I'm so sorry I overreacted. But the thought of
never seeing your beautiful body again** blah blah blah.

I delete all of them and set up a spam filter in my email
for the jerk. I grab my swimsuit and head to the school pool.
It's a Saturday, and as I punch in the code, I see I'm the only
one there. I dive into the water, searching for solace. The
warm water greets me. With each stroke, I try to put Teddy
behind me.

As I'm swimming, someone else comes in and jumps in
the water. The guy in the blue swim cap from the other day
splashes toward me.

"Hi!" he says.

I really wanted to be alone today, but Blue Cap doesn't

take the hint. He swims alongside me, yelling out unsolic-
ited swimming advice.

"Harder with your left arm!"

"Hold your breath here! Don't inhale!"

"Now fill your lungs! Good!"

It's annoying, and I finally turn to him, breathless. "Will
you stop?" I shout.

He holds his hands up. "Sorry. I . . . I was just trying to
help," he mumbles.

He looks hurt.

"I'm sorry, I just broke up with my boyfriend," I grumble.

"Shit, I'm sorry . . . ," Blue Cap says.

His face brightens, and he adds, in that sorry, not sorry
alpha way that guys do, "Clearly it's his loss."

I look away. Too soon. Quietly, I swim to the edge of the
pool and get out.

As I'm sitting in the locker room drying my hair, I get a
group text from Florence.

HOUSE PARTY TONIGHT!!! MY PLACE!!!

I smile. She's forwarded it to all the parachutes. After
what happened with Teddy, I could use a little distraction.
Maybe Jay will be there.

I text Florence back, OK but no pics on Insta.

Jess quickly texts back, Girl chill. I swear on my Olaplex
washed, Evian rinsed hair. 🧖🧖

I order an Uber. Blue Cap's waiting for me when I

get out of the locker room.

"Hey," he says. "I'm sorry I offended you."

He mumbles his name, but I don't catch it. And I don't want to ask him to repeat it either, because I don't want him to think I'm one of those Asians who are really bad with American names. Instead, I point to his bag, which reads, *American Prep Swim Team* on it.

"Do you know how I can try out for the team?" I ask.

"Oh, you should totally try out next year!" he says. "You'd be great!"

I feel a pang of disappointment. "Next year?" I ask.

He nods reluctantly. "Yeah, sadly all the spots are filled for this year," he says. "But come August . . ." He smiles and finger-guns me with both hands. "We'd love to have you."

I stare at him, wanting to believe him. But the cynical part of me thinks all men are scum, and he's probably saying that because he has "yellow fever" or some other despicable epidemic. My phone dings with my awaiting Uber.

"I gotta go," I tell him.

He walks out with me and waves at me as I run toward my Uber. When I get inside, I look back at him and a smile escapes. He's still waving.

Later that night, Nancy and Jess come over. We're getting ready for Florence's party together. As we're putting on our makeup, Florence FaceTimes us.

"Florence!" Jess shrieks into the phone. "Did you get

enough alcohol? I'm gonna get so lit!"

Dani walks by my room.

"Oh, hey, I'm gonna be home late tonight," I call out to Dani. "My friend Florence is having a party."

"Did you say Florence?" Dani asks.

I nod, looking over at Jess. Does Dani . . . know Florence? Jess shakes her head at me. *Hell no, we're not inviting her.*

Dani walks back into her room as my phone dings. It's my dad texting me.

Hi, sunflower, heard your good news about your English class. Can't wait to celebrate with you in person next week. I have a business meeting in LA.

I look up from the text and announce to Nancy and Jess, "My dad's coming next week!"

Nancy squeals while Jess continues touching up her makeup. I can't tell if she's jealous or she gives zero shits about dads.

"C'mon, let's go," Jess says. "Florence is waiting for us."

"Is your boyfriend coming?" I ask her.

"We broke up," she says.

"Oh, I'm so sorry," I say.

"Don't be. I found out that the fucker was still charging my parents for personal training sessions. Can you believe that?" She throws her head back and laughs. "Have to hand it to him, pretty slick. He got like five thousand dollars for screwing me."

Nancy's jaw drops. "He should give it back!"

"Not worth it." Jess shakes her head. "I'm over it."

As Jess orders an Uber for us and starts heading out, I look down at my phone, fighting the urge to reread my dad's text. Is he really coming next week? The thought is both thrilling and stressful—I so desperately want him to show up, to celebrate my English test with me. I want him to see my new life here and be proud of me—I'm doing it, on my own, just like he wanted! But what if he cancels at the last minute? Nine out of ten times that's exactly what he does.

In the car, I look over at Jess, swaying to the music. She looks amazing, rocking her Helmut Lang open-back mini, her eyelids sparkling in the powdery light. She does *not* look like she just got out of a relationship. I wish I could be like her, like I don't have time to be sad.

"I just broke up with my boyfriend too," I tell her.

Jess gazes at me. "What happened?" she asks.

I shrug. "I wanted to slow down . . ."

"And he didn't want to?" Jess asks. The driver glances in the rearview mirror at us as he turns onto Florence's street. "Fuck him!"

"Fuck him," Nancy seconds.

"FUCK BOYS!" The three of us scream as the car pulls into Florence's driveway. Florence runs out to greet us. She giggles when she hears us saying we're done with boys.

"Agreed! From now on, I'm going full-on les," Florence jokes.

Jess hugs Florence and replies, "Um, no, that's not the answer."

Florence leads us into her house. Her house is three times bigger than Dani's, and there's tequila, vodka, rum, wine, and champagne set up. A few parachutes have already arrived and are standing around the spacious living room.

"How'd you get all that?" I ask Florence.

"Online," she says. "My mom left me her ID and when they come and deliver, I just tell them I'm her."

"They can *never* tell Asians apart," Jess chimes in, making herself a martini.

As she's sipping her drink, she looks up and sees a familiar face. "Look, it's Jay!" she exclaims. Jess waves to Jay, who is there with a bunch of his friends.

Jay smiles and walks over. "It's you again," he says to me. "From English class."

"Not anymore," Jess informs him. "Bae so smart, she just tested out!"

"Is that right?" Jay asks, his eyes twinkling. "Then we should celebrate!"

twenty-eight

Dani

Mr. Connelly looks up from his desk when I push the door open to his classroom.

"Oh, good, you're here," he says. "I was beginning to worry you wouldn't show."

I slide my backpack off my shoulder and take a seat in the front row. Of course I'd show. This is for Yale, for my future. I take out my cue cards and ask if we can get started, and Mr. Connelly, for the most part, keeps it professional. He listens attentively to my speech, giving me feedback and suggestions. There are no weird comments about "Junior" or digs at my focus level—thank goodness.

When we're done, I sit down and unscrew my water bottle, thirsty from speaking nonstop for forty-five minutes.

Mr. Connelly walks over from his desk and slides into the seat next to mine. "Hey, I'm sorry again for what I said the other day," he says. "I guess I can get a little overprotective."

I muster a smile and say it's okay.

His face brightens, and he claps his hands. "Let me make it up to you. There's an Italian restaurant—"

"No," I say. I think about Ming and what she said about establishing boundaries. She's right. I have to do it, even if it's with the guy I most admire.

Mr. Connelly looks down, hurt, and I vacuum in his disappointment.

"Hey, but maybe we can all have lunch as a team, before the tournament on Saturday," I offer. I can't believe I'm suggesting dining with Heather as an alternative.

Mr. Connelly nods as I reach for my backpack and get up out of the seat.

"I'll see you at training later," I say to him as I leave.

At lunch, Ming is talking excitedly about her new part-time gig at the host agency. They're paying her $11 an hour, and while she doesn't get to screen potential host families, she does get to call up parachutes and remind them to pay their rent, since she speaks Mandarin.

"Most of them are okay with their host families," Ming says. "But I talked to two girls yesterday who wanted to switch."

"Really? How come?"

"They wouldn't say," she says. "But they're coming in to talk to me this weekend. I hope it's nothing like what I have with Underwear Kevin." Ming sighs. "If only I had my own place like Florence . . ."

At the mention of Florence's place, I chew my lip. Ming still doesn't know about Florence's house party this weekend.

"You should see it, her house is incredible," Ming continues. "She even said the other day if things ever got really bad with Kevin, maybe I could move into her place. . . ."

I don't know about that. She can't even invite Ming to her party.

"What is it?" Ming asks.

I look up at Ming. I so don't want to tell her, don't want to hurt her, but I also hate seeing my best friend get played. Florence never walks with her to class. Never sits next to her at lunch. Never so much as waves to her!

Gently I tell Ming about the party.

Ming doesn't say anything for a long time. She reaches up and touches her necklace with her fingers. She has a gold necklace with a small violin on it that her mom gave her before she left. Whenever she's nervous, she touches it. As she strokes the tiny violin, I look down. I should have just kept my big mouth shut.

"Whatever," Ming says. "I wouldn't have gone anyway. I had to practice for my solo for the spring concert."

"Totally," I say.

As Ming takes her tray and stands up, I peer at her face. She's looking over at Florence, sitting with Claire and laughing. For a second Ming looks like she's going to march over there, but then she puts her head down and walks over to empty her tray instead.

Later that afternoon in debate training, I shift my weight, leaning against the podium, as I squint into the light. Mr. Connelly has just cut me off and told me to start over for the third time. I don't get it. He was fine with my speech in our private session. It's the same speech. Word for word.

"I don't know, it's just not doing it for me," he says, shaking his head. He turns to my teammates and asks them, "Is it working for you guys?"

"No!" Heather hollers, sitting up, her forehead glistening like a sugar-sprinkled ensaymada.

"It doesn't feel authentic!" another one of my teammates, Gloria, calls out.

Oh, please.

"That's it," Mr. Connelly says, nodding. "It doesn't feel authentic. I need to feel your words with your *every move*."

On or off the stage? I wonder. I pull my cardigan closed and cross my arms, staring down at my cue cards. I speak into the microphone and ask him to give me one more chance—I can do this, I know I can do this! But Mr. Connelly motions for me to get down.

"You've had enough tries for one day," he says.

As my weak legs carry me off the stage, I breathe into my fist, wondering, What did I do wrong?

o o o

Later that day, the bus drops me off in front of Sun Grove Mobile Park. I'm holding Zach's economics book in my arms, which he had accidentally left when we were studying. But really I'm here because I need to talk to him. Ming's at practice with Mr. Rufus for her solo. And I don't know how to deal.

The mobile park is a lot bigger than I thought. There are, like, two hundred RVs in the lot. I ask some boys sitting on an old picnic table whether they know where I can find Zach, showing them a pic of him from the school online portal. They point to an RV parked three lanes down, laughing as they ask, "What you want with that fool?"

Zach answers the door in a tank top and shorts. His face sort of panics when he sees me, the way my mom's does whenever the property tax accessor comes around. His eyes jump from the empty beer bottles outside to the plastic bucket over which he's drying his swim trunks, and I immediately feel bad for not calling before I came.

"I'm sorry, I came to give you this." I hand him the textbook.

I hear his mom's voice from the trailer.

"Zaaaccchharrry," she slurs.

Zach holds up a finger to me. "Just a minute," he says.

I hear banging and footsteps inside the small trailer. What's going on in there?

"Is everything all right?" I ask.

"Fine, fine," Zach calls out.

The front door swings open. Zach reappears, sweat beads collecting on his face.

"Actually, no," he says. "It's my mom. I think she's really high."

He goes back inside the trailer, and I follow him. I see his mom, arms and legs spread out on the floor. She's rail-thin. Her eyes are bloodshot, her skin full of rashes and ghastly white. Next to her is a trash can that she's been puking into. The stench hits me in the face; I temporarily forget all about Mr. Connelly and rush over to help.

"Can you get her up?" Zach asks. He pours water from the tap into a glass and wets a rag.

I bend down and lift his mother with my arms.

"Whoooo'ss she?" his mother asks.

"This is my friend Dani, Ma. We're going to help you sober up," Zach says. I hold up his mother's head in my hands while Zach gently pours water into her mouth. "C'mon, we need you to drink."

"What did she have?" I ask.

Zach shakes his head. "No idea."

He wets her face with the rag while his mom mumbles incoherently. "I didn't do nothing . . ."

My eyes slide down her arms to the needle spots near her veins.

"She's been getting better, honest," Zach insists. "She's been holding down a job, going to meetings. But . . ." He wipes the corners of her mouth. "She relapses sometimes."

Zach's mom closes her eyes. We lift her onto the bed so she can sleep it off. When she's quietly dozing, I ask Zach whether they've thought about rehab.

"You know how much rehab costs?" he balks at the suggestion. "We don't have the kind of money for that."

He tells me they have no family nearby, and as I look around the trailer, it's bare, save for a few swimming medals and a poster of Michael Phelps on the wall.

We leave Zach's mother in the trailer and go outside. I sit on the curb next to Zach, staring at the sky above us shifting and changing colors. Zach takes a rock and throws it on the ground. "I didn't want you to see me like this . . . ," he mutters. He looks so naked sitting there, his pain exposed, I want to wrap a blanket around him.

"So what's going on?" he turns to me and asks.

Suddenly, I don't feel like telling him. My issues seem so small compared to his.

Zach bumps his shoulder lightly against mine. "C'mon, out with it," he says.

I look down at the dirt, stalling, not knowing where to begin. I don't want to tell Zach that it started with him coming to see me at training, because then he won't come see me at training. And I liked that.

"I'm just having a rough day. My debate coach was crazy harsh to me at training," I say. Then quickly shake my head. "It's nothing."

"No, that's real," Zach says. "I get that. My coach can be

an ass too. Once, he said, if I don't swim faster, he's going to kick my poor ass back to the trailer park."

I turn to Zach. He said that? I tell him I'm sorry his coach is such a douche. Though at least with swimming, there's a clear winner, unlike debate, where it's up to the judge.

"I don't know how Mr. Connelly can go from loving my speech to hating it, in the span of less than four hours. What happened? What'd I do?"

"I wouldn't overanalyze it. Guys can be dicks sometimes."

I chuckle and nod, though I don't want to believe it. Mr. Connelly is not a dick.

"I'm sorry," Zach says, putting an arm around me. He looks up at the red and gold rays in the sky and all the trailers parked beside us, and I lean against his shoulder. "I promise, one day, we're both gonna get out of this godforsaken place."

twenty-nine

Claire

Jay and his friends partied with us all night at Florence's house. Jay stayed by my side, pouring me drinks. Every couple of hours, he asked me if I was hungry and wanted to get out of there and grab a bite. But I didn't want to ditch my friends.

"Such a gentleman," Jess said, leaning up against me as we waited for our Uber. Nancy and the other parachutes had already gone home. I could smell the sticky sweet alcohol on Jess as she whispered in my ear, "I think he likes you."

I laughed. "I think you're drunk."

"That may be true too," she said, stumbling.

My phone dinged. Speak of the devil. It's a text from Jay. You looked cute tonight. Text me so I know you got home safe.

I showed the text to Jess, who laughed into the velvet sky.

"I knew it!"

"He just wants to make sure I get home safe," I said, rolling my eyes.

"Girl, he wants some late-night Snapsex!" Jess teased.

Yeah, well that's not happening. Jess cozied up to me, and we both looked at the stars. In China, it's so rare to see stars because of the pollution, but here they sparkle like diamonds.

Jess whispered softly, "Hey, Claire, I'm really happy for you."

"About Jay you mean?" I asked. "Or my English class?"

"No, about your dad," she said. "My old man would never come all the way over here to have dinner with me."

Oh, Jess. I quickly reminded her my dad has a business thing.

She shook her head. "Still."

As we waited for our Uber, I put my arm around Jess and hugged her close. She tucked her head in the nook between my shoulder and chin. I hoped she knew, I've got her. Even if her parents don't, I've got her.

I didn't return Jay's text that night, or the next day. After what happened with Teddy, I think I'm going to lay off boys for a while. I remind myself I'm here for an education. I'm here to be the hero of my own journey—I don't need some guy. And now that I finally got into the class I want, I'm not going to blow it.

I go to the bookstore on Sunday and buy all the books on the English III syllabus Dani gave me. I bet she gets straight As, that Dani. She doesn't have to deal with idiot boys getting mad at her if she just wants to talk. She's going to be so massively successful when she grows up.

My dad says success isn't about what you know but who you know and the relationships you form. I think about our date later this week. So far, he hasn't canceled yet. Just seven more days until he gets here.

On Monday, I go to my new English class. There are seven white kids in my class, a black kid, two Hispanic kids, and three Asians. I look hopefully at the Asian American girls and recognize Emma Lau, the one who argued with Jess in the cafeteria. She's in this class too? Great.

"Listen up, everyone!" Mrs. Wallace shouts, an intense-looking white woman with gray hair and reading glasses, which she holds tight in her hands and points at us like a baton as she talks. The students take their seats. "Today we have a new student in the class."

She turns to me. "Why don't you tell us a little bit about yourself, Claire?"

I look down at my laptop in my arms, feeling the intensity of all the eyeballs on me.

"Hi, I'm Claire," I start to say. "I like to watch American movies."

"Over here they're just called movies!" one of the white kids in the back calls out. The whole class laughs.

"All right, that's enough," Mrs. Wallace says. She points to an unoccupied desk toward the back. "Take a seat."

Despite the glances and snickers from the other kids, the hour passes quickly. I try to channel my inner Dani and sit up as straight as I can, ignoring them and focusing on Mrs. Wallace. She talks about *The Great Gatsby* and how it's a reflection of the social elitism of the time. As she's talking, I raise my hand.

"Yes, Claire," she calls on me, surprised.

"Actually, I think the elitism still happens today. The way people look down on 'new money,'" I say, doing air quotes with my hands, and feeling very American. "Just because they amassed their wealth quickly. That's more reason to respect them, not less. It means they're smart and they worked hard."

Emma Lau raises her hand to respond.

"But let's be honest, who are these new-money people in *Gatsby*?" Emma asks. "They're people who come and drink his wine, eat his food. They don't even bother with an invitation; they just show up. And when he dies, no one even comes to the funeral. *That's* why they're not worthy of respect, they're fundamentally self-absorbed, hollow people whose only care in the world is consuming material goods." Emma turns to me and adds, "Just like the crazy-rich Asians at our school."

Hot blood heats my face. I look to the teacher, and when she doesn't say anything, I wait in suspense for my own voice to emerge, but the rage chokes my throat.

o o o

"That bitch!" Jess exclaims at lunch when I tell her what Emma said. She gets up from her seat and zeroes her eyes in on Emma. I pull her back down.

"And the teacher just sat there?" Nancy asks.

I nod.

Florence shakes her head. "Unbelievable," she says, texting on her phone. Whoever she's texting is not texting her back, and Florence frowns in frustration at her phone.

Jess shoots death stares at Emma sitting at the ABC table. "She's going down!"

Florence looks up from her phone and reaches for her boba tea. "Why do they always have to distance themselves from us?" she asks, chewing her boba. "Don't they realize that when white people look at us, we all the same? We all yellow to them?"

Nancy looks to me. "She's just trying to intimidate you, Claire," she says. "But it won't work. We're tougher than iron."

Florence nods, chewing on her boba while I look down at the green WeChat app on my phone. At times like these, I miss Teddy. I miss his little Chinese messages throughout the day comforting and reassuring me. I glance over at Jess and sigh. How did she get over her boyfriend so quickly? I know it was only physical, and the guy was scamming her parents, but she still slept with him. Does sleeping with someone make it easier or harder to get over them? I wonder.

thirty

Dani

On the Friday before the tournament, I change into my black debate dress and run down the hallway to meet my teammates and Mr. Connelly to go to the airport. We're flying to Seattle for a tournament, our last one before Snider.

As I'm walking down the hallway, I see Claire standing by Emma Lau's locker. I've never cleaned Emma's house because her mother insists on cleaning it herself, but once she called up Rosa and asked if she could book us to help her cook for a Bible study party. When Emma opens her locker, rice comes gushing out onto the floor.

Emma screams at the thousands and thousands of little white grains.

A crowd gathers. Emma is freaking out. She steps on the grains in her platform sandals, nearly losing her balance. Her eyes zero in on Claire.

"Did you do this?" she demands.

Claire, who's standing there with her friends, shakes her head. She looks every bit as bewildered as the rest of us. I know for a fact it wasn't Claire. She doesn't even know where we keep the rice in the kitchen, and she certainly hasn't ordered any from Amazon.

Mrs. Mandalay arrives at the scene in time to break up the crowd. "All right, that's enough!" she says. "Let's get the janitor to clean this up."

As Mrs. Mandalay ushers the crowd out of the hall and the janitor cleans up the mess, I glance over at Claire.

"You okay?" I ask her.

"Dani, we're all waiting for you!" Mr. Connelly calls me from the end of the hall. "Hurry up!"

I leave Claire and run after Mr. Connelly and my teammates.

On the flight to Seattle, Mr. Connelly sits between me and Heather. Heather makes small talk with him while I look over my notes, reviewing last-minute case studies. Usually, on these off-site tournament trips, there's a parent chaperone, but Mrs. Berstein, Gloria's mom, had to cancel at the last minute because something came up with her other daughter.

The flight attendant walks down the aisle, and Mr. Connelly orders a Bloody Mary. He turns to me and tells me our team assignments. Thankfully, I'm not paired up with Heather this time. Instead, I'm paired up with Josh, and we're told we're going up against Marlborough, the elite all-girls private school in LA.

Mr. Connelly swirls the Bloody Mary in his hand. "The team they have this year is quite good," Mr. Connelly says. He looks at Josh. "Don't worry, I have full confidence we'll still beat them!" He smiles. "If we place, we'll go out and celebrate. Seattle's fun!"

The tournament kicks off the next morning, and Josh and I hold our own against the Marlborough team. Mr. Connelly's right: they are pretty good. But our diligent planning in prep pays off. And unlike Heather, Josh does *not* steal my points. By the end of the first day, we've broken into the semifinals! Mr. Connelly suggests we all go out and grab some Seattle seafood instead of just eating the bland conference food.

"Sounds great!" Josh says. "We'll meet you in the lobby at six thirty!"

At six thirty, I'm waiting in the lobby for Josh and the rest of my teammates, but only Mr. Connelly walks out of the elevator. He's wearing a blue shirt, unbuttoned at the collar, and jeans.

"Where's everybody?" I ask.

He makes a pained expression. "Heather's not feeling well. Josh wanted to come, but his girlfriend's having some sort of meltdown, so he has to stay and Skype with her. And Audrey and Jake and the rest of them said they have a big physics exam. So they're just going to get some sandwiches and study."

"Oh." I know Audrey and Jake and the rest of my teammates are in AP Physics. I'm the only one in AP Bio.

"Looks like it's just going to be me and you, Thunder Girl!" Mr. Connelly beams. "C'mon, the Uber's here." He takes my arm and leads me outside to a waiting car.

Inside the Uber, I try to pull the hem of my white cotton dress down with my fingers. If I had known it was just going to be me and him, I would have worn something much longer. I glance at Mr. Connelly sitting next to me playing on his phone.

The Uber takes us to the financial district and, oddly enough, pulls up right in front of another hotel. "I thought we were going to get some seafood," I say to Mr. Connelly.

"We are," he says. "I just want to check out this place!"

I get out of the car and follow Mr. Connelly into the swanky hotel. He heads into a lounge full of people.

A bar?

"It'll be fine. You're with me," he assures me.

I shake my head, but Mr. Connelly insists.

"Relax. You can order a lemonade."

Reluctantly, I follow my coach into the bar. I take a seat on one of the plush leather sofas, digging my phone out of my bag and keeping it in my hand at all times. I feel more like an underage date than a pupil as Mr. Connelly sits down next to me.

The waiter appears. Mr. Connelly orders a vodka tonic for himself and a lemonade for me. The waiter doesn't ask any questions about my age or tell me I shouldn't be here.

"You were incredible today," Mr. Connelly says when the waiter leaves, beaming at me.

"Thanks," I say, trying to look as casual as a teenager can be in a bar. Despite our location, it's nice to hear such affirmation, especially after how our last training session went.

Mr. Connelly grabs a handful of bar peanuts. "I knew you could do it. Never doubted it for a second."

"Not even at our last team practice?" I ask.

The light from the backlit wall shines on Mr. Connelly's frown, and I regret bringing it up. "I was just saying that so the others wouldn't think I was giving you preferential treatment. We have to be very careful about that type of thing at the school. You know how some parents can get."

Really? Is that the reason?

The waiter returns with our drinks, and Mr. Connelly holds up his vodka tonic. We clink glasses.

He takes a long swig and studies me. His eyes fall on my hair, which is usually up in a ponytail or in a messy bun, but tonight is down over my shoulders. "You look nice," he says. "You should wear your hair like that more often."

The comment makes me self-conscious, and almost by reflex, I grab a fistful of hair and hold it up in a hand ponytail. Mr. Connelly reaches jokingly for my hair with his own hand, like, *Nooooo.*

Our fingers touch slightly, and he looks at me, his eyes lazy with alcohol. He moves over closer to me, almost like he's going to kiss me, and I drop my hands and stare at the condensation on my lemonade glass.

"You've had too much to drink," I mutter softly.

He laughs and swirls his vodka. "I have not," he says. He asks me to wear my hair like that tomorrow.

"I don't think so," I say, shaking my head.

"Why not?" he protests. "You afraid of looking good *and* sounding good?" He holds his drink up at me. "You're going to be dangerous in about ten years."

I feel his eyeballs traveling up and down my upper body, and I squirm in my seat. This is getting really weird.

"You know, if you'd been around when I was seventeen, oh man . . ." He reaches over and places his hand on my leg. I freeze, staring down at his hand. *Shit!*

As calmly as I can, I start to get up.

"Where are you going? I thought we were going to go get seafood!" he calls after me.

The thought of seafood now makes me want to hurl. I storm out of the bar and into the hotel lobby.

"Dani," Mr. Connelly shouts at me, but I keep walking. When I get outside, he catches up to me, grabs my arm, and pulls me around.

"Stop, Dani, you're overreacting," Mr. Connelly says. "It's not like that!"

I turn to him with wet, angry eyes. It's not like *what*?

"Please, let's not make this a bigger deal than it has to be," he begs.

"I'm going back to the hotel," I say. "Don't follow me."

I walk the two and a half miles back to the hotel in my cheap Payless leather pumps, tears docking onto the pavement.

thirty-one

Claire

Jess and I are the only ones still in the school parking lot after Dani leaves with her debate team. Nancy and Florence left shortly after Dani, looking rattled. They should be rattled. *I'm* rattled. What was Jess thinking? It took the janitor three trips to the dumpster to get rid of all that rice. In the end, we had to help him. Emma glared at me as she got into her mom's car. "You're going to pay for this."

Jess gazes at the blazing afternoon sun and pulls out a thin pollution mask from her purse. She offers one to me, and I smack it onto the ground.

"You could have gotten us both in so much trouble!" I say to her.

Jess rolls her eyes. "Don't be such a wuss. That bitch deserved it. Now she'll know never to mess with you again." She runs a hand through her hair and examines her tinted roots in the sun. "A thank-you would be nice."

A *thank-you*? "You don't get it, do you? We're juniors. Our grades, the decisions we make—they count toward college!" Quietly, I blow out the words from the rawest part of me. "You may not care about that, but I do."

Jess turns and walks to her car. "Whatever," she says, unlocking her Porsche. She gets in, doesn't offer me a ride, and speeds off.

I fume all the way home. There are no Ubers available nearby, so I'm forced to walk. With each step, I think about how much I miss my friends back home. None of them would do such a thing.

Worries and anxiety swirl through my head that weekend. What if my dad doesn't show? What if he does show and Mrs. Mandalay called him about what happened? I think about calling Emma to apologize, only to put back the phone. I'm so shaken that when the doorbell rings on Sunday night and Dani announces my dad's here, I look down in a panic. I'm not ready!

My dad frowns at me standing in the middle of my room in my *The Future Is Female* sweatshirt.

"You're wearing *that*?" he asks.

"Hi, Dad!" I exclaim. I hold up a finger. "Give me one minute to change!"

One minute, of course, turns into twenty as I slip into an evening dress, heels, throw on some foundation and lipstick. The whole time, my dad's tapping his feet outside my door, talking in Mandarin. "I told you I was going to be here at six thirty to pick you up. Our reservation's at seven, and now there's going to be traffic. You have school tomorrow. I have to get you home by nine. I sent you two reminders. I don't know how you're going to function in college if you're like this!"

I open the door. My dad's face softens. I'm in a baby-pink Dior dress with the matching pink Prada bag that he got me, the one my mother encouraged me to keep. His eyes smile in recognition.

"You look beautiful," he says in English.

We walk arm in arm to the living room, where Dani is planted on the couch, lying feet up, with her laptop on her stomach.

"Hey, Dani," I say. "I'm just going out to dinner with my dad."

She makes a noise, a distracted "uh-huh," as her fingers continue typing on her keyboard. I consider for a second inviting her to join us but figure she's too busy. She just got back from Seattle.

"Have a good night!" my dad says to her.

I follow him out to a waiting Uber. We drive over to a French restaurant called the Cellar. My dad orders a bottle of wine and takes his time smelling the aroma before taking a sip. It's always strange watching someone smell wine. Closing his eyes. Inhaling the earthy scent. Lips parted in anticipation. Feels oddly intimate, and I look away. I think of what topics we can talk about. I spent so much time worrying if he's going to cancel that I never prepared for him coming.

"So your mother tells me that you're settling in nicely," he says, taking a generous drink and handing me the glass so I can have a sip.

I drink the wine and nod. He signals the waiter and orders for the both of us, as he always does whenever we go out.

"Yeah, it's nice here," I say.

"See? What'd I tell you?" He beams. He's in a pale yellow button-down shirt and a navy tie, which he loosens, just a bit. "This is the kind of thing I wish I had done when I was a kid." He takes a long, deep breath and his belly swells. "Would have really given me a chance to see what's out there! To explore!"

I resist the urge to ask, *You don't think you've done enough exploring?* I reach for a breadstick.

"How was your business meeting?" I ask.

"Good!" he says. "We went to this company, Timaratech, have you heard of them?"

As my dad talks, I drink from his glass. Once he gets going, he can monologue all night. I nod along as he describes the office he went to, the people he met, grateful when the food arrives.

"These ABCs, they all want to impress you with their Chinese," he says, chuckling.

I put down my fork and look up at him, wondering if I

should tell him. "Actually, I had a situation in class with this girl who's an ABC . . . ," I say.

"Really?" my dad asks.

I nod, trying to figure out how to tell him. I don't want him to get too angry. On the other hand, he did come all this way to see me, and this was something that was bothering me. And better he hears it from me than Mrs. Mandalay. I open my mouth, and as I'm about to tell him what happened with Emma, he launches right back to describing his business meeting again.

"Anyway, so there I was, and you should have seen these kids, how eager they were to show off their Chinese, and it was one mouthful of bad Chinese after another, I mean truly pitiful."

I stab my filet mignon with my knife.

"At least they got to talk to you," I say bitterly.

He swirls the wine with his hand. "What are you talking about? We're talking right now."

"No, *you're* talking," I say. It's been like this for as long as I can remember. It's always about him. I shake my head. I can't believe I thought this time would be different, that tonight he might actually want to know how my life is. "You haven't asked me one thing about my life or my school."

"I asked when we first sat down!" he protests.

"That was a statement—'I heard you're settling in nice here.'"

"To which you replied yes. So I moved on!"

"Yeah," I mutter. "You always move on."

My dad glares at me. "Watch it," he warns. Neither of us say anything for a minute. I stare into the wineglass, drawing strength from the potent red, feeling ever so emboldened and scared at the same time. I've never talked to my dad like this before. Is it the wine? Is it America? Whatever it is, my dad does not like it. He takes his napkin and throws it down on top of his plate. "You know what, I don't have to take this, not from a seventeen-year-old who I pay to school, feed, and clothe." He points at me. "I'm busting my ass to send you to this American private school—"

"Which I never asked you to send me to," I retort.

He gets up from the table—*OMG, is he just going to leave me here?*—and takes out his wallet. He takes two one-hundred-dollar bills, tosses them on the table, and puts his wallet away. Then remembers he needs to give me spending cash. He takes his wallet back out and counts $2,000, and I'm sitting there mortified—the whole restaurant's looking at us. As my dad stuffs the $2,000 into my pink Prada bag, I feel like a whore.

"I'll tell your mother you said hello," he said.

"Wait!" I reach out and grab his arm. I jam my hand inside my purse and pull out the fish-oil capsules I had gotten for my grandmother and shove them into his hand. I didn't forget. Because despite what my parents think, I actually am a good Chinese girl.

thirty-two

Dani

The juices of envy churn in my stomach as I watch Claire with her dad. His pride. Her happiness. Their linked arms as they walk out to dinner together.

I throw my head back onto the couch, thinking of Mr. Connelly and how we got here. He was the closest thing to a dad to me, and he knew that. Did he take advantage of it, or was I just so desperate to find a father figure in my life that I ignored all obvious warning signals?

I lie on the couch for hours, hugging my knees to my chest as my mind replays all our previous training sessions. Was the light too powerful all those times I stood up onstage in the auditorium? Could he see through my shirt? Should I not have hugged him or high-fived him after practice?

The bigger question, the one that pricks like a fish bone in my throat, is *Now what?* What does this mean for Snider . . . and for Yale?

I open up my laptop to check my email. There's an email from Mr. Connelly. I sit up.

To: Danielle De La Cruz
From: Bill Connelly
Subject: Checking in

Hi Dani,

Just wanted to check in with you. You did SO great this weekend; I'm so proud of you! Don't let anything else color your takeaway from this weekend, which is that YOU KICKED ASS. I believe in you so much! Call me if you ever want to talk. I'll see you at practice on Monday!

Best,

Mr. Connelly

I stare at the email, at his encouraging words and jokey language. I read it over five times. *Am I missing something here?* It was like it was written for a whole different weekend! How could *this* be the email I receive after what happened?

The phone rings. It's Ming.

"Hey, you wanna hang out?" Ming asks. "Florence is busy with her friends, and I'm tired of being second—"

"You won't believe what happened to me!" I cut in.

My voice shakes as I tell Ming about Seattle and read her the email from Mr. Connelly. And even though it's my best friend, it's scary saying the words out loud, and I squeeze my eyes shut as I wait for her reaction.

"Okay, first of all, breathe," Ming says. "I know you wanna hit Reply—"

"Oh, I'm going to hit Reply! And tell the creep to fuck off!"

"But, Dani, think about your future. Is there a softer way?" Ming urges. I shake my head, anger pumping through my veins.

"I already tried the softer way. It didn't work!" I tell her. And besides, I'm a debater—I have principles!

"I know and this is so fucked up. I'm so sorry," Ming says. "But you gotta remember, we're not like other students."

I swallow.

"When we fall, we free fall . . . ," Ming reminds me.

I get off the phone with Ming and stare back at my computer. Slowly I tap Reply. I start the email calmly and cordially, like Ming suggested, trying to hold back. But then the debater in me takes over.

To: Bill Connelly
From: Danielle De La Cruz
Subject: Re: Checking in

Hi Mr. Connelly,
I was confused to receive your email. I don't think you understand the magnitude of what happened this weekend.

Maybe you had too much to drink, but I was sober. You tell me that you believe in me, that you see something special in me and you're willing to train me, but when you do or say things that make me think you may be interested in something else, it hurts my ability to trust you.

Going forward, I hope you'll have as much respect for me as I do for you.

Your student,

Dani

PS. Please note I will no longer be needing the private debate coaching sessions from you—thank you for those. I found them really helpful. But given what's happened, I think it's best to stick to our group training. I'll still see you at training.

My fingers sit on the keys when I'm done. I stare at the words, wanting to cover them and, at the same time, wanting to make the font big AF. I reread the email, mind running through Ming's words and all the ramifications if I press Send—Snider, scholarship, Yale, future—all the while, my heart pumps, *Do it!*

My cursor jolts back and forth from Trash to Send.

Fuck the softer way.

I press Send.

thirty-three

Claire

After my dad dumps me at the restaurant, I wait in the chilly night for an Uber, teeth chattering in my short Dior dress. Finally, I manage to get one. I call Jess in the back of the Uber.

"Jess! I need you," I whimper into the phone. I'm so sorry I got into that stupid fight with her over Emma Lau. I feel a sob building as I tell her what happened. "Can you believe the bastard just left me in the restaurant?"

"Hang on, girl, I'll meet you at your place," Jess says.

She's waiting for me in my room when I get home. I take off my Dior dress and change into pj's. Jess helps me wipe the mascara stains and makeup off me. We watch Chinese movies on my computer, cussing our trash dads. She sleeps over, the two of us talking late into the night until we finally fall asleep.

Dani wakes us up the next morning. She raises a sharp

eyebrow at Jess. "Is she slumming it here too from now on?" she asks.

I scrunch my eyebrows. What's Dani talking about? Jess takes a slipper and throws it at Dani, who quickly closes the door before it hits her. Jess gets up, yawning. As the two of us change for school, she examines some of my new clothes, bought online. Not everything I've purchased has been amazing, but I haven't quite figured out how to return things yet.

"That's it, we're going shopping after school," Jess announces. She picks up my Amex card on the top of my bureau and smiles mischievously. "And guess whose money we're going to spend?"

Oh, it's on!

In English class, I try to block out the death stares from Emma and focus on what Mrs. Wallace is saying about *Gatsby*. Today we're discussing Myrtle and how she's always aspiring to be a part of the upper crest but she'll never be fully accepted by Tom, who only uses her and takes pleasure in her powerlessness.

One of the white kids raises his hand and draws a parallel to colonialism. "Kind of like Britain and India. Or . . ." He tries to think up another pair. "The European powers and China in the 1800s."

"China was Europe's mistress?" the other kids ask.

The whole class looks at me, and I slide down in my seat.

"They were called concessions," I say. "The French and the British forced China to open up after the Opium War."

"Open up how?"

"I'll force you to open up!" a boy cackles from the back.

Jess meets me after class. As we're talking in Mandarin, Mrs. Wallace walks out of the classroom. She frowns at us.

"You should be speaking in English, Claire," she scolds me.

I instantly stop talking, lips hot with humiliation. Jess gasps as Mrs. Wallace walks away. "Who the hell made her the language police?" Before I can stop her, she turns and yells at Mrs. Wallace in Mandarin, "Hey, woman, it's a free country! Why you think we came here?"

Later, Jess drives us over to Plaza East Covina. I get a text from my mom.

Heard you gave your dad a hard time at dinner.

I text back, He walked out on ME at dinner.

She types back, He went all the way over there to see you, after he'd been on a flight for thirteen hours!

I put away my phone. Why is she always defending him? Jess pulls into the mall. We hit Nordstrom. Jess shops like my mother, picking me up jeans, tops, and shorts, with no regard for price. As we're shopping, I see someone looking over at us from across the floor. It's Jay. I poke Jess, who spins around.

"Hey!" she greets him in Mandarin.

"Hey," he says back, but he's not looking at her. He's looking at me. "You never texted me back the other night."

"I was tired."

"I was worried about you . . . ," Jay says. Jess jabs me lightly on the ribs and makes an *aww* face.

"So what are you doing here? Shopping in the girls' section?" Jess teases him.

"I'm getting something for my mom," he says. "It's her birthday. Actually, maybe you guys can help me."

Jess nods. "Sure!"

We follow him over to the fine-jewelry section, where he points to a pair of drop-diamond earrings. The sales girl opens up the case and retrieves them.

Jay turns to me and asks, "Will you put them on?"

"Me?" I ask.

I look over at Jess, who is fiddling with some of the other earrings. She's too distracted by the jewelry to follow what's going on. I look to the sales girl and nod. As she cleans the earrings and hands them to me, Jay leans in closer to me.

Carefully, I put them on. Jay examines them, studying my face. His face is so close to mine, I can feel his breath. I stare at the diamonds glistening in the reflection in the mirror. Gently he touches my ears.

"They look beautiful on you," he says.

Jess clears her throat. "But are they too young for your mom?" she asks, craning her neck to see from the other side of the display counter.

Jay considers this. They are on the fun side of ear-rings. *My mom* would like them. Jay picks up another pair instead—classic solitaire diamonds. He tells the sales girl to wrap them up. Jess smiles, pleased he listened to her.

As we walk out, Jay thanks us for our help. We watch as he gets inside his blue Lamborghini and drives off.

Jess pretends to swoon onto the hood of her Porsche. "He is so *hot*," she squeals.

"Can't believe he's getting his mom such expensive ear-rings," I say. The diamonds he chose were close to $20,000.

"Mama's boy," Jess says.

"Total mama's boy," I agree. Although, that's not neces-sarily a bad thing. I think about my dad and how he almost never goes and visits my grandmother.

"You want him, don't you." Jess grins. "Admit it."

I blush.

She giggles as she gets into the car. "Girl, if you want him, you're going to have to let him touch a lot more than your ears!"

thirty-four

Dani

The next day, at school, Mrs. Mandalay walks up to me in her power suit and pumps. I look up from my phone. Mr. Connelly still hasn't replied to the email I sent.

"Oh, hey, Dani, I heard all about Seattle," Mrs. Mandalay says.

I wait for a hopeful second that Mr. Connelly might have said something to her.

"You guys beat Marlborough! Well done!"

Guess not.

"I have to say, things are looking good for you for Snider!" She marvels at me. "Wouldn't that be amazing to have on your college app?"

I linger. If there's ever a time to say anything to her, now's the time. Mrs. Mandalay's phone rings, and she lifts up her index finger. "Sorry, I have to take this." She clicks on her phone, the vein on her forehead popping as she answers,

"This is Joanna Mandalay. Yes, we're very excited to have your child join us in May! We've talked to the agent, and everything's ready for her, including her host family." She turns and click-clacks her pumps back to her office.

Ming runs over to me from the bathroom after Mrs. Mandalay leaves. "Oh, Dani, you won't believe what happened," she says. Her face is wet, like she'd just washed it. Still her eyes are swollen.

"Is it your violin?" I ask her.

She shakes her head. She tells me she finally confronted Florence about not inviting her to her party, and Florence came over to her place and apologized. She was really sorry and asked how she could make it up to Ming. The two of them started fooling around, that's when Underwear Kevin walked in on them.

"He got so mad, he kicked Florence out and told me I could have no more visitors," she says. "And this morning he removed all the locks on the doors."

"*What?*"

Ming nods, running her hands up and down along the goose bumps on her arms. "He says we're going to have an open-door policy from now on."

"Fuck that," I tell her. I take her hand and lead her down the hallway to Mrs. Mandalay's office. "We're going to get you out of there *right now*."

thirty-five

Claire

To: The American Prep Student Body (undisclosed emails)
From: Mrs. Candice Wallace (English Department)
Subject: INTERNATIONAL STUDENTS—PLEASE READ

Dear international students,

PLEASE be more considerate of others when choosing which language to speak at school. I know it must be challenging for you to speak English, as it is not your mother tongue, but you attend an American school now, and it is rude for you to use a language others cannot understand. Also, it is best for your future if you speak English 100 percent of the time you are at school. Isn't that the whole point of attending an American school? In the interests of your educational and future professional goals, please try to use English.

Regards,

Mrs. Wallace

○ ○ ○

OMG. This is about *me*. Mrs. Wallace sent it because she heard me and Jess talking outside her class in Chinese. My phone rings. It's Jess.

"Are you looking at this trash email?" Jess exclaims. "Is this because of us? She's out of her mind! Claire, you seriously need to move back to our class—"

"I'm not moving back!" I say.

"Well, you can't just stay in the bitch's class!"

I look over toward Dani's room and tell Jess I'll call her back. Quietly, I walk over with my laptop and knock on her door.

Dani opens her door.

"Have you seen this?" I ask.

She reads the email from my laptop, then walks over to her own laptop, horrified, and reads it again.

"I think it's about me. What do you think I should do?" I ask her.

"You have to fight this. This is discrimination!"

"Fight this how?" I ask.

Dani tells me I need to go to the administration. She says she just went with her friend Ming, who's a parachute too and was having problems with her host family. Mrs. Mandalay was sympathetic.

I shake my head. "I don't know." A few weeks ago, I thought nudging was rude. And now to go and complain about a teacher?

"Trust me," she says. "It'll be okay."

When I hesitate to respond, Dani asks, "Want me to go with you?"

We wait outside Mrs. Mandalay's office, me tapping the floor with my white Alexa Chung patent leather pumps, and Dani studying the quotes painted on the wall outside the office, hands interlaced on her lap.

When the door opens, Dani is the first to stand. She waits for me to collect myself, then we walk inside together, my hand clutching a printout of Mrs. Wallace's email. I can't believe I'm doing this.

Gently, I slide the email across Mrs. Mandalay's desk. I glance over at Dani, who nods encouragingly.

"Mrs. Mandalay, I think this email is really . . ." I pause. Dani had suggested a bunch of adjectives at home— "offensive," "discriminatory," "hostile"—but in the moment, they all feel too harsh. "Not nice."

Dani leans forward and points to the line in the email that reads, "It is best for your future if you speak English 100 percent of the time you are at school. Isn't that the whole point of attending an American school?"

"This implies that English is the best language for our future," Dani says. "That is unsubstantiated and one can even argue that it is a form of cultural imperialism."

I stare at Dani. Whoa!

Mrs. Mandalay puts up her hand. "Thank you, Dani."

She looks quizzically at her. "And why are you here again?"

"For moral support," she says.

"Again?" Mrs. Mandalay asks.

"Again."

I take a deep breath and look to Mrs. Mandalay. "This email has caused me and the entire Chinese student community a lot of distress. We feel publicly humiliated by it—"

Before I can finish, Mrs. Mandalay says, "You're absolutely right. I was appalled myself when I received this email." Mrs. Mandalay pulls out a copy of the student manual and turns to page 73. "American Prep has a zero tolerance policy for harassment and discrimination. We want every single student in our school to feel like they're being culturally respected. Mrs. Wallace will be suspended at once."

I look to Dani in surprise. Did she just say *suspended*? Dani gets up from her seat to shake Mrs. Mandalay's hand.

"Thank you so much," I say to Mrs. Mandalay, shaking her hand too.

Mrs. Mandalay beams at us and opens the door to her office.

"My pleasure. It's my job," she says.

Walking out of Mrs. Mandalay's office, a smile sweeps across my face as I pull Dani in for a hug. I thought it was going to be like in China, where you walk in with a thorn up your ass and you walk out with a brick.

"Thanks so much," I tell her. "I couldn't have done it without you. That line about cultural imperialism—that was so great."

She laughs.

Jess, Nancy, and Florence come running down the hall. Dani's friend Ming walks over too, and Florence shyly introduces Ming to us—apparently, they know each other. Excitedly, I tell everyone the good news. The girls flip out. Jess starts jumping up and down and pulling me toward the cafeteria.

"This is huge! We have to tell the rest of the parachutes!" she says.

As the girls head toward the cafeteria, I turn to Dani and thank her again. "If there's anything you're ever going through that I can help you with . . ." My voice lingers.

Dani falls quiet for a minute, then shakes her head.

"I'm good," she says.

thirty-six

Dani

Florence and I help Ming move out that weekend. I'm so happy Mrs. Mandalay agreed to up Ming's housing stipend so she can switch host families. And I'm thrilled she did the right thing and suspended Mrs. Wallace for that ridiculous email. It's funny, everyone's always saying Mrs. Mandalay is such a hard-ass. But she can be surprisingly swift and decisive in difficult situations. Maybe I should tell her about Mr. Connelly—he still hasn't replied.

"Careful with that picture frame," Ming says. I look down at the small silver frame in my hands. It's a picture of Ming as a little kid and a tall man. They're both playing the violin.

"Is this your dad?" I ask Ming.

"Oh, let me see!" Florence says, walking over. Florence puts a finger over young Ming in the picture and coos. I smile. I'm glad those two made up. It's clear how much

Florence likes her. I hope she'll invite Ming to her house parties from now on.

"That's my uncle," Ming tells us, taking the picture and wrapping it carefully in Bubble Wrap. "He's the one who taught me how to play the violin."

"Is he coming to the spring concert?" I ask.

Ming's face falls. "No."

"How about your parents?" I ask. There must be a way to fly them out from China—it's Ming's big solo! Again Ming shakes her head.

With a sigh, Ming puts the rest of her stuff in a box and carries it out to the living room, leaving me and Florence alone. Florence turns to me.

"Hey, so . . . don't tell Claire about me and Ming. They don't know that I'm um . . ." Florence blushes.

"Of course not."

"Not that I think they'll have a problem with it," she clarifies. "I'm not sure."

"I don't think they will," I say. I can't speak to that girl Jess, but I do live with Claire, and she's pretty vocal at dinner about diversity and acceptance, especially after that horrible email Mrs. Wallace sent. "And if they do, you'll know they're not your real friends."

"Yeah . . . ," Florence says, looking away.

Ming comes in to get the last box in the room.

"You guys ready?" she asks.

"Ready." Florence smiles.

o o o

Later that weekend, Zach does his physics homework at my house while I research case studies for Snider. Mr. Connelly hasn't said a word about Snider still, even though the deadline is looming.

I go to the fridge. My mom's out late cleaning again. She left us with some food to heat up. It's just going to be me. Claire's probably going out with her friends to celebrate. I look over at Zach. I think about telling him about Mr. Connelly, but I don't want to be reminded of it. I don't want to utter the words, as if by uttering them out loud I make what happened in Seattle more real. For the same reason I haven't told my mom either. I just want to be able to pretend it didn't happen.

Instead, I bring over the leftover palitaw my mom made to the living room. Zach looks at the sesame-and-coconut-covered sponges and pops one in his mouth. He closes his eyes as he chews. The afternoon light shines on his nose, revealing a faint dusting of freckles. I can't believe he's sitting in our living room.

He puts his physics textbook down and points to our TV. "You guys have Netflix?" he asks.

I nod. One of our few luxuries.

Zach reaches for the remote. "Mind if I watch?" he asks, turning the TV on. "I just need a break." *Titanic* is playing. Zach points to Jack and Rose on the screen and grins. "I love this movie."

"What? Really?" I ask, amused. I glance over at Jack and Rose shivering in the water. There's only one door, and only one of them can survive.

I put down the plate of palitaw on the coffee table. "And of course it's gotta be Rose who survives. God forbid we let the smart, scrappy, poor guy live and kill off the rich, beautiful idiot."

I think of Heather as I'm saying this, but Zach turns to me, all offended. "Rose is *not* an idiot," he balks.

I chuckle. Didn't figure him to be such a diehard fan. "She is," I insist.

"How so?" he asks. He stops watching and turns his attention to me.

I point to the door in the movie. "First of all, she could have totally scooted over," I say. "Look at that door! You can easily fit two people on that door!"

Zach glances at the door and considers this.

"Second of all, she tries to kill herself by trying to jump off a ship. Why? Because she's tired of fancy cocktail parties?" I ask. Please, it's not like she's a full-scholarship student at American Prep.

"Whoa!" Zach says, throwing his hands up.

I giggle. I like riling him up, it's fun. I move closer toward him.

"Let's consider what would happen if they actually did both make it off the ship together, shall we?" I gaze over at Zach as I talk. It almost feels like we're a real couple.

Like we're dating. And we're having one of those couple's debates that is going to become like our song.

"And Jack would probably have had to go off and fight in World War I. Maybe Rose would hook up with Cal again—"

"But she didn't hook up with him," Zach points out. "We know because Old Rose is in the movie."

Dang it. I forgot about Old Rose.

"Well whatever. We don't know what Old Rose did or did not do. She looks like she's had a bunch of boyfriends."

Zach bursts out laughing. *"What?"*

"Seriously, she's got that look." Now I'm just spewing nonsense. Zach is on the floor, laughing his ass off. And I'm starting to laugh too.

It feels good to laugh, to forget about Mr. Connelly and what he did and what's going to happen to Snider. Zach puts a hand over his stomach, and pleads, "Stop, stop . . . you're too much!" But I don't stop. Instead, I move onto the floor with him. Our arms brush lightly against each other.

"And what's with her throwing diamonds in the ocean?" I continue. I smile at Zach, rolling around on the carpet, shrieking with laughter. "Seriously, she could have donated that diamond to some free-women-from-boring-cocktail-parties charity."

"You are a piece of work, Dani, you know that?" he asks.

Our eyes meet, and I lean in toward him to kiss him. Zach makes a sharp move to reach for the remote, accidentally knocking into my head. "Ow!" All of a sudden, the door swings open and in walks Claire.

She looks at Zach, confused for a second.

"It's you!" Zach says, jumping to his feet. "What are you doing here?"

thirty-seven

Claire

I stare at Blue Cap, standing in the middle of our living room. For a second, I think I've entered the wrong house.

"I'm Zach, remember?" the boy says. "We met at the pool."

"You know Claire?" Dani asks, surprised.

I'm confused. "Is he your boyfriend?" I ask Dani.

"What? No!" Zach denies quickly. Too quickly. Dani retreats behind one of the couch cushions.

I leave the two of them and go to my room. I open my laptop, poring through the emails and messages from parachutes, saying how much it meant to them that I stood up to Mrs. Wallace. When I hear Zach leave, I call out to Dani.

"Dani, come look at this," I say, lying in bed, pointing to my computer. There's an email from a parachute saying her science teacher has been making fun of her accent for six months.

But Dani doesn't come in. Instead, she walks right by my room.

"I've got an assignment due," she says as she closes her door.

I sit on my bed wondering what I've said.

In English class the next day, we get none other than Ms. Jones! I almost whoop out loud when I see her. Ms. Jones is in a blazer and wearing hoop earrings, her braided hair tied in a bun on top of her head. She smiles as she tells us she'll be teaching us while Mrs. Wallace takes a leave of absence.

"Now I know you guys have been reading and talking a lot about *The Great Gatsby*, but Gatsby's old! I want to hear about *you*. When's the last time you felt like you wanted the respect of a group of people whom you just could never get to take you seriously? I'll tell you, for me it was five p.m. on Friday, when they called me and asked me if I wanted to take over for Mrs. Wallace."

We all sit up.

"I'd been substituting here for a while. Some of you guys might have had me," she says, winking at me. "But I never thought they'd give me a more permanent position."

Ms. Jones opens up to us about herself. She tells us that she used to be a public school teacher, until she had her kids. Then she took some time off to be with them, and when she wanted to go back, it was hard to find a job. The public schools weren't hiring due to budget cuts.

"And the private schools, well the private schools wanted

to hire people who looked . . . more like them," she says.

My eyes are transfixed, riveted by her story. I can't remember the last time an adult was so real with me, not my old teachers in China and certainly not my parents. She talks about institutional racism and how it's affected her life, to the point where she almost didn't believe Mrs. Mandalay when she asked her if she wanted to teach here as an adjunct teacher.

She asks us if we've ever felt like that, like no matter what we did, it would never happen for us. People won't think we're good enough.

One by one, hands go up. A couple of kids say they feel like that with their sports coaches sometimes. When it's my turn, I say my parents.

Ms. Jones nods, like she's been there.

"Your assignment this week is to forget about this person," she says, "and focus on you. I want you to write a short story in which Gatsby doesn't care about Daisy."

I think about this as I walk out of class. I squeeze by Emma, who, incidentally, also said her parents.

As I open my locker, a small box falls out. When I open it, I find a pair of earrings.

My breath hitches in my throat.

It's the drop-diamond earrings I tried on at the store for Jay.

I open up the note.

Thought these looked good on you.

—Jay

thirty-eight

Dani

It eats at me the way Zach said no when Claire asked if he was my boyfriend. The face he made, like it was preposterous, something that could only be possible in the land of make-believe. This, juxtaposed with the way his eyes lit up when Claire walked into the room, practically purring, *"It's you!"*

What does it mean that she and Zach know each other? I tell myself to forget it. Who cares? I used to pride myself on not giving a shit what guys think, not wanting to be just another pretty face.

And yet, when Claire walked through that door in her skintight jeans and crop top, silky black hair flowing down her back, and Zach's eyes turned into walnuts, I would have *killed* to be her.

I look at Claire the next day in the cafeteria while Ming talks about her new host family.

"They're so much nicer than Underwear Kevin," she says, pouring a packet of sesame oil on her noodles. "I'm thinking of making an app that allows parachutes to rate their hosts. Wouldn't that be cool? Florence says she might be able to help, she's good at coding."

Mr. Connelly walks into the cafeteria. He still hasn't replied to my email. In debate training, he avoids eye contact when I'm speaking. Occasionally, he offers a comment but never anything substantive. Not like before.

"I'll be right back," I tell Ming.

I walk over to Mr. Connelly. He looks up at me from the granola-bar stand.

"Hey, Mr. Connelly," I say to him. "I was just wondering . . . did you ever get my email?"

Mr. Connelly frowns. "Not here," he says. He turns and leads the way out of the cafeteria. I follow him to an empty staircase.

"Did you read my email?" I ask again.

"Yes," he says. His voice is ice. He puts his thumb and index finger to his forehead, like the very mention of the email is bringing on a migraine. He takes a deep breath. "Why would you do that? Why would you write that to me?"

I look up at him, confused.

"After everything I've done for you, I can't *believe* you'd put that in an email!" he says, raising his voice. He struggles to stay calm. "If you were mad, you should've come talk to me. You should've called me." He stares at me, letting the full extent of his disappointment sink in. "You don't do this."

Tears threaten in my eyes as I nod.

He walks out.

thirty-nine

Claire

Jay's in the parking lot, getting into his Lamborghini. I run up to him with the jewelry box in my hands. It's so sweet, but I can't accept them.

His face falls when I hand him back the earrings. "But they looked so good on you!"

"They're way too expensive," I say.

"That's for me to decide, not you," he says. He points to his car. "Get in. I'll give you a ride home."

The passenger-side door opens up, and I slide in. I've been inside luxury sports cars before, but never a Lamborghini. They're rare in Shanghai, and my dad, for all his love of luxury goods, never really got into sports cars. "Who am I trying to impress? The other people on the road?" he'd cackle.

Jay, though, is really into his car. As the Lamborghini roars to life, Jay backs out of the parking lot. It's an incredibly loud car, and Jay shouts over the noise.

"So do you have a boyfriend?" he asks as he switches between lanes, finding any opportunity to accelerate, even on local streets.

"No." I return the question, "Do you?"

He laughs.

I point to Dani's street ahead and tell him to turn right. He nods but then ignores me and keeps going straight.

"Hey, you're going the wrong way," I tell him. "My host's house is back that way."

"I know," he says as he steps on the gas.

"So where are we going?" I ask. "I thought you're taking me home."

He looks over at me and grins. "I am . . . eventually," he says.

I feel the outline of my phone in the front pouch of my backpack and clutch it tightly. I remind myself there's nothing to be nervous about. He was a gentleman back at Florence's party. Ten minutes later, we arrive at his house. It looks more like a country club than a private residence, with tennis courts, a huge pool, and a Jacuzzi.

"Is this your host's house?" I ask, eyes widening, as I get out of the car.

Jay shakes his head.

I look around the driveway. There are no other cars. "You live here? By yourself?"

He click-locks his Lamborghini. "My mom comes and

visits sometimes," he says. I follow him inside.

The inside of the house looks even more immaculate than the outside. The floors are white marble. The furniture is sleek and modern, and light pours in from the two-story glass windows.

Jay throws his backpack onto the couch and goes into the kitchen. He comes back with two bottles of Pellegrino. He tosses me one. As I drink, he gazes at me.

"You wanna go for a swim?" he asks.

"I . . . I didn't bring my swimsuit," I tell him.

He runs up the spiral staircase. "Hang on."

He comes back with a brand-new navy-blue Stella McCartney swimsuit, which he swears his mom ordered but has a million of and won't care if I take it. He himself is shirtless and in trunks. He has *such* a nice body, and I try not to stare.

I take the swimsuit and change in the upstairs bathroom.

He's already in the pool waiting for me when I come out. The afternoon sun stretches across the sky, and beads of water glisten off his chest. Jay smiles when he sees me.

I jump in. The water is warm and soothing. I close my eyes, thinking about how the past week has turned around. Mrs. Wallace is gone, I have a new English teacher, and now I'm swimming with Jay Li. I let the happiness wash over me as I enjoy the first minute underwater. My toes and fingers stretch.

I do laps, back and forth. Jay tries to catch up with me, but I'm too fast.

"You're a good swimmer," he says when I finally catch my breath.

"Thanks," I say. "I used to train until . . ."

"Until?"

"Until my mom said I should quit," I tell him. "She said swimming doesn't look good on girls. Gives them broad shoulders."

"She's right. It does," he says, pretending to examine my shoulders. "But you don't look too bad." He swims up close to me and playfully splashes me with water. "I wouldn't have invited you here if you did."

I laugh.

Later, we get out of the pool.

"Hey, you hungry? I know a great place in Santa Monica, right on the beach," Jay says, tossing me a towel.

"Santa Monica? We won't make it back till ten!" I follow him into the kitchen.

"Who said anything about making it back?" he says with a grin. "There are some great hotels on the Westside. Have you stayed at Shutters?"

I stare at him. He's kidding, right?

"We can get separate rooms," Jay says, rolling his eyes. "C'mon, you deserve it. You're a hero for what you did to Wallace!"

He walks over to the fridge, pulls out a bottle of white, uncorks it, and pours two glasses. He hands me a glass. "What do you say?"

I hold the glass up to my nose. I can tell he's one of those guys who are not used to hearing the word "no." And it would be *so* easy to just say yes, to sip chenin blanc all day, get in his Lambo, and drive to the beach. But then what about school tomorrow? What about Ms. Jones's assignment?

"Another time," I say, putting the glass down.

Jay drops his head and nods.

"I'll drive you back," he says. He grabs his keys, like he wants to go now. I look down. I'm standing in his kitchen still in my bathing suit, dripping wet.

"No it's okay. I can get an Uber," I offer. Quickly, I unlock my phone, open the app, and order myself a car.

He puts his glass down and turns and walks away without another word, leaving me alone in the kitchen.

I head upstairs to change. As I'm leaving, I peek inside one of the bedrooms. Jay is sitting on his bed, playing video games. There are Pocky boxes and half-eaten bags of Fritos on the floor. A pair of dumbbells sits in the corner.

"Hey. My car's here. I'm gonna go," I say gently.

He doesn't look up.

I wait a minute, and when he still doesn't say anything, I turn around.

As I'm walking out, he calls after me, "Close the door

on your way out . . ." No *Goodbye.* No *I'll see you at school.*

I shake my head as I get into the Uber. What's wrong with him? I throw my head back on the leather seat and sigh. As I reach for my water bottle in my backpack, a box falls out. It's the box with the earrings, along with a note.

Sorry, I'm unreturnable, just like these earrings.

—*Jay*

forty

Dani

Today's the day. Mr. Connelly is going to announce who's going to Snider. I hold my breath at training as he reads the names from the piece of paper in his hands.

"Josh Williams . . . Risha Laghari . . . Audrey Anderson . . ."

Josh, Risha, and Audrey whoop in excitement. Mr. Connelly calls out two more names, until he gets down to the final one.

Please . . . please . . . I need this.

"And the final person is . . . Heather McLean," he says.

I race down the hall, wiping my sweaty, humiliated fingers on my pants, as I try to catch up with Mr. Connelly after practice. I fly straight into Zach. My books drop out of my arms, and Zach kneels to pick them up.

"What's wrong?" he asks. "You okay?"

I shake my head. As he hands me back my books, I tell him quietly I didn't get picked for Snider.

"Because of Heather?" he asks. He scans the hallway for her, and I press my fingers into my books, too embarrassed to tell him, no, it's because Mr. Connelly hit on me.

Zach shakes his head. "But she cheated! That's so messed up," he says.

Ming runs over to us from the band room.

"Dani! Guess what? Mr. Rufus just told me he managed to get the school to pay for my parents to come to the concert!" Ming announces, lugging her violin case behind her. Her happy news is absorbed by the fog on my face.

"What's wrong?" she asks.

Ming puts her violin case down. "Is it Mr. Connelly?" she asks.

I nod, my chin quivering.

She takes me by the arm and leads me over to a quiet corner so we can talk as Zach calls out, "Let me know if there's anything I can do."

Later that day, I go to see my college counselor, Mr. Matthews. It's time I tell someone. I'm always saying to Ming and Claire to fight back. I can't let Mr. Connelly take this from me. Mr. Matthews looks up at me from his desk, confused.

"I'm sorry, when did this happen?" he asks, massaging his neck. Mr. Matthews is a tall, thin man with an unusually veiny neck that he likes to hold, like a hand warmer, when he talks to people.

"A week and a half ago, in Seattle," I say.

Mr. Matthews frowns. "And you're saying Mr. Connelly came on to you?" he asks. "Where? At the tournament?"

"At a bar."

Mr. Matthews takes his hands off his neck and scolds me, "Dani, you know you're not supposed to be going into bars."

"Mr. Connelly dragged me there," I tell him.

"He dragged you," Mr. Matthews repeated, like he didn't believe me.

I nodded.

Mr. Matthews gives me a serious look. "Dani, these are serious allegations you're making. If Mr. Connelly really did what you say he did, you'll need to tell Mrs. Mandalay, and there would be a formal investigation."

I gaze down at my lap, wavering. I think about what Mr. Connelly said to me in the stairway. I'm silent for long enough that Mr. Matthews lowers his tone.

"Look, I know you're upset about not making it to Snider. But just because you didn't get picked . . . ," he starts to say. His voice trails off.

Wow.

I walk out of his office.

forty-one

Claire

It's a little after midnight and I'm working on my English paper for Ms. Jones, due tomorrow. I've read through it six times already when my phone dings.

Hi, my dad texts.

I tap Pause on Spotify. We haven't spoken since he walked out on me at the restaurant.

Your grandmother says she likes your fish oil, he types.

I roll my eyes. Why can't he just say *I'm sorry* like a normal person, instead of using fish oil to bait me into talking to him?

That's good, I text back.

How's school? he writes.

Good, I write back. I'm liking my new English class.

He doesn't even know about the email or Mrs. Wallace getting replaced. So much happens when we're busy being mad at each other . . . what's the point of recapping afterward? But then if I don't recap, an entire lifetime can pass by, it'll just be "Oh, hi, yeah, I lived and then I died."

Do you need anything? Any new books? my dad writes.

This is my dad's way of saying he cares about me.

Sure, I write back. Not because I actually need his help getting me books—we both know I'm capable of using Amazon, but because it's my way of saying, *Fine, care about me.*

I need more books by F. Scott Fitzgerald.

Done! I'll get my secretary to order them for you! A box set!

I put away my phone and turn back to my paper. I remind myself that there are five languages of love. My parents' just happen to be financial.

My phone dings again. This time, it's an iMessage from Jay.

You're up late, Jay texts.

I smile. You too, I write.

A few seconds later, he writes back: Come over.

I stare at the text. Three dots appear.

We don't have to do anything. We can just sleep, he adds.

Yeah. RIGHT.

Admit it, you're thinking about it right now. Us sleeping together, he writes.

I let out a laugh. He's such a player.

You're so busted, he types.

I type back, I can come over tomorrow after school again and we can go for a swim?

Can't tomorrow. Mom's in town, he writes.

Aww.

Then three dots appear.

You should meet her.

Maybe I was wrong about Jay, I muse with Jess over Face-Time as I'm getting ready for school. I thought he just wanted to fool around. But now he wants me to meet his mom. Jess makes me pull out every single thing in my closet and show her so we can decide on what I'm going to wear. In the end, I go with my white Rag & Bone pants, a blue lace-trimmed linen Chloé top, and Phillip Lim suede mules. I fidget in class, rocking my leg as Ms. Jones collects our papers.

"I can't wait to read yours, Claire," Ms. Jones says.

I smile. "I worked really hard on it."

"Good," she says. "You can only get out of life what you put into it."

After school, Jay's mom comes to pick up Jay in a white Escalade.

"Mom, this is Claire Wang," Jay introduces me to his mom.

His mom holds out a hand. She's in head-to-toe Chanel— she's what my mom would call a Chanel whore. I note the rock on her hand, at least five carats, too big for my taste, but my mother would be impressed.

"So wonderful to meet you, Claire," Mrs. Li says. "We're going into the city tonight. Won't you join us? Do you like sushi?"

"Sure," I say, glancing over at Jay, who flashes me a smile. I'm still not sure what this is. A date?

"Great," Mrs. Li says. "It's settled, then."

At half past five, Jay and his mom come to pick me up. As I climb into the back of the Escalade, Mrs. Li gives the driver directions to Matsuhisa in Beverly Hills.

"You've been to Nobu, right?" Mrs. Li asks me.

"Nobu, yes, of course," I say. My mom has taken me to the one in Hong Kong on our many shopping trips to the city.

"Well this is actually his original restaurant," she says. "In my opinion, it's better than Nobu. Nobu's gotten *so* touristy."

I nod in agreement, and Jay smiles at me, amused. He's wearing a button-down blue shirt and slacks, and he looks *so damn fine*.

Mrs. Li takes a compact out of her purse and powders her nose. "Actually, there used to be a really great little sushi place at the Santa Monica airport. What was it called?" she turns to Jay and asks.

Jay shrugs.

"Anyway, it was closed a few years ago. The owner got sentenced for serving whale meat. Can you believe it?" She shakes her head and sighs. "Such a pity, because you could just land your plane and eat, you know? It was right there. Tell me, does your family fly private or commercial?"

It takes me a while to realize she's asking me a question. I put a hand to my chest. "Me?"

She nods.

"We fly commercial," I tell her. "Always Cathay or Singapore Airlines."

She seems a little disappointed by my answer.

"But only business or first," I quickly add.

She sits with the answer, pursing her lips in such a way that I almost wonder whether the whole monologue about the sushi place was just a long-winded way to ask if we also had a private plane. Is that what this dinner's about? Her trying to figure out where exactly on the social ladder we are? If that's the game . . . I sit up straight. My mom invented this game.

We talk about Mrs. Wallace's email. Jay's mom says when she saw it, she was appalled and called Mrs. Mandalay right away. *Huh.* Maybe Mrs. Mandalay listened to her, not me.

Jay makes it clear who *he* listened to. "We were all cheering Claire," Jay says proudly. Mrs. Li smiles and closes her eyes. She tells the driver to put on some music so she can relax. As the soothing voice of Diana Krall fills the car, Jay slips his hand into mine.

At dinner, Mrs. Li does not fuss with the menu. She tells the chef, who's on a first-name basis with her, to make whatever he thinks we would like. The chef nods and disappears into the kitchen. Soon, an endless parade of mouthwatering sushi arrives along with a heavy dose of Mrs. Li's questioning.

"So where do you live in Shanghai?" she asks.

I tell her the name of our villa complex, adding that it's where a famous Chinese actress has her house too. Years of watching my mother name-drop has trained me well.

"Oh, yes, I know her husband," Mrs. Li says of the actress. She turns to Jay. "They have a daughter your age, you know."

Jay's more interested in the tuna sashimi, which he picks up expertly with his chopsticks and holds up to my mouth.

"Try this, Claire," he says.

I take a bite. The tuna melts on my tongue.

As I reach for a piece of sushi, Mrs. Li pulls out her phone and starts showing me pictures of their summer vacation in Tuscany.

"Here's us on our sailboat," she says. I know where this is going.

"And where do you guys like to summer?" Mrs. Li asks.

And there it is. I smile at her, three steps ahead. "We like to come here actually. We have a house in San Francisco," I tell her, the answer already prepared in the car. "My parents like to go to Napa. Last summer, we spent a week in Alaska. It's beautiful up there." Some of it is true. We have spent summers here, but we don't have a house in San Francisco.

"San Francisco, really," Mrs. Li repeats to Jay, pleased. She beams at him—the first genuine smile of the evening. Underneath the table, Jay squeezes my hand.

I dab my mouth with my napkin, smiling into it. I know I passed the test.

It's nearly ten by the time we finish eating, and instead of driving all the way back, Mrs. Li checks us into the Peninsula. She gets a suite for her and Jay and a room for me. The next morning, we all go shopping on Rodeo Drive. Mrs. Li and Jay hit Louis Vuitton, Bulgari, Bottega Veneta, Dolce & Gabbana, and Tom Ford, while I tag along behind them.

"Aren't you going to get anything?" Mrs. Li asks. She looks curiously at my empty hands. I just went shopping with Jess the other day . . .

Mrs. Li puts up a finger. "This is too mass luxury. I get it."

Mrs. Li glances at Jay and says with a wink, "She has taste." Her eyes light up. "Let's go somewhere more boutiquey! I know just the place for you."

We pile back into the Escalade and Mrs. Li tells the driver to take us to Fred Segal. At 13,000 square feet, Fred Segal can only be described as a mecca for serious fashionistas. My eyes boggle at the dresses, skirts, pants, and shirts, rows upon rows of art—not clothes, *art*. Mrs. Li snaps up tops, scarves, pencil skirts, and gowns for me. She's got impeccable taste. Almost every single thing she picks up, I adore.

"You have such a nice figure," she compliments me. "Stop hiding it in those shapeless boxy pants!"

She thrusts a clingy cashmere turtleneck mini dress in my direction and tells me to go try it on. Jay waits for me outside the changing room. When I step outside, his jaw drops.

"You look amazing," he says, staring at my legs.

The dress goes only to my thighs.

"Are you sure it's not too short?" I ask.

"Oh, I'm sure," he insists. "It's not too short."

He snaps his fingers and motions for the sales person to ring it up. "She's wearing this out," he tells them as he puts his hand on the small of my back.

When the sales clerks wrap up all the other pieces, I gaze down at the dresses and shirts Mrs. Li handpicked for me. Where am I going to put all this stuff? I rack my brain trying to think of an excuse not to get it all, but then they'll think I'm cheap and question all the stuff I said at dinner. So I pull out my American Express card and set it down on top of the clothes. Maybe I can ship some of it back to China.

"Oh, what are you doing?" Mrs. Li laughs, slapping my arm lightly.

"She's sweet," she says to Jay. With a flutter of her lashes, she lets me know, "I've already settled the bill."

I look at her, so surprised. "You didn't have to do that!"

I glance over at the total on the receipt the cashier hands Mrs. Li: $5,876. Actually, she kinda did. My dad would have called me up and given me an earful.

Jay drops me off at home later that day with a kiss on the cheek. He has the look on his face of a boy who's spent the entire day with his mom and finally gets to be alone with his girl. Is that what I am? His girl?

"I'll see you later?" he asks.

I nod.

"My mom really likes you," he says.

"I like her too," I say with a smile. "When's she headed back?"

"Tomorrow," he says. His eyes fall slightly. I can tell he and his mom are close. He hands me my Fred Segal shopping bag.

"Thanks," I say, taking the bag from him. "For everything."

The clothes. The dinner. The hotel. The earrings. "I don't know how I'm going to make it up to you," I say to him as I wave goodbye.

"I have a few ideas," he answers with a grin.

forty-two

Dani

I study the motivational quotes outside Mrs. Mandalay's office as I wait. It's my third time in two weeks sitting outside her office, and I've nearly memorized them all by heart. I remind myself that both times I've been here, she's given Ming and Claire what they wanted. Still, my fingers grip the corners of the chair. This time is different. This time it's for me. And I'm not a parachute.

"Please come in," she says.

I get up and suddenly have second thoughts about coming. I tell myself it's going to be okay. She's a woman. She'll understand more than Mr. Matthews.

I take a seat in Mrs. Mandalay's office. She looks at me in the kind of distracted way of a busy headmistress who doesn't really have time to congratulate me on yet another tournament well done. But that's not what I'm here for. I try to hold my trembling hands steady in my lap as I tell her what really happened in Seattle.

Mrs. Mandalay takes off her reading glasses. She sits there soaking in the information. "So you want to quit debate," she finally says.

"I— No, I don't want to quit debate. I love debate," I tell her. "I want to go to Snider . . . ," I say, hesitating before adding, "preferably with a new coach."

"That's impossible. Even if we can find a new coach, the season's almost over. And Mr. Connelly is the finest debate coach we've ever had, one of the best in the country."

Did she not hear me? "But, Mrs. Mandalay, his *hand* was on my leg."

My voice hitches as I say the words, thinking of how I went to sleep that night in the hotel room, my eyes glued to the silver light beneath my door, petrified Mr. Connelly was going to come to my room.

She jots a few notes down on her notepad. "I'll have a word with him, and I'll make sure it doesn't happen again," she says. "And I'll see what I can do about Snider."

I nod, grateful. As Mrs. Mandalay gets up and walks around her desk to open the door for me, she offers me some advice. "I'm sorry you have to go through this. But there will be a lot of situations in life that make you uncomfortable. And the sooner you learn not to let them derail you, the better."

I think about her words as I walk out.

∘ ∘ ∘

After school, I meet up with Ming at Budget Maids and tell her what Mrs. Mandalay said.

"That's wonderful!" Ming says, dragging the bucket of cleaning supplies out to Eduardo's car. "I'm so glad she can help!"

"We'll see," I say, retying my hair in a bun. Now, every time I let my hair down, I think about Mr. Connelly and the awful night at the bar. I've even resorted to sleeping with my hair up. "I'm trying not to get my hopes up."

"He'll listen to her. She's the boss," Ming says. She closes the trunk door and makes a face. "Speaking of bosses, my boss at the host agency shot down my host-rating app idea."

"What? But that's such a great idea!"

"I know!" she says, as she grabs an extra pair of cleaning gloves from the office and stuffs it in her back pocket. Ming always wears several pairs of gloves when she cleans, to protect her violin hands. She tosses me a pair. "I literally know girls who are afraid to take a shower in their own houses and have to shower at school because they're worried about their creepy host dads."

I shake my head.

"But the boss says the app is unnecessary and will only create trouble," she says. "I'm still going to make it. Florence is going to help me. We want to create a safe space to report issues." She leans in closer so Eduardo and Rosa don't overhear. "Especially for queer parachutes."

Eduardo walks out of the office. "You girls ready?" he

asks. Ming and I jump into the SUV, and Eduardo drives us over to nearby Diamond Bar, where we're told we have to clean a five-bedroom house. In the car, Ming tells me about her weekend with Florence. When we get there, we realize it's not a five-bedroom house. It's actually a maternity hotel.

"What's a maternity hotel?" I ask, looking around at the empty cribs and suitcases in the bedrooms.

A maternity hotel, Ming explains, is a house where mainland Chinese mothers hole up in America until they're ready to give birth. This is the first time I've heard of such a phenomenon. I ask Ming why an expectant mother would want to leave her family and friends to come here and have her baby in a house full of strangers.

"So the baby can have US citizenship," she says matter-of-factly. Ming explains that in mainland China, only kids with foreign passports get to go to the international schools.

"Fascinating," I say. I think of my own mother and how she traveled from the Philippines to Hong Kong and then to the United States and how proud she is that I have US citizenship, saying the government could never take it away because I was born on this soil.

The madam of the house, Mrs. Woo, scolds Ming in Mandarin to quit yakking and get to work. "You guys have three hours! The mothers have all gone out shopping. They'll be back soon, and they want their rooms clean. Hurry up!" she says.

Ming and I get to work changing the sweaty sheets off the sunken beds. As I'm wiping down the gummy bathroom counters, I ask Ming about her parents coming to the spring concert.

"It's going to be their first time in America!" She smiles as she grabs a plastic baby bath bucket and scrubs.

"Are you going to introduce them to Florence?" I ask.

Her face falls. "No," she says. I put down my rag and look at Ming through the cloudy mirror. Ming sighs. "I'll just tell them she's my friend. It's easier this way."

Easier for whom?

I stand there, waiting. Finally, Ming stops scrubbing and tosses her sponge into the baby bucket.

"Okay, you want to know? When I was seven, my uncle came out to the entire family. And you know what happened? My whole family disowned him. He was told never to come back to any family functions. I wasn't even allowed to say goodbye to him, even though he's the whole reason I started playing the violin. They didn't want me to xue huai, to be corrupted by him."

My heart breaks listening to her tell her story. "I'm so sorry," I say.

"Now you know why I'm never telling my parents," she says. "Or going back. I'm not going to live the rest of my life in a sham marriage, just so my parents can save face. I'd rather stay all by myself in the US."

I reach out and put a plastic-gloved hand over hers. She

picks up the sponge and starts scrubbing again.

"It's a small price for freedom," she mutters as she scrubs, looking around at the grimy bathroom and stuffy bedroom, which reeks of diapers and throw up. "And we all have one."

forty-three

Claire

"When were you going to tell me you're dating Vincent Li's son?" my mom shrieks over the phone.

I put down my psychology assignment. "How'd you know?" I ask.

My mom sends me a link. "There are pictures of you guys shopping in Beverly Hills on Weibo! Do you know who his family is?"

I shrug. "I have a vague idea."

"A vague idea!" My mother laughs. "Here's a clear one. His father owns Li Incorporated, a massive real estate and telecommunications conglomerate. Half the high-rises in Beijing and Shenzhen are owned by his family." She sounds practically hyper. I picture her sitting on the terrace, sipping Dom, smiling at the artificial lake next to our villa. "Oh, this is the best possible news! I'm so proud of you, honey! I knew you could do it!"

She gushes as if I'd gotten into Harvard, which of course, in her mind, is what this is.

"You haven't even asked me yet if I like him . . . ," I remind her.

My mother laughs. "Guys are like school admissions. Get in first. Then worry if you like them back," she says. I chuckle. "Your grandmother is going to be *so* excited."

"Wait, let's just not tell everyone just yet," I say to her. I'm not sure I want to broadcast this before I even know what it is.

"Oh, but we have to tell her!" my mom insists. "Imagine the envy on your aunts' faces!" She giggles. "Oh by the way, I forgot to tell you. I'm coming in two weeks! I'm meeting Auntie Pearl in New York for shopping, but I have a six-hour layover in LA! We can have dinner! I can finally meet Jay!"

Jay greets me with a smile when I walk to his car after school. He was the first person I texted after my English teacher, Ms. Jones, handed me back my story, the one I'd stayed up all night working on. She'd given me an A and called my writing "raw" and "heartbreaking." Jay texted back, Show off ☺. Followed by, Proud of you. He puts his hand on my leg as he drives.

"Keep your eyes on the road," I tease him.

"My eyes are on the road," he says. His right hand, however, is sliding up my thigh. I let it rest there and stare down at his hand. He has long piano fingers. I ask him if he plays.

He shrugs. "Doesn't every Asian kid?" he replies, then starts playing a chord on my thighs.

It kind of tickles, and I wiggle away. I ask if his mom got to the airport okay. He leans over and whispers in my ear, "Yes. And now we have the whole house to ourselves."

The anticipation flutters inside me as he drives. I tell him my mom's coming in two weeks and she wants to meet him. Jay takes my hand, kisses it, and says okay. Five minutes later, we arrive at his house.

Walking into the empty house, Jay drops his keys on top of the marble table, then turns and kisses me.

He's a very good kisser. Whereas Teddy was always rooting around in my mouth with his tongue like it was some sort of scavenger hunt, Jay caresses me with his experienced lips. I put my hands around the back of his neck as he pulls me hungrily toward the couch. Slowly, he moves his lips down my neck. My breathing changes. I close my eyes, feeling the heat spread as his fingers move under my shirt.

"Wait, stop," I pant.

This is moving way too fast. I put my hand on his chest to try to put some space in between us. He tries to kiss me again, but I turn away slightly.

"I think we should slow down," I tell him.

He looks at me confused. "Why?" he asks.

He stares down at the huge bulge in his pants, as if to say, *CASE IN POINT. WHY?*

"I'm not ready," I say, my pupils flashing. I get up and go into the kitchen and pour us both some water. When I return, he's standing in front of the window, looking out at the pool.

"I'm not really into the innocent thing," he says.

I set down the glasses, carefully considering the statement. "Well, I'm not really into the call-girl thing," I reply tartly.

He laughs. "Don't kid yourself. You're not a call girl, not even close," he says.

I look down at my glass. "Have you had them?" I ask.

"Call girls?"

I don't know, it's possible! We've only just started hanging out. Maybe that's what all the mirrors on the walls are for?

Jay looks almost offended. "No," he says firmly.

And I feel bad for asking.

His eyes soften. He reaches out and takes my hand. "Are you a virgin?" he asks.

I nod. I wait for him to say something, and when he doesn't, I feel really exposed. I hug my chest. "I mean, I've done stuff before, but just not . . ."

He arches an eyebrow. "What kind of stuff?" he asks.

My face turns hot. It crosses my mind to tell him about sexting with Teddy, but that's almost more embarrassing.

He smiles at me. "A real virgin, interesting . . . ," he muses to himself.

"I take it you're not," I ask him hesitantly.

He shakes his head. "I am *definitely* not," he says. I fall quiet, bugged by his reply. Why'd he have to add "definitely"?

I cross my arms, suddenly mad at myself for coming. An hour ago, I was feeling so good, proud of my first A at my American school and now my English high is gone and in its place is a horny, sulky angst I can't explain.

Jay walks over and puts his hands on my cheeks. "Hey. It's okay."

Slowly, I look up at him. The sex-crazed look has vanished. In its place are kind, gentle eyes.

"We can take it slow," he says as he pulls me in for a hug.

I lie floating in the school pool the next morning, thinking of Jay, his lips, the way they pressed hungrily into mine. The need, the urgency in his body when I pushed him away. And he stopped. He didn't say forget it, like Teddy. He was intrigued.

I close my eyes, feeling the water underneath me, the mist on my eyelids. The water is so warm, I could lie here all day. I reach with my fingertips to feel the smooth glass surface. In an hour the swim team will be here, but for now, I have the pool all to myself. I run my hand down my wet body.

"Hey!" a voice calls out.

The unexpected interruption breaks my floating position.

It's Zach. He jumps into the pool with his blue cap and starts swimming toward me.

"I was hoping I'd find you here," he says with a smile. "What were you doing?"

"Just floating," I tell him, face flushing. I still haven't figured out what the deal is between him and Dani. She's been so distant lately.

I glance at the clock. It's six forty-five. I promised my mom I'd Skype with her before school. I start swimming toward the edge of the pool.

"You're not going to keep swimming?" he calls after me.

I shake my head. "Nah, I've already done like twenty-five laps," I lie, getting out and covering myself with a towel.

Zach turns and starts doing laps back and forth. I linger for a second, watching his toned body tearing through the water, before heading to the locker room.

Later that week, Jay invites me over to his house for dinner. We eat out on the terrace. Jay orders in—scallops with risotto and cauliflower and pomegranate salad. I set the table while Jay gets a bottle of Château d'Yquem Bordeaux Blanc from the wine cellar downstairs.

I raise my eyebrow at the expensive bottle of wine. "You sure your parents are okay with us drinking that?" I ask.

Jay uncorks the bottle and pours some into a glass. He holds the glass up to his nose, closing his eyes and inhaling the smell, just like my dad. On Jay, it's a far sexier look.

"Yeah, they're totally cool," he says. "My dad's been teaching me to drink wine since I was seven."

I laugh, thinking it's a joke, but he looks at me dead serious.

"I was trained in all the grapes and regions, the acidity and the tannins. Most of all, how to hold my alcohol."

That sounds *awful*—to be seven years old, plastered with alcohol? Jay shrugs.

"Being drunk is a weakness. My dad doesn't believe in weaknesses," he says, handing me a glass.

I take a sip. "Mine does," I mutter.

Jay peers at me.

"Never mind," I say. "So what does your dad believe in?"

He ponders this. "Strength and control," he replies.

After dinner, we curl up in front of the TV. I drift asleep. Maybe it's the wine or all the late nights of studying finally catching up on me. When I wake up, it's midnight. I'm lying in bed. I look around, feeling slightly disoriented as I register that I'm in one of the guest bedrooms, down the hall from Jay's room. I panic, looking down at my clothes. I'm in navy-blue satin pajamas. But my bra's still on. *We didn't . . . Did we?*

I get up out of bed to find Jay. As I walk down the hall, I hear him talking on speaker.

"Sorry, sir. I haven't had a chance to go to the site yet. I'll go soon," Jay says in Chinese.

Who is he talking to?

"Stop screwing around. The future of this family depends on you," the thick Beijing accented voice booms on speaker. Is that his dad?

"Of course. I understand," Jay says. "I'll go tomorrow."

"Have you been doing your exercises?"

"Yes, Dad," Jay says.

"I'm going to test you when you're back. If it turns out you've been lazy—"

"I haven't been lazy."

Jay's dad exhales. "Your mother says you've been hanging out with a girl," his dad says.

I freeze at the mention of me and lean against the marble wall.

Jay doesn't say anything.

"You know I don't care who you take to bed, but don't let it get too far," his dad says. "Women are a weakness."

"Yes, sir," Jay says.

I tiptoe back to my room as he ends the call. Crawling back under the covers, I try to close my eyes and go back to sleep, but I can't. All I can think about are the words, "I don't care who you take to bed . . ." Who *says* that to his son? And is that all this is?

Jay wakes me up at the crack of dawn.

"Hey," he says. "Get up, sleeping beauty."

I squint at the misty morning light streaming in through the airy white curtains.

"Want to go on a run with me?" he asks. He's in jogging pants and a T-shirt.

I sit up and look around the room. "What time is it?" I ask.

"It's nearly six," he says.

I groan. So early? I put my head back on my pillow. Ever since I stopped Skyping with Teddy, I've been sleeping in until seven. Then I suddenly remember. "Did we?" I ask him.

He looks at me, amused. "No, we did not," he says. "But if you want . . ."

He leans over. His lips open with desire. My body trembles as he climbs on top of me in bed. He kisses my lips . . . my ears . . . my neck. As we kiss, his legs wrap around mine. He presses into me. We both want more, but he stops.

"Get dressed," he says. "There's cereal and juice downstairs. I'll be back in thirty."

"Hey, who was that on the phone last night?" I ask. I wasn't going to say anything but it'd been bothering me all night.

"Oh, that's just my dad," he says. "He can be a bit . . ." He makes the sign for crazy with his finger. "You know how it is."

I smile. I do know. After Jay leaves, I stretch my arms and legs in the luxurious sheets. It almost feels like I'm back in Shanghai, and I bask in the familiar comfort. I take a shower, standing in the rain shower for several minutes, the water dripping down my body as I think about Jay and replay our kiss from this morning.

forty-four

Dani

Mr. Connelly gathers us after training on Wednesday.

"Hey, guys, I have something important to discuss with you regarding Snider," he says.

My teammates and I form a circle around him. The Snider people smile smugly, looking at the rest of us like, *You can probably sit this one out.*

I ignore them and hold my head up high. *Please, let Mrs. Mandalay have talked to him.*

Mr. Connelly takes a step forward and gazes down at his leather loafers, like he's sorry for what he's about to say.

"After a lot of thinking, I've decided to make some adjustments to who's coming to Snider," Mr. Connelly says. My teammates suck in a sharp breath and hold it. "Dani will be coming with us."

A smile sneaks out the corners of my mouth before I can

stop it, but Mr. Connelly doesn't look at me. He keeps his gaze glued to my other teammates, his body language says, *I so did not want to do this.*

"Unfortunately . . . ," Mr. Connelly adds, "we can only send six, so this means one of you guys cannot go." Hands fly to my teammates' mouths. All around me, heads shake. No, no, no, no, no, no. I want to run up to the podium, grab the mic, and yell no too. This is not the way this is supposed to go down!

"Heather," Mr. Connelly calls. Heather's head jerks up. The look in her eyes is of pure terror. "I'm so sorry, but you're not able to go to Snider this year. I know you're dis- appointed, but—"

The rest of Mr. Connelly's words are drowned out by Heather's rage. "This is *bullshit!*" she screams.

I reach for my backpack and start walking out of the auditorium. I can't believe he did it this way. He could have sent an email. He could have written to the organizers and tried to add more people. Instead, he had to turn everyone against me. Heather comes charging after me. She catches up with me in the hallway, grabbing my backpack and pull- ing me to a stop.

"What the hell did you do?" she demands to know.

"Nothing!" I say. My eyes shift to all my teammates standing behind her.

"Nothing, my ass! He just gave you my spot!" Heather exclaims. She points a finger at me. "My mom's going to have a word with Mrs. Mandalay about this, and when she finds out—"

"Mrs. Mandalay already knows," I cry.

"Knows what?" Gloria asks. My teammates' eyes burrow into me.

I shake my head, trying to keep it together. Then decide, fuck it. Better they hear it from me than from the headmistress. Slowly, I back up against the wall, my body sliding down to the cold white floor as I tell them what happened in Seattle.

I stare at their shoes, Common Projects and Gucci Aces, as I wait for them to respond. Gloria speaks first.

"You never mentioned anything when we were up there," she says quietly.

"Yeah, and you debated so well the next day," Josh adds.

I know where this line of reasoning is going. As I look up at their disbelieving faces against the harsh fluorescent lights, I grab my backpack and run.

My mom is in the kitchen, putting away her groceries, when I get home. I fall face-first onto the couch.

"You want pinakbet tonight? You think Claire would like that?" she calls out.

I can't think about food right now. I just want to build a fort of sofa cushions and curl up inside.

My mom pokes her head out from the kitchen. "Or how about batchoy? That's probably easier," she says.

I close my eyes. For once, I wish she was out cleaning. Anywhere but here.

My mom walks over. "Hey what's wrong?" she asks.

What's wrong? My teammates didn't believe me! They think I made up what happened to me just so I can go to Snider!

She looks into my eyes. "Dani, whatever it is, you can tell me."

No, I can't. Because if I tell her, she won't let me go to Snider with Mr. Connelly. And then I won't be able to go to Yale. And I won't be able to change our lives.

"Everything's fine, Mom," I say, getting up and going to my room. I hear her walking over, but I close the door before she can come in. I stand against the door, crying silently, listening to her worried breathing on the other side before she finally retreats back to the kitchen.

That weekend, I'm on Chrome, trying to decide whether to forward my teammates the email I wrote to Mr. Connelly. Would that prove anything?

I open a new tab and type in sexual harassment in high schools in California. The first article that comes up is on the Marlborough all-girls school scandal, where a teacher had an inappropriate relationship with a student. I think back to the plane to Seattle when Mr. Connelly told us we were debating Marlborough—and to think that he was going to try to pull something twenty-four hours later just like the Marlborough teacher! And now I'm being punished for my ability to compartmentalize things!

"You debated so well the next day!" Josh had argued. I want to pound my fist onto the keyboard and scream, *Because I had to! Because my mom works eighty hours a week cleaning your room! I HAD TO!*

I'm so overwhelmed that I pull up Microsoft Word and click on New Document. I write in a trance, the words shooting out of me. It feels good to let it out, to purge and process the pain and humiliation of what happened. My room fills with the sound of a heavy rainstorm as I tap the keys, fingers giving life to the emotions I've been bottling up.

When I'm done, I stare at my essay. I move the cursor over to delete it. But it's too good to delete. It feels wrong. I go back to Chrome and click open a new tab. Heart pounding, I type xomegan.com, an anonymous Reddit-like site for teenagers.

Do I dare?

forty-five

Claire

Jay takes me, Jess, Nancy, and Florence, and a bunch of his friends out for hot pot that weekend. He's a gracious host, picking up pieces of radish and tofu for me and the girls with his chopsticks and setting them on our plates. He even personally mixes our hot-pot sauces for us, saying it's his grandmother's secret recipe.

Jess leans over and whispers in my ear, "He's a keeper!"

I smile. Nancy and Florence stare enviously at us as Jay holds up a piece of shrimp for me and puts it in my mouth. I lick his fingers. Jay smiles. I know he's craving more. But I want to do things differently this time, after what happened with Teddy. I want to take things slow and savor every moment.

Jay discreetly settles the bill before it even arrives at our table. As we're leaving the restaurant, I notice Florence texting in the corner.

"Who are you always texting?" I ask her.

She blushes and puts her phone away. "No one," she says. "Just a friend."

"You ready?" Jay asks. I wave to my girlfriends and get into his car.

I sleep over that night, and in the morning, Jay wakes me up with a kiss. He's holding his car keys in his hand.

"Want to go on a trip with me?" he asks.

I sit up in bed and put a sweatshirt on. "Where are we going?" I ask.

"Newport Beach," he says. "I gotta look at something for my dad. C'mon, it'll be fun."

"But I have a history paper due on Monday," I tell him, gazing over at my backpack in the corner.

He shrugs. "So bring your books," he says.

I get changed and throw my backpack into the car. As he drives, I ask him about this place we're going.

"It's just a place my dad's thinking of buying," he says.

I think back to his phone call with his dad the other night.

"He's very particular," Jay adds.

I got that. "Has he always been like that?" I ask.

"Yeah." Jay shifts gears as he drives. "When I was little, he used to make me do my homework in the snow in my underwear," Jay says.

"What?"

"To make me faster at it," he says. "Especially the math. Said I was too slow. And if I cried, he'd keep me outside. Even in the dead of winter."

I remember when he first said that thing about being naked in the cold when we were playing two truths and a lie in English class. At the time, I thought he meant something sexual. Now, looking over at him, I feel so bad he had to go through that.

"How old were you?"

He keeps his eyes glued to the road. "I was eight," he says quietly.

Eight? Who would do such a thing to an eight-year-old?

"At ten, I had to swim across a ten-mile lake. Sailed a boat solo from Hong Kong to Macao when I was twelve. Anything to make me stronger . . ." His voice lingers. "That's why he sent me here by myself. To toughen me up."

He turns onto the highway, and I can feel the engine rumbling behind us as he kicks the car into high gear.

"And what happens if you say no?" I ask him.

Jay glances at me. "My dad's worth four billion US dollars. He's not exactly the kind of guy you say no to."

"So?" I ask. "He's still your dad . . ."

Jay reaches to turn on the radio. The sound of DJ Khaled fills the car, making it hard to continue the conversation. I look out the window, thinking about my own dad. He had his secretary track down and send me a box of first-edition Fitzgeralds, which my mom told me not to bend or even open, because then I can't resell them later. A lot of good they'll do me in English. I peer over at Jay, wondering if he feels similarly stifled sometimes.

"Ms. Jones, my English teacher, asked us a question in class," I shout to him over the noise. "'What does it mean to live well? And on what terms?'"

Jay reaches to turn down the radio, but he doesn't answer the question. Instead, a mischievous look crosses his face as he lifts his hand off the steering wheel. "Hey, you want to drive?" he asks.

"No!" I exclaim, and reach to put his hands back.

He laughs. "I'm going to teach you how to drive," he says. He turns to me and adds, "Can't have a girlfriend who doesn't know how to drive."

It's the first time I've ever heard him call me that, and our eyes meet. Jess predicted that he would call me his girlfriend within the week. I stretch my legs up onto the dash, feeling the fireworks in my chest. Jay glances at my bare legs, distracted.

"Keep your eyes on the road," I tell him.

He grins, leans over, and kisses me, nearly swerving over to the next lane because the car's so wide.

We arrive forty-five minutes later, at a shopping mall called Fashion Island.

"We're here to go shopping?" I ask him, confused.

"I guess you can say that," he says, eyes twinkling. "We're shopping for a shopping mall."

I laugh.

"I'm serious. My dad's thinking about buying it!" he says. "C'mon, let's go!"

"This whole thing?" I ask as I run after him. There must be three hundred shops in the open-air mall, plus movie theaters and restaurants.

"Give me your phone," he says. This mall's so big, he installs Find My Friends in case we get separated.

As we walk around the complex, Jay's own phone keeps ringing. Every time, he taps Ignore. "You can answer it if you want," I say to him. "Maybe it's your dad calling—"

"It's not my dad," he says. He quickly shoves his phone into his pocket. "It's nobody."

We poke around the mall for the next hour, checking out bathrooms and elevators. Jay takes pictures of large cracks on the ground and counts the number of people in stores. He tells me the strategic investment team has already gone through all the papers.

"But the reason why my dad's been so successful is he doesn't just look on paper," Jay says, examining the walls for water stains.

Wow, Jay really cares about his family business. I'm impressed.

As he swipes to take another picture of the exterior wall, his phone rings again.

"It's a girl, isn't it?" I guess. Only a girl would have the willpower to keep calling after the fifteenth rejection. He doesn't say anything. I feel a twinge of jealousy and try to shrug it off. "It's okay. You can take it."

"I don't want to take it," he says.

He throws the phone at me with a grin.

"Here you take it," he says.

"I don't want to take it!" I protest. I try to give it back to him, but my finger accidentally taps Answer.

Reluctantly, I lift the phone to my ear. "Hello?" I ask.

Upon hearing my voice, the girl, whoever she is, hangs up. I look down at the name on the screen. The name on the screen reads "Tall. High cheekbones. Jimmy Choos."

"Who's Jimmy Choos?" I look up at Jay. "You name girls based on what they're wearing?"

His face turns red as he mumbles a response. "I meet a lot of girls. It's so I don't forget what they look like."

"What am I in here as?" I ask. I start searching my number. Jay reaches to grab his phone out of my hand but it's too late. I find my number listed under "Claire. Cute smile. Virgin."

"What the fuck?" I yell at him.

"I'm sorry! I'm just really organized," he says.

"You're organized? This is *insane*," I tell him. I continue scrolling through the many, *many* girls in his contacts, and they're all tagged "meis." *Mei* means "hot girl" in Chinese.

"What the hell? *Bubble butt? Button nose? Dimple cheeks*?" I read from his phone. A few shoppers turn and stare at us. "And why are we all tagged meis?"

Jay plunges his face in his hands.

"It just helps me find the contact faster. It's more efficient!"

"More efficient?" I put up my hands. I can't believe this. "For what? When you text them for a booty call?" I meant it as a joke, but when he doesn't respond, my eyes go wide. "Oh my God! That's exactly what you do!"

I throw the phone back at him and pull my own out to get an Uber. I have zero interest in being with someone who labels girls based on the shape of their ass. I don't care how nice he is to my friends at hot pot.

"Stop! What are you doing?" he asks as I walk away.

"You can find yourself another mei," I yell as I head toward the parking lot.

As I'm walking out, Jay runs toward me and pulls me aside.

"Fine, you know what," he says. He grabs his phone and holds it up so I can see. I watch as he does a quick search all for meis. There are 129 entries. 129! He highlights them all, and before I can say a word, he presses Delete.

"There," he says. "All gone."

I put my hand to my mouth.

The soft ocean breeze blows loose strands of my hair in my face as Jay pulls me close and wraps his arms around me.

"I don't want those girls anymore." He looks into my eyes and says, "I want you."

forty-six

Dani

I hustle across the field to Mrs. Mandalay's office. She sent me an urgent email to meet; I'm assuming it's to talk about Snider. Zach calls me as I'm walking.

"Hey," I say. "Did you read it?" I posted my anonymous piece on xomegan.com last night and sent him the link, figuring my writing can finally fill him in on what my mouth can't seem to.

"Where is it?" he asks. "The link doesn't work. I've been looking for it all day and I can't find it."

I stop walking. "What do you mean it doesn't work?" I ask. I look down at my phone and try to load the link myself, but the page comes back with "Error—We Couldn't Find the Page You Requested." I must have sent the wrong link, because it was there when I checked it last night.

I glance at the time. *I'm late.* I tell Zach I'll call him

back later and hurry the rest of the way to Mrs. Mandalay's office.

As soon as I walk inside, Mr. Connelly is standing there. Shit.

"What were you thinking?" Mr. Connelly asks me. I look down at the piece of paper in his hand and see the familiar logo on the top—Xomegan.

"How did you get that?" I ask.

Mrs. Mandalay informs me that one of the investors of xomegan.com is friends with the school. A private equity fund. My mind trips over itself, a traffic crash of information. How's that possible? Mrs. Mandalay takes the essay from Mr. Connelly and reads.

"'He took advantage of my admiration and respect for him, exploited my trust,'" Mrs. Mandalay reads my words. She shakes her head at me. "Do you know how much trouble you could have caused for the school if they hadn't taken this down?"

"You're lucky we don't sue you for slander!" Mr. Connelly adds.

"It's not slander if I'm telling the truth," I reply, defiant eyes staring up at him. He should know, he taught it to us in debate.

Mrs. Mandalay frowns. "I thought we gave you what you wanted. You're back on the team. You get to go to Snider. Haven't we been good to you?"

I feel myself shrinking in the chair, as they both lay on the guilt. I think of all the things they've both done for me in years past—big and small—and a knot forms in my throat I can't dissolve.

"All that time. All that energy I poured into you. And this is how you repay me?" Mr. Connelly asks.

"What about *my* time?" I ask. "I trusted you. I believed you."

It's the first time I've confronted him since the incident. I stare at him, as the anger burns in my eyes.

Mrs. Mandalay stands up and holds open her door, telling me to go back to class. As I get up to leave, she takes my essay, rips it up, and warns, "I better not find this on another website."

forty-seven

Claire

I text Jess as Jay and I drive up and down Balboa Island, a tiny island in Newport Beach with waterfront houses, sail-boats, and idyllic streets. Jay leans over and kisses my cheek, and I want so desperately to forget what happened, to lose myself in this picture-perfect postcard. But the question nags at my brain, who are those other girls?

They're probably just his exes, big deal! Jess texts back. He deleted them for you! That's so good!

But 129?! How does he have that many?! I text back.

He probably didn't sleep with them all!

Three dots appear.

If he did, she texts, then DAMN. He probably has great technique!

I peer over at Jay. He flashes me a smile, and I feel my anger soften. It's difficult staying mad at him when I'm in a place this beautiful and I'm cruising down the street with a guy this gorgeous. Who just deleted all his exes for me. Jay pulls over the Lamborghini.

"What are you doing?" I ask.

He unbuckles his seat belt and mine. "Get up. We're switching seats," he says with a grin. "I'm teaching you how to drive."

My hands grip my seat belt. "What? Now? Here?"

He pushes up his car door, comes over to my side, and pulls me out of my seat.

"Sure, why not," he says. "You couldn't ask for more peaceful streets."

Reluctantly, I walk over to the other side and slide into the driver's seat. As the engine revs, I beg Jay with my eyes.

"Please, I've never done this before," I tell him.

He grins. "You've never done a lot of things before. Time to start changing that," he says with a wink. He pushes a button on the center console to put the car into automatic.

As I release the break and step lightly on the gas, the car flies down the road. I scream and turn to Jay. I really don't want to crash his car.

"Slow down. You're doing fine," Jay says. He puts his hands over mine and helps me steer.

The whole time, I'm looking at the road and I'm trying not to freak out. "I don't think learning to drive in a Lamborghini is a good idea!" I tell him.

"Maybe not, but we're doing it," he says.

He commands me to stop, slow down, and speed up, and

turns the steering wheel with his hands over mine. After a while, I start to get it. I drive the car up and down empty streets, learning to control the speed, which isn't easy, given how forceful the engine is. Slowly, Jay lifts his hands off mine. And I'm doing it! I'm driving!

I laugh.

"You're a fast learner," he says. He sits back in his seat and grins. "I know what I'm getting you for your birthday."

I turn to him and say, "No. No. No. Please don't."

"Keep your eyes on the road at all times!" he barks at me.

"Sorry!" I force my eyes straight ahead. As I make my way down the street, I notice a beautiful house up the road. There's a For Sale sign on the lawn.

"Stop here for a second," he says.

I pull up in front of the house and we both get out. The Cape Cod–style blue-and-white house sits in front of the water. Jay and I hold hands as we walk across the lush green lawn.

"Hey! There's an open house right now," I say, noticing the sign on the door.

We walk inside. The house is stunning, with gleaming hardwood floors and sunlight pouring in from the windows. The real estate agent glances at us, but is too busy talking to someone else to come over to say hello. Jay and I show ourselves around the house. He runs his fingers along the walls and the wood, pointing out to me the Dutch door entry, the handcrafted French oak cabinets.

He studies every corner and angle mechanically, scientifically. This is obviously not his first open house. As we walk, I offer random possibilities for remodeling, trying to sound like the real estate expert I'm not. But I've picked up enough from watching my mother redecorate our villa.

"You could put a window seat right there," I say, pointing to a quiet spot in the corner with lots of sunlight. "And you could store things under it."

Jay's impressed. "You're good at this," he says. He pulls out his phone and starts taking pictures of the house. When we get to the master suite, I hop onto the bed and stretch out my legs. Jay calls his dad, and I listen to him go through the specs of the mall as I text with Jess on my own phone.

What are you guys doing now? Jess texts.

Looking at real estate, I text back.

OMG #goals, she texts.

I smile.

"Oh, and there's a house we found, Dad, right on the water," Jay says to his father on the phone. "It's beautiful."

He snaps his fingers for the flyer, and I hand it to him.

"Built in 2016," he says. "Four bedrooms, five baths; 4.2 million US dollars. Excellent foundation." He walks over to the window, glances at the direction of the house, and adds, "And good feng shui."

As he's talking, it's hard not to be taken with him. Dashing young scion, charming and boyish. No wonder he has so many girls chasing him. Maybe I should just let that go.

I close my eyes and imagine our future together, driving around, looking at real estate.

Jay grins at me. "Claire already has some ideas for remodeling," he adds with a wink.

There's a long pause, during which I worry his dad's pissed that I'm here. But then Jay's face relaxes into a smile.

"Sure, I'll send you the pics right now," he says. He gets off the phone, runs toward me, and jumps on the bed. "Guess what? We're buying it!"

"What?" I exclaim. "Just like that?"

"Just like that," Jay says. A dreamy look crosses his face. He kisses me, and he whispers, "Can you see us living in a place like this?"

The door bangs open and the real estate agent walks in. He sees us making out on the bed.

"What the hell are you two doing in here?" he barks at us. "This is Newport Beach, not Chinatown! Get off my bed!"

Jay turns to face the real estate agent and says, "Actually, it's my bed. I just bought the place."

"Did you see the way he looked at us?" Jay fumes as he drives. We're in the car heading over to the Ritz-Carlton Laguna. I can feel his anger in the way he grips my hand. "No matter how fucking rich we are, they still treat us like second-class citizens."

I've never seen him get mad like this before. He takes a

water bottle and crushes it against the seat. I put my hand on Jay's lap, trying to calm him.

"Take it easy," I say.

"No!" he yells, flinging my hand away. He steps on the gas, and the car goes *vroooom*. "I hate this country sometimes! America's the only place in the world that can make me feel like a shoe polisher."

I laugh, trying to defuse the anger. "Well, that was pretty baller for a shoe polisher! Did you see the look on his face when you told him you're buying the place?" I ask. Jay's tense face dissolves into a grin.

"It was pretty fucking baller!" His shoulders relax, and my heartbeat comes back to normal as he takes my hand and kisses it.

We arrive at the Ritz-Carlton, where Jay checks us in to the ocean-view executive suite. It comes with a couch in the living room, which Jay swears up and down he's going to sleep on; I can take the bed.

We order room service. While we wait for the food to arrive, I take out my history books from my backpack. I try to read, but it's hard to concentrate. I'm still thinking about Jay's fit in the car. He was *so* angry. I thought he was going to crash the car.

Jay pats the spot next to him in bed. He's more peaceful now as he lies there, feet crossed, gazing at me. "I'm the only homework you should be concerned about," he says. "Come here."

I put my textbooks down and go to him.

As I climb into bed, he starts kissing me. I kiss him back and nibble his ears. Then, ever so gently, he starts pushing my head down. I know where this is going, and I stop.

He throws his hands up at me in frustration. "What do you want, a proposal?" he asks.

"I thought we were going to take it slow," I remind him. I get up and walk back over to my history books.

He holds his hands out to me. "But I have needs . . . ," he whines.

I ignore him and try to concentrate on my homework. Five minutes later, he jumps out of bed and announces he's taking a shower. He strips in front of me, taking off all his clothes. I feel the temperature rising in the room.

"You sure you don't want to join me?" he asks.

I look longingly at him. He has *the most amazing* body. But there's also something delicious about waiting, as I'm starting to discover.

"Yes," I say. I smile sweetly at him. "I'm good."

"You're going to pay for it, you know," he says, grinning as he walks into the bathroom. "All this making me wait. I haven't thought of how yet. But you're going to pay for it."

I put a pencil in my mouth and bite down gently. "Can't wait."

forty-eight

Dani

Ming tunes her violin in the band room after school, waiting for Mr. Rufus to approve the changes she's made to her sheet music, while I research who the xomegan.com mole is on my phone.

"I can't believe they took it down," she says, playing G on the strings and adjusting the peg.

"I know! It's so Big Brother!" I pull up the corporate site for xomegan.com and scroll through the About Us.

Ming closes her eyes and plays a dramatic piece on the violin, her eyebrows rising and falling. When she opens her eyes again, she asks, "And what does a private equity fund care about a teen-chat forum?"

"Or American Prep, for that matter," I mutter.

Mr. Rufus walks out, hands Ming the sheet music, and gives her a big thumbs-up. Ming puts her violin and bow back in her case. Walking down the hall together, we see

Florence with her friends. She's deep in conversation with Jess.

"Hey!" Ming calls out to her.

"Hi," Florence says politely, and keeps walking.

Ming shakes her head. "I don't get it. She introduced me that one time, but she still never lets me hang out with her and her friends." Ming stops walking and turns to me. "You think it's because I'm poor?"

"*No.* That's not it."

"We've been dating for almost two months! I want to get to know who all her friends are."

I gaze over at Florence with her squad and sigh. "Well, I know one of them," I say, eyeing Claire. She's been gone a lot. I don't know where she disappeared to this weekend. I hope she's okay. I turn back to Ming. "Maybe Florence just needs a little more time."

Later that day, I walk into the auditorium for our usual debate training, only to find it empty.

Where are all my teammates? Snider's in a month. I look down at my phone. There are no emails in my in-box from Mr. Connelly or any of my teammates.

Did they move practice to Mr. Connelly's class, since there are only six of us going to Snider?

I grab my backpack from the floor and hustle over to Mr. Connelly's classroom, but it's empty too. And his door is locked.

Huh.

I go over to the main office, nearly colliding into Claire and her friends as I'm running.

"Watch it!" Jess yells at me. She throws her backpack down and looks like she wants to get into it with me.

"It was just an accident," Florence says in my defense.

"Sorry," I call out as I keep running. At the main office, I ask the assistant if she knows whether the debate practice got moved. I tap my fingers while she checks.

"Looks like debate's been moved from Wednesdays to Thursdays in the auditorium," the assistant says. She looks at me. "Did you not get an email about this?"

My face reddens. "Nope, I did not," I say to her.

If that's how they're going to play it.

forty-nine

Claire

Every time I close my eyes, it comes to me. Jay's arm around my waist. Legs twisted together. Waking up in his sheets, feeling so adult, it almost feels like we're playing house. I stare out the window in class, thinking about our weekend in Newport.

We didn't have sex. But we did take our clothes off and sleep together, falling asleep in each other's arms and waking up together. I'm proud of myself for my self-control. And I'm proud of Jay too, the fact that a guy will listen to me. Sometimes I think the *only* reason Jay listens to me is because I say no to him. What else differentiates me from the other 129 girls? Why delete them and not me?

My lower lip trembles when I think about all the things we could have done . . . if I let myself say yes.

"Claire!" Ms. Jones calls out.

I look up at her, face flushing.

"I said you're working with Emma on the group project."

What?

I glance over at Emma, who celebrates our new partnership with a great big middle finger under the table. *Wonderful.*

Walking out of English class, I take the stairs to psychology. As I'm about to walk into the stairway, I see two girls holding each other in the stairway. It's Florence and that girl Ming, the one Dani's always hanging out with. And they're *making out.*

I turn and back out of the stairway.

Oh my God, is Florence gay?

In the Uber on my way to Emma's house, I replay all the conversations I've ever had with Florence. How could I have not known? I'm tempted to text Jess—does she know? Then decide, no, if Florence wants to keep this a secret from us, I have to respect that, as much it hurts that she's kept such a fundamental part of her from us, her girls.

I gaze out the window as the driver turns on the windy roads. Emma refused to meet me anywhere else but her house, saying she didn't trust me not to plant rice or some other stupid prank. The Uber driver asks me where I'm from.

"Shanghai," I tell him.

"Shanghai, isn't that where Jackie Chan's from?" the guy

asks, looking at me in the rearview mirror.

"I'm pretty sure he's from Hong Kong," I reply.

The driver shrugs. "Shanghai, Hong Kong, it's all the same."

I shake my head. *Actually, it's not.*

"Tell me, why y'all like coming to America?"

I don't answer him. I look out the window, hoping he'll stop talking to me.

"You guys come here, buy up our houses . . . go to our schools," he continues. He pauses for a second. "Don't they have schools in China?"

I open my mouth, then close it. I put on my headphones instead.

"Pardon me," he says, holding up a hand. "Didn't mean to offend you." He looks in the mirror at me. He puts his hands together and does a little bow. "Konichiwa! We appreciate the business."

"That's Japanese—" I start to say. Forget it! I think about what Jay said. How no matter how much money we have, we still get treated like second-class citizens here.

We pull up to Emma's house, and I get out. She lives in a Spanish-style house with a little bonsai garden up front. Nowhere near as big as Jay's but bigger than Dani's and cute. Very zen, which unfortunately she is not.

She comes outside with her arms crossed, proclaiming I'm twelve minutes late. "I have piano after this, then bio, and then SAT prep," she says. "Hurry up."

I follow her inside. We sit down in the dining room. As I get out my laptop, Emma's mom, Mrs. Lau, a stout and chatty woman, comes over to say hello. She offers us plates of fruit with little toothpicks stuck in them, like Tressy used to prepare. Emma obviously hasn't told her mom about the rice, thank God.

"Thank you, auntie," I say to her, popping a strawberry in my mouth.

"My pleasure, it's so great to see you girls study hard together," she says in English, smiling at me. I think back to Emma scolding her mom in the school parking lot about speaking Chinese in public. "You know Harvard only take eight percent Asian American this year?"

She shakes her head at this tragic news.

"Which is why you need to get perfect SAT," she says to her daughter. "ACT too, just to double-prove you good."

Emma groans. "Mom, will you leave us alone?" she asks.

"Some Asian I know, they even change their last name from Yang to Young," she continues, showing no indications of leaving. She stares her daughter in the eye. "We Lau, we can't do that. We clearly Chinese. That why we can't make any mistakes!"

Wow, Asian moms are the same everywhere.

"Thanks, auntie," I say, smiling. "These strawberries are really good!" I know the quickest way to get rid of a Chinese mom is to compliment her on her food and ask her for more.

"They were on sale at Whole Foods!" She beams at Emma and adds, "I borrowed Auntie Ling's Prime membership."

Emma shakes her head, clearly embarrassed. Mrs. Lau looks at me.

"I'll pack some up for you to take home!"

Emma exhales after her mom disappears into the kitchen, sliding down in her chair. "Oh, thank God. She drives me up the wall . . ."

I nod knowingly at her. "I have one too."

Emma glances at me but doesn't say anything.

As we work, Mrs. Lau vacuums and does the housework. She does the dining room first, then the living room, and the stairs, plugging and unplugging the vacuum as she goes. I'm impressed. I've never seen my mom vacuum, though she always claims she's a good housekeeper because she hired a good housekeeper. I can't believe my mom's going to be here next week and she's going to meet Jay. Emma asks me a question about theme. As we're flipping through the text together, we hear a scream from upstairs.

Mrs. Lau comes charging down the stairs with a shoe-box.

"What's this?" she asks Emma, shoving a shoebox in her face. Mrs. Lau starts pulling out packets of condoms from the box.

Emma's face immediately goes red. She looks like she's going to pass out.

"Are you having sex?" her mom demands.

I look to Emma, then jump up and say, "No, I am."

Mrs. Lau stares at me, her hands crushing the condom packets in her fists.

"Yeah, I just had a few extra, so I gave them to Emma. You know, just in case she ever wanted to"—Emma shakes her head alarmingly at me—"sell them."

Mrs. Lau sits down. She puts a hand to her chest out of relief for her daughter and deep concern for me and my deeply troubled soul. "You, Claire, you need to stop," she says to me. "Sex is like drug. Once you have it, you can't stop. It's just sex sex sex sex sex sex sex SEX SEX SEX!"

Her eyes bulge bigger and bigger with each "sex." I turn to Emma, who's got her hand over her mouth. We're both trying so hard not to crack up.

"Seriously, Claire, you need to respect you self, respect you body!" Mrs. Lau says.

"I do," I say, pointing to the shoebox full of condoms. "Hence the condoms."

Mrs. Lau shakes her head at me and lets out a profound sigh. "This makes me so sad," she finally says. She takes the shoebox and hands it to me. To her daughter, she adds, "I don't want you studying with her anymore. You will xue huai."

My forehead puckers at the Chinese phrase for "learn bad." Later, when we're standing outside her house, Emma thanks me.

"That was . . ." She covers her embarrassed face with her hands. "OMG, I don't even have the words."

We both burst out laughing as I hug the box of condoms. "I'm keeping these," I say.

Emma chuckles. "Oh, please, they're yours! I seriously thought my mom was going to kill me," she says, shrinking at the thought. "Thanks again." She lingers. "And I'm sorry about what I said in class."

"Me too. About the rice," I say.

My Uber ride pulls up.

"I'll see you at school?" she asks.

I wave as I throw my backpack in the car along with my box of condoms. "See ya," I say, getting in. I roll the window down and flash one of the condoms at her. "I'll be the one getting it on in the bathroom."

Emma laughs as my ride drives away.

fifty

Dani

Mrs. Mandalay walks up onto the stage of the auditorium, flashing a smile. It's our annual headmistress commendation awards ceremony. I look over at Ming, wiping her palms on her jeans, her leg bouncing in the auditorium seat. I smile, we're both expected to get headmistress commendation again this year, the only silver lining in this semester of hurricanes.

I look around and roll my eyes at Zach, who's five rows behind me, making googly eyes at Claire. He should know she has a boyfriend. And judging by how often she's over at Jay's house—she usually texts me when she's spending the night—I'd say things are going well with them. As Mrs. Mandalay welcomes us to the assembly, I scan the auditorium for Mr. Connelly. I still can't believe he changed the time and day of practice without telling me. Has he always been this cruel?

Mrs. Mandalay clears her voice. "As you know, every year the faculty picks ten students from each year group to award the prestigious headmistress commendation to," she begins. "Among the qualities we're looking for are dedication to academic excellence, drive, perseverance, exceptional talent . . ."

Ming looks over at me, and I smile reassuringly at her. She's going to get it again. If the school's flying her parents out for the spring concert, that's a sign of how much they value her. As for me, though I'm probably not high on Mrs. Mandalay's fave list this year, the headmistress commendation has more to do with GPA. And I'm holding steady at 3.9 unweighted.

"Here to announce this year's headmistress commendations is Mayor Stein," Mrs. Mandalay says. The doors in the back open and Mayor Stein, our newly elected mayor, walks in. The crowd erupts in applause as the mayor takes the podium.

"It's an honor to be here today," he says. "American Prep isn't just a school. It's a local treasure, one that's *lifted* this entire town to what it is today—a diverse, business-friendly community that warmly welcomes immigrants!"

There's a round of applause from the parachutes.

As Mayor Stein gushes about American Prep's many contributions to East Covina, I turn to Ming and whisper, "Why's the mayor here for this?"

"Maybe he's the xomegan.com mole!" Ming jokes.

Our classmates sitting next to us give us odd looks. As Mayor Stein calls out all the seniors who have earned head-mistress commendation this year, my eyes glide across the room to my debate teammates, tensing in their seats in eager anticipation of their names being called next.

"Moving on to the juniors," Mayor Stein says. "For the juniors this year we have . . . Ming Liu."

Ming stands as Mr. Rufus claps for her from the front. I smile and squeeze her hand as she walks by and goes up to the stage to collect her award.

Mayor Stein reads out three more names: Emma Lau, Sophie Zhao, Tiffany Davis from geography, whose room I cleaned with Ming not that long ago. I didn't expect her to get it, and, judging from the look on her face, neither did she. Mayor Stein names five boys from our year group before pausing to take a drink from his water bottle.

I feel a squeeze in my chest as I wait for the last name to be called out.

"And last but not least, Heather McLean."

Nervously, I walk up to Mrs. Mandalay afterward and tap on her shoulder. I wasn't going to talk to her about it but I worry if I don't, I'll always wonder. She's chatting with Mayor Stein, telling him about her latest fund-raising efforts.

"Mrs. Mandalay, may I speak to you for a sec?" I ask.

Mayor Stein busies himself with his phone while Mrs.

Mandalay turns to me. "What is it, Dani?" she asks.

"I just . . . I'd like to know why . . ." I'm so embarrassed, I don't even know how to ask.

"Why you didn't make headmistress commendation this year?" she finishes for me. "Well, it's like Mayor Stein said. We're looking for students who embody the values of the school."

"I—"

"Who *love* and honor our school," she continues, cutting me off. "And are real ambassadors for the school."

I swallow. I take it that writing online about your teacher hitting on you doesn't count as ambassadorship. Mrs. Mandalay turns back to Mayor Stein.

Zach walks over to me and puts a hand on my shoulder.

"I'm sorry," he says. "But, hey, if it makes you feel better, I never get headmistress commendation!"

No, that does not make me feel better. I pull away from him and walk out of the auditorium. I'm so upset afterward that I skip debate training, even though I know they're having it today in the auditorium.

Instead, I head to work, taking out my frustrations with Lysol. It's a little after six when I'm done cleaning. Famished, I stop by Dave's Food Hall, the local grocery store, to pick up a salad.

I grab a container and start piling on avocado, pistachios, and croutons, hoping the extra toppings will fill the hole of my not making headmistress commendation this year.

I don't know how that's going to look on my college apps. Mr. Matthews is always talking about upward trajectory. Lately, it's been one never-ending, downward nightmare. I pick at the pistachios with my fingers, trying to eat a little off, as they charge by the pound.

As I'm eating, Mr. Connelly and his wife walk in. I fight the urge to go up to him and ask, Was this you? Did you ask Mrs. Mandalay to take away my headmistress commendation as retribution? Instead, I duck behind the pet food aisle as they walk by, too angry to stay, too mortified to leave. Sandwiched between the dry dog food, I sit as close to the shelf listening to the two of them talk.

"How many bottles do you think we need?" Mr. Connelly's wife asks him as they stroll by the alcohol section.

I hear the clanging of bottles being picked up. "Depends on if your mom's coming," he says.

"You're one to talk," his wife snaps. "I see you at night, pouring yourself a gin and tonic, pretending it's a club soda."

"Give me a break, will you? I got me-too'ed," Mr. Connelly says.

I can't believe he's using it as a verb, like *he's* the victim. I crouch into a ball and push myself deeper into the shelf, as they roll their cart past my aisle. When they walk by, I poke my head out. I glance at the automatic double doors. Now's my chance to make a break for it. I can't wait in line to buy my salad; there's no time. They might see me. I stuff three more bites in my mouth, put my salad container down next to the pet food, and make a run for it.

"Hold up." The store security guard comes up to me as I'm walking out.

"Me?" I ask.

"Yeah, you," another security guard walks over and says. He wiggles a finger. "Follow us."

I follow the two security guards into a back office, glancing over at Mr. Connelly and his wife, who, luckily, are on the other side of the store and don't see me. They lead me into a small room in the back of the store, behind the milk and yogurt fridge. As I sit down on the metal chair, the security guards turn to me.

"We saw what you did," one of the guards says.

"What?" I ask.

"Don't play dumb with us. You ate the salad back there without paying for it. We have it all on camera," the guy on the left with the red hair says, pointing to the CCTV cameras. He rewinds one of them and presses Play. There I am on the grainy screen, shoveling salad into my mouth in the pet food aisle like a starving weirdo. My ears turn red.

The redheaded security guard crosses his arms. "You think you can come in here and just consume our product without paying?" he asks, leaning into me. He's a big guy. Sweat trickles down my back.

"Answer me!" he screams into my face, and all of a sudden, being seen by Mr. Connelly is no longer my greatest problem.

My eyes jolt from the screen to the guards. "I'm really sorry. I just took a few bites. I was going to pay for it—"

Red snorts at his colleague, a mop-haired guy with a mustache.

"That's what they all say," he says, pointing to the wall next to him. There, on the wall, was a four-by-five grid of faces. Mug shots. Embarrassed-looking people, holding signs that read, "I stole from this store."

"We have another one up at the front of the store," Mop Head informs me proudly. "That's where your face is going to go unless you pay up."

Hands shaking, I get my wallet. I pull $10 out and give it to them. That should cover the salad.

The security guards shake their heads. "Oh no," they say.

A smile sneaks out the corner of Red's mouth; clearly he's enjoying this. "The penalty for theft is ten times the price."

Ten times? The pistachios inside me turn into stones.

Red turns to his colleague, who fishes out my salad from a plastic bag sitting on his desk. I clench my teeth as I wait for him to weigh it. It comes out to one and a half pounds, which puts it well over $13. *Goddamn it*. I knew I shouldn't have added the avocados!

"That'll be thirteen forty-eight times ten." Red punches it into his calculator. I didn't need a calculator. My mind was already in full-on alarm mode. "That's $134.80."

"What?" I exclaim. "I don't have that kind of money!"

Red shakes his head at me and looks down at my bronze

arms. "You guys always do this. You come over the border from Mexico—"

"I'm Filipino, not Mexican," I correct.

Red rolls his eyes. "Same thing," he says. Mop Head grunts in agreement. My skin boils.

"What's it going to be? Pay up or the wall?" he asks.

My eyes slide over to the wall. I think about my debate teammates and my teachers, Mr. Connelly, Mrs. Mandalay, walking into the store, looking at the sign, and cringe.

"I'll pay," I say. I peel my wallet open once again. I only have $20. Unlike Claire, I don't have an Amex or any other credit cards. I take my phone out of my bag. First I call Ming, but she doesn't pick up. She's probably still at violin practice with Mr. Rufus. I try Zach next.

The phone rings and rings.

Pick up, pick up.

Zach doesn't pick up either. I try my mom, regretting the words I'm going to have to say. *So, Mom . . . I'm at the store. I need you to bail me out for shoplifting a salad.*

When she doesn't pick up either, I really start panicking. The last thing I need right now is a shoplifting record. How's *that* going to look on my college apps? I try the house, but no one's home.

"Her battery probably died," I explain to the security guards. They yawn. Red reaches over on the desk for his camera, getting ready to take my pic, while Mop Head grabs the sign.

"Wait, wait, wait!" I beg. Frantically, I tap on my phone. "Let me try one more person."

Claire answers on the third ring.

"Wei?" she asks in Chinese.

"Um, Claire? It's me Dani," I say. "I need your help. I'm in some trouble and I . . ."

I feel my throat closing in. I don't know how to get the words out.

"Where are you?" Claire asks.

I tell her the name and address of the store.

"I'll be right there," she says.

Claire arrives at the store ten minutes later. She strolls into the back office in her block heels and looks at me—I want to crawl into the fetal position.

"How much?" she asks the security guards, pulling out her wallet.

She doesn't ask what happened. Doesn't ask why.

"Your friend here owes $134.80," Red tells her.

Without a word, Claire pulls a hundred-dollar bill and a fifty from her wallet and hands them to the security guards. She doesn't wait for change, she just grabs me and pulls me out of there.

When we're out of the store, I turn to her and say, "It's not what you think. I'm not a shoplifter."

"Of course not. I never thought that."

"I was going to pay for it—I swear! But then I saw someone in the store and I—"

"Listen," Claire says, holding up a hand, stopping me. "You don't have to explain it to me." She taps on her phone for an Uber, then looks up at me. "I've listened to enough of your speeches to know that." She smiles.

My eyes open wide. "You have?"

Claire nods. "Oh yeah, all the time. It's the best part of living at your house."

Her words surprise the hell out of me. "I thought you didn't like living with us," I say quietly. "You know, from your WeChat posts," I add.

She flushes. "I was just writing that for my friends back home. It was stupid; I'm sorry." Her phone dings. It's her Uber driver. She asks me if I need a ride. I shake my head no.

"Thanks again for coming. And I'll pay you back!" I say to her. I put my hands together. "Please don't say anything to my mom about this."

She shakes her head, like she would never.

"Or to Zach," I add.

As her Uber driver pulls up, Claire opens the door and turns to me, shielding her face from the sun with her hand. "Zach, is he like your boyfriend or something?" she asks.

I shake my head. I shift my weight from one foot to the other, wondering whether I should tell her I like him. But when I look up, she's already inside the Uber.

I wave as she drives off. She texts me from inside the Uber, Next time you want to go crazy in a grocery store, call me and we'll go crazy together. Especially in the chocolate aisle!

I smile. I was wrong about Claire.

fifty-one

Claire

I was happy to be able to help Dani. She's done so much for me, not the least of which was help me get an amazing English teacher. Jess is waiting for me in my room after I get back from the grocery store, not to go shopping, but to study. Dani's mom, who came home to get her phone, let her in. I'm helping Jess prep for the English placement test. More parachutes have been testing out, not just in English but in math, science, and history too. It's wonderful to see so many parachutes taking charge.

Now when the bell rings, instead of the usual stampede of jet-black hair heading one way and blonds the other, there is jet-black dotted throughout the blond and brunette, which makes me smile. I've been trying to encourage Jay to test out too, but when it comes to school, he's not too bothered. He tells me he's going to take over his dad's company when he gets out of college, a plan that I'm sure will impress my mom at dinner. And for that role, his old man says it's more about instinct than book smarts.

"You're late," Jess says, pointing to her Cartier tank.

"Sorry," I say, putting my purse down. "I lost track of time."

"Where were you?" she asks. I shrug, not about to tell her Dani's secret. Instead, I delete my WeChat moments on my phone and point to the English books on my desk.

"Did you get started?" I ask.

Jess smiles mischievously and walks over to Emma's box of condoms. "No, but I did discover these!" She opens the box. "Thank God you finally popped your cherry," she says. "But seriously, Claire, these are so cheap. I'll get you some better ones from Japan. The Kimono MicroThins? They won the Oscars of condoms."

There's an Oscars of condoms? I chuckle. "Thanks, but they're not mine," I say, putting away the box.

Jess looks confused. "What do you mean? You and Jay still haven't had sex?"

I don't say anything.

Jess's jaw drops. "What's wrong? He can't get it up?" she presses.

"No! It's not that!"

"Then what is it?"

"I thought you came here to study," I say.

Jess plops herself down on my bed. "Claire, you're dating the hottest guy in school. And he's crazy for you." She looks at me and asks gently, "Is it the other girls on his phone?"

That certainly doesn't help. I walk over and look out the window.

"I know it's hard, but you're going to have to trust him. Those girls are in the past."

Jess's phone dings, as does mine. We both look down at the urgent message from Nancy.

HELP! My parents saw my Insta!

Jess speeds over to Nancy's host's house on the other side of town. Florence meets us at Nancy's. We find her sitting on her bed next to a fortress of handbags, which she appears to be categorizing with her laptop. She puts down her laptop when she sees us.

"Hey," we say to her, taking a seat next to her on her bed. Nancy looks up and clutches an LV bag as she cries. "My parents got a VPN to go on Instagram. When they saw my posts, they flipped out. 'This is what we're paying forty thousand US dollars plus room and board for?' they said," she wails. "They called me an ungrateful piece of American trash!"

Jess tries to calm her down. "Did you explain to your parents it's all just a way to get followers and when we get enough, we'll delete all our posts and start fresh? But we'll still have the followers? We need at least 20k to be influencers!"

Nancy rubs her eyes. "My parents don't know what that

means. They're not like your guys' parents." A tear falls onto her LV bag, and she quickly dries it with her hand. "I don't come from a lot of money. My parents left me with my grandparents when I was four years old to go to Beijing to work. They took out a billion loans just to send me here."

Jess, Florence, and I look at each other. "But what about all your clothes? All your bags?"

Nancy picks up the LV bag she's holding and shows us. "All knockoffs from Shenzhen or rented from online." She pulls out the rental card from the inside pocket of the leather bag.

Jess gasps. "You rented this?" she asks, taking the bag in her hand. "Why?"

The answer, too embarrassing to say, was *for us*. I toss the bags aside and pull Nancy in for a hug.

"You don't have to rent that stuff," I say.

"That's easy for you guys to say. You already have it!" Nancy says. Her eyes slide over to her desk, where her wallet lies open. Both her Visa and Mastercard are cut up into a thousand pieces, next to a pair of scissors. I think back to all the times she said she forgot to move her credit card from one bag to another. "I don't know how it got so out of control . . ."

"You should have just told us," Jess says, shaking her head at Nancy. "I would have totally lent you some of my—"

"No," I say, cutting Jess off. That's not the thing to say. I look into Nancy's eyes and tell her, "It doesn't matter what you carry."

Nancy peers over at Jess, whose eyes flit around the room at all the fake bags that litter the floor. I can tell she's trying hard to be supportive while also trying to stay true to herself, someone who would *never* be caught dead buying knockoffs.

Florence's small voice chimes in. "I have something to tell you guys too."

I turn to her, fully expecting her to come out, but instead, she says, "My parents aren't who I said they are. . . ."

"Your dad's not a hedge fund manager?" Jess asks.

"I mean he is, but . . ." Her chest rises and falls. "I'm . . . I'm his illegitimate daughter."

Jess's eyes go wide. She stares at Florence, the flesh-and-bones incarnation of her most painful scar. I can feel the heat of Jess from the other side of the bed.

"That's why he sent me here. To hide me . . ." Florence looks down, her eyelashes flooding with tears. "I know it's a lot. If you guys don't want to be friends with me anymore, I'll understand."

The room falls silent. As I reach out a hand to Florence, Jess gets up, grabs her car keys and her bag, and starts walking out.

"Jess, what are you doing?" I ask.

She holds up a hand. "I'm sorry, I need to process this," she says.

o o o

That night, as I get ready for dinner with my mom and Jay, I think about Nancy and Florence and how I had them pegged but I was totally wrong. I think about Nancy, quietly renting and returning bags, running up a huge credit card bill her parents can't afford, just so she can feel like she's one of us.

And Florence, how she *still* didn't tell everyone her other secret. Though now I understand a little more why she's so afraid. Her situation is complicated. After Jess left, she told us her dad won't even let her call him Dad in public. They put her here in America so no one would find out about her.

Dani knocks on my door as I'm putting on my boots.

"Come in!"

"I just wanted to say thank you again," she says. "You look nice! Going out with your dad again?"

I shake my head.

"He seemed really nice, by the way," she adds.

Ha, if she only knew. "I'm going out to dinner with my mom and my boyfriend."

"Is that the guy who always drives up in his Ferrari?"

"Lamborghini," I correct, then feel immediately bad for being one of those people who knows the difference and actually corrects people.

Dani reaches into her jean pocket and pulls out five twenty-dollar bills.

"This is for the other day. I'll pay you the rest later," she says.

I shake my head. "You don't have to—"

"Yes, I do," Dani insists.

She pushes the money into my hands. I can tell it means a lot to her that I accept it, just as it's important to me that she think my parents are perfect and my dad would never walk out on me at dinner. I thank her for the money and put it in my purse as the doorbell rings. My mom's here.

"It's okay, honey," my mom says from across the table. We're sitting in Mori, one of the top sushi restaurants in Orange County, and Jay's late. "You have to understand, guys get busy sometimes."

I nod, pushing the wasabi around in my soy sauce. He's *really* late. We're almost done. My mom has to leave for the airport soon or she won't make it for her connecting flight to New York. I try him again on his cell. *Where is he?*

It goes straight to voice mail.

"I don't understand," I say apologetically. "I told him five times we were going to dinner tonight."

I try texting him. My mom reaches across the table for my phone.

"Honey, you need to stop," she says, switching off my phone. "He's going to think you're needy."

My mom tosses my phone into her purse.

"When I first met your dad, I didn't call him back for days," she says, blowing on her green tea. "You have to be a little more coy with guys or they'll lose interest."

See, this is exactly why I needed Jay here tonight, so I wouldn't have to deal with my mom's psychobabble all by myself. "Jay and I don't need to play games. We're in a happy, healthy relationship," I inform my mother.

My mom sets down her tea. "Then why isn't he here?" she asks.

Ouch. As I reach for a sushi roll with my chopsticks, my mother remarks to take off the rice, I don't need the carbs.

"Your arms are looking big," she says, studying me. "Have you been swimming?"

I ignore her, popping the whole piece in my mouth and chewing loudly just to spite her. We talk briefly about Tressy and how Snowy, my dog, is doing, eventually getting to the sensitive subject of Dad. She reaches a hand across the table.

"He didn't mean it," she apologizes for him.

I roll my eyes. I feel the tears gather in the back of my eyes at the memory of that night. I waited for forty-five minutes outside the restaurant after he left, crying in the wind, before my Uber finally showed up. "Mom, it was horrible."

"I know, honey," she says. "I'm so sorry." She says she gave him an earful when he got home, and he felt really bad.

I ask her how things are going with her and Dad.

"Good," she insists. "I told him if I ever catch him cheating again, I'm out of here."

I nod. Good for her, although it's probably not the first time she's said that.

She reaches for an edamame. "Sometimes I think if I hadn't met your dad at such a young age, maybe I could have had a life of my own."

"It's not too late, Mom. You're only thirty-seven."

My mom laughs as she peels the edamame. She hands me the peas and asks me about school. I tell her about the mini revolution I started, fighting to get my English teacher suspended for writing that obnoxious email.

"You've always been feisty. I think you get it from your father," she says with a wink.

As I smile back at my mom, it suddenly occurs to me that I've spent two and a half months away from my parents.

"I'm so proud of you, Claire," she says as she waves to the waiter for the check and gives me back my phone.

"Thanks, Mom," I say.

"And I'm sorry not to meet Jay. He is an *amazing* catch." She holds up a glass of sake to me.

As we toast to my amazing new boyfriend, I try not to think about the fact that at this exact moment I literally have no idea where he is.

fifty-two

Dani

After Claire and her mom leave for dinner, my mom turns to me, sheepishly, and asks if I too want to go out. But I don't want to schlep to KFC or McDonald's, I want a real dinner. I used to dream about the day I would get my acceptance to Yale, how my mom would saunter into Budget Maids and announce to Rosa that her daughter's going to an Ivy League school, and we'd go out to a nice, white-tablecloth dinner afterward. The look of pride on my mom's face, it'd fill me up on nights when I went to bed half-hungry.

I shake my head and turn back to my laptop. I'm at the kitchen table researching LA private schools. Maybe there's one I can transfer to midyear, one that'll offer me a scholarship. My mom pulls green beans, onions, bell peppers, and coconut milk out of the fridge and starts making ginataan, my favorite. The warm coconut smell fills the kitchen. My mom pulls out a brochure from her purse, glancing at it as she stirs.

"What's that?" I ask.

She holds the brochure up, and it reads, "ADULT SCHOOL."

I close my laptop and sit up. "You're thinking of going back to school?" I ask.

My mom shakes her head. She tastes the coconut and adds salt. "No time," she says. "Too busy cleaning and trying to make enough money."

"I can pull some more shifts. Mom, I think you should do it," I encourage her. "It'll be great."

She leaves the stew to simmer, walks over, and massages my shoulders. "I don't want you pulling more shifts, my anak," she says. "You already pull enough." She works a tight knot in my neck. "How's school?"

My shoulders tense, and I squirm out of her hands. I don't want her to know I didn't get headmistress commendation this year.

"It's fine," I say, gathering up my papers and computer in my arms.

My mom looks at me. "Are you okay?"

I nod, averting her probing eyes.

She walks back to her stew and stirs. "I know you think of yourself as my greatest hope, and you are," she says. "But I don't want you to put so much pressure on yourself."

Too late for that. That night, I tiptoe into my mom's room

and put the money I made from cleaning houses that week on her desk. I was going to give it to Claire, to finish what I owe, but she can wait another week. I hope my mom will enroll in adult school. I still think she's right, that I'm our greatest hope. But in case I'm not, I hope she invests in herself.

At school the next day, Ming walks me to my locker after band. She consoles me on not making headmistress commendation.

"You'll get it next year," she says. I tell her about my debate team changing the time on me.

"That's so messed up," she says, shaking her head. "I can't imagine if I showed up for practice and the rest of the band wasn't there."

"It was pretty bad," I say, opening my locker.

"You still gonna go though, right? To practice?" she asks.

Before I can answer, something falls out of my locker. A bloody rubber hand.

Ming and I scream.

I pick up the rubbery Halloween prop. There's a note attached to the gross hand, severed at the wrist in fake blood. It reads:

OMG a hand touched me!

Followed by a motion:

This house believes Dani De La Cruz will do or say anything to get ahead.

fifty-three

Claire

Where were you??? I text Jay.

Three ??? to convey the urgency. I press Send and continue typing. How could you stand me up with my mom!? WTF?! Then I stare at the words. I can hear my mother's voice: *Don't seem needy . . . you need to be coy with guys.* I delete the words and put down my phone.

I try to focus on my psychology essay, but it's impossible. Where was he? And why hasn't he texted me back?

At school the next day, Jay's not there. Jess, Nancy, and Florence tell me to relax.

"He's probably sick or something," Nancy says. She takes out a piece of gum from her simple Coach backpack. She's returned all her rented bags from online. Honestly, the Coach bag looks just as nice. I'm thinking of getting one too.

"Or maybe his phone got hacked," adds Florence. "That

happened to my dad once."

Jess glances at her but doesn't say anything. I know she's still processing Florence's "situation," but our friendship is so much stronger than labels. I smile and reach my hand out for a piece of gum from Nancy.

After lunch, Nancy and Jess hurry back to class while I linger behind and walk with Florence.

"Hey, I just wanted to say . . . I'm here for you," I tell her.

Florence grips her MCM backpack as she walks.

"If there's ever anything else you wanted to talk about," I say.

Florence stops walking. "Did Dani say something to you?" she asks.

I shake my head. "No."

"Then . . . ?"

I look around at the crowd of parachutes walking next to us and pull her into an empty staircase.

"I saw you guys the other day," I say to her when we're alone.

Florence's face starts reddening. "OMG . . ."

"No, it's okay. I think it's great," I reassure her. "I just don't know why you didn't tell us."

Florence removes her backpack and takes a seat on the stairs. I sit down beside her. She reaches into her backpack for tissues.

"I didn't know how you guys would react," she says, tearing up. "You don't know what the last sixteen years have been like for me." She dabs her eyes. "And I finally felt . . . like I belonged. Like I was part of this club. And I didn't want to lose that."

"You're not going to lose that," I promise her, reaching over and hugging her tight.

Florence grips my arm with her hand. "I just didn't want it to get out . . . didn't want to give my parents another reason to hide me, you know?"

"Oh, Florence," I say. As we hold each other, I tell Florence about my dad's own infidelity.

Florence hands me a tissue. "Who's your dad?" she asks, joking. "Maybe we're sisters."

I laugh through my tears.

"We can check when he comes in two weeks."

"Your dad's coming?"

Florence nods. She says both her parents will be here for the spring concert. Her mom twisted her dad's arm, saying there's no chance he'll bump into any of his colleagues here.

"I'm kind of nervous. It's their first time appearing at a school function together . . . ," she confesses.

I hug her and promise her everything will be fine. We stay in the staircase trading stories, long after the bell has rung and the hallways have emptied.

After school, I Uber over to Jay's. His door is unlocked and I let myself in. I find him in the downstairs study, watching random YouTube videos on cage fighting.

"Hey," I say.

He clicks Pause on his computer. "Oh, hey," he says. "Sorry I couldn't make it to your mom's thing."

He says it like it's an informal get-together at his dentist's office rather than a sit-down dinner with my mom.

"Where were you?" I ask, trying to keep my cool, even as the thunder goes off inside me. "I tried calling and texting you."

"Yeah, I know," he says, distractedly, turning back to YouTube. "I was at a friend's."

He *knew*? And he didn't pick up? I don't know whether to be impressed with his honesty or offended that he doesn't at least lie and say his phone was dead.

"What friend?" I ask, getting out my phone and going to Insta. "A boy or a girl?"

Jay clicks off YouTube. "What does it matter?" He shrugs. "We're just friends."

So a girl then. "What's her name?" I ask, scrolling through his many followers.

Jay swirls in his chair and frowns at me. "Stop," he says to me. "Don't get all psycho on me."

My mouth hangs open. I can't believe he just said that. I turn to leave.

Jay calls after me. "Wait, Claire, stop—!" he says, but it's too late. I'm already out the door.

∘ ∘ ∘

Jay comes up to me at school on Monday and pulls me aside. I had texted him last night saying, I think we need to take a break.

"Please don't do this," he says. He puts his arms around me. Everyone is staring at us. Jess, Nancy, and Florence try to usher us into an empty classroom, but my feet remain stubbornly glued to the pavement. Jay seems oblivious to the many eyeballs on us and talks to me as if we're the only two people in the courtyard.

"Claire, I'm sorry," he says. "But you're the one who's always making me wait. And I got mad."

Jess covers her eyes with her arm, like this is too much to watch.

He pulls me in for another hug. "Please, Claire," he says. I feel his neediness in his voice, his hands, the way they grip my back.

I break free from his grasp and walk away.

At lunch, he stares at me from across the cafeteria.

"Look at him," Nancy says, popping a carrot into her mouth. "It's like he's undressing you with his eyes."

"Yeah, well, he certainly didn't undress her with his hands," Jess says, giggling.

I smack her arm lightly. "Stop."

The girls turn to me, all wide-eyed. "Is it true you didn't put out?" Nancy asks.

"I don't want to talk about it," I say.

"Leave her alone," Florence says, casting the others a firm look. "It's her body and her sexuality."

Despite what Florence says, Nancy gazes over at Jay and sighs, "Poor guy."

As I look around, the entire cafeteria of parachutes is making sad, puppy-dog faces at Jay.

Jess suggests we go do karaoke to take my mind off things. After school, we pile into Jess's Porsche and drive over to Monterey Park, where she knows a great karaoke bar with private rooms and soft white leather couches.

The owner greets us warmly, showing us into a VIP room. We order food and drinks off the menu as we choose our songs.

As Nancy and Florence sing, Jess bumps her knee into mine and asks me how I'm feeling. I shake my head. To be honest, I miss him. I keep thinking about our weekend in Newport, how he was so patient with me, so nice he even taught me how to drive. We were so good then. What happened?

A tear trickles down my cheek.

"I'm sorry, boo," Jess says, hugging me and giving me a tissue.

Nancy and Florence stop singing and wrap their arms around me too. Gently Florence reaches for my phone on the table.

"Are you sure you don't want to call him?" she asks.

"Sometimes when my girlfriend and I get into a fight, talking it out helps."

Jess stares at her.

"I mean boyfriend," Florence quickly corrects. "From before. Like in China."

I look down longingly at the phone, debating.

"Call him," the girls urge. Before I know it, my hands are on my phone and I'm scrolling my contacts. I listen while it rings and rings. The girls huddle beside me. With each ring, I feel the words in my heart hardening, like a bulb that could have grown into something but now lies as shriveled as a toasted seed.

And then I hear it. The phone's ringing. In the room.

I look up. It's Jay. He's standing in the middle of the karaoke bar.

Florence, Jess, and Nancy look equally shocked. "We'll give you two some privacy," they say, and leave us.

Jay walks over to me.

"I'm sorry, I messed up," he says, taking my hand in his.

Cautiously, I look up at him.

"I need you," he says.

"Why?" I ask.

Jay searches for the words. "You're not like the other girls. You're the only one who sees beyond all this crap." He waves his hand at the crystal chandelier hanging above the opulent karaoke bar. He pulls me into his arms and says, "You see me."

But do you see me? I want to ask. *I needed you to text me back that night.*

He kisses me lightly on the lips. "Don't you see what you do to me?" he asks. "I'm crazy about you."

He rubs my runny mascara with his finger. As he hugs me tight, he breathes into my hair, "Please, Claire, I'm sorry. Give me another chance."

fifty-four

Dani

Zach calls me while I'm cleaning, says he needs help with his history homework. He can't wait until Friday, when I'm supposed to tutor him. I'm in one of the houses in North Hills.

"Where are you? Can I swing by?" Zach offers.

"Um . . ." I glance around the big, empty house. Ming's at extra violin practice for her solo, so it's just me cleaning. "Okay." I give him the address.

Twenty minutes later, I answer the door in my maid's uniform. Zach's eyebrows shoot up when he sees me.

"I feel like I'm stepping into a porno . . . ," he jokes.

I jab him lightly in the ribs and pull him inside before any of the neighbors see us. Zach puts his backpack down and whistles at the size of the house.

"Hot damn," he says, marveling at the size of the pool.

He follows me up the stairs to the bedrooms. While I

change the sheets, he asks me questions about American history. The time goes by faster with him here. Zach helps me tuck in the sheets and gets extra rolls of toilet paper for me from the downstairs supply closet. He asks me how debate's going.

"Not well," I mutter. I can't *believe* my teammates put a fake hand in my locker. It's bad enough they changed practice on me. And the shit that they wrote? I'm tempted to skip the rest of the training sessions altogether. Lately, I've been wondering whether I should even go to Snider. "Sometimes I think about quitting. . . ."

"You can't quit!" Zach protests. "Then they'll win!"

I look over at him as I smooth the sheets. It's nice how much he cares, though he still doesn't know the full extent of it. He just thinks my teammates are all cheating. He doesn't know what Mr. Connelly did.

"Hang in there," he urges, throwing the comforter on the bed. "Snider's in what? Like three weeks?"

I nod, taking a deep breath. I remind myself there's quiet bravery in staying on the team. It's not selling out.

I climb onto the bed and carefully arrange the half-dozen pillows.

"Why do rich people need so many pillows?" Zach chuckles. He looks out the double glass doors of the bedroom terrace at the trees and sparkling-blue pool below. "Man, can you imagine how different our lives would be if we lived in a place like this?"

"That'd be sick," I say.

Zach gets up and starts strolling through the house. "My mom would sleep right there," he says, pointing at the master bedroom, which has its own Jacuzzi. I follow him as he walks down the hallway, amused. "Home theater system in this room so I can watch the game with the guys," he says, pointing to another bedroom.

I chuckle. "I'd make this my debate-prep room," I say. Zach flashes me a thumbs-up. We continue walking.

"Gym!" he calls out when we pass the upstairs study, grinning as he runs a finger up and down his chest. "Gotta keep the ladies happy!"

I pause. Zach sees my face and is quick to reassure me. "Hey, don't worry. You're going to have a bunch of guys lined up to date you too," he assures me.

I don't want a bunch of guys. I only want one.

Claire calls me later from her boyfriend's, whom I've still not met. I know he drives a Lamborghini. But he never comes in. He just drives up, texts her, and waits in the car.

"What's up?" I ask Claire, scrolling through my email. A bunch of private schools got back to me, unfortunately none of them have a scholarship spot open at this time.

Claire says in a hushed voice, "Hey, can you come over? I need you to bring me my makeup bag and . . . some tampons. I don't want to have to run out and get some. That's so embarrassing."

Isn't it tragic that for all we've advanced, girls are still embarrassed by their menstrual cycles? I close my laptop.

"No prob," I say. "I'll be right there."

I put her stuff together in a bag and catch the bus. As the bus inches up Mount Diablo Lane in North Hills, I gaze out the window at the familiar palm trees and perfectly manicured lawns. I've cleaned so many houses on this street.

The bus drops me off, and I walk up the steep driveway to the address Claire gave me. It isn't until I walk up the steps to ring the doorbell and nearly trip on a small dragon statue that my stomach plunges.

Oh. My. God. This is the house where Ming and I walked in on the guy having sex!

The front double doors open, and Claire steps out.

"You're here!" She smiles, taking the makeup bag from me. She takes my hand and leads me inside. "Come meet Jay."

I shake my head.

"It's okay . . . ," I say, but she drags me toward him.

Claire's boyfriend walks down from the top of the spiraling staircase. It's him! I didn't get a good look at him that day—I was too busy trying to shield my eyes from all the skin—but judging from the way he's staring now, he recognizes me.

"Jay, this is Dani, my roommate," Claire says. "She just came to drop some stuff off for me. Can you give her a ride home?"

"No, it's okay. I can just take the bus," I say.

"Nonsense," Jay insists, and grabs his keys. "I'll take you."

Reluctantly, I follow him to his car. He waits until Claire's back inside the house before confronting me. "You better not say a word to her," he says. His tone is assertive, all power and privilege, and I cross my arms. My turn for cross-examination.

"Who was that girl?" I ask him.

"She's nobody!" he exclaims, face reddening. "Look, if you tell Claire, she's just going to freak out. And anyway, I wasn't serious!"

"Oh bullshit, you wanted a threesome," I snap. Or a four-some. Whatever the technical term would be. Cautiously, I look at him. "Have you had them before, threesomes?"

His pause says it all. Jay reaches for his wallet. "What's it going to take?" he asks.

It's infuriating that he thinks he can buy my silence. "I don't want your money!"

He runs a frustrated hand through his hair. "I was just joking around that day. It was the uniform! I didn't really want you and your friend to sleep with me." He looks me up and down. "No offense, but you're not exactly my type."

What. An. Ass.

"Please don't tell her," he begs. "Claire and I are very happy together."

"Who was the girl?" I ask him again.

"Just some girl I hook up with from time to time," he says with a shrug.

From *time to time*?

"But it's over now!" he swears.

I side-eye him, trying to decide if I believe him. I gaze back at the house toward Claire. "An essential part of a happy relationship is honesty and communication," I remind him.

He scoffs and throws back at me, "An essential part of being a good maid is discretion."

fifty-five

Claire

Something's different after Jay and I get back together. He's more on edge. I can feel it in the way he jerks away from me now whenever I touch him in the morning, like he doesn't want to be teased. But I'm not teasing him. I'm working up the courage to take the next step with him. And I feel like I'm ready.

That night, as we're kissing in bed, I straddle him in my La Perla bra and panties. Slowly, I move my head down, kissing first his neck, then his chest, then his . . .

"What are you doing?" Jay asks, sitting up.

I bite my lips shyly.

He studies my eyes. "I thought you wanted to wait . . . ," he says.

"I do," I say. I cover my face with the silk comforter, embarrassed, and peek out. "But maybe we can try . . . other things . . . ?"

Jay smiles. He lies back down and puts both hands behind his head, and I scooch down on the bed. I'll admit I don't really know what I'm doing, but I've read enough stuff online and seen enough movies. Jay watches me. It turns me on to see him so turned on. He groans as I take him in my hands and part my lips.

Afterward, we lie side by side in the damp silence. I resist the urge to face him and ask him what's wrong. *I* thought it was pretty hot, which was why I was so surprised when barely three minutes into it, he pulled his boxers back on and said, "It's okay. You don't have to do that. I'm good."

I'm good? What is that supposed to mean? Am I that bad at sex? I pull the covers up over my head, sighing into the night. I can feel his own labored, frustrated breathing next to me. I want to turn to him and ask for editorial comments, just like Ms. Jones always gives us on our writing.

Instead, I think about the 129 girls on his phone. Who are they and what are they doing with him? He must be doing something, because he just turned down a blow job.

At school the next day, I tell the girls what happened. Jess offers to give me tutorials with a banana, if it'll help.

"I feel like you guys are just in this weird sexual phase," she says.

I slump my shoulders forward and look over at Jay, sitting with his friends in the cafeteria. God, I hope they're not also dissecting what happened. Do guys do that?

"Maybe you should just have sex with him," Jess says. "Get it over with!"

"Yeah," Nancy jumps in. "I think you're building it up in your head. It's too much pressure!"

I shake my head. I can't imagine having sex with him now. What if he stops in the middle and says, "I'm good"? I drop my face in my hands.

"C'mon, it'll be really hot. You can buy some candles and dress up for him in your sexiest lingerie. . . ."

"I already did all that," I say.

Nancy cocks her head. "And what were his words exactly?"

I repeat them verbatim to the girls.

Jess sighs through her teeth, *yikes*. I put my head down on the table. I wish my mother were here. She'd know what to do. It'd be weird, but she'd tell me exactly what to do to fix this.

"Maybe he's just not into BJs?" Florence asks.

"What guy is not into BJs?" I mutter from behind my arms.

"I once had a guy tell me my mouth was too hot," Jess says, cracking up as she says it. Jess opens her mouth wide, inviting us to feel the temperature.

Florence tosses out another wild theory. "Maybe he's saying you're so special, you don't have to do that. Like you're wife material, not mistress."

We all stop talking and look at her.

"Okay, we have to talk about this," I say, sitting up.

"Yes, we do," Jess says. Everyone falls quiet as Jess turns to Florence. "*Everyone's* wife material. Me, you, your mom, everyone." As she lifts her eyes to meet Florence's. "And if one day you meet a guy and he doesn't understand—"

"About that. There's something else I need to tell you guys," Florence says, taking a deep breath.

I reach over and squeeze her hand. *You can do this!*

"I'm gay," she says.

Jess and Nancy stare at her.

"Is this a joke?" Jess asks.

"No," I quickly say.

Jess turns to me. "Wait a minute, you knew about this?" she asks. "I'm the last person to find out?"

"I didn't know either. Though thinking back," Nancy says, putting a finger to her chin, "you did have that big-ass poster of Kristen Stewart in your room."

"I liked *Twilight*." Florence shrugs.

"Me too," I say.

"I still can't believe you didn't tell me earlier," Jess says.

"I didn't know how you'd react."

"Hello, do you not know me at all? I am such an ally. I *love* Karl Lagerfeld, may he rest in peace," Jess says, making a cross on her chest.

Florence chuckles.

Jess points to me and Florence, smiling. "So, Claire, if

the blow jobs don't work out for you, you can always give this one a call."

Florence takes a carrot and throws it at her. "Shut up!" she says, laughing.

We all start cracking up, and when the laughing dies down, we lean over to give Florence a hug. I'm so proud of Florence for coming out, and of Jess and Nancy for being so cool with it. Jay walks over from his table as we're hugging and looks at us, amused.

"What are you guys doing?" he asks.

The girls pull away and say hi. Jay leans over and whispers, "Hi, babe." I put a hand on his arm, pulling him close. As he gives me a slow, lingering kiss, I feel my insecurities melting. Maybe the girls are right. Maybe I'm overthinking what happened last night.

"I'll see you later at my house for dinner?" he asks.

I nod.

"Good, because I'm cooking," he says.

My friends go "aww" as Jay walks away.

Jay's in the kitchen making caramelized carrots when I walk in. A beautiful roast chicken sits on the counter.

"What's the special occasion?" I ask, gasping at the chicken. I pose in front of it with my phone and try to take a selfie. The smell brings me straight back to my grandmother's kitchen in Shanghai.

"No reason. Just wanted to do something nice for my

337

gorgeous, brilliant girlfriend." He smiles.

He leans over, kisses me, and takes my phone from me so he can take a proper picture of me with the chicken. When he's done taking my pic, he doesn't give me back my phone. Instead, he starts browsing my camera roll.

"Hey, give that back," I protest.

He laughs, tapping on an album called "Childhood Photos."

"Was this you when you were a kid?" he asks. He shows me the pic. I cringe. It's one of the few pictures of me with my old eyes. I was about seven.

He studies my face. "You look so different," he says. "You better not have gotten plastic surgery. I don't want ugly kids when we get married," he teases.

I snatch the phone away from him. "Give me that," I say. "And who said anything about marriage?"

Jay blushes slightly.

"I want my wife to be a virgin," he says, setting the table. "My mom was a virgin when my dad met her. She's never slept with anyone else."

"How do you even know that about her?" I ask, fascinated and low-key disturbed.

"They met when they were seventeen." Jay shrugs. "Exact same age as us."

My phone dings.

"Who's that?" Jay asks. "Is it Dani?"

When I don't reply, his face clouds over with worry.

"I don't like that girl. Don't trust a word she says."

I chuckle. "Why? What's she got on you?" I'm only teasing, but he gets upset.

"Nothing! I'm so good! I didn't even make you finish yesterday!"

About that. I'm glad we're finally having this conversation. I bite my lip and look up at him. "Why didn't you?" I ask.

Jay puts down the napkins. He pulls me in and kisses my ear. "Because you're too sweet to be doing something like that," he says. "Besides, I could tell you were getting kind of tired."

I throw up my hands in protest. "I was not!"

I glance down at his phone and ask shyly, "Did you ever do stuff with those other 129 girls?"

He shifts uncomfortably.

"Just tell me . . . ," I prod. I kiss him lightly on the arm. "I promise I won't be mad."

The oven timer goes off. Jay looks relieved. He puts on the oven mitt and retrieves the tray of caramelized carrots.

"Can we talk about it later?" he asks. "Look at all this great food I made. . . ."

I look down at the succulent carrots glistening on the table. "Okay."

The dinner is delicious, but we don't end up talking about the 129 meis later because as soon as we finish eating, Jay receives a text. He tells me it's from a friend and he needs to go and meet up with them in LA. I follow him around the house as he grabs his keys and his wallet and gets ready to go.

"When will you be back?" I ask him.

He shrugs.

"I don't know," he says. "But I wouldn't wait up."

I furrow my eyebrows. *Wait a minute, is he planning to spend the night?* Before I can even ask, he's out the door.

I stay up late waiting for him to come home and eventually drift to sleep on the couch. When I wake up, he's not there. He's not at school the next day either. I try his cell, but he doesn't answer. Jess and the girls throw out wild theories of where he's at.

"He's at some new Coachella we don't know about," Jess says.

"He didn't want to invite you because it's this weird music they make from rain and ice, and he didn't want you to make fun of him," Nancy adds. Jess laughs so hard, she nearly spits out her water.

A small smile escapes. Rain Coachella sounds a lot better than the raging orgy I imagined him at with all his meis.

"Or maybe he got abducted. The bad guys are holding him for ransom," Florence guesses. "His parents are probably wiring the money right now!"

That night, when he's still not back, I call my mom and ask her what to do. She's back in Shanghai and fretting over the three pounds she gained eating out in New York.

"He's probably off on a boys' trip or something," she says.

I sigh into the phone. "Can you come over?" I ask.

"Oh, honey, I wish I could," she says. "But I just got back! I can't leave your father all alone again so soon, you know that."

"How is he?" I ask.

"He's been good," she says. "Anyway, I'm sure Jay will be back soon."

That's my *line,* I want to say. That's what *I'm* supposed to say to *her.* As we hang up, I think about all the days my mom used to just sit by the window and wait and wait and wait for my dad. I used to wonder how she could do that, and now I'm doing it too. By the third day, I really start to fall apart. I want to go home, but I want to stay at his house, if only to scream at him when he gets home. I toss my swimsuit in my bag and head to the pool. It's a Saturday and Zach is there again.

"I've missed you!" he says, taking off his goggles. "How've you been?"

I don't respond, and he swims over to me. "Shitty week?"

I nod.

"I'm sorry," he says. His face brightens. "You want to know what I do when I'm having a shitty week?" He pushes himself out of the pool and reaches out a hand. "C'mon, I'll show you."

I stare up at him in his wet trunks, water dripping down on me.

Hesitantly, I reach up. For the rest of the afternoon, we take turns doing belly flops in the empty pool. It's the only time in the last three days when I don't think about Jay.

Jay finally resurfaces the next day. He comes home on Sunday bearing flowers and bullshit, about how he was hanging out with his friends when his grandpa called and said he wasn't feeling well, so he had to hop on a flight and go home to see him. I know it's bullshit, because his passport was here the whole time. I know because I'd gone through his entire room, looking for incriminating photos of him and his 129 meis.

I walk over to the bureau, find the passport and throw it at him. He picks it up and puts it back on the bureau but doesn't offer any further explanation. Instead, he strips out of his clothes and goes to take a shower. I sit on the floor in the bedroom, holding his shirt up to my nose, trying to detect any traces of perfume.

Jay insists we go out. I say no. I want an explanation, not dinner. But he jumps in the car and I scramble after him, worried he'll disappear again. I'm not through discussing this with him! He drives us down to Fashion Island, where he pulls me into Cartier.

"What are you doing?" I ask him.

He points at one of the bracelets to the shop guy—an 18k solid-gold bangle with little diamonds around it. He hands the guy his black card, doesn't even look at the price. The shop guy takes the bracelet out of the case and gives it to Jay.

"This is the Cartier forever love bracelet," Jay says to me, holding up the bracelet. *"Forever."*

Our eyes lock as he says the word. Jay slips the bracelet on my right wrist. The tiny little diamonds sparkle in the light.

Jay leans in and kisses me. "I'm sorry I left you," he says as he screws the bracelet tight around my wrist. "But I'm back now." He drops the tiny 18k gold screwdriver into his pocket and pulls me toward him.

As he wraps his arms around me, he whispers into my ear, "You're mine. All mine."

fifty-six

Dani

I'm in my room researching the private equity fund that owns xomegan.com. I finally went to debate practice, though a lot of good it did. Everyone else had been emailed the motion in advance except me. Mr. Connelly said he must have accidentally left me off the email chain. Oops.

I can hear Claire yelling on the phone in her room. Who's she talking to? I bookmark the page I'm on. It's the website of Phoenix Capital. I've managed to narrow it down to this private equity real estate fund, which strangely enough, is not headquartered here in the US but in Hong Kong.

"I just want to know where you were this week! Why won't you tell me?" Claire shouts.

I take off my headphones and listen to her conversation.

"If we're going to be together, we have to be honest with each other," Claire says. "I need to be able to trust you!" Her voice cracks on the last words.

344

After they hang up, I walk out of my room and knock gently on hers.

"Hey . . . you okay?" I ask.

Claire walks over and opens the door for me. Her nose is red, and she's holding a tissue in her hand.

"Just typical boy stuff," she says, blowing into the tissue.

I sit down on her bed as Claire applies lotion to her tear-stained puffy eyes and tells me what happened with Jay.

"It bugs me so much that he won't tell me where he went," she says. Her eyes slide over to a picture of her parents on her bureau. "Maybe because I have trust issues . . ."

"No, it's not you." I shake my head. I think back to Jay's bedroom, the smug look on his face when we walked in on him having sex. "You're smart to not trust him," I tell Claire.

She shifts her eyes from her parents' picture to me and scrutinizes my face. "What do you mean?" she asks. Claire's instincts hone in on me. "What do you know?"

"Nothing," I mutter. Quickly, I get up from her bed.

Claire follows me to my room. "Tell me!"

"Nothing!" I insist. But Claire won't stop pressing me. She corners me in my room, and I buckle under the pressure of her intense eyes. The lotion in her hand falls onto the floor when I tell her what happened in his bedroom that day.

"He asked you guys to *join in*?" Claire asks. "Why didn't you tell me earlier? When you realized it was him?"

Claire gets up and walks back to her room, slamming the door.

"I'm sorry, Claire," I say through the door. "I've just been going through a lot. I was going to tell you!"

"No, you weren't! You were going to keep this a secret from me. I thought you were my friend!" she yells from the other side of the door.

fifty-seven

Claire

I used to think Jay looked peaceful when he sleeps, his baby face so innocent. I used to feel special sleeping next to him. Now I think of all the others who have been here before me.

"Wake up." I jab his shoulder with my fingers.

He stirs, opens one eye, starts to smile, then sees the storm on my face.

"What's wrong?" he asks, sitting up.

"Dani told me," I say. "You asked her and her friend to join in?" I could feel the heat of his body, the veins on his forehead pulsating as he digests this.

He throws his head back onto the pillow, closes his eyes.

"She's lying," he says.

I pull his pillow out from under him and whack him with it.

"No, *you're* lying," I say. "Where were you last week? Tell me!"

He gets up out of bed, throws on a robe, and walks out of the room. I follow him.

"Were you with your whores?" I ask. "Your 'meis'?" I do air quotes with my fingers.

"Will you shut up?" he yells back. He throws on a pair of pants and a shirt.

"I deserve an answer! Who were you with?" I press.

He crosses his arms at me. His jaw locks. "You *deserve* an answer?" he mocks. "Why? Because you're my 'girlfriend'? You won't even let me have sex with you!" I feel the cold marble under my toes. He takes a step toward me as he hurls the words at me. "Don't ever tell me what I can and cannot do!"

Shaking, I reach for my phone. "I'm leaving."

Jay walks across the room and grabs his car keys. "Don't bother," he says, storming past me.

Hate courses through my veins as I push myself through the water.

"Good! Keep kicking!" Zach says. He stands by the edge of the pool timing me. "Wow, you are on fire today!"

I claw my way to the edge, strokes powered by my burning rage as I play back Jay's words. *Don't ever tell me what I can and cannot do.* I open my mouth, gasping for air. The smell of chlorine fills my lungs.

Zach jumps into the pool. He's in his red trunks. I notice he has only two pairs of swim trunks, unlike Jay's eighty-five. It's late afternoon, and it's just the two of us in the pool.

"Nineteen seconds, not bad," he says, grinning. He doesn't notice my tears because of the water. Boys can be so oblivious.

He glances down and points to my wrist. "You'd go faster if you take off your bracelet."

I shake my head. "I can't," I say.

My mouth starts to quiver. I turn away from him.

"What's wrong?" Zach asks.

A sob builds. My body shakes uncontrollably as I yank on my bracelet. I wish I could take off this nightmare.

"Hey, whoa, it's okay." Zach puts his arms around me. Our bodies bob in the water as he tries to calm me down.

Our eyes meet, and I feel it. There's a second. A second when I can pull away, say no. I used to sit at home in Shanghai thinking about this second and wondering why my dad could never pull himself away. But in that moment, I couldn't either.

Zach kisses me.

His lips brush mine. It is not ravenous like Jay's. It's slow and soft, a stolen kiss, comforting in ways I could neither comprehend nor explain.

As soon as I open my eyes, though, the guilt unspools in my chest. What have I done?

"You and Dani . . . ," I start to say.

"We're just friends," Zach quickly reminds me.

The warm water sloshes around us. He pulls me in toward him. Our foreheads touch. Warmth radiates toward my lips, sweet, delicious warmth. But this time, I pull away.

I push myself up out of the water and run toward the changing room.

I run all the way home and lie on my bed in my room, hugging my legs, chin wedged between my knees, staring at the wall I share with Dani. It was a mistake. A lapse in judgment. A moment of weakness. I'm never going to tell anyone, not even Jess.

My phone rings. It's Jay calling for the eighteenth time. I ignore it, like I've ignored all his texts. Fifteen minutes later, I hear banging on the door. He's here. Dani pokes her head in my room. "You want me to tell him to go away?" she asks. I nod.

I hear her answering the door, telling him I'm not here. Jay raises his voice at her. "You said you were going to keep your mouth shut!" he yells at her.

She says something that I can't hear.

It burns inside me, the fact that the two of them have been hanging on to this secret. And how do I know Dani and her friend didn't join in that day? Maybe they did. I shake my head, hating what this is turning me into. The person I swore I would never be. I walk outside to confront them, hands gripping my cardigan tight around me.

"Dani, what are you doing?" I ask.

She stands in the sun blinking at me.

"Why are you still talking to him?"

"I'm not!" Dani says.

Jay shouts to me in Mandarin. "Nothing happened, okay? Look at her! You think I'd be interested in *her*?"

I grab Dani's hand and pull her back to the house. Once inside, Dani asks me gently, "You want to talk about it?"

I shake my head at her. No, I do not. Not with her. As she walks back to her room, I lie on the couch, wondering where on a scale of shittiness is my kissing Zach versus her not telling me about Jay.

The next day, I find Zach at the pool, fully clothed this time. It's a lot harder to swim fully clothed, but Zach's coach makes him do it sometimes for practice.

"What happened cannot happen again," I tell him.

He looks up, water dripping down his brow.

"Why?" he asks.

There is no why. It just can't!

"Because I don't want it to," I say.

He puts his head into the water, submerging himself. I stare at the ripples on the surface, trying to make out his face.

When at last he resurfaces, he looks all calm, as if nothing happened, and asks, "You hungry? Want to get a bite to eat?"

"Huh?" I ask.

He pushes himself out of the water, shakes his head, and gets me all wet as if he were a golden retriever. I scream. Zach smiles at me.

"C'mon, let's get something to eat. My treat," he says, leading the way.

I open my mouth to say no, then I realize I'm actually kind of hungry. I haven't had anything to eat all day. I follow him out of the pool.

He takes me to Norms, a diner so American, it's like walking into a country song. He gets the cheeseburger while I order the spinach salad.

"You're gonna need more carbs if you want to swim faster," he says.

For as long as I can remember, my mom's been trying to get me to eat less carbs, saying my butt is too big, my arms are too big—something's always too big. Even Jay teases me about my calves sometimes. I raise my hand and change my order to a turkey burger. I tell the waitress to hold the fries.

Zach smiles. "That's more like it."

We sit in silence, pruned fingers clutching our ice waters, waiting for our food to arrive.

"So how long have you been swimming?" he asks me.

I shrug. The waitress arrives with our food. I stare at Zach's fries, curly and golden crisp. Zach laughs, takes a bunch and puts them on my plate.

"How old were you when you started?" Zach tries again.

"Three," I say as I reach for a fry.

"And why'd you stop?" he asks in between bites of his burger.

I debate whether to tell him. "My mom made me quit because she said I would get big shoulders if I kept swimming. And that's not a good look on a girl. . . ."

He puts down his burger. "Wow," he says, so loudly the couple from the next table looks over. Zach shakes his head. "First of all, you look amazing. Second of all, who cares about broad shoulders? Just the feeling of being in the water, doing what you love . . . *that's* the most beautiful thing ever."

I look at him with glowing eyes. No one's ever said that to me before.

"That's sexy," he adds.

I blush. A cozy quiet falls over us.

"I'm glad you're swimming again," Zach says as he reaches across the table and touches my hand.

fifty–eight

Dani

I pore over the annual-fund donation pamphlet in the school library. It's a list of donations made to the school last year, embarrassingly organized by student, amount, and parent. I look up my name and cringe at the big fat zero next to it. As if that's not bad enough, there's an asterisk next to my name announcing to everyone I'm a *full-scholarship student*, in case there was any doubt from my ripped socks.

I flip to Heather McLean and see that her family gave $50,000 to the school last year. No wonder she made head-mistress commendation.

Ming and Florence walk into the library holding hands. It's good to see the two of them no longer hiding their relationship. Florence kisses Ming on the cheek and waves goodbye to her as Ming walks over to me.

"How are you doing?" Ming asks me, sliding into the seat next to mine.

"I'm okay," I say. I lean toward her. "How are you?"

"So great." She beams. "It's amazing not to have to sneak around. I'm even thinking of telling my parents when I pick them up from the airport Saturday night."

"Really?"

Ming nods.

"When did you decide this?" I ask her.

"When she took the plunge and came out to all her friends," Ming says. "I'm so proud of her. Her parents are gonna be at the concert too."

"I'm so happy you're finally going to tell your parents. Are you scared?" I ask.

Ming shrugs. "What's the worst that can happen? We're already a continent apart, right?" She pauses and adds, "And it's not like they can cut off my tuition . . . I'm already on a scholarship."

"True," I chuckle. She points to the donation pamphlet.

"What's that?"

"Oh, I'm still trying to figure out the connection between xomegan.com and the school," I say. I look up and see Heather. I quickly put the donation book away as she walks by.

"Can't wait to see you lose at Snider, Thunder Girl," she hisses.

I roll my eyes, sick and tired of her harassing me. "Can't wait to see you get busted for lying on your college applications."

Heather stops walking. "What did you say?" she asks.

"Buying recommendation letters?" I turn to Ming. "What do you think? Is that a felony?"

"It's got to be," Ming says, nodding.

The blood on Heather's face drains. "I don't know what you're talking about."

I reach into my backpack and take out the hideous rubber hand she stuffed into my locker.

"Here, you can keep it." I throw it at her. "Unlike you, I don't need a helping hand."

Ming high-fives me as Heather walks away.

I grin and go to put the donation pamphlet back. As I'm placing it on the shelf, I thumb through it one last time. I stop on a page called Headmistress's Circle. It's a list of major donors who gave more than one million dollars to the school last year. There are five names I don't recognize on the list, followed by a company name.

Phoenix Capital Limited.

That's the private equity fund that's one of the shareholders of xomegan.com! According to the pamphlet, last year they donated a whopping *1.5 million dollars* to the school. Why would a private equity fund donate $1.5 million to a random private school in East Covina?

The band room shakes with the cacophony of voices and instruments as Mr. Rufus tells us to settle down. He announces he's making some changes to our seating arrangement for the spring concert this Saturday. I sit up, putting the donation pamphlet I'd borrowed from the library back in my backpack. I pick up my flute. *Please don't move me away from Zach. Please don't move me away from Zach.*

"Zach," he calls out.

I look over at Zach, sitting on his chair texting. He looks up, distracted.

"I'm making you fourth-chair clarinet," Mr. Rufus tells him. "Go ahead and move one chair over."

"Yes!" Zach jumps up and high-fives the other clarinets, and I cover my face, trying to shield my disappointment. As he scoots away from me, triumphantly holding his clarinet, I realize he has no idea how I feel about him.

This is ridiculous. I should just tell him. The next time we're alone. If Ming can tell her parents about Florence, I'm brave enough to tell Zach my feelings.

fifty-nine

Claire

Jay finally gets through to me on my cell later that day.

"Where the hell have you been?" Jay asks. "I've been calling you like a hundred times."

"I've been busy," I say.

"Well, get unbusy," he replies. "My dad's coming to town next week and—"

"I don't really want to meet your dad. . . ."

Jay sighs into the phone. "Please, Claire," he says. "It's important. I don't want to do this alone."

Oh, but when it's *my* parents, it's okay to bail on me? Jay tells me to be at his house on Tuesday night and wear something nice. After he hangs up, I stare at the ceiling and groan.

On Tuesday, I don't go over to Jay's house. Instead, I head over to the pool after school. Zach's there, as usual, waiting for me. It's become our thing, swimming together after school and grabbing dinner afterward. Sometimes I paid, sometimes he paid. I've come to like American diners, especially the free lemonade refills. So far we've had five dinners together. During our conversations, I tell him about my life in Shanghai. He says he has a tough relationship with his mom too. He tells me he's here on a scholarship, which I think is really amazing. I guess that's why he takes swimming so seriously.

The more we talk, the more I find myself drawn to him. He's so different from Jay. The way he talks about swimming. Getting a full-ride scholarship somewhere. I love his passion and his drive. Even the way he talks about pulling up his grades. It's clear he has a lot of respect for Dani. He swears up and down they're just friends. And I believe him, even though I thought I detected a trace of something when I walked in on the two of them watching *Titanic*. But maybe I was wrong, I think as we work on the butterfly stroke.

Zach helps me get into position. Gently he puts his hand on my stomach. It tickles, and I giggle.

"Quit squirming," he says.

He moves his hand, and I laugh some more, accidentally dunking my head into the water. He reaches a hand out to me, and I wrap my legs around him. Our eyes lock. Gently, he pushes my body to the edge of the pool, leans in, and kisses me. The kiss starts off soft and gentle, then becomes firmer. I moan, breath quickening, until it's clear: we both want more.

He looks around. It's just the two of us in the pool. I can feel him pushing into me. He moves his hand down to my chest, and I close my eyes.

"Is this okay?" he asks, looking into my eyes as he touches me.

I nod.

"Have you ever . . . ?" he asks.

"No," I say. I search his baby-blue eyes. There are tiny specks of gold as his irises expand and contract. "Have you?"

"No," he says. It fills me with such comfort and relief that I'm finally with a guy as inexperienced as me. That we might both enjoy something together that we've never tried before and remember it for the rest of our lives.

Gently, Zach moves his hand down. The warm water laps around us. His fingers find my bikini bottom.

"Do you want me to stop?" he asks. His warm lips press against mine.

"No," I say.

And then it's happening. He's inside me. We move in perfect harmony, my legs wrapped around him. With every thrust, he asks me if this is okay, and I bite my lip, the happiness exploding inside me, for I am with someone I trust, someone who respects me, and someone I admire.

Afterward, Zach drops me off at home. We linger in the car, kissing, then I walk inside. Jay's sitting in the living room waiting for me. Dani's mom let him in. My face flushes at the sight of him. I remind myself that I have nothing to feel bad about. He's not my boyfriend anymore. Not after what he said to me.

"Where have you been?" Jay asks. "It's Tuesday. My dad's here. You were supposed to be at my house an hour ago."

He glances at my wet hair.

"Did you go swimming?" he asks. "In the school pool?" He makes a repulsed face, like I'd just gone swimming in a swamp.

I walk by him and go to my room.

"I'm tired," I say. "I don't feel well. I don't think I can—"

Jay follows me into my room. He closes the door and starts going through my closet, trying to pick out something for me to wear.

"You're not listening to me," I say.

He turns to me and pleads with me, pressing his hands together.

"Please. Just one dinner."

sixty

Dani

The smell of chlorine stings my eyes, filling me with regret. Regret at having gone to the pool after school, thinking I was going to watch Zach practice and then tell him I like him, only to see him with Claire. The look on her face as she opened her legs, the sounds they made.

I stood in the back of the pool, silently watching them. The light from the window shone on Zach's blond hair, creating an aura around him, as he pushed inside her. And I just stood there, my feet soaking wet, arms lifeless by my side. I should have screamed. I wanted to scream. I even opened my mouth, but no sound came out. I was too bewildered.

Afterward, I sat in the corner of the locker room, too shocked to leave, too chicken to stay. Claire came in and she didn't even notice me—that's how wrapped up in her own world she was. I watched her as she showered. Her perfect body. Hands running up and down her back as she lathered herself with soap.

Later, she stood in front of the mirror, staring at her reflection, her rosy cheeks flushed pink. She was probably thinking about Zach, playing back details that I can never recall.

And I'm filled with the most untamable envy.

sixty-one

Claire

Just one dinner. I still can't believe I agreed to go with him. We arrive at Jay's house. My chest rises and falls in my white chiffon dress as I think about what just happened with Zach. Jay tells the professional catering crew that has taken over his kitchen that we're here.

Jay's dad walks down the stairs. He's tall like his son, looks about forty-five, impeccably dressed in a blue suit and silk tie. He glances at me and manages a thin, tight smile before his face defaults back into a frown. We sit down in the formal dining room, which Jay and I never use. We usually eat on the terrace or around the kitchen island. Jay sits next to me and puts his hand on my lap.

"So Jay says you went with him to see Fashion Island?" his dad asks. "What'd you think of it?"

"I like it," I tell him. "It's beautiful and right on the water."

He shakes his head to his son and points to me with his fork.

"Women. All emotion and no logic," he says to Jay as he cuts his filet mignon.

I feel the heat rush to my cheek.

"You know what 'right on the water' says to me? It says distraction. Who wants to go shopping when the beach is right there?"

"Actually, Claire has a good eye for real estate. She's the one who spotted the house I told you to buy in Balboa. It's a good investment property," Jay says, beaming at me.

Jay's dad takes a generous gulp of his wine.

"I took a look at that house," he says.

"And?" Jay asks his dad, his eyes round and hopeful.

Jay's dad makes a face. "Terrible," he says. "First of all, there's grade sloping back toward the home. This is going to lead to all sorts of foundation problems. It already is! Some of the windows are out of the square." He glances at Jay. "Frankly, I'm shocked you didn't notice. Maybe if you weren't so . . . distracted."

Jay's nose flares. He stares straight ahead at the Zhang Xiaogang painting on the wall and doesn't say a word.

"I'm disappointed in you, son," Jay's dad continues. "You wasted my time and my energy." Maybe it's the wine or the echo in the formal dining room, but his voice grows louder and louder as he scolds Jay.

"I was just trying to—" Jay says.

"I know what you were trying to do! You were trying to show off to your new girlfriend. You were thinking with your dick and not your head!"

Jay's eyes plunge to the table. It's heartbreaking to watch.

"No, he wasn't! We looked everywhere!" I say. "At the cracks, the floor. We didn't see any windows out of the square!"

"Yeah, well, you didn't look hard enough," Jay's dad says. He frowns at Jay, pointing at him with his knife. "You're lazy and soft, just like your mother."

Later, I find Jay in his room. His dad's downstairs on a call with Beijing. His voice booms in thunderous bursts we can hear even in the master suite. I take a seat next to Jay on his bed. Neither of us speak for a long time. Then, ever so gently, Jay takes my hands in his. "Now you know why I need you," he says.

His eyes are red and swollen.

"I'll wait for you as long as you need," he says, his voice raw.

He buries his head in my lap, and I hold him.

Dani and her mom are both already asleep when I get home. I fall onto my bed. My legs are bone-tired, both from the dinner and . . . other activities. But I can't go to sleep yet. There's something important I have to do. I pull out my phone, and Jess answers on the third ring.

"Hey, it's me." I chew nervously on my lip. "Do you happen to have the morning-after pill?"

In the excitement and passion of our underwater adventure, we did not exactly use protection.

"Yeah, of course. I have some from Hong Kong," she says. "I can give it to you tomorrow."

I breathe a sigh of relief.

"I thought you and Jay were having a fight," she says. "Did you guys make up?"

"It's not Jay . . . ," I whisper.

"Oh," she says. Her bed squeaks. I picture her sitting up. "Who is it?"

I press my lips together, anxious and excited to finally share my secret. "I met someone from the swim team, this guy Zach Cunningham," I tell her.

"A white guy?" she asks.

"Yes," I say.

She doesn't say anything at first.

"Be careful, Claire. Don't ruin what you have over some white guy you don't even know," she says. I know she's been burned before, that that's where this is coming from, but it still stings. "Jay *cares* for you. He adores you."

"He adored me enough to go AWOL for three days," I remind her.

"But he came back," she says. "I see the way he looks at you. That's real, Claire. If I were you, I wouldn't throw that away."

I think about Jess's words as I drift to sleep.

She hands me the pill at school the next day, along with a heavy dose of guilt. "If this is going to happen again, you need to tell Jay. He deserves to know." She's right. I know she's right. As I twist open my water bottle and pop the pill in my mouth, I wonder, Is *it going to happen again?*

I find the answer in the form of a red rose inside my locker.

> *Can't stop thinking about you. Meet me after school.*
> *—Zach*

I smile.

"Where are we going?" I ask Zach. He holds out the passenger-side door of his Honda Civic for me. As I get in, I'm reminded of a Chinese saying my mother used to say when I was a kid.

I'd rather cry in a Mercedes than smile on a bike.

"You'll see," Zach says. He leans over and kisses me.

As Zach drives, I roll down the windows, something Jay never let me do in his Lambo. He didn't want the fumes getting in from other cars. I prefer Zach's Honda. For one thing, it's quieter. You can actually have a conversation.

We talk about the SATs, which we're both planning to take in October in time for college apps, and swim tryouts early next year. He tells me next year the team's going to get a new coach.

Zach parks at Peter F. Schabarum Regional County Park and says we're going hiking. I reach for my pollution mask. I don't usually wear it, but it's 3:30 p.m. and the midday sun is roasting.

"What are you doing?" Zach asks when we get out of the car. He points to the gray mask on my face.

"It's just to protect against the sun," I tell him.

Zach rummages through his backpack and fishes out a tube of sunscreen. He tosses it to me.

"Put this on, and you'll be fine," he says.

I slather some sunscreen on my neck and arms but don't take off my mask.

"C'mon, you're not seriously going to hike with that on, are you?" he asks. "It's gotta be like a hundred degrees under there!"

I shrug and keep walking. Overheating is a small price for beauty. But Zach won't let it go. Every few steps, he looks over at me and sighs.

"But I want to see your face," he complains.

"Yeah, well, you're not going to want to see it when I'm old and covered with aging spots!" I recite almost word for word what my mom always says.

He puts his arms up. "Whoa, whoa, whoa, hang on a sec, Snow White," he says. "Where is this coming from?"

I shake my head at him, frustrated he's giving me such a hard time. Jay never questioned my pollution mask. He wore one himself when we were walking on the beach in Laguna. His was blue and from Japan. Jess, Nancy, and Florence each have one. Even Dani's mom makes her wear a hat.

I turn to Zach. "Do you have any idea how much money my mother spends on laser treatments? They're not just expensive, they hurt!" I tell him. "I have to protect my skin now if I want to look good later."

Zach chuckles when I say this, which only makes me angrier.

"You're going to look good later," he assures me. I roll my eyes and keep walking, thinking back to what Teddy once said about white guys, how they can't tell the difference between a pretty Asian girl and an ugly one.

"Hey, wait up!" Zach calls, running toward me. He reaches for my arm and pulls me aside. "You think I like you because of the color of your skin?" His eyes search mine. "I like you because you're smart. Because you're kind. Because you can swim like a fish. And you're brave. You're the bravest person I know. You're here all by yourself in this strange, foreign country."

A lump forms in my throat.

"So you can put on all the masks you want but it's not going to matter. I can still see what's inside you. And that's why I like you," he says.

It is the nicest thing anyone has ever said to me, and as I

370

put my hands around his neck, I want him. Now. I rip the mask from my face and we start kissing. His soft lips nuzzle my neck, and all of a sudden, it's happening again. Breathlessly, Zach pulls himself away to get a condom out from his backpack this time. He leads me over to a patch of grass underneath a tree and starts peeling off my pants.

As we're undressing, we hear someone on the trail.

"Shit! Someone's coming," he says. He fumbles with his pants as I pull mine back up. We collapse on the grass in each other's arms, giggling.

sixty-two

Dani

There are dirt stains and grass stains on Claire's shirt and pants when she finally gets home.

"I saw you guys, you know," I mutter from the couch.

Claire looks at me, puzzled.

"In the pool." I turn to her. "Why would you do that?"

She gives me a bunch of crap about how she and Zach have been seeing each other for a while, how they're both swimmers, as she walks toward her room.

I couldn't care less about their aquatic connection. "Did you even use a condom?" I ask her.

She stops walking. Unbelievable. Of course she didn't. That would require thinking and being responsible, which she's clearly not capable of.

"I took care of it," she informs me. "I'm fine."

I stand up from the couch. "Well, I'm not fine," I turn to her and say. My lips quiver. I look away, emotions unknotting inside. All I can think about is the two of them at the pool. I haven't been able to do anything, not eat or sleep or even get ready for Snider. "Do you have any idea what this year has been like for me?" I cry. "You stole my boyfriend!"

"He's not your boyfriend," she says. Claire retreats and hides behind the door in her room. "You guys were just studying together."

It infuriates me the way she says it.

"Fuck you, Claire!" I scream. "I wish you never moved here!"

sixty-three

Claire

"Jay?" I call out as I walk into his house. It's a little after 8:00 p.m. He had texted me earlier asking me to come over, saying he needed to talk. I was so shaken up after the confrontation with Dani that I said okay. I need to grab some of my stuff anyway.

"Up here," Jay calls from the master bedroom.

As soon as I walk into the room, I sense it. In his bloodshot eyes. His nostrils. His clenched jaw. He *knows*.

"How could you do this to me?" he yells. "I thought you were the one!"

I shake my head. *But how? How'd he find out?* My breath catches in my throat as I realize. Dani must have told him.

"All this time you were telling me you wanted to wait, and I believed you, I never pushed you," Jay continues, staggering around his room as he blinks back the tears. "Meanwhile, you were taking your clothes off for some piece of white trash!"

He charges at me. I can smell the alcohol on his breath.

"No!" I exclaim. "It wasn't like that!"

But something in Jay snaps. He grabs me and throws me onto the bed. "You wanna be a whore? I'll treat you like one," he says.

"What are you doing?" I ask, my eyes darting as he starts undoing his belt. The air sizzles with the coming violence. Oh my God. What's he doing?

"Stop!" I yell. My eyes fill with terror. I try to wriggle free, but he's too strong. He holds me in place, hands pinning my wrists to the bed. I scream, kicking at the sheets. My scream does little to deter Jay.

"Tell me, did he make you come?" he asks. "Your little white boy?"

I feel my heart leave my body. His fingers find my panties, and he yanks them down.

"Stop, Jay, please stop," I beg.

But he doesn't stop. He doesn't stop.

Afterward, Jay makes me take a shower. I am filled with the most excruciating shame as I stand under the rain showerhead, the water trickling down my arm to the diamonds glistening on my wrist. I wish I could slide down the drain like the water. I wish I could leave this house without facing him. I stay in the shower long after the water's gone cold, terrified to come out.

Eventually, when I do emerge, Jay's sitting in the living room waiting for me.

"I'm so sorry," he says, looking up at me. He stands up and walks over as if to give me a hug. I turn away from him, physically repulsed. My heart thuds in my chest. Jay takes the hint and backs off. "Do you need a ride home?"

I shake my head.

We both fall quiet. What do you say to someone after he's raped you?

I reach for my phone and order an Uber. The driver calls me a minute later, and I tell him where I am. That I'm able to stay so calm in the minutes and hours after both shocks me and gives me hope. Maybe it's not so bad. Maybe I'll get over it.

Later, in the back of the Uber, the tears come.

sixty-four

Dani

Claire mopes in her room all weekend. Doesn't come out. My hands shake as I dial Zach's number. I tell myself I'm doing the right thing. He deserves to know about Claire and Jay. I'm doing this for transparency and for truth. Deep down inside, I know the real reason.

"Meet me at the library," I say to Zach when he answers. "There's something I have to tell you about Claire."

Zach clenches his fists in his car. We're in the parking lot of the public library. I can see the whites of his knuckles in the sun.

"How many times?" he asks.

I avoid his gaze. All I can think about is how much it hurt to see him with Claire in the pool.

"How many times did she go over there and sleep with him?" he demands. His blond hair falls over his watery eyes. Is he . . . crying?

"I don't know, maybe ten? Twenty times?" I hadn't exactly kept count, but there were a couple of weeks when she was over there nearly every night.

"Twenty times?" He punches the steering wheel, a loud *beep* erupts from the car. "Jesus Christ."

I won't lie. It feels satisfying to be able to hurt him as much as he's hurt me.

"She told me she broke it off," he says.

"Well, she didn't. I saw her go over there after she came back from the pool."

"After she came back from the pool?" He bites down on his knuckles. "After we—? She told me I was her first!"

He presses his lids with his fingers, and tears drip onto the steering wheel. I look away. I know he's in pain, but it hurts so much that he has no idea what I'm going through. How *I'm* feeling in all this.

"I was at the pool too," I mutter.

Zach opens his eyes, cheeks coloring. "What?" He looks over at me. "You *saw* us?"

"I came by to tell you something . . ."

Zach blinks in confusion. I debate whether to even say it now. Admitting my feelings seems moot. But not admitting them feels like something I might regret forever.

"I liked you, in case you hadn't noticed. And I thought maybe you . . ."

Zach shakes his head.

"I just assumed . . . you know, because we were spending so much time together," I ramble on, justifying my hypothesis. *Stop talking. Stop talking.*

"Yeah, because we're good friends," he says by way of explanation. We sit for a long time in the hot, stifling silence. I feel the burn of the sun on my legs. Zach finally turns to me. "What am I going to do?" he asks.

I want to tell him, *Let her go. You deserve better.* For me. But I know that's not what he wants to hear. "You'll get through this," I say instead. "And you'll come out stronger."

Zach shakes his head. "But I don't want to come out stronger," he says.

"Yeah, well, sometimes we don't have a choice," I snap, opening the door to the car and getting out.

At the spring concert that night, Zach avoids my gaze as he holds his clarinet stiff in his hands. No sound seems to be coming out of it. I'm not sure if he's even playing it. I look over at Ming. She looks beautiful in her black concert dress. Her eyes close as she plays, like she's in her own private world. I hope it went well with her parents today when she told them about Florence.

I peer at the audience. Mr. Connelly is not there, thank goodness, and neither is Claire. Florence and her parents are in the back. Florence is recording Ming's performance on her phone. So are two Chinese people in the front row. They must be Ming's parents. I smile at them. I wish my own mother was in the audience. She was supposed to come, but at the last minute Rosa called her in to clean up a VIP client's house party.

As Ming stands up to play her solo, filling the auditorium with the sound of heaven, Florence puts a hand to her heart.

After the concert, at the cocktail reception, Ming pulls her parents over toward Florence's parents. Florence's dad is dressed in an expensive suit and doesn't seem to be saying much to anyone, while her mom makes small talk with Mrs. Mandalay. I walk over to join them.

"Florence!" Ming calls out. "I want to introduce you to my parents!"

Two reluctant Chinese people inch forward, but Florence's eyes are glued to her own parents. Her dad is looking down at his watch, frowning. Her mom is scanning the crowd for someone more important to talk to.

As Florence's parents reluctantly shake hands with Ming's parents, Florence offers no explanation as to who Ming is and quickly pulls her parents away.

"Let's go," she says to her parents.

The look on Ming's face as she watches Florence walk away from her is devastating. Ming's dad frowns and scolds his daughter in Chinese. As her parents leave, Ming turns to me and tearfully translates what her dad said.

"He said, 'That girl has the good sense not to embarrass her family.'"

sixty-five

Claire

For days, I don't get up. Don't leave the house, don't switch on my phone, don't move, except to go to the bathroom. Every time I think about what happened, my stomach twists into a knot so tight, I feel like I am going to hurl. I don't ever want to go back to school, don't ever want to see Jay again.

Gently, I massage my wrists. The bruises have mostly gone away. But the bigger wound, the one inside, is just starting. I curl into a ball, crying myself to sleep at night, thinking about my own stupidity. When I wake up, my eyes flit around my room, landing on this shirt and that bag—all the stuff that shithead bought me, that I *allowed* him to buy, as the bile inches up my throat.

Dani knocks on my door. I turn to my side and hide my head under the covers.

"It's Wednesday. Are you just not going to go to school?"

she asks. She informs me that technically, in California, it's a crime not to go to school. "It's called truancy. . . ."

I bunch up my sheets. I'm so tired of her technicallys. *Technically, you are a bitch.* Tears pool on my pillowcase. "Fuck off, Dani," I yell, adding under my breath, "You'll never know what you did to me."

I wait until I hear Dani's footsteps leave, then pull down my cover so I can breathe again. When she and her mom are both out of the house, I pick up my phone to call Jess. My phone beeps and dings when I turn it back on, alerting me that I have a million messages and voice mails.

I swipe past my voice mails to go to my iMessages. There are twenty-five from Jay.

Are you ok? 10:30 p.m. Friday

Call me. 11:52 p.m. Friday

I'm worried about you. 9:05 a.m. Saturday

Can we talk? 12:30 p.m. Sunday

I just want to know that you're ok. 4:32 p.m. Monday

I'm sorry if I hurt you. 6:39 p.m. Tuesday

CLAIRE! I'M FREAKING OUT! TALK TO ME!!! 10:25 p.m. Tuesday

You have to know how I was feeling. 6:38 a.m. Today

The last message makes me want to throw my phone at the wall.

I tap Reply and write, DON'T EVER CALL ME AGAIN.

Then delete it without sending it, because the thought of engaging with him again, even on text, makes me ill.

Instead, I text Jess to come over, telling her it's an emergency. As I wait, I pick up the dresses and tops and bags he got me and put them in a box. I write FREE on top of the box and drag it outside. Shielding my eyes from the sun with my hands, I dump the box on the curb. The sun feels so foreign to me, its warmth almost insulting as I cut across the grass in my bare feet.

Jess's Porsche pulls up. She turns off the car and gets out, carrying coffee and scones from Starbucks. I burst into tears at the sight of her.

"Claire, babe, what's wrong?" she asks, ushering me inside.

She sets the coffee and scones down on the coffee table. She tries to hand me a pastry, but I shake my head. I can't keep anything down. I'm an incoherent mess as I try to form the words. In between the hiccups and the sobs, she makes out what happened, and the whites of her eyes grow large.

"He *raped* you?" she asks, spilling her coffee. She sets it down. "How? When?"

Jess holds me, crying, as I tell her. I show her all the text messages he's sent me. The first thing she does when she takes my phone in her hands is she blocks him. And just to make sure he really gets the message, she takes her own phone and sends him a text—YOU ARE NEVER TO TEXT, CALL, OR COMMUNICATE WITH CLAIRE AGAIN.

I'm grateful to have her take charge, but what am I going

to do when I see Jay on campus? She can't block the sight of him in real life.

"Who else knows?" Jess asks.

I shake my head. "No one."

"Good." Jess nods, strategizing what to do. "I won't say a word, not even to Florence or Nancy. The good thing is you guys don't have any classes together. I'll stay by your side when we're at school, and if he tries to come up to you, I'll bitch-slap his ass to China."

She makes it sound so easy, but the thought of going back to school and seeing him again is like swallowing broken glass.

"I don't want to go back and see him," I say.

"So . . . you're going to switch to another school?"

"No!" I say. Why do *I* have to switch to another school? He should switch. He should go to jail as far as I'm concerned! I feel the heat of my anger exploding inside me as I hug my chest with my arms.

Jess looks down at her knees and says quietly, "This is why I told you to go and talk to him . . . before he found out some other way."

My eyes jerk up at her. Wow. The judgment.

"What? I'm just being real with you. If you'd been more careful—"

"I was careful!" I jump up from the couch and shout at her.

I don't need this right now. I walk over to the door. As I

hold the door open, Jess gets up reluctantly from the couch and says she's so sorry and to call if I need anything. After she leaves, I throw away her scones and coffee and stare at the wall, feeling so alone.

I go to find Zach after school. I tried calling my parents but couldn't get through. I think back to my mother's words when she first sent me here, *I'm one phone call away. If something goes wrong, I'll be right over.* I want to shout *Bullshit!* at the sky.

Stepping out of the Uber, I'm disoriented for a second. Zach had said Sun Grove, but that can't be right. There are no houses in Sun Grove, only mobile homes and tents. I've never seen a mobile home up close before, only in movies. I turn around, trying to wave down the Uber driver before he leaves so he can take me out of here, and then I see him. Zach stands next to a trailer, washing out his red swim trunks.

"Zach?" I call out.

His face turns the same shade as his trunks when he sees me. The door to his trailer swings open, and a really strung-out-looking white woman comes stumbling outside calling for him.

"Zach, where the hell are my cigs?" she slurs. I can smell the stench of alcohol on her.

"Go back inside, Ma," Zach tells her. "I'll be right there."

I stare at the woman. *That's* his mom?

As Mrs. Cunningham lumbers back inside, Zach turns to

me. His eyes look up from the sandy dirt.

"Hey," he says. His voice is low and laced with hurt. "Dani told me about Jay."

I close my eyes. My head throbs. That bitch just doesn't stop! The roots of my hair feel like they're being pulled out from inside my head.

Zach glances at the trailer, at his mother, sitting by the window watching us. She's found her cigarettes, and she's making little smoke rings with her mouth as she studies us.

"You lied to me," Zach says. "You told me I was your first."

"You are my first! You have to believe me," I say. Desperately, I search his eyes. "We weren't doing anything! We were just sleeping next to each other!"

"Yeah well, in this country, you sleep with one guy at a time," he mutters with disgust.

"I'm so sorry, Zach," I say, chin quivering. Before I realize it, I'm full-on crying. The tears gush down my face. I don't know how to stop. I cry so hard, Zach puts a hand on my back, concerned.

"Whoa, whoa. What's wrong?"

I shake my head, and he pulls me in toward him. It comes out in bits and chunks, half in Chinese and half in English. In my hysterical state, I cannot string together more than three words in either language without sobbing. When Zach hears the word "rape," his body goes cold.

"Tell me exactly what happened," Zach says.

He pulls me toward a bench by the side of the trailer. We sit down. One by one, I push out the words, drawing strength from the shock and horror and anger pooling inside me. Zach breathes in and out as I tell him the details. Through the blur of my tears, I can see the rage on his face.

"We have to go to the police!" He jumps up.

"No," I say, pulling him back down. The last thing I want is to have to sit in a cold, dreary room with some creepy cop as they ask me to show them exactly where Jay touched me.

"We *have* to," Zach insists. "We can't let him get away with this."

I look up cautiously at him.

"Have you told your parents?" he asks. "What about the school? Have you told the school about this?"

I shake my head. I haven't told anyone. I've just been bathing in a pool of my own shame.

Zach grabs my hand. "We have to go tell the school," he says.

I appreciate his using the word "we," but really this is my decision. And I've been thinking about it. What if they don't believe me? I should have gone and gotten a rape test done, but I looked it up, and in order for a rape test to be effective, I should have done it within seventy-two hours. It's been five days. Any DNA evidence is gone by now.

"It's going to be okay," Zach says, scooping me into his arms. As he holds me, I nod into his hair, desperately wanting to believe the words.

sixty-six

Dani

Ming paces back and forth in my bedroom while I text Zach. I was supposed to tutor him today, but he canceled.

"I can't believe Florence left like that! She wouldn't even introduce me to her parents as her friend!" she says. "I shouldn't have told my parents."

She tries Florence again, but she doesn't pick up.

"It was so stupid," Ming cries, lying on my bed and blinking back tears. "Now my parents know my secret . . . and for what?"

I put down my phone. "What'd they say when you told them?" I ask her.

"That I've gotten too Americanized and I need to stop."

Ming's phone rings. But it's just Mr. Rufus calling. Ming presses Ignore.

"What are you going to say to Florence?" I ask.

"That it's over," Ming says, throwing her phone into the

388

side pocket of her violin case. She curls up into a ball on my bed, pressing her chin to her knees. "For good."

I reach over and put a hand on her back.

"All my life I've just wanted to make my parents proud . . . ," she whispers as I rub her back. A tear escapes my eye. I feel that. I totally feel that. Ming wraps herself in my blanket. "And now I can never do that."

"Of course you can," I tell her, hugging her. But no matter how many times I say it, she shakes her head and says she can't.

After Ming leaves, I try Zach once more, but he doesn't pick up. I sit down at my computer and try to go over debate case studies. My team training sessions have been so abysmal, I'm kind of on my own for Snider. Chrome alerts me that I have email. I go to my Gmail and see a group email from Mr. Connelly reminding us of our flight reservation next week and what to bring to Snider. I'm glad he didn't leave me off the email chain for once. There's also an email from Google. I'd set up a Google Alert on Phoenix Capital Limited.

I click on the news article, from a Chinese business website.

To facilitate continued expansion of its portfolio assets, international real estate firm Phoenix Capital Limited has raised $128 million in a Series B round backed by Morgan

Stanley. The round was led by Hong Kong venture capital firms Dragon Investments and Asia Pacific Capital, bringing the firm's total equity funding to over USD $378 million. The firm said in a statement the new investment will go to expanding its real estate portfolio in Hong Kong, London, Tokyo, Shanghai, as well as up-and-coming markets such as Ho Chi Minh City, Vietnam, and East Covina, California.

East Covina, California? That's so weird that we're in a major press release, on the same list as Hong Kong and Tokyo, which have some of the highest real estate values in the world. I know Ho Chi Minh City is on the up and up, with Vietnam quickly becoming a factory destination for cheap labor. But what do *we* have?

I open a new tab and load Zillow. Red dots fill my screen, most of them million-dollar homes in North Hills that are for sale or rent. I click on a random one and call the real estate agent listed.

"Xander Vander Real Estate!" the guy answers.

"Uh, hi . . . I got your number from Zillow—" I start to say.

Before I can even finish my sentence, Xander bombards me with a level of enthusiasm I am not prepared for. "Are you looking to buy or sell? I have several houses over in North Hills! All spectacular and within twenty minutes of the esteemed private school American Prep! May I show you some?"

"Actually . . . I just had a question," I say. "Have you heard of Phoenix Capital Limited?"

Xander thinks for a minute.

"Doesn't ring a bell," he says.

"It's an Asian real estate fund," I tell him. I scroll through the article. "It says they're investing in real estate here in East Covina."

"That may very well be," Xander says. "We do a lot of work with Asian real estate funds. Most of them are affiliated with Li Incorporated. Are you sure it's not one of their subsidiaries?"

I scribble down the words Li Incorporated.

He tells me that Li Incorporated is one of the biggest real estate conglomerates in China, and they've been investing heavily in the city.

"Why?" I ask. Seems bizarre that Chinese real estate companies would be so interested in our small town.

"Good schools, of course!" Xander chuckles. "Nothing sells houses faster than good schools!"

sixty-seven

Claire

My mom lets out a sob when I finally tell her. I have three boxes of tissues on my bed for the call. Still, when she cries, nothing I could have prepared can soak up the pain inside.

"Oh, Claire," my mom cries. "Are you okay?"

I shake my head even as I force out a "Yeah."

"Does anyone know?" my mom asks.

"Just some friends."

There's a pause. "Don't tell anybody else," my mom says. "How will it look?"

I put a fist to my mouth. My mom covers up the phone with her hand. Her muffled voice asks into the phone, "How did it happen?"

"Is that Claire?" my dad asks in the background. I hear lowered voices—I assume my mom's telling him what happened. My father picks up the phone.

"Claire, it's me. Dad," he says. My chin quivers and I try

to stay strong. It's the first time we've spoken verbally since the restaurant incident.

"Hi, Dad," I say.

"Your mom's just told me what happened," my dad says.

"Don't tell your grandmother," my mom cuts in.

"Of course I'm not going to tell Nai Nai!" I say. I can't believe they're even thinking of my grandmother at a time like this.

"Listen to me," my dad says.

I sit up in anticipation of sympathy and advice from my daddy to his only daughter. He'll come through. I think back to when I first got home from Korea after my eyelid surgery and he sat with me, telling me how brave I was. He'll know what to say in my time of need. I know he will. Instead, what I get is, "These things happen. We're not mad at you."

Not mad at me?

"Your mother and I will talk to Jay's family. I'm sure we'll sort it out," he says. "The important thing is do not make a scene."

"No, the important thing is you're okay," my mom corrects.

"I am not okay," I yell.

I hang up on my parents and stand in the middle of my room shaking. I speed-dial Zach, then remember he's in class. I still haven't gone back to school, though I keep getting messages from the headmistress's office asking where I am. Every time I think of going back to school, my stomach twists into a knot so tight, I have to crouch down. I pick up my phone and instead of emailing back the headmistress's office, I email Ms. Jones, my English teacher.

Hi Ms. Jones,
Can we meet somewhere off campus to talk? I'm going through something and urgently need to talk to someone.
Thanks.
Claire

Ms. Jones and I meet at Starbucks. I sit across from her, my hands around a steaming hot coffee mug. As I tell her what happened, I stare into the hot abyss of my coffee, wishing I could fall in. Ms. Jones reaches a hand out to me, gasping. When I get to the part where Jay pins me to the bed, tears drip into my latte. I told myself I wasn't going to cry again, but my eyes are not capable of staying dry. I don't know if they'll ever be dry.

"And then . . . he raped me," I say, my lips trembling.

"Oh, Claire," she says, reaching for me with her arms. "I'm so sorry." As she holds me tight in her arms, she tells me over and over, "It's not your fault."

It feels so good to hear that, to have an adult tell me it's not my fault. I wish I could stay like this, feeling the warmth and comfort of her words, like a shield.

"I'm here for you no matter what you decide to do,"

she says, looking into my eyes when we finally both let go. "Have you thought about what you want to do?"

I shake my head.

"I think the first step is to go back to school and tell Mrs. Mandalay what happened," she says.

"I don't want to go back." I shake my head. My fingers press into my coffee mug, feeling the burn on my fingertips. "I don't want to see him at school."

"That's exactly why you need to come back!" she says. "Claire, you have certain rights as a student. One of them is the right to feel safe. If you come back and tell the school what happened, I'm sure they'll take the necessary actions to suspend or expel Jay for what he did."

I look up at her.

"Claire, you're not alone in this," she says. "The school wants its students to feel protected. Look how quickly they got rid of Mrs. Wallace. They have an *obligation*."

Emotion pokes through as she says the words and I want to believe her.

"That's why they have administrative proceedings and other disciplinary procedures—they have systems in place to protect their students."

I think about how decisively Mrs. Mandalay kicked out Mrs. Wallace after she wrote that email.

As Ms. Jones reaches over and puts her hand on top of mine, I look into her eyes. "I'm so sorry this happened to you. But you're a strong girl, Claire. 'Stronger than iron,'" she quotes from one of my essays. I smile at her from the blur of my tears.

"You're going to get through this."

Later that night, my parents call. I ask them if I can move out of Dani's and check into a hotel for a few days. I can't live with her anymore, not after what she did to me. They say okay. When I tell them I'm thinking of going to the headmistress to tell her what happened, they're not so quick to agree.

"Hold on, before you do that," my dad cuts in. "Let me speak to Jay's dad next week. If there's a way to do this quietly . . ."

It infuriates me that he somehow thinks there's a better way to do this and it involves my silence. "What if I don't want to do this quietly?" I ask.

"Claire." My mother's voice jumps on the line. In the background, I hear the clinging of forks and knives and chopsticks. Are they *entertaining*? "Be smart about this. We're just trying to protect you."

I hear my grandmother's voice in the background. "Is that Claire? I want to speak to her."

"No, Nai Nai, now's not a good time," my mom calls back.

I hear my mother close the door and she turns her attention to me. "This isn't like the email with your teacher. If you make a big stink about this, everyone will know," she says. She holds the phone closer to her mouth and whispers, "Do you really want your name synonymous with rape?"

She hisses the word "rape" like it's a dirty word that we can't even say, let alone report. I cry into my fist. It chokes my neck, their shame.

"Don't do anything until we discuss first," my dad says.

As my parents wait for me to respond, I think about all the years passed. All the birthday parties where they chose the guest list, not me, all the school photos, where I closed my eyes so there would be no physical evidence of my once single eyelids.

All I've ever been to them was a pawn, not a daughter.

sixty-eight

Dani

I find the movers at my house when I get home. "What's going on?" I ask, standing in the doorway as the movers wrap up Claire's Sealy mattress in Bubble Wrap and drag it along the carpet.

Claire ignores me and directs the movers to pack up her stuff into boxes.

I follow her to her room. Is this really necessary? We had a fight. And now she's moving out?

"Look, I didn't mean what I said . . . ," I mutter to the carpet. "I was angry."

Claire ignores me and continues packing. She has her sunglasses on and I can't see her eyes. She pushes past me to her closet, knocking into me with her shoulder.

"Claire, please!" I call out. I think about my mom and how devastated she's going to be when she finds out she's lost her tenant. "My mom's going to freak out when she comes home and finds out you're gone!"

"You should have thought about that." Claire glares at me, taking her dresses from her closet and stuffing them into boxes.

I walk over and try to block her from getting more of her dresses, but Claire mistakes it for me wanting the hangers.

"You want the hangers?" she asks. She takes a plastic hanger and throws it at me.

It hits me on the leg, and I wince. "Ow!"

"Here's another one!" Claire says, holding up another hanger.

I throw up my hands. "Fine, you want to move out? Move out!"

I retreat back to the living room and watch her from the couch. When the last of the boxes has been moved out, Claire looks around the house one last time. I hope she'll say goodbye and leave a note for my mom, but she just takes the house key off from her furry rabbit keychain and places it on top of the coffee table. And leaves without a word. No forwarding address. No nothing. Just walks out as hastily as she had arrived.

I throw my head back against the couch, head throbbing. I listen to the silence of the empty house. The hum of the refrigerator. The drip of the faucet. I tell myself I should be happy. No more having to wash her plates or step on her contacts on the floor. Or waiting around for the bathroom while she runs the hot water for an hour to steam her face. Instead, I wrestle with a splitting headache that lasts for hours.

When I wake up on the couch hours later, my headache is mostly gone but an eeriness clings to every surface of the house like a sticky film. I reach for my phone to call Ming. There's a message from Xander the real estate agent asking me whether I'm still interested in looking at houses.

I think back to what he said about Li Incorporated. I grab my laptop and pull up their website. I open another tab to google their founder. I don't find much on their website, but Google spits out a picture of their founder, Vincent Li, standing next to his wife and son— Wait a minute, is that . . . ? I zoom in on the image to get a closer look at his son when the home phone rings.

"Hello?" I answer distractedly.

"Hey, I need to speak to Claire." The voice gets my attention. It's Jay. I put down my laptop.

"She moved out," I tell him.

"What do you mean she moved out?" Jay asks.

"She *moved out*," I repeat. I gaze at her empty room. All that's left of her is the faint stain on the carpet where she threw up that first night.

"Where'd she move to?" Jay asks. Suddenly his voice takes on an entirely different tone. "Is she with that white boy?"

"No!" I exclaim. Then it occurs to me, Jay knows about Zach.

"If you see Claire, tell her that I need to talk to her," Jay says.

"Wait, before you hang up!" I open my laptop back up. "Is your dad by any chance Vincent Li? Does he own Li Incorporated?"

There's a pause on the phone. "Yeah, why?"

Oh. My. God.

"Nothing," I say to Jay.

sixty-nine

Claire

I put my stuff in storage and check in to a nearby hotel while I wait for my mom's real estate agent to find me a house. The real estate agent says it's going to take a couple of days, during which I continue to skip school (my parents email the school to tell them I'm sick), watch TV, and order room service.

My mom says hotels make you forget reality—what happens in a hotel, stays in a hotel. I wonder if that's something she tells herself so she can avoid thinking about what my dad does in them, but I try to apply the same logic. I take long swims in the outdoor pool. I float on my back as I gaze up at the clouds, thinking about my childhood and enjoying the warm weather and how nice it is to not be at school, until I remember why it is I can't go to school. At the thought of Jay, all the horror comes flooding back and my body plunges. Water goes up my nose, and I gasp and cough.

The pool staff rushes over to me and asks if I'm okay. I get out of the pool and run back to my room. Is this what the rest of my life is going to be like? Moments of happiness punctured by the memory of what happened, like a bomb which can detonate at any time.

Sleep's been hard. Zach brought me some melatonin, but it doesn't really work on me. I long instead for my grandmother's special blend of Chinese rosebud, wolfberry, and white peony root tea, but I know I can't call her. I've been forbidden from contacting her. Not that I'd want to talk to her about what happened.

Jess FaceTimes to tell me Jay's been asking about me.

"I told him to go fuck himself," she says. She's kept my secret and not told anyone, not even Nancy and Florence, who keep texting me, Where are you? What's going on? "He looks like shit by the way . . . ," she adds.

My phone dings. It's my parents on the other line.

"I'll call you back," I say to Jess, and switch the call.

"Good news," my mom announces. "We found you an apartment two blocks away from school. They're getting it ready now. You should be able to move in a few days."

"Oh, and listen," my dad adds. "I talked to Jay's dad."

I sit up and wrap my robe around me tightly.

"He assures me what happened will not happen again. Jay is very sorry. You're safe to go back to school."

I'm safe?

"I'm only going back if he's kicked out of school." I tell

my parents I've been doing a lot of thinking about what Ms. Jones said and I think I want to press it with the school.

There's silence on the other end.

"What will that accomplish?" my dad asks. "Sure, it'll feel good for five minutes. But what about afterward?"

I brace for a lecture on how uncomfortable it's going to be to have to recount my story to all the various administrators of our school. But that's not what he says.

"Everyone will know you're damaged goods," my dad warns.

My hands go cold as my mom quickly apologizes for him and says, "He didn't mean that. We just don't want you to get hurt!"

But it's too late. I bite my mouth so hard, when I get off the phone, there's blood on my lip.

Mrs. Mandalay makes small listening noises in her office the next day as I tell her what Jay did to me. Zach offered to come with me, but I wanted to do this by myself. I've now told the story five times to people, and each time, I can feel myself getting stronger.

"And that's when you say he raped you?" Mrs. Mandalay asks.

"Yes," I say, proud of myself for keeping it together. Surprisingly, during the most important meeting of them all, my eyes stay dry. Mrs. Mandalay asks me what I did afterward. She's a lot more clinical than Ms. Jones, asking for times and details almost like a doctor would. I tell her I took a shower and went home.

"Did you go to the police?" Mrs. Mandalay inquires.

"No," I say. "Not yet."

A pause. "I see," she says.

"Should I go to the police?" I ask.

She jots down some notes. "You can if you want," she says, looking up at me. "Is that what you want, Claire? To have a long, drawn-out police investigation?"

I shake my head. Not when she puts it like that. She seems colder than when I was in here for the Mrs. Wallace email thing. Does she not believe me?

"If you go to the police, they'll want to know a bunch of things. Why didn't you get a rape test done? Why'd you wait so long to come in? Why did you *stay* in Jay's house afterward and take a shower? Not to mention, what were you doing in his bedroom to begin with?"

I press my index finger and thumb to my forehead. They're the exact *whys* I've been asking myself these last few days.

"I just don't want to have to see him anymore," I murmur. I look up and plead with Mrs. Mandalay. "Please, can you make him switch to another school?"

Mrs. Mandalay shakes her head. "We can't just kick him out of school. This is America. We believe in due process," she says. She reaches for a copy of the school rules. "Now, on page thirty-eight, you'll see that whenever there's an internal student dispute, students are encouraged to take the matter before the administrative board."

Ms. Jones had mentioned something about the administrative board. The headmistress tells me it consists of teachers, administrators, and student representatives and works just like an actual court. They hear testimony from both sides.

"So it's like a school court?" I ask.

She nods.

"And Jay will be in the room?"

"Yes," she says. I groan at the floor. I was afraid of that. "And either side can call witnesses."

"There are no witnesses."

"Well, you can have character witnesses." She slides the school rules pamphlet across her desk. "Trust me," she says. "This is the best option."

As I take the pamphlet from her, she reminds me that California truancy laws prevent me from staying home any longer.

"You mean I have to stay at school today?" I ask.

"I'm afraid so," she says.

My mouth forms an O. I promised myself I would not come back to school until after Jay was kicked out. I only came back today to meet with Mrs. Mandalay.

"Claire." Mrs. Mandalay looks me in the eye. "If you really want to do this, you're going to have to be stronger than this. You're going to have to face him at the meeting eventually."

I reach for my backpack, putting the school rules pamphlet inside. Stepping out of Mrs. Mandalay's office, I lift my eyes, squinting at the full on-ness of school. Classmates screaming. Laughing. Taking pictures of each other in the photo booth of their MacBook Airs. I stare at them, envying their normalness. This is just a regular school day for them, not a warzone they have to share with their rapist.

Florence is the first one to spot me.

"Oh, thank God, where've you been? My parents came for the spring concert and—" She stops talking when she sees my face. I shake my head, the words trapped in my windpipe. Florence leads me over to a quiet picnic table way out in the field.

Jay runs up to us as we're walking.

Florence lets go of my hand when she sees him. "I'll let you guys have a moment," she says.

I shake my head at her, *No, don't leave me!*, but the words are swallowed up by the shock of Jay standing next to me, talking to me, like *nothing happened.*

"Hey," Jay says. "I just wanted to apologize for what happened." He reaches out a hand to touch my elbow, and I jerk it away so violently, I drop my phone on the ground.

As he reaches to pick it up, I shout at him, "Leave it."

Jay puts up his hands. Florence, Nancy, and Jess watch us from across the field. The sight of his hands brings me straight back to that night, the way they pinned me down, holding me in place while he violated me. I lunge forward, feeling my breakfast rising in me. It comes shooting out of me. As Jay reaches to hold back my hair, I shout at him, "Get the fuck away from me!"

My face is ashen white, hair a disheveled mess, the sick drying on my shirt as I march back into Mrs. Mandalay's office for the second time today.

"I want to proceed with the ad board," I say. Mrs. Mandalay puts down her pen and folds her hands on her desk.

"Are you sure about this?" she asks.

"Yes." The idea of spending the next few months in the same school as that creep, while he walks around pretending nothing happened, is impossible. I get physically ill around him. Any hope for an undisturbed rest of my education withered and died today on the field.

Mrs. Mandalay presses a button on her desk phone, tells her secretary to hold her calls. She turns to me and once again reminds me, "You're going to have to face him during the trial."

I know. I tell myself there's nothing to be scared of. I've already faced him. Of course, telling him to fuck off on the field is not the same thing as listening to him deny having raped me to our teachers.

"You think you can handle that?" she asks.

I clench my hands into tight fists.

"Yes," I say.

"Okay, then," she says, retrieving her calendar from her

desk. She glances at the dates. "How's Thursday?"

Walking out of Mrs. Mandalay's office the second time, I'm met by Florence, Nancy, and Jess outside. My squad pulls me in for a hug as I tell Nancy and Florence what happened.

"That motherfucker!" Nancy cries. "Are you going to switch schools?"

I shake my head. "No. I'm going up in front of the ad board."

"Hey, how'd it go?" Zach runs up to me and asks me. He's just come from training, and his hair's still wet. My friends stare at Zach as he leans over and gives me a kiss.

"This is Zach," I introduce to them.

Jess looks down at Zach's ripped JanSport backpack and used Nike sneakers, the swoosh so faded it looks more like the crooked mouth of a smiley face. And even though she doesn't say it, I can see it on her face: *You left Jay for him?*

seventy

Dani

"Hey," I say to Zach in band, putting away my tournament papers for Snider. "How come you keep canceling our tutoring sessions?"

He doesn't reply.

I glance over at Ming, rubbing her puffy eyes as she gets out her sheet music. Last night, she finally talked to Florence about walking away at the concert. Ming asked Florence why she did that. Was it because she didn't want her parents talking to Ming's parents and finding out they weren't exactly rich? When Florence couldn't give her a straight answer, they broke up.

Zach turns away from me.

"How's Claire?" I ask. Again, he doesn't say anything. "I got a call from Jay. He knows about you guys . . ."

This gets Zach's attention. He points his reed at me. "You're still talking to him? Don't you think you've done enough damage?" he asks me.

I stare at him. *What'd I do?*

Mr. Rufus walks up to the conductor's stand and orders us all to sit down. He holds up his baton and nods to Ming, who lifts her bow. She takes a deep breath and plays the first soulful note.

I sneak glances at Zach as I lift my flute. I can't believe I'm back to sneaking glances at him in band again. I deliberately play an off note, hoping to get his attention. But no matter what I do, he doesn't look at me.

Claire lingers in the shadows of the hallway, like she's hiding from someone. I'm glad she's back in school. She peers into the big faculty conference room, the one Mrs. Mandalay only uses for special occasions, like an ad board meeting.

"Dani!" Mr. Matthews, my counselor, walks up to me in the hallway and greets me. "Everything okay? You feeling better?"

I muster a polite nod while looking over his shoulder at Claire. She catches me looking at her, frowns, and walks away.

I glance down at the file in Mr. Matthews's hand. It reads: CONFIDENTIAL—BRIEFING MATERIALS FOR MEMBERS OF THE ADMINISTRATIVE BOARD ONLY.

"Is there going to be an ad board proceeding?" I ask.

Mr. Matthews sighs yes. I try to probe him for more

details, but he moves the file sharply away from me. "Dani, you know I can't comment on an ongoing investigation," he says, changing the subject. "Hey, I'm sorry you didn't make headmistress commendation. Maybe next year."

I look down. "Yeah . . . maybe," I say.

"But at least you get to go to Snider!" he says. "It's in two days, isn't it?"

I nod. My mom printed out the plane ticket this morning and set it on my bed.

My eyes slide back over to the ad board room. Now Jay's standing in front of it, looking inside. His finger's moving in the air, like he's counting how many seats are inside. Something's definitely up.

"Hey, Mr. Matthews, do you know anything about Li Incorporated?" I ask.

Mr. Matthews's face hardens.

"Why do you ask?" he says. Before I can answer, he says stiffly, "I think you should focus on preparing for your upcoming tournament." He excuses himself and walks away.

seventy-one

Claire

Jay's making the rounds, going from table to table, talking to parachutes. They informed him yesterday about the ad board meeting that's happening on Thursday and I guess he's lobbying for character witnesses. At lunch, the other kids talk in hushed whispers, murmurs that dull when I get close and sharpen the minute I walk away. Jess sighs.

"Maybe you should back down," she says, watching Jay out of the corner of her eye.

Florence stirs her soup, her eyes puffy and red. Apparently, she and Ming broke up.

"No way." I shake my head. I look over at the ever-growing table of Jay sycophants, most of them guys, but also a couple of girls. What'd he promise them? A flight home on his private jet? "I'm not worried. I've got you guys, Zach, and Ms. Jones."

Speaking of Ms. Jones, she catches up to me later that

day and tells me she's going to talk to Mrs. Mandalay and request that she be a part of the ad board.

"Now that I'm teaching here full-time, I'd like to be a part of the decision-making process of the school, especially on matters involving student safety," she says. "I looked at the rules and there's no requirement that ad board members needed to have taught at the school for a certain period of time. It just says faculty members."

I throw my arms around her—it's the best news I've heard all week! "Thank you so much!" I say. If Ms. Jones is in that room on Thursday, it would mean that I would have at least one adult on my side.

I wish her good luck as she goes and talks to Mrs. Mandalay. The smile on my face vanishes when I get back to my locker and see the Chinese words smeared on the front of my locker:

Cock Tease

Frantically, I try to rub it out, but it's written in permanent marker. I scrub and I scrub, as the other students pass by and stare. The white kids thankfully can't read it, but all the parachutes can. They shake their heads at me as they walk by.

Dani sees me and joins me in scrubbing, but I yell at her, "I don't need your help!" She stops scrubbing and quietly walks away. Five minutes later, she comes back with a dry-erase whiteboard marker, which she tosses at me.

"Try tracing over it with this," she says.

I try tracing over the characters after Dani leaves. It works. When the words finally come off, Jess, Nancy, and Florence walk up. The four of us stand back and look at my locker. The words are gone but I'd overscrubbed and now there's a faint white outline against the beige metal.

Florence looks nervously at me. "You sure you still want to go through with this?"

Later that day, I'm moving into my new apartment, two blocks away from school. It's a two-bedroom town house overlooking the lake. The real estate agent, a white lady named Sarah, gives me the keys and asks if it'll be just me. I tell her yes and brace for a lecture about the dangers of living alone as a teenager, but she couldn't care less. She shows me how the stove and the oven work and leaves the number of the local housecleaning agency on the fridge. It happens to be Dani's agency. I toss it out.

After Sarah leaves, the movers drop off my stuff and the delivery guys from Pottery Barn show up to deliver the rest of the furniture I ordered. As they're moving the couch inside the house, I hear a sports car speeding down the street. My body shrinks with dread. I look up to see my worst nightmare parking in front of my town house.

"We need to talk! You've been ignoring all my voice mails!" Jay shouts, walking toward me.

I'm so shocked he's here, I'm disoriented for a second. Then angry. Violently, hysterically angry. This is my home!

How dare he come here? I look to the mover guys and the delivery people and want them all to get out so I can lock the door, but the door's open wide, and Jay's running up the stairs, and before I know it, he's standing in the middle of my living room.

"You can't be here!" I say to him.

The movers and delivery guys look up at us.

"Is there a problem?" one of them asks.

"Yes!" I say. "I don't want this guy here!"

Jay explains to the movers, "She's my girlfriend. We're just having a fight."

The movers nod sympathetically—*Been there, bro*—and get back to unpacking. I reach for the phone to call the cops.

"Please, Claire! Hear me out!" Jay pleads, grabbing the phone out of my hand. Tears brim in his eyes. He puts his hands together and begs me for two seconds.

We go outside.

I hold on tight to my jacket, my arms across my chest in a brace position. "How'd you find me?"

"My family has real estate connections all over town," he says, handing my phone back to me. "We know every real estate transaction that occurs."

I roll my eyes. Of course he does.

"Claire, look, I'm sorry. I lost control. You hurt me, and I just . . . I lost it." His voice rises and falls. "Haven't you ever lost control before?"

I shake my head. No, I've never raped anyone before.

Jay puts a hand to his head and grabs a fistful of hair. There's remorse in his eyes, I can see it. But that doesn't make it any more bearable. "I haven't been able to sleep. I haven't been able to eat . . ."

"I don't give a shit about your appetite."

"I know, I'm just saying, I'm hurting here. I'm *already* hurting. You don't have to go and ruin my life," he says.

I shake my head at him. It's so unfair he puts this on me—*he* did this. *He* ruined his own life. One of the mover guys squeezes by us, and Jay moves closer to me. "Please, I'm in so much shit with my parents."

"As you should be!"

He plunges his eyes, and he's silent for so long that I turn around and start walking back. "If you care about me at all, if you have even an ounce of feeling toward me, you'll call this thing off," he mutters.

I turn around. "I did care for you, Jay—"

"Yeah, funny how you showed it."

We're done here. "I'll see you on Thursday," I say, slamming the door behind me.

After Jay leaves, I sit on my new couch for the next hour, trying to figure out how the hell I'm going to survive being in the same room as him for hours when I feel gutted after a five-minute conversation.

seventy-two

Dani

I search for Claire. According to Messenger on my phone, she hasn't been online in five days. I switch over to email.

To: Claire Wang
From: Danielle De La Cruz

Hi Claire,

I saw you looking into the ad board room. Are you in some sort of trouble? I saw Jay looking in there as well. I don't know what happened but you should know Jay's family is heavily invested in the school. They've been selling houses to Chinese families, packaging them as some sort of American dream home + American dream school deal. They've poured millions into American Prep through various subsidiary companies. They practically own the school!

Call me when you get this message!

—Dani

I type *PS*, debating whether to include a postscript. In the end, I decide against it and send the message as it is, hoping the urgency of my words can convey to Claire what I'm too proud to say outright: *I'm sorry.*

I head down the hallway after I send the email. Maybe I can catch Claire before she goes home. Instead, I bump into Zach.

"Zach!" I call. He looks up from the water fountain. "Do you know where I can find Claire?"

He wipes the water from the corners of his mouth and starts walking away.

Is he just going to ignore me? I rush after him. "What's wrong?"

"What's wrong? She's kind of going through a lot right now, that's what's wrong. You should know." He walks briskly and I struggle to keep up.

"Know what?" I ask, picking up the pace.

Zach stops walking.

"Hey, do you know anyone on the ad board?" he asks.

Shit, so it's true. I tell him only Mr. Matthews. But if she's going before the ad board, she should know the administration is ten times more powerful than she thinks.

Zach shakes his head like he doesn't understand. I pull

him into an empty classroom and finally tell him the whole truth about everything that happened to me this year. About Seattle, xomegan.com, the real reason they took away my headmistress commendation. Everything.

"Oh my God," he says. "Why didn't you tell me?" he asks. My gaze falls to my feet. I don't have the words to explain why I kept it a secret. It wasn't like by keeping it small, it disappeared. Instead, it just burned a hole inside my pocket.

"I'm so sorry," Zach says, putting his arms around me.

As Zach holds me, I breathe into his sweatshirt. I think about all the times he's cheered me up this past year, lifted me when I felt defeated. As I pull away from him, I say, "I hope you and Claire are happy together." I say it from the most genuine part of me, the part that misses both of them.

"Thanks." Zach smiles.

He pushes open the door to the hallway. "I'm sorry again, Dani," he says. "I wish you had told me earlier so I could have helped you."

I raise my eyes. "You did help me," I tell him.

Zach gives me another hug and wishes me well at Snider. "I'm proud of you, De La Cruz," he says. "I'll be rooting for you."

seventy-three

Claire

Early on Wednesday, the day before the ad board meeting, I go to find Ms. Jones. My parents are still really unsure about this whole ad board thing, but I reassured them that my English teacher's going to be on it. I push open the door to my English class, but instead of finding Ms. Jones at her desk, I find Mrs. Wallace.

"Where's Ms. Jones?" I ask.

"Home!" she exclaims. "I'll be teaching this class again."

I immediately make an excuse to go to the bathroom. In the bathroom stall, I tap into my in-box, closing my eyes as I hit refresh and wait for my emails to load. *Please please . . . let it not be true.*

And then I see it.

Dear Claire,
I'm so sorry to be writing you this email. At five o'clock

yesterday, I was dismissed from the school. The official reason was that my services were no longer needed as Mrs. Wallace's suspension has been lifted. The unofficial reason, I suspect, may have to do with my trying to get on the ad board.

Please do not feel at all responsible—I am only telling you this because I feel it is important that young people know the real facts of a situation, not the sugarcoated version. If I had to do it all over again, I would do the same thing because I consider it my utmost duty as a teacher to protect my students. After all, if we cannot offer even this basic level of care in our schools, what right do we have to call ourselves educators?

Good luck tomorrow. I know you're scared but trust you are doing the right thing and every rational, impartial adult who hears your story will believe you. I certainly do. Do you still remember the thing I taught you about the hero's journey? Well, this is it. You are the hero, and tomorrow you will find the strength to take back control of your journey. I have faith in you. It has been an honor teaching you.

All my love,

Sharisa Jones

I read and reread the email from Ms. Jones. How could they do this to her? She was the best teacher I had! My in-box notifies me with another email from Dani and I tap Junk Mail before I even read it. I quickly reply back, thanking Ms. Jones for all her help and apologizing for what happened. The bell rings. As I pick up my backpack and walk out of the stall, I try not to think about what this means for tomorrow.

The night before the ad board meeting, I wake up in a cold sweat. I don't know how to explain it, this inexplicable fear I have. It grows inside me, breeding worries and anxieties I can neither articulate nor control whenever I think about what Jay will say tomorrow. Will he deny anything ever happened? Or fill the room with lies, saying that I consented to it, that I asked for it, even enjoyed it?

And if he does, will I sit passively, eyes glazed over while he spews these lies? Or will I lunge forward and put my enraged hands around his throat?

I call Zach in the middle of the night. He stays on the phone with me while I try to calm down.

"It's going to be okay," he says. "Have faith . . . it's like your English teacher said. Any rational adult will see you're telling the truth."

"Thanks, Zach," I whisper. He's been steadfastly sweet to me, coming by every day, sitting with me and my friends at lunch, even though Jess eyes him like he's a statement button I picked up at Gap Outlet.

"Hey, I talked to Dani today," he says.

"And?"

"I think you should talk to her."

I sigh into the phone. I'm not ready to talk to her. I don't know if I'll ever be ready. Instead, I bid Zach a good night and hang up to try to catch some sleep. I tell myself there's nothing to be scared of tomorrow. The worst thing that can happen to me has already happened.

seventy-four

Dani

Ming takes me to the airport. We linger in Starbucks until the last minute, so I don't have to join Mr. Connelly and my teammates any earlier than I have to.

"How do you feel?" Ming asks.

"Like I really don't want to go on a five-hour flight with those assholes."

"Don't think about them," Ming says. "You're not debating for them or for American Prep. You're debating for you."

I lean in to hug her. "Thanks."

As I gather up my boarding pass and start walking toward the gate, Ming calls out to me, "Hey, Dani!"

I turn around.

"Show 'em you don't need a parachute to soar!"

∘ ∘ ∘

It takes five and a half hours to fly to Boston, during which time I ignore the whispers from my teammates and Mr. Connelly downing one Bloody Mary after another, two rows up. I repeat Ming's words in my head—*I'm doing this for me. I'm doing this for my mom, for Yale, for a future I can't afford to give up on.*

When the plane lands, I text Claire again on Messenger. Still no response. She's not checking her messages. We get two Ubers to the hotel. As we pull up, I see the banner hanging on the Charles Hotel: *Welcome to the 5th Annual Snider Cup: The Nation's Top Debating and Public Speaking Tournament.* I take a minute to take it in. This is it. I made it.

Mr. Connelly assigns me to a room with Audrey. When we unpack, Audrey wrinkles her nose at my polyester-rayon black dress. She hangs up her own Theory stretch wool dress in the closet and points to my cheap Payless shoes.

"You might want to draw over your shoes with a permanent marker," Audrey says.

My face reddens. My pumps are so overworn, the fake black leather's peeling off.

"No, thanks," I say, picking up the shoes and hugging them close to my chest.

At the opening ceremony, the Hotchkiss kids huddle next to us going over last-minute motions. I peek over at their motions.

This house believes the state should lace water supply with a chemical that homogenizes people's intelligence to the intelligence level of an average university graduate.

This house would force all companies worth over $1 billion to list publicly.

This house believes that developing countries should heavily disincentivize rural to urban migration.

Holy shit. These motions are so much harder than the ones we've been studying. Audrey and Josh are on their phones talking to their private debate coaches. My airways are closing up. Heat crawls up my neck as I realize I may be out of my league here. My phone rings. It's my mom.

"Hi, honey! I just wanted to wish you good luck!" she says. "I'm sorry I can't be there, but I know you'll do well!"

The enthusiasm in her voice collides with the impossibility of the motions I've just seen. I think of all the extra nights she's worked to save up so I can come here, all the things she's had to give up, including her own education, and I'm filled with the most soul-crushing guilt.

"I don't know if I can do it, Mom . . . ," I tell her. My voice wobbles.

"What are you talking about?" she asks. "Of course you can do it!"

I glance at my teammates on the phone, their coaches feeding them arguments, giving them talking points. "The other kids, they all have extra help."

"You don't need extra help!" my mom says. "And besides, you know things that they don't know. Things you can't learn from a textbook! You can do it—I know you can!"

I cover my mouth, shaking my head into the phone. There's so much she doesn't know. My mom hangs up, and I turn back to the table. Mr. Connelly looks over at me, opens his mouth like he's going to say something reassuring, and then closes it. Instead, he turns to my other teammates and builds them up.

That night, I grapple with major imposter syndrome. As I listen to Audrey's loud snoring, the doubts swirl through my head. *What am I doing here? Do I really have what it takes?* Eventually, these questions lead to even bigger questions of *What's even the point? They're just words!* Even if I win, will it make one iota of difference? I glance over at Audrey, in her silk pajamas and fuzzy eyeshades. Tomorrow, she'll get up and say a bunch of woke words she doesn't believe, and everyone will clap and smile and feel good about themselves, while the world continues to spin in the sexist, racist, classist mess that it is.

I toss and turn on the hotel bed. I close my eyes and picture my mom, but that only stresses me out even more when I think about returning home empty-handed, having wasted her hard-earned dollars. Finally, I find solace in the most disgusting of places . . . Mr. Connelly's old words to me: "You're better than all of them."

As I drift to sleep, I wonder whether in replaying his once cherished words to me, am I forgiving him? Am I betraying myself?

seventy-five

Claire

On the day of the ad board proceedings, I'm in the bathroom, checking my email in one of the stalls, getting ready
to head to the meeting, when I hear two parachute girls
walk in.

"Can you believe she's actually going through with it?"
one of them asks the other in Chinese. "The *ad board*?"

I peek out through the crack. I recognize the girls from
my year, but I don't know their names.

"She's not going to win," the other one says as she reap-
plies her lipstick in the mirror.

"I hope not. If she wins, what if it gets out? It'll make
the school look so bad, and all our degrees will be worth
way less."

My jaw drops. *That's* why they don't want me to win?
Because their degrees are going to be worth less?

"I don't know why she doesn't just switch schools," one

of the girls says, flipping her hair to one side. She turns on the faucet to wash her hands.

"Or stay and just, like, avoid him," the other one suggests.

"Totally."

I want to laugh at the absurdity of this conversation, me pressed up against the bathroom stall while these two girls discuss how easy it is for me to cruise on through the rest of high school and "blend in" like I'm a tree lizard. I grab my backpack and unlock the door. The two girls freeze. The water collects in the sink.

"Claire! We didn't know you were in here!"

I walk over to the sink to wash my hands as nonchalantly as I can. As I walk out, I turn to the girls and say, "Excuse me, I have to go devalue your degrees."

Adrenaline and fear press me forward as I head over to the faculty conference room. The fear that if I don't do this, *this* will be my normal, having to listen to people talk about how I chickened out while hiding in a bathroom stall.

Jess and Zach are already inside, waiting for me when I walk in. I smile and take a seat next to them.

"Nancy and Florence texted," Jess says. "They're on their way."

I nod. Jay hasn't arrived yet, thankfully, but the ad board members have. There are four faculty members on the board. They are Mr. Matthews, the school counselor; Mr. Francis, a PE teacher; Ms. Sloan, a teacher I don't know;

and Mrs. Mandalay. The door opens and in comes the student representatives. My eyes flash with surprise when I see Emma Lau, the girl from my class.

She gives me a small, guarded smile as she takes a seat—I can't believe she's here! Jordan Bekowski, the other student rep, sits down beside her. Nancy and Florence quietly come in after them.

"Great, are we all here?" Mrs. Mandalay asks.

The door opens. I draw in a sharp breath as Jay walks in.

"Sorry I'm late," Jay says.

He takes a seat across from me. I sit up, trying not to be intimidated as Zach stares Jay down. The door opens again, and a bunch of other parachutes follow Jay in, faces both familiar and new. They must be his character witnesses. Mrs. Mandalay calls the meeting to order and goes over the rules of the proceedings.

"Claire, since you are the claimant, we will start with you. Can you please walk us through what happened the night of Friday the fifteenth?" she asks.

I pull out my speech. I'd prepared it in advance and rehearsed it a thousand times in my room, like Dani always did before a big debate. As I read my statement, my voice is nowhere near as strong as hers. It wobbles with emotion. Still, I manage to get the words out. When I get to the part where he pushed me onto the bed, Jay interrupts me.

"Excuse me, I didn't push you onto the bed. You climbed

onto the bed with me," he corrects.

Mr. Francis leans forward. "So you're saying it was consensual?" he asks Jay, scribbling on his notebook.

"No! It wasn't consensual!" I object. I stare into Jay's eyes, daring him to lie to my face. And he does. Effortlessly.

"Yes," Jay answers.

I turn to the teachers. "He pinned me down. I screamed no! So many times!"

Mrs. Mandalay motions for me to calm down.

"And then what happened?" Ms. Sloan asks.

"Then I took a shower," I say.

"Where? At your house?" Mr. Francis says.

I shake my head. "At his place," I say.

Mr. Matthews's eyebrows squeeze together into a tight, confused wrinkle. "Why?"

"I wanted to get him off me," I say. He would too if a squid had just slithered all up and down his body. I wanted to take a million showers.

Mr. Francis clears his throat. "Yeah, but why did you do it *there*?" he asks.

I glance at Jess. *Help!*

"I'm just saying, if you'd just been . . . violated . . . wouldn't you want to get out of there as fast as possible?" Mr. Francis looks around the room and the student rep, Jordan, nods.

"I did get out of there," I say.

"Yes, eventually. You went home," Mr. Francis says, glancing down at his notes. He looks up at me. "Why didn't you go to the police?"

"I . . . I . . ." I feel my throat go dry.

"She just didn't, okay?" Zach jumps in.

"I have text messages," I say, pulling out my phone. I show them all of Jay's texts to me after the rape.

"That was over something else!" Jay insists.

Mrs. Mandalay tells me to put my phone away. "Zach, let's hear from you. You and Claire are . . . friends?" she asks, looking down at our hands, touching on the table.

"Yeah," Zach says.

"Excuse me," Jay interjects. "They're more than friends, they're sleeping together. Claire was cheating on me with him."

"That's not true!" I interject.

"Oh, please, I saw you two at the park," Jay mutters under his breath.

I turn to him. He *saw* me? I think back to that day at the park when we heard someone coming. "OMG, was that you?" I cover my mouth. "You've been following me?"

All this time I thought it was Dani who told him about me and Zach but it wasn't Dani. I think back to that night at the karaoke bar. At the country park. This week when he came over to my house. He's been following me all along. But *how*?

And I remember he installed Find My Friends on my

phone that day when we went to Fashion Island. Mr. Francis says something, but I can barely hear it above the loud thudding in my ear. I feel like taking my phone and hurling it at Jay.

"Claire, is this true?" Mr. Francis asks again. "Were you cheating on Jay with Zach?"

I swallow hard. "Jay and I's relationship was already over."

Jay snorts. "Yeah, right. That's why you were over at my house, eating my food and drinking my wine when my dad came," he says.

"Excuse me," Jess jumps in. "Homegirl can afford her own booze, thank you very much."

Mr. Matthews clears his throat. "I think we're getting a little off track. Let's get back to the night. Jay, you're saying Claire came over to your house around seven p.m. and had consensual sexual relations with you."

Jay nods.

"Why would she do that if she was also sleeping with Zach?" he asks.

"Because she felt bad for cheating on me," he says. He looks directly at me. "For leading me on for so long."

Mr. Francis raises an eyebrow. "Leading you on?" he asks, sitting up with renewed interest. He looks up from his notebook at me and Jay. "How so?"

As Jay proceeds to paint a picture of me as some sort of selfish, cruel tease who preys on the innocent and vulnerable hearts of young heirs, I lunge from my seat, feeling a homicidal rage I've never felt before.

"You bastard!" I say to him.

Mrs. Mandalay orders me to sit down. But I don't. I've heard enough.

seventy-six

Dani

Three debates in at Snider, I'm holding my own, raking in best speaker points, even as my teammate, Josh, refuses to prep with me. I get a text from Zach.

Dani, the ad board screwed Claire! he writes. I don't know what to do!

Three dots appear.

I glance at my watch—I have less than a minute before my next debate. Call me! I type.

My phone rings right as the organizer walks into the room. "Dani, Josh, you're up next!" he calls.

I tap Ignore Call.

The organizer tells us our motion and puts us in a prep room to prepare. As Josh and I sit down to prep, I pull out my phone to call Zach.

Josh frowns at me.

"You're not supposed to get any outside help," he says.

"I'm not getting outside help, asshole. I am *helping* the outside," I say, texting Zach.

Zach doesn't respond. I try Claire as Josh gets up and goes outside. I assume he's going to the bathroom, but he comes back with the organizer who frowns at me and confiscates my phone. Did Josh just tell on me?

"No phones please," the organizer says, reminding me of the tournament rules.

"Please, just one call!" I beg, but he shakes a finger at me and walks out.

I glare at Josh, who smiles smugly at me.

When prep time is over, Josh and I walk into the main debating room. I'm first. I step up to the podium and begin my speech. The whole time I'm debating, I'm trying not to look at Mr. Connelly, who claps and cheers. He's putting on a big show for the other coaches. When they announce that I'm the winner of the round, Mr. Connelly whistles.

"My girl!" Mr. Connelly hollers.

It's so gross how he's trying to "claim" me, marking his territory around me like I'm a tree, when privately he offers not a single word of support. The opposing team shakes my hand, while their coach offers Mr. Connelly his congratulations. The organizers usher us back down to the banquet hall.

"Wow! What a start, Dani!" the head organizer compliments me. "You did an amazing job."

Mr. Connelly smiles. "We're all so proud of her," he says,

putting his hand on my back.

I squirm away from him and dive into the crowd, moving farther from Mr. Connelly when we enter the banquet hall. The main adjudicators are up on the stage tallying up the scores. I scramble to the front. As the main adjudicator steps up to the podium, the room falls quiet.

"Can I please have your attention everyone?" he asks, tapping on the mic. I look up at the judge, hope pounding in my ear. "Based on the individual and team scores, the following contestants may now advance to the finals. Rachel Gordon of Exeter. Joseph Siegel of Deerfield. Danielle De La Cruz of American Prep."

Oh my God! I made it! I turn around and, out of habit, automatically scan the room for my coach. Mr. Connelly is in the back of the room, shaking the other coaches' hands. The head organizer calls out seven more names and rushes us backstage. He tells us we have five minutes to prepare our speech, on the motion "This house will not consume the works of artists who have committed sexual crimes."

The organizer announces our speeches will be broadcast on Facebook Live. Excitedly, my fellow contestants and I scribble our names on consent forms being passed around. Mr. Connelly rushes backstage.

"You know who I was talking to out there? The debate coach of the Yale team," he says. He puts his hands on my arms and shakes me. "Yale, Dani! *Yale!*"

My breath catches in my throat.

"I told him all about you. He's been watching you," he says. "He likes what he sees."

His eyebrows shoot way up, the way they do in practice when we surprise him with an impressive speech. I used to kill to make his eyebrows go up like that.

"If we play our cards right, you could be looking at a full ride to Yale next year, and I could be looking at a coaching gig with New Haven Promise, their local high school outreach program." Mr. Connelly beams. "Wouldn't that be amazing?"

We. It sneaks into my euphoria.

He peers at me, all serious. His big-coach-game face is back on. "You want to run through the points? What do you need?"

"I'm fine," I say.

Mr. Connelly nods and leaves me to prep. "You're gonna be amazing," he says, giving me a thumbs-up as he walks out. "My bright, shining star!"

As he pushes open the backstage door, he turns. "Oh, and, Dani?"

"Yes?"

"I forgive you," he says.

I close my eyes after he leaves, trying to center myself and find solace. I tell myself to forget Mr. Connelly and just focus on Yale. I have one shot to go out there and deliver a powerful speech.

But as I turn the motion around in my head, I can't shake

the pins and needles in my fingers, the demoralizing notion that *he* forgives *me?* Does he have any idea what the last few months have been like for me? The choking anxiety of having to sit with this, day after day, weighing my options. If I go nuclear, what about the blowback? What about my scholarship? The crushing fear that they'll come after me with every dollar of their million-dollar endowment and bury me?

"Dani, you're up!" An organizer taps on my shoulder and jolts me back to reality.

Panicked, I turn to him. "I need more time!"

He shakes his head and taps on his watch. "Let's go," he says, and leads me to the front of the stage. The blinding spotlights hit me as I walk over to the podium. I look out at the audience, at Mr. Connelly in the back and the debate coach from Yale standing next to him.

I think of Ming's words—I don't need a parachute to soar.

seventy-seven

Claire

In the end, it wasn't even close. Of the four faculty members and two student representatives of the ad board, only one voted in my favor—Emma.

It gives me some comfort that Emma Lau, of all people, chose to believe me, and I cling to it. That it wasn't unanimous. That I was able to go into a room, stare into the eyes of my assailant, and tell him that what he did to me was not okay. And the sky did not collapse. That's something, isn't it? All this I remind myself, even as the pangs of regret cramp my stomach. The ad board was not a path to justice. Rational, impartial adults did not believe me. And tomorrow when I go to school again, I'll still have to see him.

I unlock the door to my apartment and plummet on the couch as the phone rings. It's my mom calling.

"Claire, guess what? We got you a place at another school," my mom announces. "Your dad and I just gave a donation to Terry Grove High and now you have a spot!"

I lower my head back against the couch. "Oh, Mom, you won't believe the shitty day I've just had," I exhale into the phone as I tell her the verdict.

She mutters a curse word in Chinese. "I know you're hurting, honey, and I'm so sorry. That's why I didn't want you to go to the ad board. But just think, you could have a fresh start!" my mom says.

How do I tell my mom I need more than a fresh start? More than a spot? More than something money can buy? I need *her*. Tears fall down my neck.

"Your father pulled a lot of strings to get you in this late in the school year," she continues. "If you transfer now, you can put all this behind you. No one *ever* has to know about this."

As my mom talks, I put the couch cushion over my eyes, trying to swallow the lump in my throat as she makes plans to, once again, airbrush my past.

seventy-eight

Dani

In debate, there is a moment before you open your mouth, when you're bathed in the spotlight and the microphone amplifies your breath, and you look out at the audience and you can either choke or you can slay.

I lean forward into the mic, slow and steady.

"Earlier this year, my teacher, my debate coach, Mr. Connelly, who taught me everything I know about debate, who's here in the audience today"—I look at Mr. Connelly. He flashes me a grin. The crowd starts to cheer, then freezes when they hear my next words—"sexually harassed me."

There's a collective wave of gasps.

There's no turning back now. I speak clearly into the mic, describing what it felt like to have my coach, my hero, proposition me. To find myself—me, a strong, opinionated debater, the kind of girl who takes no shit from anyone onstage—a victim of sexual misconduct offstage.

Mr. Connelly flinches as I tell the audience how it all started with him believing in me.

"It used to take my breath away, that someone could believe so much in me," I say, staring at him. "It made me feel invincible."

I describe what it was like trying to navigate sexual misconduct as a scholarship student. Is it possible to keep training with him? How would that work, do we establish ground rules? I'll let you hit on me in exchange for killer feedback? Hold my hand for rebuttals? The crushing fear that the alternative would mean he'll punish me, take away my scholarship, or worse, ruin my future.

My voice quivers as I describe what it's like to lose a coach. Not just any coach. The one man who's ever believed in me. In my weakest moments, I would lie awake at night, fighting the urge to grab my phone and text him, *It's okay, I forgive you*, whatever it takes just to hear those four magical words again—"my bright, shining star."

As I talk, I feel something change in me. I always thought that if I went out there and spoke my truth, I'd be filled with a kind of shame that I can never undo, but instead, I feel lighter. Like the crushing stone that has been weighing me down for months is finally being lifted. And the anger that has consumed me is morphing into something else—hope.

"Sexual crimes are not just a hashtag on Twitter. They are real. They can happen to anyone, even the strongest, loudest of us," I say. "We need to combat it. We need to make victims feel safe to come forward. We need to boycott the work of artists who commit sexual crimes, and remove those in positions of power who use their authority to abuse our trust. So that new, emerging artists have a chance to thrive."

The audience claps wildly. Many people stand. Mr. Connelly ducks out of the room. When I'm finished, the chief adjudicator, Mr. Burroughs, comes onstage and takes the mic from me.

"Thank you so much for those electrifying speeches! Let's give these incredible young men and women another round of applause!"

An organizer leads me backstage to where all the other debaters are waiting for the results. Some of them offer words of condolences for my suffering; others look at me like they're not sure what to say to me. I keep my eyes to the ground, listening to the pumping in my chest. I try not to think about my teammates, Mr. Connelly, my teachers watching back home, my mom—oh God, my mom. What's she going to think?

Suddenly, I hear the judges call out, "And now, the moment you've all been waiting for. The winner of the fifth-annual Snider Cup for Excellence in Debating and Public Speaking is . . ."

I suck in a breath.

"Danielle De La Cruz of American Prep!" he announces.

I won. I fucking won!

seventy-nine

Claire

Tears stream down my face as I watch Dani's speech on my Facebook feed. This whole time, I can't believe we've been suffering silently on two sides of the same wall, drowning in separate puddles of the same shame.

The questions Mr. Francis asked me during the ad board proceeding, they were questions I'd asked myself a million times—what were you doing in his bedroom? Why didn't you scream louder? Kick him in the balls, dig your nails into him, run out of there? Why didn't you do all the things society tells you to do when you get raped, having never been raped themselves?

Instead, my body lay there limp, worried if I shoved and kicked, it'll take longer, it'll be worse. My mind drifted out of my body, like the two were entirely separate, and my psyche went back into my childhood, to me playing in the garden with Tressy; walking my dog, Snowy; little reminders that I still have things to live for. And later, when it was over, I didn't leave because the thought of having to face him downstairs was so repulsive, I lingered in the bathroom. I stood in the shower telling myself that I was strong. And that everything was going to be okay. See? I'm washing it off—the shame, the humiliation, all of it. I'm washing it off because I'm a strong woman.

And I was strong.

It's later that I fall apart in the interrogation room of my own mind. So to hear Dani's words—*it can happen to anyone, even the strongest, loudest of us*—it was like turning on a light in the pitch-black cave. I never for a second considered there might be others in the cave.

I pick up my phone and text Dani.

We need to talk.

eighty

Dani

"What the hell were you thinking?" Mr. Connelly comes barging into my prep room. I look up from my text exchange with Claire. I can't *believe* what happened to her and what the school decided. It takes a minute to register the tone of Mr. Connelly's voice, the fury on his face. "I let you come to Snider, and this is what you say about me?"

Calmly, I tell him to please step out.

"Me step out?" he snorts. "You wouldn't even be here if it weren't for me! I should have never let you come!"

I jerk backward from the sting of his words. His eyes are bloodshot, his forehead sweaty as he points a finger at the door. "Go back out there and take it back," he orders.

"I'm not going to do that."

"Then you've ruined me!" he cries. "After everything I've done for you." His hands tighten into fists. "You were nothing when I found you. I *made* you."

The words cut into my most sensitive, vulnerable tendon. I try to shake it off, but I can't. "Stop. Shut up!" I move to the other side of the room.

"I've created a monster," he continues. He's standing inches from me, and I can feel his wet spittle on my face. "A disloyal, heartless monster."

"Leave. I'm warning you. Or I will call security."

"You wouldn't dare."

I snarl at his arrogance, his self-pity. That's what really gets me, the self-pity. I can't believe he thinks *he's* the victim. Nice white man creates brown super debater only to have her turn on him and unleash her powers against him. I open my mouth and scream, "SECURITY!"

Two organizers come charging in. They recognize Mr. Connelly and put their hands on his arm. "Sir, we're going to have to ask you to leave," they say firmly.

As Mr. Connelly walks out of the room, he turns to me and hurls the words, "You ungrateful bitch."

My mom's waiting for me at home when I get back to LA. She's sipping salabat, which is this Filipino ginger tea she only ever makes if she's about to have a serious conversation with me. I guess we're finally having our talk.

"Come," she says, patting the spot next to her and handing me a mug of salabat. I put my bags down and take a seat. I blow on the tea, closing my eyes, breathing in the warm ginger.

"So you watched the speech?" I ask softly.

She nods. "Yes, I watched it." She puts her mug down and turns to me. "Why didn't you tell me?"

Her voice cracks on the question. She wipes a tear from her eyes.

"Mom, I'm so sorry," I say, burying my face in my hands.

"When did it start?" she asks.

I tell her it started when he was coaching me privately and then when we went up to Seattle, that's when he put his hand on my leg. I tell her I tried to go to Mrs. Mandalay, but she got all mad at me for posting it on xomegan.com, and that's when she took away my headmistress commendation.

My mom shakes her head. "I don't care about the headmistress commendation. This whole time . . . you've been lying to me?" she asks. She reaches for her mug, doesn't drink, just holds the cup to steady her trembling hands. She asks me questions. *Did he ever send you pictures of himself? Does he have any pictures of you?*

As I'm answering the questions, I start tearing up. "I'm sorry, I don't know why I'm crying," I say. I try to wipe the tears from my eyes, but my mom reaches and pulls my hand down so I can't rub.

"It's okay to let it out," my mom says. "You don't always have to be so strong."

"But I do!" I say. "I need to be strong for the two of us."

Tears rolls down my mom's sunken cheek. I grit my

teeth. My biggest fear, far greater than losing a competition, is hurting her.

"You are the strongest girl I know," she says. I shake my head. My mom puts down her mug and holds my hand in hers. "Being strong doesn't mean never hurting."

I stare down at her hand on top of mine, brown and wrinkled from washing too many dishes in too many strangers' homes. "I'm hurting, Mom," I whisper. It's the first time since I was a little girl I've ever admitted to my mom that I am feeling anything other than 100 percent. And it's terrifying. I gaze cautiously up at my mom, worried she might break.

But my mom does not break. Instead, she takes me into her arms. "I know, my anak," she says, taking my glasses off and stroking my hair. "But you will get through this. You wanna know why? Because you are so brave and you are so smart and you are"—she pauses for a second, searching for the word—"what is is that you kids call it these days, bad butt?"

I laugh through my tears. "Badass," I tell her.

"You are badass." She smiles.

As I hug my mom, my phone dings. I look down at the email from the headmistress's office.

To: Danielle De La Cruz
From: Office of the Headmistress
Subject: URGENT

Dear Ms. De La Cruz,

You are hereby notified that your academic scholarship has been suspended with IMMEDIATE EFFECT. Please see Headmistress Mandalay at her office upon your return to discuss your suspension and the conditions you must meet in order to return to school.

Stacey Webber

For and on behalf of

Headmistress Joanna Mandalay

eighty-one

Claire

Jess pulls up to the In-N-Out drive-through window and orders for us. We get burgers and fries to go and eat them in the car while the girls try to cheer me up about the hearing.

"You were so brave," Nancy says.

"And inspiring," Florence adds. "You made me think about some things I need to do and say in my own life."

"So now that it's over, what are you going to do?" Jess asks. "Are you going to move to another school?"

I look down and don't say anything. Is it really over though? I know I'd gone to the ad board and failed. But watching Dani's speech these last few days, it's made me rethink what I want. Is it simply not having to see Jay again at school or is it more than that?

Jess drives by the local police station and I point to it.

"Can we turn in here for a sec?" I ask Jess.

Jess gives me a wild look but turns like I ask. She parks

next to a police SUV and switches off the car. We sit in the hot afternoon sun staring at the entrance to the police station. I don't make a move to get out.

"It's okay if you want to go in," Florence says gently, putting down her burger. "We'll support you."

"Is that what you want?" Jess asks.

I shake my head. I know there's nothing in there that's going to magically undo what happened or make it all better. And yet, I just want to sit for a minute and visualize going in. To know that I have the power to walk in there and take back control. Even if it's not today. Even if it's not tomorrow.

After all the shakes and fries and burgers have been demolished, I turn to Jess and tell her to drop me off at home.

"Are you sure?" she asks.

I nod as she restarts the car.

Zach comes over later. I'm texting with Dani—she's coming by tomorrow so we can finally talk. I hear a knock on my door. I get up and open the front door to find my mom standing there with two suitcases.

"Mom! What are you doing here?"

My mom glances at me and Zach, who grabs one of her suitcases.

"Hi, Mrs. Wang! Here, let me help you with that," Zach says.

My mom holds her suitcase out of the way and won't let go. I take her suitcase and gently mutter to Zach, "Maybe you better go."

Zach nods and waves goodbye as he runs down the stairs to his Honda Civic. My mom studies him, taking off her sunglasses as she peers at his ride, remarking to me in Mandarin, "Didn't think you'd get a new boyfriend . . . so soon."

I shake my head at her. "If you're here to lecture me—"

"No, I'm not here to lecture you," she says, kicking off her shoes. She takes a seat on the couch, reaches into her purse, sprays Evian mineral water mist over her face, and rubs her eyes. With a deep breath, she tells me, "I'm thinking about leaving Dad."

"What?" I drop the suitcase, absorbing the full impact of the news.

"It's been a long time coming," she says.

I shake my head. "I don't understand. What happened?"

My mom crosses her legs and sighs. "Well, if you must know, I found texts on his phone. I think he's having another affair."

"But why *now*?" I ask. After all these years, when she's consistently turned a blind eye, what's changed?

My mom exhales. "I guess hearing you insist on going to the ad board thing, I realized, maybe I don't need to be so afraid. I don't just have to take it, I have other options."

I study her, like it's a freeze frame in a movie. I want to

believe her words, but they sound so foreign coming out of her mouth.

"But you were so against me going to the ad board," I say.

"I know because I knew it would be painful, and I didn't want you to be hurt," she says, looking down at her hands. "But then when you actually did it, and I know you didn't win but still . . ." She shakes her head, blinking back the tears. She gives herself a minute to collect herself. "I asked myself if my daughter, a seventeen-year-old, is not afraid to do something so scary, what am I, a thirty-seven-year-old, so afraid of?"

I put a hand to my mouth. "Oh, Mom," I say.

"Your nai nai thinks I'm crazy," she adds.

"Well, I think *she's* crazy," I tell my mom.

My mom bursts out laughing.

She reaches out a hand and pulls me close to her. "I'm so sorry I didn't come earlier," she apologizes as she hugs me. "But I'm here for you now. Whatever you want to do."

As she says the words, it sets off a flood of tears I've been desperately holding in. My mom holds me in her arms as I cry, and I feel my heart fill with the kind of love I thought I'd never be able to get.

eighty-two

Dani

The door to Mrs. Mandalay's office swings open. I look up, and Mrs. Mandalay's secretary informs me I can go in. She shakes her head as I walk inside, like I've just been busted for selling pot instead of winning a national debating tournament.

Mrs. Mandalay is standing at her desk, holding a copy of the *Los Angeles Times*, which she slams down on her table. The headline reads, "Local Girl Wins Snider Cup, Accuses Teacher of Sexual Misconduct."

"You have some nerve," Mrs. Mandalay says, taking off her reading glasses and flinging them on her desk.

"Every word I said was true," I tell her.

Mrs. Mandalay points for me to sit down and pulls up her calendar. "Clear your schedule on Tuesday," she says. "You're going on air and taking it all back."

"I'm not gonna do that!"

Mrs. Mandalay points at me with her newspaper-ink fin-gertip. "Dani, this is serious. I just got off the phone with the police. They want to interview you," she says. "This is no longer just fun and games."

I stare at her. *When was it ever fun and games?*

"You need to walk back what you said."

I feel the room start to spin.

Mrs. Mandalay offers to lift my suspension if I go on air. "Just tell everyone the truth. That you wanted to win the tournament so bad, you got a little carried away . . ."

I shake my head. "But I didn't get carried away!"

Mrs. Mandalay puts a hand to her face. "I can't believe you're being so selfish. This isn't just about you. Think of all the kids who *need* this school. Why do you think I'm always fund-raising? So I can find and help the next Dani."

"So help me," I say.

Mrs. Mandalay shakes her head. "Not like this."

I feel the burning in my chest as I stare at her oak bookshelf. So many great books on education and justice, apparently none of them mean a thing. "No, but you will help Jay." My eyes cut into Mrs. Mandalay's. "I know his dad owns Phoenix Capital. He's the one who took my email off the site."

Mrs. Mandalay doesn't answer. Tiny beads of sweat form on her forehead. She keeps her gaze steady on her hands, folded tightly on her desk.

"What'd he donate to get his son off the hook? A new

wing to the library? Another football field?" Claire and I have been texting. I lean in and go for the kill. "This school has a culture of allowing sexual misconduct."

"A *culture*?" Mrs. Mandalay erupts. She jumps up from her desk, looking like she's about ready to hurl a paper weight at me. "You think it's any different at Yale? Or any of the Ivy League schools?"

I freeze at the mention of Yale.

"Life's ugly sometimes," she yells. "You wanna build something great? You have to be willing to sacrifice!"

She jabs her finger into her fancy wooden desk, and I stare at her conviction. That's what astounds me—she actually thinks she's doing the right thing. As I get up to leave, I say, "Yeah. You sacrificed us."

Later, I'm standing in front of Claire's apartment. She answers the door in rubber dishwashing gloves. I stare down at the gloves—now there's a sight I never thought I'd see.

"My mom's here, she's sleeping," Claire says in a lowered voice, pointing toward the bedrooms. I follow her inside. Claire goes to the sink and takes off her dishwashing gloves, throwing chunks of a cut-up lemon down her sink.

"You're running a lemon down your garbage disposal?" I ask, impressed.

She smiles at me. "I might have learned a thing or two from watching you."

She joins me on the couch and puts her arms out. "Oh,

Dani," she says, hugging me. "I'm so sorry about what you went through. I wish I had known—"

"Me too," I say to her, hugging her back. There's so much I want to say to her, starting with I'm sorry too. "I wish I could take back all the mean things I said right before you moved out. You were going through *hell*, and I was too hung up on Zach to even see it. I can't imagine what that must have been like."

"Actually, you can," Claire says. "You're the only one." She tells me she finally went back and read my email.

"Now you know why the ad board was rigged."

"And what about you? What did Mrs. Mandalay say?"

I shake my head. "Nothing meaningful," I tell her. "But I do have an appointment at the police station tomorrow."

She sits up. "The police station, really?"

I nod. "They saw my speech and they want to know what happened."

"Are you scared?" she asks.

I want to say, *Psh, I'm a debater. I live for moments of justice like this.* But that would be ignoring and hiding the other half of who I am, a girl without a parachute. A student of color. A daughter of a single mom. Someone who needs her scholarship. And has no safety net whatsoever.

"A little," I admit.

"It's going to be okay," Claire reassures me. "You're going to do great, just like you did at Snider."

I reach out a hand. "Why don't you come with me?" I

ask. "We can do it together."

Claire looks away. I recognize the hesitation on her face, even though she's different from me. She has a parachute. But what I've realized this year is even if you're born with one, things can happen that can cut holes in yours.

"You think I should try? Is there enough evidence?" she asks.

I want to tell her of course she should try. This is America. Here, we believe in liberty and justice for all. At the same time, I want to be real with her. If she goes to trial, Jay will lawyer up and probably outspend her ten to one. And yet. I think back to the feeling in my veins at Snider when I got up there and spoke my truth, knowing my voice was my armor—it didn't even matter what they decided.

"I think we should both try," I say to Claire. "Even if we don't win."

Claire gives me a half smile. Slowly, she puts her hand over mine. As we lock hands, her phone rings. I look over and see Zach's face flashing on her screen. Claire's reluctant to take it.

"You can take it," I tell her.

Claire shakes her head and silences the call. "No. I just want to talk to you right now. You're important to me." She looks in my eyes. "Always have been," she adds shyly. As we lean over and give each other another hug, Claire apologizes once more. "I'm sorry for hurting you. If I had known Zach meant so much to you, I would have never started something with him without talking to you first."

"It's okay," I say. "I'm happy for you guys."

My mom says that apologies are like coconuts, best served ripe. But dried and hardened, they can be pretty sweet too.

Walking home from Claire's house, Ming forwards me a video. It's of Ming playing her solo at her concert and over the beautiful music is Florence's voice talking about how much Ming means to her.

"She sent this video to her parents last night," Ming says on the phone. "After Claire's trial, Florence told me the real reason she didn't want to introduce me to her parents that night. It wasn't because she's ashamed of me. It's because she was afraid I'd look at her differently if I found out her parents aren't married." Her voice cracks. "Oh Dani . . . isn't this video the sweetest?"

I smile and blink back a happy tear. "It really is," I say. I swipe to look at the video again. Wow. The things we don't know about each other. And the real reasons we do what we do.

My phone dings with an awaiting message. I think it's Claire, texting about when we're going to the police tomorrow.

"Hey, Ming, can I call you right back? I'm so happy for you!"

I hang up with Ming and look at the message, but it's not from Claire. Instead, it's a Messenger request from someone named Bree. I open it to read.

Hi Dani, I saw your speech and really need to talk to you.
Mr. Connelly was my debate coach from 2014–2016.

I don't reply. It's probably one of his old students, looking to scream at me for tarnishing the image of their beloved coach. I don't need that right now. I need to be in the right state of mind if I'm going to go to the police tomorrow.

That night, as I'm lying in bed, my mom comes into my room.

"Do you want me to go with you to the police tomorrow?" she asks.

I shake my head. "No, Mom, it's okay." I know how the police make her anxious, being a first-generation immigrant and all. Frankly, having her there will make it harder for me to say what I have to say, because I'll be worried about her listening to my testimony and getting emotional instead of focusing on the facts.

"Are you sure? I can get the time off from Rosa," she says. "I know I haven't been coming to your things at school, and I'm sorry. I'll make more time from now on."

I smile. "Thanks, Mom, but I got this one," I tell her. "I would love for you to come to my next tournament though."

At the thought of my next tournament, my face falls. Will there *be* a next tournament for me?

My mom pats my back and says good night. As I'm

reaching to turn off the light, my phone dings. It's that girl Bree again.

Please. I really need to talk to you. Can we connect?

I sit up and stare at the "please" with a period. I tap Accept. The next thing I know, my phone rings and Bree's voice comes on the line.

"Dani, I watched your speech at Snider and I just . . ." She starts to cry.

"It's okay; I'm okay," I assure her. I tell her after I left the bar that night, Mr. Connelly backed off. "Thankfully, he didn't try anything else."

There's a long pause.

"Well, he did with me," she says.

eighty-three

Claire

On the day I'm supposed to go with Dani to the police station, my mom wakes up and walks into the living room in her silk robe.

"Dani came by yesterday," I tell her.

"How is she? It's terrible what happened to her," my mom says, shaking her head.

"We're thinking about going to the police," I say.

My mom doesn't respond. I know she's still uneasy with the idea of me going to the authorities, but she's been quietly calling up lawyers. I know because I see the caller ID on my mom's phone when it rings. Still, the admissions letter to Terry Grove is taped prominently to the refrigerator, beaconing an easier solution every time I reach for a LaCroix.

"Do we have any espresso?" my mom asks. "I can't think about going to the police without caffeine."

I shake my head.

My mom makes a face. It's been interesting being room-mates with my mom these last few days. She still functions as though Tressy is here, leaving her towels and clothes on the floor everywhere. I hope I wasn't like that when I first moved in with the De La Cruzes.

"We should get on that," she says. "Do they sell coffee machines at Trader Joe's?"

I chuckle. Ever since I took her to Trader Joe's, she's been obsessed. She even asked me who Joe was as she walked around in her red Versace feather skirt, looking like an out-of-place peacock while the other shoppers stared.

The doorbell rings.

My mom and I glance toward the door. "I hope it's not another package from your father." She rolls her eyes. My dad has been sending her apology gifts. He called twice, begging her to come back. Both times she put him on the phone with me, and he whined and complained that we both ditched him. I told him, don't worry, we'll be back soon, even though I hoped it wasn't true. I hope my mom will stay for a while.

"Hey, maybe next week, we can go out to dinner with Zach," I suggest as I go to the door.

I open the door to find the mailman standing there. He hands me a letter, posted by registered mail.

"Actually, I'd really like to go to the school and have a word with Mrs. Mandalay about how she handled this whole thing. Maybe I'll go in with Dani's mom. She's got

467

to be pissed too. . . ." Her voice trails off when she sees my face as I look down at the letter.

"It's from Jay," I tell her.

"A confidentiality agreement?" Jess asks. She slides her sunglasses off. We're at Pinkberry, sitting outside.

I nod. The letter, sent from Jay's family's attorney's office, proposed a nondisclosure agreement between me and Jay, whereby I agree not to reveal the facts relating to the dispute of what happened the night of Friday the fifteenth in exchange for a monetary settlement.

"How much?" Jess asks.

"Two million dollars," I tell her.

Jess's eyes go wide. Her frozen yogurt spoon falls out of her hand. "Claire, that's fucking great!" she exclaims. "Are you gonna take it?"

I push the yogurt around in my cup with my spoon, watching it melt. "I don't know. To not be able to talk about what happened? With anyone? Not even the police?"

"Claire, it's two million dollars!"

When I don't say anything, Jess leans forward. "Do you remember what I said before? About how there's always a private solution?"

I nod, recalling the conversation we once had about her dad.

"Sometimes the private solution is just as good as the public solution," Jess urges.

"And what is the private solution here?" I ask her.

"The private solution is you take the motherfucker's money, transfer to another school, and move on. That's enough money for you and your mom to buy a nice house! Start over!"

I shake my head. "But I don't want a nice house . . ." My eyes slide down to my watch. It's four thirty. Dani's going to the police at five. If I want to meet her over at the police station, I have to leave now.

Jess lets out an exasperated sigh. "What do you want then? He already said he's sorry . . ." She grabs the letter and thrusts it at me. "This is how sorry he is. Do you really want to go through a public trial? Your name will forever be tattooed to what happened . . ."

I consider my reply. "I can never get my name completely away from rape," I tell her. "But maybe I can get it closer to, you know, justice."

Jess laughs. She waves around her yogurt spoon as she says, "Girl, justice is something Americans invented to sell movies."

eighty-four

Dani

Bree Johnson meets me outside the police station the next day. She's a senior at UCLA now. We ended up staying on the phone until 5:00 a.m., until our eyes were empty and our throats were raw. Like me, she admired Mr. Connelly. He told her she was special, that she had a talent for debate he'd never seen in any of his other students. He used that to build trust with her, which he then violated during a tournament in San Diego, when he came up to her hotel room. She let him in, thinking he just wanted to run motions, but instead he cornered her and kissed her.

We hold each other in the police parking lot, clinging to the flesh-and-blood confirmation that we weren't alone in what we went through, that it wasn't our fault. I look down at my watch. I was hoping Claire would be here too. I told her we would be here at 5:00 p.m. Where is she?

"You ready to do this?" Bree asks.

470

I smile at her. I can't believe I did this with my words. I brought us together.

I try Claire once again on my phone. I have been texting her all day to see if she wanted to come with us, but she hasn't replied. A car pulls up, and I think it's her but instead, it's Ming and Florence.

"I couldn't let you do this alone," Ming says.

I turn to Florence. "Is Claire coming?" I ask.

Florence shakes her head. "I don't know," she says.

I scan the parking lot one last time, at all the cars and the hot sun reflecting off the windshields.

C'mon, Claire, where are you?

eighty-five

Claire

I hug Jess as we leave from the yogurt shop.

"Trust me, the private solution is always the best," Jess says. Her phone rings. It's her dad calling—the first time all semester. She greets him with a big smile on her face. "Hi, Daddy! I miss you too! What? You were just in LA?" Jess's face falls. She quickly hides her disappointment. "Oh no, it's okay, next time. I was busy studying anyway."

The crushed look on her face, as well as her chirpy words, stay with me as I get inside my Uber. I think about the torrent of emotions going through Jess, all the things she wants to say to him now but can't. It's like looking into a mirror. How many times have I chosen the path that saves the most face? Pretended along and swallowed? The private solution may work, but it *feels* like shards of glass, cutting you up inside.

"Wait, can I change where I'm going?" I ask my Uber driver.

I get to the police station just as Dani and the girls are walking toward the main entrance.

"Dani!" I shout. Dani turns around. I see Florence with Ming! The girls let out a big cheer as I step out of the Uber.

"We thought you weren't coming!" Dani says.

"I'm here now!" I say. Dani hugs me, followed by Florence and Ming, and I quickly introduce myself to Bree. It's crazy seeing us all together, knowing what we're about to do. I inhale deeply, letting the empowerment expand in my lungs.

I know the odds are stacked against us, if we go to trial, Jay and the school will outspend us, the media shitstorm will squeeze us, the jury will question us. Still, there's something so powerful about ripping up the two-million-dollar offer and marching through those doors. To be able to take back control and not let any person, school, or trauma dictate my life—that's why I came to America. I slip my hand in Dani's, who joins hands with Bree. One by one, we all join hands. As we walk together to the police station, my heart beats with the power of five.

The police officers look up at us as we walk in. We tell them we're here to file a complaint. A young officer named Officer Torrence comes rushing out of his office and introduces himself. He leads us into a conference room.

"Thank you all so much for coming in," he says. "About six months ago, I received an anonymous tip from one of the teachers at American Prep saying there was misconduct at the school. I've been investigating the case, but I never had any idea of the magnitude." He looks to Dani. "Until I heard Dani's speech."

Officer Torrence puts us in a waiting room and takes us individually to get our statement. Bree Johnson, the UCLA senior, goes first. While we wait, Florence and Ming and I chat about their app. Ming says it's for parachutes and host families.

"That's amazing," I tell them. I tilt my head at Dani, jokingly asking her what she'd rate me.

"I'd give you one star for keeping your room clean," she teases, to which I protest, "Hey!"

Then Dani looks at me, more serious. "And five stars for bravery."

I smile.

Officer Torrence walks out. "Claire," he calls. "You're next. Are you ready?"

I get up from my chair. I look over at Dani, who squeezes my hand and mouths, *You can do this* as I walk by and follow Officer Torrence into the interview room.

When it's over, we walk out of the police station together. We hug goodbye, promising to text the minute we hear anything. Bree drives back to UCLA, while Ming and Florence get in an Uber to go back to Florence's place. Dani offers me a ride home, and I hop into Dani's mom's Toyota Celica.

Dani doesn't start the engine right away. Instead, she sits in the hot car, texting.

"What are you doing?"

"Texting my mom and searching pro bono lawyers," Dani says, fingers tapping on her phone.

Gently, I reach over and put a hand over her phone. "Hey, breathe. You're not in this alone anymore," I remind her.

It takes Dani a second to process this, and when she does, she puts down her phone. Her face relaxes.

"How do you feel?" I ask.

She thinks about the question for a long time. "Like I'm starting a tournament and I'm finally on a team I like," she answers. "With someone with as much skin in the game as me."

Wow. It's an honor hearing her put it like that. And a little terrifying.

"And how do you feel?"

"Relieved," I say, then gaze down at my hands and start thinking about my mom's face when I get home—I hope she will have a proud smile, but I'm still not sure. "And like I might be sick," I confess.

Dani starts looking around the car for a bag.

"I'm kidding, I won't!"

Dani finds a brown paper bag and holds it up. "It's okay. If you do, I've got you."

I smile and reach my arms out to give her a hug. "I'm so glad I finally started talking to you."

"Me too."

As she starts the car, I put my feet up on the dash. Two girls from opposite sides of the earth, emerging from the ashes, *stronger*.

Author's Note

In 2016, four "parachute" Chinese kids in Los Angeles were sentenced to prison for the violent bullying of a fellow Chinese parachute student. The judge said the case reminded him of *Lord of the Flies*. Ever since then, I've been researching parachutes, interviewing current and former parachutes, their parents, host families, and teachers, as well as visiting schools, including the school where the four kids attended. What I discovered from talking to these students was how unique their experience was growing up, grappling with issues of homesickness, privilege, identity, peer pressure, all while trying to navigate a new country on their own.

Currently, China sends the greatest number of international students to US high schools. Around two in five international students enrolled in American high schools come from China. The number of international high school students from China rose by 48 percent between 2013 and

2016.[1] The American schools I visited view this new, full-pay pipeline as a godsend, but it comes at a steep price. Many of the Chinese students I talked to struggled with loneliness, alienation, or worse. Recent headlines of foreign exchange students getting sexually assaulted, raped, gone missing, or murdered are just some of the reminders of the perils parachutes face.

And it's not just parachutes. The stories of Dani and Claire mirror the experiences of so many young women and men all over the nation. In 2017, the Associated Press uncovered seventeen thousand reports of sexual assault at schools across the United States. The AP found that "schools frequently were unwilling or ill-equipped to address the problem. Some administrators and educators even engaged in cover-ups to hide evidence of a possible crime and protect their schools' image."[2]

While most of these cases were perpetrated by other students, an alarming and increasing subset are being perpetrated by teachers. In 2014, almost eight hundred school

1. Chris Fuchs, "Report Finds China Sends Most International Students to U.S. High Schools," *NBC News*, August 14, 2018, https://www.nbcnews.com/news/asian-america/report-finds-china-sends-most-international-students-u-s-high-n792681.

2. Robin McDowell, Reese Dunklin, Emily Schmall, and Justin Pritchard, "AP Uncovers 17,000 Reports of Sexual Assualts in Schools Across US," Boston.com, May 1, 2017, https://www.boston.com/news/national-news/2017/05/01/ap-uncovers-17000-reports-of-sexual-assaults-at-schools-across-us.

employees were prosecuted for sexual assault.[3] According to a study commissioned by the Department of Education, 10 percent of students surveyed said they have experienced sexual misconduct at the hands of school employees. Of the students who said they were abused, 38 percent were elementary students and 56 percent were in middle or high school.[4] Many of these predatory teachers get dismissed and rehired, a system known as "passing the trash." It's a devastating problem that affects both public and private schools, including some of the most prestigious boarding schools in the nation.[5]

At the same time, *Parachutes* is also a very personal story for me.

Seventeen years ago, in my 1L year, I was sexually assaulted at Harvard Law School. My attacker was another fellow Harvard Law School student. I was only eighteen years old at the time. I had skipped several grades, overcome

---

3.   Barbara Goldberg, "U.S. Cracks Down on Female Teachers Who Sexually Abuse Students," Reuters, April 21, 2015, https://www.reuters.com/article/us-usa-crime-teachers/u-s-cracks-down-on-female-teachers-who-sexually-abuse-students-idUSKBN0NC14H20150421.

4.   Erin B. Logan, "Without Warning System, Schools Often 'Pass the Trash'—and Expose Kids to Danger," NPR, April 6, 2018, https://www.npr.org/sections/ed/2018/04/06/582831662/schools-are-supposed-to-have-pass-the-trash-policies-the-dept-of-ed-isn-t-tracki.

5.   Elizabeth A. Harris, "At Hotchkiss School, Sexual Misconduct and 'Missed Opportunities' to Stop It," *New York Times*, August 17, 2018, https://www.nytimes.com/2018/08/17/nyregion/hotchkiss-school-sexual-misconduct.html.

poverty, and beaten the impossible odds to get in. The last thing I expected would happen to me at Harvard Law was sexual assault.

I remember my attacker telling me afterward, "I should probably go to church for what I just did to you." This followed by "And you should probably take a shower." I did take a shower. I wanted to take a million showers.

The showers did little to assuage the fact that we went to the same school. That his apartment was across the street from my dorm. That he sat behind me in one of my classes. In the months and weeks that followed, I saw him nearly every day, walking around like nothing happened. I saw him at law school events and law firm interviews. Whenever I saw him, my stomach would twist into a knot so tight, I felt like I was going to hurl. And then I'd gulp for air, nearly choking.

Still, I did not formally file charges against my attacker because I was young, I was scared, and I had reason to believe that my attacker had a close and material relationship with the senior management of Harvard Law School. Instead, I went to the university nurse, got the rape tests done, told the dean of students what happened, switched dorms, and filed an anonymous report to the police.

The next two and a half years became a delicate dance of hide-and-seek, tiptoeing around my attacker, asking friends if they saw him in the library, and studying his patterns of migration like a zoologist. It might have worked if we were in the jungle or a big city, but Harvard Law School spanned about a street and a half.

Finally, in my third year of law school, with graduation fast approaching, I decided I had to do something. I couldn't bear the thought of seeing him at graduation. I didn't want my immigrant parents to have to see him, to have to watch their daughter get her diploma while sharing a stage with the guy who sexually assaulted her. So I talked to the new dean of students as well as the new dean of Harvard Law School.

Despite all the warnings of how long it would take if I brought charges and how difficult the process would be, I decided to formally bring charges of sexual assault against my attacker to Harvard's administrative board. Harvard's admin board is its very own mini court system, the "jury" made up of faculty members and students. In order to proceed with the ad board, the law school required me to write and sign a document saying I would not bring a formal criminal complaint with the police and that I was proceeding only through the administrative board.

The case was emotionally draining. It required me to sit in a room in front of my attacker and listen for hours as he called me a liar. In the end, I lost. The university decided that there was not enough evidence to suspend or expel my attacker, despite the fact that I had gotten rape tests done, told the school nurse, switched dorms, and even written my attacker an email after the assault saying, "What you did to me was horrible, unwanted, and illegal" to which he had responded, "My heart is bleeding."

Then, the other bomb dropped: the university was now investigating me for "malicious prosecution." The days that followed were the darkest ever as I waited for the faculty to vote on whether to yank away my own diploma all because I dared bring up the fact that I was sexually assaulted while at Harvard Law School.

When I was finally found not guilty, a faculty member actually came up to me and congratulated me. "Congratulations! You get to graduate! Let me give you a bit of advice," he said. "Move on!"

And I did, sort of. After I graduated, I moved as far away from Boston and New York as I could, to Hong Kong. I moved away from law too. I started teaching kids. I started writing. I started having lunch at normal hours again, because I didn't have to worry about bumping into him. I stopped looking over my shoulder. I got married, had kids. Before I knew it, a decade flew by and I didn't think about my attack. I stuffed what happened to me in a box and buried it deep in my closet.

It remained peacefully buried until 2014, when I read the op-ed in the *Boston Globe* in which Harvard Law professors argued against Harvard's stricter policy for sexual misconduct. Some of the professors who signed the op-ed were the same professors who ruled on my case. "We believe that [the stricter] sexual harassment policy adopted by Harvard will do more harm than good," they wrote.[6] Reading their words was like reopening a wound.

Then, later that year, the Department of Education found that Harvard Law School was "in violation of Title IX of the Education Amendments of 1972 for its response to sexual harassment, including sexual assault."[7] In response, Harvard Law School issued a statement: "Harvard recognized that we could and should do more."[8]

Tears streamed down my face when I read these words: they are the closest to an apology that I'd ever gotten from the institution that I felt wronged me, an institution I had admired since I was a little girl.

While I can't get back those three years of law school, I hope that through writing *Parachutes*, more schools will prioritize protecting the students, not the brand.

6. "Rethink Harvard's Sexual Harassment Policy," October 15, 2014, http://www.law.harvard.edu/faculty/bartholet/Boston-Globe _Op-Ed_Sexual-Harassment.pdf. Matthew Q. Clarida, "Law School Profs Condemn New Sexual Harassment Policy," *Harvard Crimson*, October 15, 2014, https://www.thecrimson.com/article/2014/10/15 /law-profs-criticize-new-policy/.

7. "Harvard Law School Found in Violation of Title IX, Agrees to Remedy Sexual Harassment, including Sexual Assualt of Students," US Department of Education, December 30, 2014, https://www.ed.gov /news/press-releases/harvard-law-school-found-violation-title-ix -agrees-remedy-sexual-harassment-including-sexual-assault-students.

8. Jake New, "Settlement at Harvard," *Inside Higher Ed*, December 30, 2014, https://www.insidehighered.com/news/2014/12/30 /law-school-reaches-agreement-education-department-do-more -protect-victims-sexual.

Acknowledgments

This book would not exist if it were not for the complete, unwavering love and support of my literary agent Tina Dubois. Tina, thank you for getting this book from the very beginning. Thank you so much for believing in me. This book took a colossal amount of courage for me to write; knowing that you were on the receiving end of each draft was the only way I could do it. I am enormously grateful to have you as my agent.

To my editor Ben Rosenthal, thank you for seeing the potential and pushing me with each draft. Your sharp editorial instincts and feedback transformed this book. Thanks for your bravery and willingness in allowing me to tackle hard topics and letting me take risks, and supporting me always. I treasure the trust you've placed in me; it is an honor being one of your authors.

To my publisher Katherine Tegen, thank you so much

for publishing *Parachutes* and being such a staunch in-house advocate for this book. It means the world to me to be a Katherine Tegen author and I thank my lucky stars every day. To my greater HarperCollins team—Jacquelynn Burke, Ebony LaDelle, Valerie Wong, Tanu Srivastava, Laura Mock, Amy Ryan, Kathryn Silsand, and Mark Rifkin, it is such a joy working with you! Thanks for bringing my girls Dani and Claire to the world!

To my dear friend Lucy Fisher, your support and thoughtful feedback meant everything to me. Thanks for helping me have this baby. I am so crazy-happy excited to go on this wild journey with you! To Doug Wick, thank you for entertaining us all at dinner; it contributed greatly to the editorial process. Many thanks as well to Lucas Wiesendanger and everyone at Red Wagon.

To my agent John Burnham, thank you for championing me and my work every day and working tirelessly on my deals. To my greater ICM team, Ava Greenfield, Alicia Gordon, Lia Chan, Roxane Edouard, Bryan Diperstein, Ron Bernstein, Tamara Kawar, Morgan Wood, and Alyssa Weinberger—thank you so much for being on my team and supporting *Parachutes*! I love you guys!

To my dear friend and attorney Richard Thompson, thank you so much for your guidance and wisdom over the years. You're so much more than a lawyer to me and I cherish our friendship immensely.

Many thanks to my colleagues John Chew and Paul

Smith at the Kelly Yang Project and to all my students that I taught for thirteen years—you inspire me beyond words. To my mentors and professors Bruce Cain and Paul Cummins, how I treasure our long, thought-provoking conversations on all aspects of academia, including how schools struggle to tackle sexual misconduct.

A million thanks to all the students, host families, parents, teachers, and members of the community I talked to while doing research for *Parachutes*; thank you for opening up and sharing your experiences with me.

Finally to my family—a huge thank-you to my parents for not freaking out when I told them I was writing a #MeToo book about sexual assault in schools. To my kids, Eliot, Nina, and Tilden, thanks for being patient with Mommy while I drafted this book. To my husband, Stephen, who met me when I was still a law student at Harvard and encouraged me to go to the administrative board—thank you for believing me from the start. And for believing in me all these years.

Special thanks to the Orinda Library, where I wrote this book. Those of you who know me know that libraries are dear to my heart. After my assault, I took refuge in the Harvard Law School library. It was the only place on campus where I felt truly safe. My deepest thanks to the librarians all over the nation who provide much needed comfort and safe spaces to patrons—I would not be where I am today without you.